# The Deadliest Art

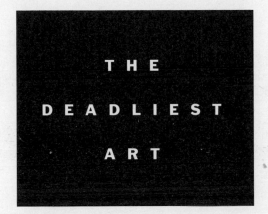

# THE
# DEADLIEST
# ART

## NORMAN BOGNER

*A Tom Doherty Associates Book*
New York

THE DEADLIEST ART

This book is printed on acid-free paper.

A Forge Book
Published by Tom Doherty Associates, LLC
175 Fifth Avenue
New York, NY 10010

www.tor.com

Forge® is a registered trademark of Tom Doherty Associates, LLC.

Library of Congress Cataloging-in-Publication Data

Bogner Norman.
    The deadliest art / Norman Bogner. — 1st ed.
        p.cm.
    "A Tom Doherty Associates Book."
    ISBN 0-312-86856-1 (acid free paper)
    1. Provence (France)—Fiction. 2. Bruges (Belgium)—Fiction. 3. Venice (Los Angeles, Calif.)—Fiction. I. Title

PS3552.O45 D4 2001
813'.54–dc21

                                        2001023200

First Edition: July 2001

Printed in the United States of America

0  9  8  7  6  5  4  3  2  1

*For Natalia Aponte*
*with affection*

# ACKNOWLEDGMENTS

Dr. Benjamin L. Cohen, my lifelong friend, was present at creation when this was merely an idea. He encouraged me to go forward and also provided medical research materials and insights into the problems confronting those who are different.

I would like to thank Andy Nevill, owner of the Tattoo Asylum in Venice Beach, California, for his invaluable assistance, generosity, and guidance in exploring the world of tattoos and piercing. When he was not available, his colleagues, Swag Knowles and Bill Beccio, patiently answered my questions and allowed me to watch them work.

Lon Bentley, the legendary makeup artist and hairstylist to the stars, patiently took me through the intricacies of how people can and do frequently change their appearance.

Dr. Gary O'Brien contributed valuable information regarding dental procedures.

Dr. Yale Bickel was generous with his time and advised me about the effects of acids and drugs.

*Where Do We Come From? What Are We? Where Are We Going?*

—title of painting by Paul Gauguin, 1897

# PROLOGUE

**It was a rosy** early June day in Aix-en-Provence, the wind a lackadaisical whisper daintily shuffling the leaves along the Cours Mirabeau before the hordes of tourists arrived to trample them and unsettle life. The visitors would be clamoring for the flavors of Provence, creating prohibitive prices for bottles of water, and swatting each other with berets over sacks of herbs that they'd never cook with, but which would adorn their kitchens, listing over the copper pans. The pans would turn green, the herbs fester, the house might lose its structural integrity, but the memory of Provence would be alive.

The placid mood of the town, however, had one spot that dispelled the present mood of sleepwalking and sloth. The incomparable Chez Danton, the locals' favorite restaurant for a rendezvous, had become a shelter for the homeless gentlewomen who had once plied their trade at Louise Vercours's brothel. After her murder, the establishment had been closed and was in the process of being converted into a hostel for university students. This change of amenities did little to abet the adventures of married men; they could still slink over to the ladies to discuss their theoretical divorces and steal a kiss. An invitation to dine on a platter of sizzling Charolais filets was not to be lightly discarded by mesdemoiselles barely able to pay the rent. They leeched a meal and promised future delights. This was one of the legacies of Louise Vercours, once the madam of Aix.

Louise's fortune and collection of masterpiece paintings had gone to Michel Danton. He had been overwhelmed by the gesture and hardly knew what to do about it. He was a criminal investigator for the Special Circumstances Section of the Police Judiciare.

For the past seven years he had been commander of this elite unit, which handled the most intractable homicides in Provence. He had promised his fiancée, Jennifer Bowen, that he would retire as soon as a successor could be appointed. The previous summer they had both been wounded, and almost lost their lives, when the student Jennifer was chaperoning and the girl's psychotic boyfriend had gone on a grisly, murderous rampage.

The estate, cattle, and vineyards Louise had owned she settled on Michel's parents. Even in death Louise had influenced their lives. Nicole Danton, Aix's queen de cuisine, had been her lifelong friend. Nicole and her husband Philippe had worked for years to build Chez Danton. Although the business was successful, the grueling hours had taken a toll on them. The Dantons were on easy street in every way, with the exception of the unremitting trench warfare in the kitchen.

But today, Chez Danton had become a madhouse of shrill Marseille fishmongers, food purveyors, men bullying along wheels of cheese on dollies, and ice sculptors in Michelangelo smocks brandishing chisels and hammers over blocks the size of icebergs' calves. The sound volume of these artisans was enough to rouse a zombie from a temporary snooze.

However, the brawl in the kitchen overpowered even this din. No one without a mission would have tolerated the domestic discord between the Dantons. These legendary clashes over cooking had never been banished despite the docile academic environment of Aix-en-Provence. The town's historic past, its melodious fountains, and its air of repose provided no balm to the Dantons' feud.

At issue was the wedding menu for Michel and Jennifer. At the moment, the engaged couple were rushing around the city doing last-minute errands, relieved to have left the Dantons to duel in the kitchen.

"I will not serve Lobster américaine in this establishment," Philippe bellowed. "Just the sound of it makes my skin crawl. Think of our reputation. We'll be cut off by Fournier's on the Quai de Belges and every decent market in the region . . . ridiculed by mobs of cuisiniers in Provence. We could have them picketing. No, that's my last word."

Nicole tore off her blue-striped apron and a furious calmness settled over her, like the torpid air preceding the mistral which drove people into a seasonal catatonia. She was a tall woman with a svelte figure, a lovely retroussé nose, alabaster teeth, and a milky complexion. Neither sun nor endless kitchen hours had dappled her skin with anything more than a few casual wrinkles. She rolled down the sleeves of her pale green Prada blouse. Yes, she could afford Prada now.

"Damn it, Philippe, it's a Provence dish invented by a Frenchman. Pierre Fraisse was his name."

"No, no, he cooked it in *Chicago* for Al Capone!" Philippe protested, now somewhat shaken by his scholarly wife. "I'm not going to disgrace our name by serving it."

Both in anger and in precoital ferment, Philippe's muscles bulged and his big jaw assumed the unyielding structure of the Mont Ventoux massif. He was not simply stubborn in the way that stupid men can be, he was granite itself. His good looks, however, did not offer a reprieve from his gritty sauces or ferocious temper.

Nicole tried a feminine approach. "Jennifer wants it. Your future daughter-in-law —"

"Bring some substance to our kitchen discussions," Philippe growled. "Jennifer's from California, what else would she want? I thought that Michel was educating her in our ways. Isn't that in the marriage contract?"

"There is no contract," Nicole replied wearily, her energy at ebb tide.

"He should have one. Last week, Jennifer had the audacity to request meat loaf? I asked if it was something they hunted in America. I can imagine what a savage her mother must be."

Philippe had an abiding respect for women, but successfully concealed it. They had their place, that was his philosophy. Nicole's head drooped and she wandered away from the range. Sensing a browbeater's victory, Philippe took the opportunity to open the seawater tanks to welcome the flotilla of spiny purplish indigo crustaceans creeping out of their iced crates. He reminded Nicole of Monsieur Paris, the pet name of the guillotine operator, in those bygone days when heads rolled and the public cheered the blade.

"I'll do my celebrated Lobster Cardinal with truffles and a cold lobster mousse with a velouté sauce."

"Then I'll make l'américaine," Nicole said.

"In someone else's kitchen—with my blessings."

She picked up a stick to check the responses of the death-row inmates.

"Philippe, you're crowding the lobsters."

"Let them learn what the métro in Paris is like during rush hour. It builds character."

"Lobsters *don't* need character. Philippe, they'll be dead before they're cooked."

"I've never lost one yet."

Nicole left it at that. She did not have the courage to inform her husband that Jennifer's mother, imminently due in from San Francisco for the nuptials, had written, inquiring if sushi was a possibility as a starter.


**The bizarre profusion** of murders in Aix-en-Provence last summer had caused great agitation among the populace. Despite the fact that the killer, Darrell Vernon Boynton, and his accomplice, Maddie Gold, were dead, shopkeepers had to reassure their evening customers that all was well. The locals appeared to walk a bit more warily and were obsessively suspicious, reporting to the police loud voices, and any signs of household discord. Everyone was on guard about funny looks; some of the residents carried cameras with them—just in case—to photograph mischievous tourists.

This preposterous reversal of the usual process amused Michel Danton and puzzled the sightseers, who wondered why anyone wearing a beret would be snapping pictures of *them* as they lingered over a drink or were disgorged from a bus on the shady Cours Mirabeau. Many of the foreigners drawn to the magical city put this down to yet another charming Provençal trait omitted from guidebooks.

In some manner everybody had become a detective, and the local police kept their Marseille brethren very busy, demanding autopsies for ninety-year-olds who passed away in their sleep, claiming they had been poisoned or suffocated by avaricious relatives. Hospital attendants were also alarmed; whenever a patient died, they were suspects in foul play.

Michel Danton was frequently interviewed by the media and despised pontificating, but he had to calm down the locals: "Mass hysteria, the madness of crowds, the murky hallucinations of neurotic people . . ." He had become a talking head. Whenever he could get away, he hid out at the family farm in St-Rémy with Jennifer. They would prepare a picnic and return from the woods, dripping with sweat and evening dew—naked.

Much to his chagrin, Michel had been elevated to heroic status and there was talk of erecting a statue in his honor beside La Rotonde. Meanwhile, he fretted about resigning from the police and taking a dreary job as an investigator for the judge. He didn't know how he could tolerate the stultifying boredom of everyday life, an existence without risks. But he had promised Jennifer never again to knowingly place himself in jeopardy. It was a dismal culmination of a distinguished career.

Putting aside such considerations, Michel craved the excitement and the passion an investigation always brought with it. The hunt, the pursuit, the use of his imagination and insight were a rare combination of talents. It was a strange quixotic gift, elevating him to the role of visionary. His métier was solving murders, and the prospect of abandoning this accident of perfect pitch struck him as unjust. It would have been like telling Tiger Woods he should have been a car dealer or suggesting that General de Gaulle would have made a wonderful grocer. Seldom given to rash self-assessment, Michel felt like a great natural athlete whose future would be confined to a clerk's desk.

But he was passionately in love with Jennifer and, more significantly, had given her his word. The search for a replacement had unearthed several arrogant administrators—not detectives—with airs and attitudes, who thought a few years in the heartland with a high crime-solving ratio might launch their careers in Paris. Convinced that they were meant for better things, they would all be marking time.

Jennifer had been patient during the process and seldom brought up the topic. In her quiet moments, he wondered if she relived the summer when she had killed two people, one in self-defense, the other to save his life. Her silence about the events suggested that the healing process might take a lifetime. She pretended to be free and easy, but she was nervous, afflicted by nightmares. Only a week had passed since she had last awakened screaming. Perhaps the summery weather and the sunflowers would bring a respite.

**Michel was always** happy to get back to his friendly neighborhood in the Mazarin Quarter. It had been named for the archbishop who was the brother of the great Cardinal Richelieu. These two Sicilians had altered the course of French history through wars and treaties, shaping rebellious provinces into a great power. Michel paused near the Hôtel de Marignane. Did he have time for a glass of chilled Manzanilla? Never mind, there was a line of tourists at the Café Mazarin.

He meandered through the stalls. From the charcuterie the scent of the garlicky Toulouse sausages wafted out to the street. In the brimming window a galantine of boar's head was beside a tray of boudin noir and blanc; resting on a tray beside a creamy blanquette of veal, a platter of dark ruby coq au vin highlighted the succulent still life. He wondered about chancing a snack, then realized the Force Ten squall of housewives would make him late. They were nibbling slices of sausage off the scales even before anyone weighed their purchases. A counterman spotted him, struck a fencer's stance, and waved the hilt of a friendly Lonzo de Corse as a greeting. No, a chunk of it would not do before a groom's fitting. The fruit lady offered Michel a slice of Cavaillon melon from her cold storage bin. A few doors away, at the copper sign of the baguette, the baker was chatting with the cheese matriarch, and they paused to hail him. Forty years of rising at three A.M. to begin baking had given the skin under the baker's eyes the angry black hide of a gored bull.

"*Merci,* but I can't stop," Michel said to them. "I'm going to the tailor."

Michel stopped at the newsstand and was handed his *Interna-*

*tional Herald Tribune* and *USA Today*. Neither he nor Jennifer could get used to reading newspapers on-line. He yanked out the sports section to check on his beloved Yankees. He was convinced Joe Torre would take them to a third consecutive World Series victory. He studied home run stats while roving down the Rue d'Italie to Aix's master tailor.

Outside the shop, on Rollerblades, Kristen, the golden child of the tailor's mistress, was giving out flyers for barge trips and hikes in the Lubéron. Her mother ran a travel business.

"Michel," she cooed, "get some of your police friends to take a trip with my mother."

He looked at the town's Lolita and prayed for her well-being. "If you were the guide, they'd go."

Alberto Vellancio, a Neapolitan brigand, claimed he had once worked in Rome for the great clothiers: a cutter for Brioni, and then a sleeve man with the revered Kiton in Naples. Michel was skeptical of these affinities with the Leonardo and Raphael of Italian men's clothing. Nevertheless, Vellancio's prices were steep. For years, Philippe had detested the tailor, chiding him on the cost of his clothes, but the fortune the Dantons had inherited abruptly altered Philippe's penny-pinching disposition.

"Ahhh, *il principe*, Michel."

Depending on his mood, Vellancio, an arrant flatterer, always greeted Philippe as *conto* (count of chateaubriand), *dottore* (doctor of Charolais), or *professore* (professor of prime rib); the chef lapped it up like one of his own lumpy sauces.

Prince Michel extended his hand, but the fleshy tailor was still bowing and unctuously praising him. Dressed in a ballooned white smock, with an array of lethal pins on the lapel, tape measure hanging around his neck like a stethoscope, Vellancio was almost as wide as one of the bolts of fine cloth layered on his gleaming wooden shelves. At Chez Danton the tailor and his strapping Nordic mistress always feasted on the Hercules T-bone, gnawing on it like Borneo cannibals.

The tailor's gold teeth flashed in an embracing smile. "Your esteemed father came in earlier. He ordered six cashmere sports jackets."

"Will they help his cooking?" Michel asked. "Or is he going on television?"

"They are for entertaining at the chateau. He and your mama obtain Louise's properties, you her paintings. Life is not so bad?"

So much for discretion and classified family business. It had seemed Philippe had trumpeted it from the rooftops of Aix. From working-class bourgeoisie chef to swanning millionaire landowner to the manor born. In his favor, Philippe had not set himself up with a harem of young women, taken to snorting cocaine, or gone insane gambling in Monte Carlo. Philippe's twin devotions remained bickering at his kitchen range and ravishing Nicole. His travel plans, such as they were, involved trips to survey his real estate and hiring a photographer to videotape the inventory. He had purchased a new Mercedes SUV, but drove it only when he was going to the country. At all other times it remained in the back lot of the restaurant under a canvas hood.

"Bianca!" Vellancio bellowed. "Michel's wedding suit!"

Parting the green velvet curtains from the workroom, a scrawny hand revealed a tuxedo in clear plastic. Vellancio's wife timidly appeared; she wore glasses as thick as a microscope's eyepiece and shrank back as she walked. Behind her, an arsenal of sewing machines whirred, manned by a seminary of immigrants.

Thin as a fishbone, Bianca bowed to Michel, but not before her husband demanded that she put the Pavarotti on the CD carousel. The tenor was in fine voice and not mopping his sweaty beard and spraying spittle on those in the billionaire seats.

"Please go to the changing room."

In a few moments Michel emerged, skin tingling from the sleek splendor of wild silk, and his mood lightened.

"Step, please, on the platform."

As Michel did, Vellancio's dark eyes beamed into the three-way mirror. He flung his chalk in the air, exhaled breathlessly, rejoicing in his sartorial genius.

"*Bella figura* . . . the cut, the fit. Titian himself, he should be here to paint you. Did you know that Fellini came to me after *La Dolce Vita* and said he wished I had *created* the clothes for the film? Marcello Mastroianni would have been a star."

"In some circles, he was a star."

Unfortunately, at this moment of Vellancio's self-rapture, every herb, clove of garlic, and wild root oozed from the tailor's mouth, producing a terrorist gas attack. Michel reflexively turned his head away from the dragon fumes of the tailor's past meals.

"A *minusculo* adjustment," he said, seizing Michel's balls. "The crotch, he is hanging a millimeter."

Michel turned pale and wrenched himself away from the tailor. "I forgot to wear my cup," he said, regaining his balance.

"You always joke with me, Michel."

"One more time, Alberto, and I'll arrest you."

"Stand straight, head high, *cavaliere,* and look into the mirror." With a mouthful of pins, Vellancio was exploring Michel's groin when an unnatural sound of agony detonated and the great tenor's aria from *Aïda* was drowned out.

Michel seized the tailor by the throat. "My balls, testicles! Alberto. I'm not into piercing. And you need a license for *corridas* and instruction on the use of *banderillas.*"

"You have two *testicolos. Due, due.* Ahhh, *principe,* you moved. I am like a surgeon. The patient moves, the problem is his. Now, *princessa* Jennifer is always serene during the fittings."

"You're making a dress for her?"

"Of course, where else would she go? Bianca! Bring the dress."

"No, don't!" Michel countered. "It's bad luck."

"As you like. She bleeds on her wedding night, you bleed a little."

**Jennifer Bowen stalked** among the great paintings Michel had been bequeathed. She was in the backroom of the new Chardin Gallery on the Cours Mirabeau. The hammers and saws of workmen putting the final touches on the hanging area did not intrude on her thoughts. In fact, the noise was comforting. She was still jumpy from last night's montage of tormented dreams. She had been attacked by snakes that had been thrust on her by the madman who had followed her to Aix last summer.

She was reluctant to discuss these episodes with a psychiatrist.

What could he tell her that she didn't already know about trauma and murder? *It will pass, time will heal the wounds.*

"Bullshit," she said, staring at herself in the mirror. "No one gets over these things. And it's no reason to pig out," she added, criticizing herself. She had always had a weight problem, but now with her wedding a few days off, it had blown into a neurosis. "God, do I see a double chin?"

"No, it's the light." Grace Chardin, the American wife of the gallery's owner, stood at the doorway. "And since when have you started talking to yourself?"

"I weighed one hundred and forty-five pounds this morning, Grace."

"So, you're five-ten. How would you like to weigh that much and be five inches shorter? Jen, you have to accept the fact that we're hostages—American women eating French food three times a day. We weren't designed for this kind of abuse."

"I guess you're right."

"How long are you going to be?"

"Just a few more minutes. I've got to finish these catalogue notes."

"Okay. Okay, but get these terrible thoughts out of your head. You're gorgeous."

"I'm plentiful."

"Lavish."

Jennifer's *amour-propre* sprouted wings. "Who said that?"

"Madame Desalle. Did you forget we're picking up your lingerie at her atelier?"

"Well, she's charging me enough to pay compliments."

"Oh, we're in a mood. I'm taking you to lunch at my favorite little haunt afterwards."

"Chez Danton's closed until after the wedding."

"I wasn't talking about Chez Danton. I'll be next door at Façonnable. Pick me up fast before I spend a fortune on their new blazers."

When Jennifer had first seen the paintings, she did not have the presence of mind to weigh the consequences of such an inheritance. Who could? After she hung them in the family farmhouse in St-

Rémy, and scrupulously examined each provenance, she was stunned. The collection consisted of three lyrical Renoirs from his days at Argenteuil when he was painting side by side with Monet; an exquisite Matisse *Odalisque* of his mistress; two Bonnards from his Nabi period when he and his coterie pushed Impressionism to its limits in search of new expressions, then abandoned it for bolder colors and intensely detailed surface design.

The Picasso, from his great gloomy Blue Period, was a major example of mood dictating his changing style. At a recent sale a Blue had gone for fifty-five million dollars. There was a bewitching Watteau of a young actress at her makeup table. A Degas of swirling ballerinas made Jennifer do pirouettes and crash into the furniture; an early Monet seascape of Le Havre carried the flavor and scent of sea spray; a mysterious, unknown Gauguin painted in Arles when he was living with van Gogh was like a detective story. Finally the walls were crowned with three mature, majestic Cézannes.

The fourteen paintings were worth a fortune. For insurance purposes, Jennifer contacted Sotheby's and Christie's recent auction sales. She estimated that the collection was worth somewhere in the neighborhood of three hundred million dollars. She had learned from Jules Chardin, Michel's former professor at the Sorbonne, that her appraisal was low. He thought it might bring considerably more. The prospect of such wealth was incomprehensible to Jennifer.

Only a year ago, she had been a professor at a second-rate college for problem girls with rich parents. She'd always been scrambling for money, worrying about her contract. And at thirty she brooded about the possibility of a loveless, barren future. She had won the lottery in love and money and she sought a perspective. Yes, she was a first-rate art historian with a Ph.D. from Stanford and she had a good opinion of herself because Michel had fallen in love with her, but how could she suddenly deal with the trials of good fortune?

The prospect of eventually having children with Michel made her giddy with pleasure, but raising them in a privileged environment troubled her. Worse yet, sending them to exclusive schools so that they might march through life in a social class purchased by a woman who had kept a brothel and profited from paid sex outraged Jennifer.

There was nothing of the prude in Jennifer, nor some holy feminist ideal of justice in this viewpoint. It was deeply pragmatic and not mere posturing when she asked herself: "How many lovers did thousands of young women have so that I could wake up every morning with Renoir in my bedroom?" Profiting from their sexual drudgery was distasteful.

Jennifer was incapable of this degree of self-indulgence or sticking her head in the sand. Ultimately it was human question, a question of conscience. And when this mood struck, the paintings turned rancid. As a principal in their ownership, it aroused despair. Everything had depended on Michel's decision, and she tested his love.

"It's selfish and mean-spirited to hoard these paintings for ourselves," she'd said months ago on a frigid evening in February with the mistral howling, fastened shutters clapping, sleep impossible, onion soup and lovemaking the only alternatives.

"What are you suggesting?"

"Let's show them to the public. Jules Chardin is opening a gallery. It'll help him and we can charge a hundred francs a head and donate the money to the university's endowment fund."

Michel had never thought of this and he admired Jennifer's generosity.

"But a catalogue has to be prepared."

"I'm already working on it."


**On the deserted** Beau Rivage beach in La Ciotat, a short drive from Aix, the ruckled evening waves, formerly glistening pompadours, carried the flotsam of pleasure boats to shore. Only a short drive from Aix-en-Provence, a once-popular old wreck of a hotel sulked above the sheltered cove. In its glory days, it had been a place of daytime sand castles, seascape painters, splendid picnics, and topless women bathers.

At the hotel bar an assortment of gossipy locals filtered in. They complained about their lives, the lost grandeur of the nation, and how to scourge the immigrants from Gallic soil. And now they had to cope with the thirty-five-hour week, their own truckers barricading the borders in protest. All these edicts were put in place so that unemployed aliens could be given a Frenchman's work. The Euro, as coin of the realm for the new Europe, was accepted with disgust, another debasement of the incomparable franc.

Even worse was *parité,* actually electing women to public office. Where was Marie-Antoinette as a symbol of what could happen—Robespierre, Danton, the glory days of the Directory when heads rolled? Napoleon would have taught them a lesson. The republic needed him and not the cowed prime minister, appeasing every woman. Even among the regulars, it had been generally conceded that, if there was no one to blame, the French would invent someone—along with a cause to go with it. The British boycott of Brie as a reprisal for the French ban on the English mad-cow beef brought along some "Vive la France" cheers.

Exotic affectations were not absolved from their disdain. This evening, along with U.K. beef, the extra dry, very cold martini—which had staged something of a baffling recovery in Provence—made with Ketel One, Belvedere, or the native Grey Goose—came in for a scolding. It was sweeping the coastal resorts, requiring time and effort for a busy bartender to prepare, while the beer or Pastis drinker fretted and hooted for a refill.

The source of this calamity at the Hôtel Claude bar were a pair of sandy, parboiled Brits who blundered in and arrogantly demanded them. Berlitz opened to bar phrases, the couple were behind the bar, pointing through a dusty array of bottles. They wanted martinis *styled* with triple distilled Wyborowa, no less, a gentle rinse of Noilly Prat bathed over the rocks, firm Nyons olives, and none of the wrinkled beards usually served with their pimientos drooping out like entrails. They also demanded *chilled* stem glasses and wanted to inspect the crusty Havana cigars lodged on a shelf above the rusting cognacs.

They intently watched René, the furious bartender, who, under their scrutiny, was forced to discard the ice and continue the laborious massage, cocking the shaker to his left ear like a maracas player. All the customers were fuming, but raptly viewing these aerobic follies. When would it cease? Despite the sign prohibiting the removal of glassware to the beach, no one said a word when the couple left the bar.

The regulars were happy to be rid of the limeys, with their mud-caked Air Jordans and ratty T-shirts advertising a visit to Aix-en-Provence. Even the waves below sighed when the couple pranced out, jauntily squeaking down the stone steps to forage for souvenirs. Whatever jetsam the sea had expelled, they would cart back through customs to some shaggy hamlet for a despised in-law who collected these atrocities.

Once the couple scattered to the beach with their martinis, a fizzle of voices accompanied the entrance of Claude Boisser, formerly superintendent of the vice squad in Aix-en-Provence. Claude had bought the hotel with his lifetime's savings of bribes. He was a genial host, buying the bar a round.

"This pilot on a 747 with a full load has been waiting forever for permission from the control tower to take off. He and the passengers are at the end of their rope because of the delays. Finally, he turns to the copilot and says:

" 'I'd give anything for a blow job and a hot cup of coffee.'

"The pilot has no idea that the PA is still on and all the passengers and flight attendants have heard this casual request.

"Suddenly a stewardess who looks like Catherine Deneuve sprints down the aisle to switch off the PA. As she passes an old priest, holding his beads, he calls out:

" 'And don't forget the coffee.' "

Everyone at this happy hour roared. Trust Claude to come up with a lewd joke. The bar came alive with everyone ordering more drinks while the DJ began the evening's music with a John Lennon retro. "Imagine" would open the festivities.

An aged bellman with thick glasses, wearing a faded green uniform, chivvied in a reluctant flock of well-dressed women. They almost seemed to be on a towline.

"Ah, Benedict, I thought you'd made off with my swans. I think there's a touch of Mormon in Benedict," Claude observed.

"Too many years at Louise's," René observed of the bellman's previous employment as gatekeeper of her brothel.

"I gave up penetration a long time ago," Benedict snapped.

"I'm not that fortunate," Claude replied, smirking at the liberated gaggle of women.

He had invited them to dinner and an investment lecture. When they grew bored reading his financial prospectus, prepared by his Chinese accountant, and threatened to bolt, he had locked them in the windowless banquet room. Ear to the door, he gloomily listened to the women complain that the evening had become a hostage situation. In a huff, Claude went for a walk to clear his head. Eventually he allowed his decrepit bellman to free them.

Claude splayed over the zinc bar: embracing, wooing these potential investors in his scheme to renovate the place. Girdled in baggy flea-market Armani trousers and a shirt which he wore untucked in the musical *Buena Vista Social Club* style, Claude was a lascivious but amusing man with a brazen charm. Tonight, as always, since he knew nothing of politics or current events except that they were inconvenient, he tarnished Anglo-Saxon manhood.

From the master's seat, he pointed to the Englishman down on the beach.

"*Ejaculato praecox*. These men never reach the harbor. They crash into the shoals." By this he meant thighs or other destinations remote from the port of entry.

A shriek from the beach interrupted Claude.

"Her back!" The Englishwoman's words were garbled by screams and ambushed by the sunset wind which had wildly swept up from Marseille. It was early June, the climate and sailing conditions unpredictable, rain forest fodder for Greenpeace speeches and ominous La Niña forecasters.

"If that damned girl has a glass splinter, it serves her right. Let her get back to that dirty Hertz car and find a doctor," Claude sternly observed. He had become vigilant about foreign lawsuits. "It's a public beach and not technically part of the property."

"Maybe someone's hurt," René said.

The melancholy bartender lifted the hatch and walked to the

sliding window. He had been temporarily poached from his regular employment at Chez Danton, which had closed for a face-lift while the Dantons prepared for Michel's wedding.

René observed the couple waving frantically. They were beside some bundle. He couldn't make it out. The woman was jumping on the sand. A glass splinter. For once, Claude might have been right. One of the women slipped behind the bar and collected the ancient first-aid kit, which had leaked iodine, then looked for a towel to wipe the greasy film off her hands.

She said, "Throw this down, Claude . . . René. Oh, I'll bring it myself."

A few moments later, she, too, began to screech, and the grumpy patrons trooped down to the beach. Claude remained above in the command post, the captain on the bridge, clutching a bottle of Pastis.

He had heard the dreaded word, *body*.

This was not the best news for a man who had laid on an eight-course dinner for the widows and divorcées he had hoped to fleece that evening. He had made private appointments with several of them afterward to inspect the amenities and inquire if any of them engaged in orgies, since he intended to chase out the usual family summer guests and convert the hotel into a high-class bordello, a place for pillow talk.

"We'll be eating duck with soggy olives for a week," he grunted to René.

The bartender tossed his blue-striped apron at him. "You will. I'm leaving. I've had enough of martinis and your company for a lifetime."

Claude finally ambled down to the sea, churlishly kicking sand like a child. The group from the bar had retreated to the ramshackle cabañas with the English couple. Someone was now calling for smelling salts.

Only moments before, the bloated, partially decomposed naked body of a young girl had been carried in by a wave making landfall just below Claude's rotting cabins and balding grass-skirted beach bar. This troupe of shanties managed to remain upright after the tail end of mistral had swerved out of its path; they resembled the salvaged hulls of old shipwrecked schooners.

Approaching the youthful corpse, lying on its side, Claude waved a fist. "Smelling salts, first-aid kits—I'm not running a pharmacy!"

Claude sprang back, stunned. He had been a cop long enough to have witnessed some gruesome sights, but the condition of this child was enough to make him ill. What had formerly been the flesh on her back had undergone hideous burns. She might have been set on fire or hit with a blowtorch. The girl's left nipple had been pierced and a tarnished ornament encrusted with seaweed hung from it. A faintly greenish engraving might have been the word *amour*.

He would have to telephone Michel Danton, a man he had always admired but now detested. Michel had forced his resignation from the vice squad with a charge of corruption. How else could a man live in France and buy a hotel?

After such a discovery, more than likely, Claude would find his customers looking fishy-eyed at the cloudy bar glasses. Next, they would be demanding bidets in the rooms that did not squirt up to the ceiling. Even for his future lower-depth constituency, there was a repellent aspect to sodden clothes after a bout of lovemaking.

More significantly, a dead body did not go well at the hors d'oeuvres hour over a plate of Perigeux pâté and moules with warm *frites*.

It seemed he was now a hotelier with a murdered child on what was technically not his beach. As a police officer for thirty-five years, he had made his fortune by noticing nothing. When Michel Danton came to call, Claude would trot out a host of mildewed rationalizations regarding his legal responsibility for the beach. Murdered girls, like vermin, would lead to bad publicity. Michelin and Gault-Millau wouldn't even bother to send their inspectors to the rejuvenated hotel.

Bereft, Claude groaned. He turned his head away from the dead child and dashed up the steps to the bar. The sight of the beach repelled him.

# 1

# WHERE DO WE COME FROM?

# CHAPTER 1

**In the romantic delusive** hope of re-creating an American version of Venice in California, Abbot Kinney, a man who had made a fortune in tobacco, turned property developer. Early into the twentieth century the tobacco baron had the misguided notion that Americans from all over would flock to his piers and pools, canals, and amusement parks. For a time he was successful, and one of his grand posthumous achievements became a bottleneck of homes listing over the waterways that still remain. This inspired nativity came to be known as the Venice Canals. That it was missing San Marco and the Doge's Palace, gondolas, and was deficient in Titians didn't occur to the salesmen flogging houses, or, indeed, the purchaser.

For decades amid the rotting timbers of its tract bungalows and shacks, hippies, squatters, and drug dealers — the lice of society — found enchantment. In the sixties, these forlorn dwellings, fronting onto garbage-filled waterways, flooded in winter and were blighted when drought exposed the canals' alluvial roots and the detritus of sixty years. During the Santa Ana season, the desert winds played discordant music over the decayed wasteland: Putrefying food brought swarms of insects; occasionally, severed body parts of a human being commingled with the skeletons of pets and birds; beer cans danced against broken bottles; discarded mattresses, their rusted springs quivering like medieval beds of nails, emphasized the devil-may-care attitude of the reckless natives and their indifference.

On foggy nights, and they were plentiful, the sound of gunfire neither dismayed nor outraged the community. The houses were easy to rent and even easier to purchase for thirty or forty thousand dollars in those days. Now at the millennium, even the pint-sized quarters were hard to come by for under half a million dollars. Beach property prices and sanity were never aligned in California.

Most of the former matchstick cottages had been rebuilt, pumped up with space, and resembled the bodies of their gym-crazed owners. Wolfhounds and Bouviers frolicked with wily Siamese cats on the postage-sized lawns while ducks paraded around to the delight of children who fed them bean sprouts and seven-grain chunks of bread. The present neighborhood has a quaint exclusivity, a cachet. To say that one *owns* a house in the Venice Canals immediately sparks interest at cocktail parties and marks the individual as a person of means and taste.

**Garrett Lee Brant** hadn't murdered anyone recently and it wasn't on his mind. Nevertheless, he attached the leather scabbard to his calf and inserted four long pronged needles with heads he had forged so that he could grip them and thrust them into the offending party if necessary.

He and his beautiful Eve were preparing for a millennium bash, only seven hours away and there was a lull before the cadences of a New Year's Eve party began. It presented the couple with an opportunity to count blessings and rejoice in the success they had made of their lives. It was a time of reflection for Garrett in his enchanted cottage over the canal. His beloved Eve was paying a visit to her entire wardrobe floor, one thousand square feet of it, picking and probing through the cedar-lined room of costumes in order to select her fiesta ensemble for the ball that lay ahead.

In 1993, during a property recession, with money Garrett acquired from a generous rich aunt, whom he had assisted in a suicide, he had bought a Venice teardown. His timing had been impeccable, a sortie of good fortune after years of tumultuous misery and struggle. The young fugitive of freight trains and hobo jungles became a landowner, gentry. He was one of the few to profit from the foreclosure bloodbath in Los Angeles. One man's loss, another's gain.

Priscella Carmela Adams—or Auntie, as she preferred to be

called—was a wealthy, childless widow, a Pasadena do-gooder, an elderly art groupie enchanted by Garrett's manqué Gauguin-like paintings.

After her mysterious death, Garrett crashed out of art school. He had a way with a pen, legal documents, a natural calligrapher whose talent might have served to illuminate the monastic Bibles of the Middle Ages. Yes, he frequently thought, he would have done well in those days in a monastery. Prissy's family lawyer in Pasadena ignored everything, and Garrett was bequeathed seventy-five thousand dollars. He wished afterward he had added another zero.

At the School of Fine Arts, his teachers considered him a brilliant draftsman, molded by nature for a future as an art director with an elite cubbyhole on Madison Avenue. However, his life studies professor constantly wrote *COPYCAT* on his finest work.

When she was blithely leaving a stall in the ladies' room, Garrett, wearing a ski mask, stabbed her with a six-inch copper electrical pin he had found on a building site. He missed the carotid and the pin nestled into muscle.

Garrett had learned Lesson Number One: *Never use copper wire*.

The woman recovered, and Garrett, not a suspect in the attack, quit school after the investigation ended.

As the new homeowner of a squalid house in the paradise Abbot Kinney had dreamed of, Garrett was going through his benefactor's money quickly.

Contractors were Satan's militia, all of them designed as liars. The subs sold badly cut coke, were constantly hungover, and often were no-shows. Garrett, then still a very slender gentleman, shoved the burly contractor, who had spiked the job, into the canal. He had chipped bits and pieces, wrecked the place, and left old ruptured machinery in front of the house.

The man came out of the water screaming, "You tried to drown me."

Garrett improvised: He attempted to strangle this charging bull with a dog leash and got his ass royally kicked.

Lesson Number Two: *Never try to strangle anyone without having been on a course of anabolic steroids and in possession of a black belt or two.*

Stints in acting school and a course in theatrical makeup yielded slim pickings. Garrett found occasional missions on a few independent films and wound up painting scenery with the other grunts. With property taxes to pay and squawking sewer-service collection agencies on his case, he lucked into work on the Venice Boardwalk. He loved it. Everyone looking for fun: Sun & sex & someone with $, musicians, palmists, the future, fortunes told, astrologers, massages, religious fanatics, entertainers waiting to be discovered, panhandlers, performance artists, the homeless, cops on bikes, paddle tennis, racquetball, muscle beach weight lifters, painters, cranks, magicians, people on bikes, druggies, tattooed, pierced flesh, everyone smoking blustery grass and bonking in the swamped public restrooms.

### A Career

Chomping a chili hot dog, no onions, Garrett stumbled into a tattoo parlor, where a group of desperados from a new Hell's Angels chapter waited for their insignia to be implanted on their flesh. As a potential customer, and last in line, Garrett studied a working tattooist for a few hours, observing everything.

Always a Chatty Cathy, Garrett discussed technique with the owner. In those days, Garrett carried in his backpack a magnificent set of photographs of his work as a painter. When they were planning a show, his late Auntie had commissioned some hotshot to photograph his stuff. Garrett himself was no mean photographer and he appreciated the work of others.

The owner of the tattoo parlor tossed Garrett a black artist's pen and the virtuoso proceeded to outline the badge of courage on a volunteer's forehead. Garrett Lee Brant had discovered his métier. He was hired on the spot. He settled with the tax man and the goons sent out by the collection agency.

Einstein had finally found the classroom for Physics 101.

**In two years,** Garrett slaved the madness of hours, twenty was a day, and he'd hoarded enough money from private appointments to open his first emporium.

### The Gauguin Salons

As Garrett's business flourished, he constantly remodeled the house with pros. These new contractors grew stories like redwoods. Located in a prime section of Linnie Canal, the vista revealed the elegant humped bridge. The place had grown to something over four thousand square feet, four floors, not to mention the rooftop atelier of the artist with French doors done in a lime trim, which accented the saffron medley exterior. Yellow, yellow, yellow.

Coming into the house from the two-car garage which housed his pearl gray 1989 Aston Martin (his mechanic's annuity) and Eve's practical black Range Rover, the gym and sauna reminded them that body beautiful would never go out of style.

A leap up three steps unveiled hanging copper pans refracting sunlight and the spotless kitchen filled with rainbows. Since neither of them actually cooked, it had all the agencies for caterers and reheating take-out. Eve had a positive genius for defrosting and spicing with habañero sauces.

The English-character country sitting room, plump sofas, and wing chairs echoed Garrett's bachelor-cum-old-maid period, pre-Eve. Art Deco mirrors from their antiquing forays had cast a decidedly moderne smirk on the furnishing. Eve was mirror crazy and delighted in walking around naked so that she could see herself wherever she happened to be. Garrett, on the other hand, had his demure side. His eyes caressed her.

"We're fucking beautiful, let's enjoy it," she invariably said.

When they had returned from Bangkok and made a life decision to always be together, Eve had walked through the house with a quiet sneer. Then, out of the blue, in the master bathroom, she dropped her panties, climbed on the sink, lifted her skirt, and pressed the pink lips of her delicate vagina against his shaving mirror. The magnification in the enclosed room fabricated the Garden of Eden. Garrett had never seen any woman lay open the beauty of herself in this way.

"All the stuff, clothes, shit, gew-gaws, and those Buddhas you bought me in Bangkok, you can toss into the canal. I'm not living with a monk."

\*     \*     \*

**An inglenook held** a top-of-the-line Sony entertainment center and a complex speaker system; an unobtrusive flat-screen TV kept them in touch with the disasters of daily life. The dining room, a marriage of inspirations, would have excited the appraisers of *The Antique Road Show*. English, Spanish, and French pieces formed a wayward boutique of taste buds.

Books were everywhere, including a massive collection of art volumes and biographies of the great artist Paul Gauguin. Paul, Garrett's friend, mentor, and alas, his enemy were having problems. During these moments, when artists disagreed, Garrett would turn to *Recherche du Temps Perdu* for guidance. Proust always came up with an answer to his problems.

**Eve, short-tempered,** simmering with jealousy, packed her outfits in a Louis Vuitton bag to dress for the party at Heather Malone's estate. She was very ditzy, whining, angry, and badly concealing her surrender to Garrett. She did not want to go! Heather and Garrett had been lovers until Eve's arrival. The pleasantries between the women masked total abhorrence.

The mirrored room was filled with a wardrobe of costumes and period ensembles. The racks of clothing would not have embarrassed the buyers at Barney's on his side of the room, nor hers at Stormy Leather.

Eve flaunted a black latex ensemble against her, seeking his approval. He raised an eyebrow.

"Garrett, you're in a mood. I can tell."

"Hello, *who's* in a mood? Well, how long can I watch you going through aisles of hanging racks. I feel like I'm in the middle of a French Rags sale."

"You know-all, they don't have sales! Be patient," Eve said, holding up a pair of black leather pants and a captivity belt. For her top, she selected an abbreviated Victorian corset. "Is this *trop avant garde*?"

She had been studying Berlitz French tapes for a year now so that Garrett and she could really enjoy a trip to France without him having to translate every phrase. He had been her tutor for a few days, but gave up, since he was her lover and fluent, she irascible, angry, humiliated by being slow.

"Not with blushing pink silk panties," Garrett said to appease her. Still, he had to reassert some control rather than yield to his beauty's whims.

"Well, that's done. You always read me. Garrett, thanks for being so patient." Eve's mood, always volatile, altered. "Garrett, darling, please, please, go to Heather's without me. I could kill that slut."

"I know. But she's my—*our*—financial salvation. When I was destitute and alone, Heather was there."

"Spare me this sappy bullshit. I was there, too, for you."

"Eve, don't cry."

They had agreed to attend Heather Malone's millennium prom. Garrett would greet people he'd tattooed. Actually, it wasn't work, simply a favor to Heather. In every love affair, someone loses. Eve was not about to share Garrett with anyone, certainly not Heather.

**Garrett had a** quiet, leisurely drink in his office. He nursed his martini to give Eve more time. When he returned to her dressing room, he was amazed that Eve was ready, and he wrapped his arms around her jeweled waist chain.

"You are incredible."

She gave him a borderline smile. "Garrett, you don't get it. I live to please you. I will do anything to gratify you. Now I'm looking forward to the party."

He felt himself crumbling to her power. "Eve, Eve, I know that. But please, please, let's be careful and if we do anything, it has to be together. Let's not get careless tonight. My darling, our life, our relationship, comes before anything."

Eve's reaction to orders was comparable to a pouting teenager threatened with a grounding.

"You know where I stand," she replied as though being accused of treason.

He was afraid that he had upset her and yielded. "I can't help it if I'm jealous."

"Get real."

Absolute freedom required absolute responsibility, but they were living in a universe twisted by contradiction in which time and space might prove to be strings, illusions. If gender was relative, in their society, a matter of perception, so might the cosmos.

Garrett, in his King of the Road Aston Martin DB5, whirred through the U-bends of the canals. The weather had been fitful, moody; tonight a sulky drizzle pinged over the water and the temperature had wobbled down. The sky had the inky gray ridges of a chest X-ray. Garrett wormed over the short bridges through the misty gloaming of the purified canals and embraced the new millennium with his dream woman.

Pausing at a light on Washington Boulevard, Garrett looked over beside him: cars, belching and dirty, filled with merrymakers and stereos blaring rap and hip-hop. Eve nudged him. She had her little brown bottle out. He pulled into a strip center in the wasteland of Mar Vista. Eve sucked a mound of coke into her right nostril.

She cleared the crumbs in the mirror and licked her index finger.

He smiled at her. "It's our world."

"Right. *Mon chéri,* Garr-ette"

"The millennium dawns! Eve, please, behave."

"Yes, I will. But I'm ready for something stormy and turbulent, something frantic tonight."

God help him, he thought.

# CHAPTER 2

**When Michel reached his** office in Marseille, he was immediately notified of the discovery of the young girl's body below Claude's hotel. Michel was irritated by himself. He was suffering from groom's nerves. He called Jennifer on her cell phone. She was stuck at the Marseille airport. Her mother's flight had been delayed. Rather than meet him for dinner at Le Miramar at the Quai du Port, which was near his office, she had decided to wait it out.

"The last thing I want to do is hang my mother up," she said. "It'll take forty minutes to drive into town and who knows how long to get back."

"You're a conscientious daughter."

"Maybe, if I'm looked after, I'll be a good wife, too."

Michel's testicle was still tender from the tailor's pin stab. "Remember we have a houseguest," he said in an effort to forestall any strenuous exertion.

"My mother's no prude. I'll anchor the bed."

"I told you, Jennifer, it needs to be set in a concrete base."

He listened to the sweet chime of her laughter. "Listen, you claimed you were impotent when I met you. Yeah, just like Warren Beatty. What a story I fell for."

Charles Fournier, the examining magistrate, was tapping his gold Mont Blanc pen on Michel's desk and dusting it with a Kleenex.

"I have a meeting with my new boss. Your favorite fishmonger."

"Let me talk to him," Jennifer demanded. She was bored, as everyone is, waiting at the airport.

Fournier took the receiver. "May I call you Madame Danton?"

"Very shortly, Charles. Now, don't dream up any new cases for my fiancé or I'll break your arms and legs."

"You have a dangerous reputation. I'll keep him safe. I want a report on his performance during the honeymoon to put in his personnel file." He handed the phone back to Michel.

"I'm sorry you'll miss Pierre's bouillabaisse at Le Miramar. It's the *chartered* version, approved of by my boss."

"Oh, God, I'm having an orgasm."

"Wonderful, I can preserve my vanishing sperm. We'll need a high count for the baby. I don't want our child born with a stutter and blue and brown eyes."

"I love you, you insane person. 'Bye."

The men politely skirted the case for a moment while Charles discussed the horrors of in-laws and his fanatical, personal plan for premeditated murder.

"Now you're on the record, Charles."

"Wait until you meet your *belle-mère*."

"She'll be wonderful, like her daughter," Michel said, squandering his optimism.

"Don't count on it." Charles Fournier waited a moment and sought a transition. "I called Le Miramar and Pierre said he'd keep the kitchen open until ten-thirty for us."

"Murder before a bouillabaisse sounds like bribery," Michel said.


**Michel had his** elderly Citroën-Maserati tuned the previous week and as he drove along the traffic-free coastal road, the vision of the quiet loveliness of La Ciotat relieved the anxieties of examining a dead girl. Throughout the capricious history of this beach, when summer darkness struck, it had served as a sanctuary for courtships and cuckoldry: disenchanted wives, reliving Colette's *Chéri,* surfed through young men who carried the sirens to the glossy cabañas. An exquisite, sloshed mermaid might kiss a toad.

Anyone who could walk or drive from the surrounding precincts had a romp. During these amorous nights at the beach, the husbands of these women were to be found in town at Le Miramar enjoying a robust bouillabaisse with an engaging young tartlet.

From the postwar period through the sixties and even during the rump of the nineties, these activities ruffled no feathers. Now, after its postmillennium revelry, the old place, rebaptized Hôtel Claude in honor of its new owner, was ready for a face-lift.

Michel strolled through the once-courtly bar. Shoddy pilasters draped with brittle erotic figures were in the throes of crumbling, the blackamoor lanterns had turned a whiter shade of pale. Salt water and sand blowing in from the terrace were merciless foes.

Music floated up from the beach and blinking lights from boats at sea reminded him of the past. Making his way down the steps, Michel ducked under dim lampposts coated with salt residue, which provided the sort of vision someone suffering from glaucoma might expect. The festive atmosphere and the intoxicated laughter of the people suggested an after-dinner pairing-off.

John Lennon's voice croaked the lyrics of "Imagine" through swaying warped speakers the size of camel humps.

Claude Boisser's grunting laughter was followed by that of a chorus of females. Michel, who thought he had seen every conceivable murder scene, flinched. The merrymakers still hadn't seen him. Someone else had.

In tails and sandals, Delantier, the elderly maître d' of Chez Danton, clutched his arm. The old man's head quivered as he bowed. The crisscrossed bayous over his scalp, swamped in Bay Rum, made Michel retreat. Bad day for smells, he thought.

"What are *you* doing here?" Michel asked.

"My summer holiday with riffraff."

Michel was perplexed. "Where's the body? I had a report—"

"I took care of everything before bringing down the hors d'oeuvres. Nothing for you to worry about, Michel. I heard you had your balls pricked today at the tailor."

"Good news travels fast. Did Vellancio type my blood as well?"

"No. It's a premarital tradition left over from the Normans to determine whether the groom is alive."

"Indeed. You're a scholar as well, Delantier," Michel said to the antagonistic old waiter. "Since when have you been working here?"

"While you were in Paris, the wartime conditions in the kitchen between your parents reached the level of the Normandy invasion."

"If I had my choice, I'd cancel this wedding banquet and take Jennifer to the Baumanière and have a civilized luncheon."

"Not a bad idea, Michel."


**Michel trod over** the mucky sand and shouted over John Lennon, "Everyone shut up and turn the damn music off!" The gendarmes, guarding the body, all tossed their drinks into the water. "Put on some lights, you scum!" A patrol car switched on yellow fog lights. "This is wonderful," he said to Delantier.

"I spoke to Claude and he told me I was in charge."

"Did you touch the body?"

The old man trembled. "No, Michel, I know better than that."

Claude bellowed, "Delantier, where is the sorbet? Our guests don't want to drink it through straws!"

Michel approached the bar, but the chattering group ignored him. They had Biros and were signing documents and writing checks.

Claude had a glass for Michel. "Taste this, Michel, it's a miracle. I bought this Limoncello in Sicily. Believe me, if Cézanne had ever tasted something like this, he would have learned something about lemons and painted them properly without the warts."

"You were the last one to view the body, and you didn't call it in."

"I don't know what you're talking about."

"I don't want a drink, Claude. The bar is closed! My people should be arriving shortly." His presence was a distraction to the hushed assembly. Michel's physical size and authority were unwelcome. "My name is Michel Danton of the Special Circumstances Section. You're all going to be fingerprinted and give statements to the Police Judiciaire. Oh, don't use your cell phones, either. Ladies, no more drinking. Everyone, please, stay where you are."

Michel reached for his latex gloves and approached the body. Through the water droplets blurring a plastic sheet, he saw a naked young girl partially covered in sand with hideous burns on her back.

Michel learned from the local sergeant that the English couple who had discovered the girl's body had given a statement and the name of their hotel in Aix. There was no reason to suspect that they had anything to do with this, but protocol dictated that one of his squad would interview them.

The Marseille morgue wagon girded down a hillock onto the sand. A vicious halogen spotlight illuminated the beach, giving the scene the starkness of a film shoot. Slanting silhouettes played against the changing tide and abrupt eddies of wind flapped the clear plastic covering the girl.

Michel found himself enveloped in the surrealism of murder. The early demise of a child upset the symmetry of the natural world. He was never a sentimentalist, even when he was young, but he regarded the murder of a future mother as an offense against humanity. He saw a vision of Chirico's paintings of empty space, its vacant figures, silently spawning death in the green millennium.

"Who put the plastic on?" Michel asked.

"I did," Delantier said, as though confession would purge the vision. "It came from a new roll which I opened myself."

"Good man," Michel said.

Annie Vallon, his highly charged chief female investigator, pounced onto the beach from her new convertible. This year Michel's partly schizophrenic deputy had become a redhead. She had recently returned from her holiday on one of the Danish islands. She had a stable of wealthy foreign lovers, German and Scandinavian, who spent lavishly for her favors. He had recommended her to the Paris Inspectorate as his replacement, but they tittered and asked if he was having another breakdown. Feminism might arrive in France for the third millennium. Annie was accompanied by Pierre Graslin, Michel's astute and unambitious middle-aged investigator.

"Talk about dedication," Annie said. "I had a date with a nineteen-year-old who loves older women."

"You're worth waiting for," Michel said with a smile.

"How would you know? You've never even given me a friendly stroke."

"He wants to keep your reputation spotless," Pierre said.

"What reputation? Who's dead?"

"A young girl."

Annie turned away in revulsion.

Finally, carrying his medical kit, Dr. Laurent, the dolorous medical examiner, and his techs emerged, loaded down with equipment, power packs, and camcorders.

"Michel, when the Minguella brothers prepare a bouillabaisse for your bachelor dinner, it's a case of moral turpitude to stand them up. Really, where is your honor?"

"Relax, Laurent, they'll serve us until ten-thirty."

His humor somewhat restored, the coroner, who combined lethargy and a voracious appetite, sulked beside the bar. He looked over the remains of the dinner plates, pancaked with grease. He grimaced at Claude, who was standing behind atrophied palm fronds, smoking a Gauloise and sipping a glass of Limoncello.

"Disgusting, Claude."

"What is, Laurent?"

"Didn't your cook ever hear of crisping the duck under the grill?"

"Cook? If only. He was homeless, a *clochard*."

"Whatever he was or is, he has a future as an embalmer, not a cook."

The troops concluded the forensic videos and still photos, then took the child to the morgue. The sluggish ebb tide surrendered again to the slick, wavy pompadours of the Mediterranean.

# CHAPTER 3

**In the autopsy chamber,** Michel always had the entire group of laboratory experts inspect a murder victim together. They were all present and had rescheduled their *vacances* to be in town for his wedding. The banter about him was relentless, and discussions about who was wearing what for the event were on a level with the dish that attends the couture season in Paris.

"I heard you got spiked. You're always in fashion, Michel," Dr. Louis Devoire, the serologist said.

"Yes," Michel agreed. "It's a new vasectomy from California. The tailor decided I have one testicle too many."

"Haut couture," Andrea Chang piped in. She did hair and fiber analysis and had helped to solve his last case. She was beautiful, Eurasian, and showed photos of her dress to the group. She had been picked by Jennifer to be a maid of honor.

Professor Timone Saban, in charge of DNA, wandered in with a magnificent silk tuxedo.

"God Almighty, Michel, can't a man get a dinner suit without you calling?"

The suit was white and Michel snapped, "You're not the groom or getting married in Algeria."

"Well, so much for flea market bargains. Mine fits at least."

Dr. Laurent, waiting for his moment, entered in full uniform: a black rubber apron and mask. He lifted the plastic covering from the girl.

The group had seen thousands of bodies and no one said a word.

After samples had been taken, the girl's body had been washed by attendants. There was a puzzled grin on her face; she lay on the steel table facing them as though she were the judge, demanding an explanation for this inhumanity. As Michel moved closer during the examination, changing places with his team, the coroner rifled out a cause of death.

"A pin of approximately three hundred and twelve centimeters entered the carotid artery."

The appalling yellowish burn marks reached from her pelvis, covering her entire back. Michel had been an investigator long enough to recognize an acid wash.

"The burn marks and tissue samples will be analyzed," Laurent continued. "I venture to say that the girl had her flesh scorched with nitric acid. Pathologically, from the samples I took myself, just a little while ago, I didn't detect any inflammation."

"She was carefully immersed in acid after the fact?" Annie Vallon asked.

"Yes, and there's no distinctive odor, so that again indicates she was already dead," Laurent observed.

The child's blond hair was now dry. It had a mixed golden luster under the lights.

Michel lifted a hank of it. The salt water had given it the texture of old paste. "Her hair looks . . . streaked."

"We've taken samples. But it'll be a while before we know if it's from sun or dye," Andrea said.

Michel stared at the dead girl's face. "Jennifer had her hair done a couple of days ago, so maybe I'm imagining this."

Laurent continued examining the shapely body and was about to turn her.

"Age twelve to fourteen." He switched on the saw. "I'll have to go in—"

"No, stop, Laurent. Let's study her face a bit longer," Michel said, turning the girl's head.

Michel examined the glittering teeth. "She looks like a movie star. Her teeth are capped. Her front teeth have the glow of a porcelain veneer. And her right molar has a tiny gold filling."

Laurent, who preferred to work alone with his mike and an attendant to bring coffee, was agitated. "Of course, I'll call in Dr. Fontaire to do a forensic analysis."

"As long as he doesn't come near me," Pierre said. "He wanted five hundred francs for a cleaning and some X-rays! I told him there was a Moroccan dentist would make a plate for less."

Michel smiled at his detective. He had recently had his premarital checkup and was astounded by Dr. Fontaire's new prices and equipment. Fontaire had thrown his head back and laughed. "I spent six months at the University of Southern California on a course this year and a month with Dr. Gary O'Brien, who developed a new implant technique."

"You'll have people cashing in their insurance policies to pay your bills," Michel had said.

"Only the living have to chew, Michel."

As Laurent was again going to proceed, Michel forced him to pause. He carefully examined the girl's left palm. He slid the latex glove off his left hand and held his hand beside the girl's for the curious audience.

"These callused ridges come from one thing—golf. Look at the density of them. They're spongy from the water, but they're amazing to someone like me. She's a junior golfer and been playing for years. Hitting buckets of balls on the range since she could walk, I'd bet," Michel picked up a mop handle and slowly gripped it so that everyone could observe him. "This is called a Hogan grip, named after the great American golfer Ben Hogan. He invented it and taught it to hackers like me in his book. Most golfers use it." He put down the mop handle. "Now who here can tell me about girls' junior golf in France? How about Spain . . . England . . . Brazil?"

His question linked everyone in silence.

"This little girl, with her beautiful caps and Hogan golf calluses, is *not* French. I think she's American." He turned to the medical examiner. "You can switch on your saw now."

**By nine o'clock,** Michel and the team had checked all the reports of female children missing in France. Michel placed a call to Interpol in Lyon and spoke to the division head for kidnapped children. Ten days ago, an American couple reported that their thirteen-year-old daughter had vanished in the picturesque old Hanseatic city of

Bruges in Belgium. The suspect was a woman they had encountered during a tour.

At nine-thirty, Michel received a high-quality digitized color photograph over the computer. A smiling Caroline Davis stood between her attractive parents, holding up a golf trophy.

He gathered the team around him.

"Track down the girl's parents and inform them."

**Michel reached Le** Miramar with his men. Although dinner there was always a feast, and murder invariably gave him an appetite, tonight he preferred a large uncompromising Johnny Walker. He looked at the swaying yachts and fishing boats so long a part of the bright quai walk. They now had an ominous cast. Outside the channel, off a boat like any of the thousands in the harbor, Caroline Davis had been dumped into the sea.

# CHAPTER 4

**Heather Malone was a** legend even in Beverly Hills. Once a prominent society lady, she had been drummed out of her enclave when she was caught by her husband entertaining the pool man and the tree-trimmer in tandem. Even worse, after her husband called the police, her response settled his hash.

"Since when is a good gang bang a crime against humanity?" a naked Heather demanded, clutching a detective. "There was no rape. Now get the fuck out and take my husband with you. I haven't had an orgasm since I married this loser."

The cops took Heather's limp husband outside and explained that this was a domestic matter and he had better do his homework in the future before calling 911. Heather divorced his ass and didn't ask for a penny. She was the daughter of a junk bond king who'd made off with eight or nine hundred million dollars, which he'd left to her before dying in Rio. Nobody could touch Heather.

At that moment, Garrett thought tenderly about Heather, before her surgery. When she had been svelte and amusing, they had been friends and lovers. But Garrett had changed and so had Heather. In a sense he would ensure that there were elements in his future work which reflected them as they had once been, when he composed the Minotaur in Chinese red below Heather's navel. Yes, it had been a quixotic paradise for them until Thailand, when Eve pulled them apart.

I screwed up, Heather, he thought ruefully. I'm the one to blame, Heather, not you. Oh, God, what you've done to yourself for me. *We all want to be someone else*, were her words.

It was getting on to more than a year now since Heather Malone had called Garrett, demanding that he accompany her to a plastic surgeon in Beverly Hills. She needed his support and he never refused his patroness. Heather had no time for the niceties and shoved an eight-by-ten color glossy across the doctor's desk.

"Make *me* into *her*," the once and future deb ordered the plastic surgeon.

Both he and Garrett stared at Heather. She was an extremely attractive woman with a voluptuous figure, but it didn't matter. She had turned forty the week before and this watershed altered her otherwise sunny disposition. Garrett sympathized with the doctor, who studied Pamela Anderson's photograph.

"The *Baywatch* beauty?" the doctor asked.

"You got it and donnnnnnnnnnn't even think of a breast reduction. I'm a respectable 34B, but I want much more. By the way, Pamela is on a new series called *V.I.P.* What kind of a doctor are you, don't you watch TV?"

He was examining her skin with lit magnifying glasses. "But there's nothing wrong with you. You have lovely features. Why do you want to do this to yourself?"

"Perverted people have perverse tastes, Doctor! I want to be able to get a job at Hooters when I blow all my father's money. I'm thinking of forty-two double Ds."

Garrett was alarmed. "Jesus, Heather, you're talking flotation gear."

"You love Pamela's looks."

"On her, they're fine," Garrett said.

"Well, I do a lot of flying," she replied, setting herself off on an unrestrained bout of giggling. "Think of the larger area you'll have to tattoo on me."

"Acreage," he muttered.

"A queen's Kingdom."

The doctor huddled with his computer graphics assistant to bring up digitized versions of the human face and scanned Pamela's photo into the computer. Heather turned her attention back to the surgeon, who was now sizing her up for the job and taking photographs. She yanked the camera out of his hands.

"If I have one second of pain before, after, or beyond, you and your lawyers will wish you were all dead."

The doctor estimated seventy-five K and Heather wrote out a check for half. He persuaded her to have blood and skin tests and at her insistence scheduled her for the following week.

After months of surgery and healing, Heather emerged as a replication of her dream girl. She started going to Fashion Square and the Beverly Center instead of Rodeo Drive to check out her new likeness. The sixteen-year-old mall rats were panting, climbing the escalators after her. She had Garrett drive her Rolls convertible and mooned the boys. Skateboard crashes escorted her to the exit.

**Atop Heather Malone's** mountain aerie in Trousdale Estates, the lights in Beverly Hills below twinkled; it might have been a small alpine peasant village subject to floods. The rain had ceased, but belts of fog nestled around the immense house. Garrett and Eve pulled up to the gate and security forces surrounded them. It looked as though there had been a fire sale at Gold's Gym. About a dozen men and women with pecs and biceps bulging out of their HEATHER 2000 T-shirts seemed to be patrolling for rustlers. Squeaky noises were emitted from their cell phones and night video cameras swiveled everywhere.

"Heather, it's us," Garrett said through the microphone system.

Her metallic voice rebounded through the vast area. "Let them in!"

First, however, he had to present one of the warriors with a medical certificate, twenty-four hours old, a warranty indicating the absence of AIDS. Although, Heather loved rough sex, she worried over trifles like this and no one could gain admittance without this credential.

"You're clear," said the man.

When they drove in, Eve said, pissed off, "Thanks very much, I was really sweating it. If anyone touches me or you, I'll kill them."

"Calm down. We're just voyeurs."

Heather was wealthy enough to afford a gay English butler and Rudy was in a tizzy.

"Thank God, you're here, she's been on a tear all day."

"Where is she?" Garrett asked.

"The torture chamber."

After Rudy heard his name screamed, he grabbed Garret's arm.

"I'll park myself somewhere," Eve whispered.

"Catch up with you later," Garrett said, following Rudy into the gym, where he found Heather in sweats on the treadmill. She switched off the machine and mopped her face with a red towel.

"I tell you, it's a killer being a star."

They joined her at the juice bar, where a juice girl/trainer mixed some khaki-colored vegetable slurp that resembled the Banana Republic's theme color.

"I won't join you," Rudy said. "There's still so much to oversee. By the way, Heather, that's a hideous thing to do with a cucumber."

The trainer flinched. Her days were numbered. Terrified of having him poached, Heather always agreed with her major domo.

"Yes, Rudy."

Through the window, an army of minions were affixing lights and cable wires to generators on the tented tennis court; dashing waiters were lugging in booze and food; sound checks for the bands boomed through the night.

"I have a houseguest who's dying to meet you."

"Male or female?" Garrett asked.

"Very male, very talented. He's in the darkroom I set up for him. Jan Korteman"—she carefully pronounced the J as a Y—"came over from Europe to photograph the party."

"Doesn't ring a bell."

"People who don't know say he rips off Helmut Newton." It was clear to Garrett, and a relief that Heather had taken a new lover. "I say differently. Jan will have his place in the sun."

Garrett now remembered the photos he had seen of Heather trussed up. They were taken on her last European sojourn after she had grown and entered the skin of Pamela Anderson. He had known many fetishes and had a few himself, but Heather's were certainly unique.

"Have your steam bath and I'll get Eve to make you up."

"Eve . . . please switch her off for a while."

"Now, Heather, let there be peace or I'll walk."

"Okay. Jan wants to have a serious art talk with you, so maybe you'll detach yourself from Eve for a while."

"Yes, Heather. But let me add something to Rudy's cucumber remark. It's a reckless star who treats her makeup lady *and* hairstylist with contempt."

She giggled. "Ohh, I could eat you up. . . . Garrett, darling, I was just blowing smoke."

"Eve will be civilized. You have my personal guarantee."

"Thank you," she said. "Jan has a lot in common with you, Garrett. He's also an artist of seduction and a specialist in"—Heather smirked—"the forbidden. . . . You order and he arranges it."

There was an eerie timbre in Heather's voice that made Garrett nervous. He hoped it was just girl talk, swishing the air with imaginary hickory switches.

A thin, elegant man wearing a white silk turtleneck and a black silk suit came in carrying a portfolio album. He had alps of long curly gray hair that had been lovingly cultivated and trained to crinkle down his neck like bag wrap wires. His aristocratic features were as pointed as fencing lances and his age a Chinese puzzle. His welcoming, admiring smile embraced Garrett before he clasped Garrett's hand.

"I can't tell you how much I've looked forward to meeting you." He bowed, then spread open his slightly damp, acidic photographs. "I've just come from the darkroom. I spent my entire visit shooting Heather's collection of your paintings."

Another con man, Garrett thought. Art talk bored him and he wiggled away.

A grumbling man arrived in a tuxedo and slipped through the bar hatch. Bart was Rudy's uncivil Cockney lover and Heather's man for all seasons.

"I'm also excited about meeting an artist of your distinction," Garrett said.

"Ahh, come now. You're a painter, I make photos," Jan said, his first lapse into faulty English. But his accent was British and Garrett wondered how he acquired it.

"Enough of this veggie muck," Bart said, disgruntled, flicking some string beans into the garbage sack. "Nineteen ninety Le Grande Dâme, gents."

"It is *La* Grande Dâme," Jan Korteman said as though schooling this lag for a future position with a nobleman.

"Oh, is it? Tickle yer arse with a feather/Pretty nasty weather. Oy? Listen, it's the same bluddy champers, anyhow you denounce it."

Garrett and Jan accepted chilled glasses and took the first tasting while the barman grumbled, slicing lemons and preparing olives for the onslaught of martini drinkers.

"I can't drink very much," Garrett said. "I may tattoo someone later."

"I'd like to discuss that. But first may I go through your paintings with you. The artist's perceptions of his work are invaluable to me."

"The work I did before I became a tattoo artist?"

"Of course! You're a genius and it's an honor to be in your presence." He ground his teeth with disdain. "Tattoo artist, indeed. Do you know what Andrea del Sarto said to Raphael when Raphael admired his chiaroscuro. 'I, too, am an artist, Raphael.'"

At that moment, Garrett's ego swelled by the compliments and he was enveloped in every would-be artist's bliss. But then reality dawned and he was crushed. He had yielded to the demands of the marketplace and his great talent was being debased. If Eve had been present, she would have nattered, *Show me the money in paintings.*

Garrett sighed, for Jan Korteman had struck the sensitive nerve. "You've won me over and broken my heart at the same time."

"Please, come and discuss your masterpieces. In Bruges where I have my home, you would be addressed properly: as *Maître*. You'd have an atelier with yearning students waiting to watch your next brush stroke."

Garrett knew he had lost the battle of honeyed words. "Flattery gets you everywhere."

With a snorting laugh, Jan Korteman rose into the air like a buffalo. "My dear chap, it always works if you shoot pictures for a living. Walk anywhere with a few Nikons dangling from your neck and you become the celebrity. People can't wait to take off their clothes, reveal their secrets."

Garrett allowed himself to be led into the gallery next door. He flashed over the forms of his old art school paintings, then looked away.

Garrett stated his credo. "With me, the fatal flaw is insincerity in people and art."

"And for me, reality makes an orphan of illusion."

Garrett found sycophants useful but intolerable and here he was in the grasp of an expert.

"Heather was my savior," Garrett said with a sulky look.

Jan Korteman touched Garrett's shoulder. "Heather is a holy person, a magical one."

Garrett read the man from Flanders easily. He had big plans for Heather's money, but just the same, he was a charmer.

"Seven or eight hundred million dollars certainly confers saintliness. I wouldn't be surprised if the Vatican gave her a special day," Garrett said, and the two men of the world laughed in a most civilized fashion.

**In the carefully** graded gallery light, Jan's photographs of the twenty-five paintings Heather had bought from Garrett while he was still working as an independent contractor without his own shop assumed a gravity and profundity Garrett had never recognized. Jan, with the artist's permission and copyright intact, wanted to publish them in a new book. An art critic would write a commentary to the works, and Garrett would have final approval.

"I think he or she should be independent. I don't want to tie anyone's hands."

"Well, naturally, you want to be appreciated for what you are."

"Exactly, and I hate puff pieces," Garrett said moodily. "People with airs and grandiose notions of their place in the art world. I'm an outsider."

"You belong in the center."

"Once, I thought so," he said wistfully, "then I found it wasn't going to happen."

Jan demurred. "You were meant for better things than tattooing."

Garrett became defensive. "I've made a lot of money doing it. Heather financed my first shop. It's grown enormously. Now I have a whole arcade. I owe her everything."

They paused in front of a painting entitled *The Faun*. In this dark work—a world gone berserk—the half-goat, half-man figure leaped through a forest of misshapen, gnarled trees, sunlight had turned a sickly green, the sky a stark vermilion, purple geometric stars tumbled to earth, and the faun had Garrett's luminous face. The eyes stared out of the canvas, demanding salvation.

To Jan, this was not the love that could not speak its name. This was love that screamed and blared: the love of self, psychic absorption, narcissism of the highest order.

"It was part of a series called *Requiem for Nature*," Garrett said dreamily.

"Where are the others? In your studio?"

"No, I destroyed a lot of the early stuff. They were pretentious; even worse, derivative. Eve hated them."

"Is she an art expert?"

"The opposite, if there is such a thing," Garrett replied without acrimony. "I stopped painting at her suggestion and we concentrated on creating a business."

"Well, that's an alliance of sorts, I expect," Jan said.

"As you might say in England, Eve doesn't like being on her uppers—getting by."

Jan roved to another painting and noted its Gauguin influence, the rich palette of browns and copper, the lime green, the oranges.

"Of all the painters, I love him best. I've never been able to escape from him. I've always been in his clutches," Garrett said.

"Why Gauguin?"

"He was a risk taker. He didn't give a damn about anyone or anything: family, kids, money. All for art. And his style evolved into modern art. You can keep Picasso, Cubism, Pollock, and the Abstractionists. They've all hidden under Gauguin's overcoat."

"Come to Europe, Garrett. I can show you a world no artist has ever seen."

For a moment, Garrett was stunned, and almost as reflex action, he embraced Jan. Then, regaining his awareness, he thrust him away and his aloofness was reestablished. Distance from everyone was necessary, except Eve. Garrett despised these old paintings; in his soul he knew they were dross, these compositions that Jan Korteman had praised. He could do much better work now. Garrett was uncertain whether it was the future of his work or Eve and their bond which made him emotional. Perhaps they were twins of desire.

Jan had been briefed by Heather. He must never comment or confront Garrett and Eve about their special relationship, but his curiosity was so great that he tried to ferret out details.

"How did you meet Eve?"

"In Bangkok. Are you really interested in first-meeting stories?"

"Everything about you, Garrett, astonishes and amazes me. Isn't that what art is supposed to do when the artist speaks of it?"

Garrett felt himself sucked into the vortex of Jan's unfeigned veneration.

"I wanted to study the tattoo techniques of the Orient . . . new designs. Heather gave me an open ticket to Tokyo and Bangkok with astounding travel expenses. In a way, I was looking for me."

Jan sniggered. "And some murky sex, I trust."

Garrett was amused. "Who wants to live with just blue skies?"

"Exactly. How can an artist of your talent paint a 'nice' day?"

"Bart and Rudy looked after my house, did some finishing work with some of their mates, and I flew like a bird. I wanted to see other images, different cultures. I wanted something to inspire me. An alternate reality."

"An aesthetic beyond." Jan embraced this kindred idealism. "Yes, people like us are always searching."

"The problem with tattoo art if you're someone like me is that I experience a terrible sense of loss when the tattooed person leaves. The intimacy between us is forfeited. If it were a painting and, say, the artist was attached to it, he could keep it. You can't do that with a tattoo. So a part of you dies when the work is complete. My *identity* is involved with individualizing someone."

Jan was enthralled. "It's tragic, Garrett. You shouldn't have to do that. The work belongs to you."

"They're not negatives. As a photographer you can hang on to yours. I can hardly keep my subjects prisoners, can I?"

An enigmatic smile crossed Jan's taut face. "There may be a way, so don't shut the door just yet. Tell me what happened during this *experimental* stage. Heather mentioned you had a very dark period. You almost died, taking risks."

"Yes, it was very dangerous," Garrett said pensively. "Life or death."

Garrett revealed that he had been taken ill in Bangkok. Heather had flown over, met with doctors, put him in a private clinic, and afterward, when he had recovered, she had arranged for him to have a holiday to recuperate. She picked the Shangri-La Hotel in Chiang Mai.

"You've never seen such a place. Rice fields, oxen on the grounds, the most exquisite bungalow in teak with a wonderful colonial porch, sunsets in paradise. The Thai people are so beautiful, inside and outside. Their manners are gentle. I adore their food. Even now, when I'm depressed, I chew a piece of lemongrass and it perks me up."

Jan listened raptly.

"I was at the bar drinking my third or fourth Navy Grog and I looked in the mirror. Eve was *there*. She smiled at me. I turned around to see if it was an illusion, then she became real, tactile. She didn't say a word—and this sounds deranged—but we took possession of each other."

Jan vicariously shared this epiphany and urged Garrett on.

"I kissed her hand and we looked at each other in the mirror, both of us tanned and beautiful. Now, Jan, I have to admit I was speechless. When I finally spoke, I said something stale: 'Where've you been all my life?' "

"And Eve—what was her reaction?"

"She smiled like the woman in Gauguin's *Noa Noa* and said, 'I was incubating in your psyche . . . waiting.'

" 'What is your name?' I asked.

" 'Once I thought I was the goddess Athena, but you call me what you like.'

" 'You're like Eve.'

" 'Eve it will be.' "

After a moment, Jan nodded. "Rapture."

"And beyond. We became one. I felt whole for the first time in my life. To have a woman like her as my own was beyond my dreams."

"Heather thinks she's a trifle controlling."

"A trifle?" Garrett erupted with laughter. "They're all control freaks. But believe me, it's worth the pain."

"Please, Garrett, consider a trip to Europe. We'll do the museums and galleries. Bruges is an art center of great historical significance. Memling, van Eyck, and Gerard David all painted there. William Caxton printed the first book in English in my city." Jan's excitement mounted. "Come before Lent. Our Flemish carnival is something beyond your dreams. Heather mentioned that it's the slow season in the tattoo business."

"Not many walk-ins, that's for sure. And the Venice Boardwalk is a wreck. They're redoing it and it'll kill business. But we have regular clients for our other services."

"Oh, come, now, you and Eve can spare a little time. Think of your art . . . of Gauguin. Would *he* have let commerce come first, or chucked it and said, 'I live for art'?"

Jan took a small camera out of his pocket, hidden from Garrett, and snapped a picture of the artist meditating.

"I'll see you later, Jan. Heather wants me to check her out."


**By ten, Queen** Heather was ready to make an appearance. Her makeup was concealed by a Venetian ghost mask; her costume covered in Salome's Seven Veils. An entourage of barefoot slaves lifted her onto a sedan chair and marched her to the tent to the beat of John Williams's music from *Star Wars*. The Mistress of Mischief raised her 24K gold wand and some two hundred people turned away from the giant TV screen of the Eiffel Tower alight and Barbara Walters's exuberant commentary. They applauded Heather's entrance. Through smoke and halos of dancing colored lights swirling, she at last stepped from the lowered chair. A mike was handed to her at center stage in front of the bandstand.

"*Our theme is the freedom of sexual expression*. My slaves, I set you free for one night! Let the festival in honor of our god Dionysus begin."

Holding hands, Garrett and Eve joined the revelers chanting, "Heather," as though this were a cult conclave, and in a sense it was.

# CHAPTER 5

**Bustling through immigration at** the airport, Jennifer heard her mother's husky laugh and bold idiomatic chatter with officials. There was no mistaking the queen of the Marin St. Pierre Lycée. Rosalind Bowen was a grand woman, designed for carriages, footmen and porcelain, gardeners and Mozart. She carried her battered Mark Cross makeup case and a couple of Harrods duty-free sacks. When she spied her daughter, she made no effort to catch her eye, but instead waved a scarlet Moroccan leather-bound book in the air.

Jennifer darted out of the crowd, furious because of the flight's late arrival.

"You can put your Proust down, Moms."

"Ah, *ma chèrie,* I brought *Swann's Way* to identify myself in case I was left in lost luggage."

"Moms, they read Proust in French, not translation."

"Call me Mama if you must, but not Moms. If you don't mind, I'd prefer certain introductions as your devoted, very wealthy, widowed, deeply heterosexual older sister."

"What's wrong with telling people that you teach high school senior French?"

"It's so déclassé. In any case, the bastards finally made me assistant principal. . . . And Jennifer, I want you to know right now that I'm on the prowl. Diana is hunting. I am fifty-five and in my roaring prime years."

They strolled to the baggage area. Jennifer's mother still had double-barreled glands.

"Hunting, *Rosalind?* What happened to George Rickey?"

The reference to Rosalind's eternal suitor, a portly stockbroker, brought a snarl from her mother.

"Viagra Falls. I'm too potent to spend my life stooped over the center of a bed coaxing George to victory and attending the perverse parties of his clients."

"I see," Jennifer said.

"Well, George's made me very comfortable. He had me buy some Amazon early on along with AOL." She burbled with champagne laughter. "He proposed again and I told him before I left that I'd give him my answer when I returned from Provence."

Jennifer adored the vibrancy of her mother, their friendship, free of humbug, the cornrows of her lavish blond hair flowing over her shoulders. Girl talk.

"Oh, Rosalind, I love you to death."

"Pet, I know you do. The feeling is even stronger on my side."

They hugged each other and tattooed each other's cheeks with fresh lipstick.

"Now, Jen, we have some serious business together. I don't know your detective and I'm sure I'll like him, but we can't have him behaving like a Frenchman. Treat him like a dog, snap at him, never allow him to be secure because then he'll be complacent. Don't let him think you're double-jointed, because if you were, you'd be a starring in the Cirque de Soleil. Have moods, they love to get you out of them. Don't ever shop, you were born a buyer. You have my genes. Retreat at your peril. Keep him wondering what he's done wrong and he'll worship you as the princess you are."

Jennifer never had any reason to doubt why her mother had never remarried.

"Moms, I have the man of my dreams and a Mercedes 500 as a wedding present, so let's not hang crêpe. Michel fixed my driving test. I failed because I didn't drive two hundred kilometers an hour on their freeway."

In the baggage zone, through grasping hands, Rosalind seized a porter. *"Ma baggage est grande, comme moi,"* she said, flashing a ten-dollar bill. "Is Michel outside in the car giving hell to those airport Nazis threatening people unloading at the curb?"

"No, he's very sorry not to be here. But the office is giving him a bachelor bash. They're very tame here, compared to what they have at home."

"What are they serving?"

"Probably bouillabaisse."

"My body cries out for a bracing bouillabaisse. I almost ate my armrest leaving Gatwick and was tempted to have an affair with a Scottish soccer hooligan who fed me the dregs of his Tostitos."

Rosalind's baggage arrived and everyone gasped; it stopped the carousel while two men tried to wiggle it out. It was a sky blue Andiamo, the Great Dane of their collection.

"*C'est moi. J'arrive,*" she shouted.

Jennifer watched the men strap on their hernia belts to hoist Frankenstein off the carousel.

"Did you bring your furniture?"

"Country and town clothes and something special for you."

Jennifer had to take the top down on her car, and the wearied porters lifted big boy onto the back seat, were tipped, and grumbled into the night. Rosalind took hold of Jennifer before the seat belts were snapped. She laid her daughter's head on her lap, kissed her luxuriant hair.

Rosalind's tears streamed into Jennifer's face. "Oh, my precious pet, this has all been a brave front. What's only happened to you since last year? You *killed* two people."

"It was self-defense. My student tried to murder me!" Jennifer raised her head and was now at eye level with her mother. "And Michel would have been dead if I didn't shoot her maniac boyfriend."

Her mother bowed her head. "I know. What we do for love."

Jennifer had tried to put this behind her, but with her mother she yielded to the anguish she had stored since the deaths.

"Michel is worth it all." Jennifer started the car and its engine was a sweet whisper of Michel's generosity. "Moms—and this is the last time I'll call you that—Michel is noble."

"We'll see," Rosalind said, flicking down the lit visor to repair her mascara.

"And Mother, no weight lectures, I'm a ten and not pregnant."

*    *    *

**The ancient porter** swabbing the floor of Le Miramar advised the two ladies that Michel and his crew had gone to Le Cave Espagnole to continue the revelry. It was around the corner on Rue du Lacydon and Jennifer was certain that she and her mother could get something to eat at the tapis bar. She'd introduce Rosalind to Michel and the spacemen.

"It won't be bouillabaisse, but they have these giant *gambas* and *Jamon Serrano* on little rolls."

"Say no more, Jen, or I'll walk in drooling."

A cannonade of corrida trumpets blared from speakers inside, but the long bar was deserted. A sign posted outside of the backroom said FÊTE PRIVÉE. Jennifer opened the door and entered with her mother. Through the bluish scoria of cigar and cigarette smoke, the boisterous laughter and applause of a truckload of men, they spied Michel on a small stage with four somewhat naked women who were stripping his clothes off. He was down to his boxer shorts.

The bartender spotted the women and raised his apron over their faces like a curtain, but not before Rosalind had surveyed her future son-in-law. She whispered to Jennifer, "For him, I'd leave you on the *Titanic*. Better not show me where you keep your kitchen knives."

*"C'est privée, mesdames."*

"Oh, dear," said Rosalind. "We won't tell a soul."

But it was too late. They had been spied by the examining magistrate and the coroner. Jennifer realized that an escape was impossible, for the whole room of men had turned toward them.

"Good evening, Jennifer," said Charles Fournier.

"You've rather caught us with our pants down," Laurent observed, eyeing Rosalind.

"Or at least Michel's," Jennifer said, howling with laughter. "Mother I'd like you to meet Dr. Laurent and Judge Fournier, two of Michel's ushers. And another's en route."

With mordant pleasure, Leon Stein strode over. *"Bon soir,"* he said. "I'm available for marriage counseling. My specialty," he added.

"Oh, yes, Mother, this is Dr. Leon Stein, our shrink."

"I'm delighted to meet such a distinguished group," Rosalind said with a chortle, "especially at one of your professional gatherings."

Michel was suddenly alerted to the intrusion. He pressed through the strippers and leaped from the stage barefoot, carrying his jacket and trousers. Wobbling from drink, he approached the group now milling at the entrance.

"I swear I had no idea my thugs had this in mind for me," he said, wiping his brow with a trouser leg.

"It's all right, darling."

Rosalind shook his hand. "Please don't stop. I'm from San Francisco. We invented performance art. These *events* occur there every night."

Michel bowed and kissed Rosalind's hand.

*"Madame Bowen, bienvenue. Tout le monde à Provence a attendu pour vous."*

"And I have waited for you, Monsieur Michel. Oh, please call me Rosalind."

"With pleasure." He suddenly found her in his arms lavishing Wrigley's Spearmint kisses on his cheeks. "My father is preparing a feast for your arrival," he said, gently disengaging himself.

"I'd kill for a tuna sandwich."

"We all would when he's at the range."

# CHAPTER 6

**In surveying the blithe** spawns of dark life in Heather's millennium stage setting, Garrett found himself at once at home and yet distant. This dualism enabled him to elevate himself to another plane, but he was never judgmental. He sought buried meanings in this human circus. Many of the partially clad figures displayed tattoos that he himself had done and he was engulfed by flesh imprinted with red demons on navels, spiders on thighs, sunsets on chests, chain links on wrists, mosaics of cathedrals on backs, Aphrodites, Scorpios and Leos, winged Mercurys, Thors with lightning thunderbolts, common nudes, a jumble of names, hearts, black and red roses. The quality of his gifted hand was everywhere, a vernissage of sorts for the artist.

He was deeply knowledgeable about his craft and widely read. But what was the significance of these tattoos, this body art? People who came to him were searching for some way to individualize themselves from the herd; others *were* the herd, members of a gang.

Apart from Eve, not a soul realized that this work represented pieces of himself that were lost to him. Unlike Gauguin, and other artists whose work was sought-after, hanging in museums and the collections of the rich, where would his art be in fifty or a hundred years? These bodies would be buried or cremated.

There might be photographs of his flash work: the pre-drawn graphic designs of tattoos. Perhaps books of them in other tattoo establishments might copy them. But he would not be collectible. Even the meanest gouache of a minor painter was exhibited in a home's place of honor. But he would be gone, and nothing he stood for, no credo, would succeed him. Somehow or other he had to salvage his work and live by his faith; then he would finally be whole. He thought of Iris Murdoch's reflection that "art is the final cunning of the human soul which would rather do anything than face the gods."

On the parquet floor, whiplashed by multicolored strobes, dancers gyrated in their costumes of leather and latex to the industrial heavy metal music soaring from a dreadlocked band.

Some of the men and women were exposed: their privates harnessed, pierced nipples dangling with earrings. Garrett glimpsed bordello body harnesses; leather plunge-bras; slings and stirrups, saddles and bridles; hooded executioners with their leather-masked slaves who had only grommeted air holes to breathe through; men and women in fetish corsets and skyscraper heels. It looked to him as if Stormy Leather and the Pleasure Chest had been cleaned out for the affair.

Heather caught his arm. She had removed the Venetian mask and seemed younger than her age, beautiful, even though she looked like someone else. Her spike-studded leather collar revealed the sinuousness of her neck. She wore a long violet latex suit with a valentine cut-out crotch, over which a brass chastity cage was attached. Through the gleaming bars, Garrett's scarlet Minotaur tattoo, guarding the entry to her intimate region, was unveiled by flashlight bulbs.

"What do you think?"

"Is this *Citizen Kane?* Do you want me to write a review for *Salon?*"

"Garrett, you kill me."

"I will begin with: What, no hat?" he said with a laugh.

"Eve said she'd murder me if I messed up the cornrows."

"I'd take her threats seriously if I were you."

"Well, you know I love rough sex."

"You could get yourself murdered."

Heather enjoyed dangerous talk and never backed off. "It's a lovely option. What a rush."

"Shall I ask around? It shouldn't be hard to find tonight. You've got more executioners here than they have in Texas."

"And the slaves to go with them."

Like Eve, Heather leavened his mood. "Eve did a killer makeup," he noted, looking at the stardust sprinkled on her cheeks and the rainbow eyeliner.

"Eve was very sweet. She's the best—the two of you. I don't know what I'd do without you."

"Heather, we're the ones who owe you everything."

"You were so sick, poor lamb," she said, whipping away an intruder on his knees who wanted to kiss her feet.

"For Eve and me there'll always be Bangkok."

"God, I want you so bad."

"News at eleven." He took her arm as she made the rounds inspecting the exhibitions at the circus. "Where'd you get this bunch, the La Brea Tar Pits?"

"I dig deep, sugar." She pressed against him. "How'd you and Jan get along?"

"He's very intellectual and I think I like him."

"He told me you're the real thing—a true artist. As if I didn't know that from the beginning."

"You and Jan, you're a couple?"

Heather became coy. "You and Eve are. We could all play."

"I'll discuss it with her."

"Garrett, I want to be serious for a second." With her leather whip, she shooed away a couple of flagellants who had come to pay homage. "You have to go to Europe to find your art. It's your destiny and has fuck-all to do with my sexual desire for you."

He was taken aback. "You are serious."

"Yes, I am, damn it. You are a great painter! I've always believed in you. Jan said you could be the artist the millennium is waiting for. It will arrive, but will you have the guts to take the leap?"

Garrett flicked off a blob of sweat and felt for a moment like he was on a speed high.

"Can I think about it?"

"Yes, and don't let Eve influence you. No matter what she thinks, the artist in you is being imprisoned, weeping. Once you told me you were shaped by your talent."

This unexpected side of the leather mistress invariably surprised Garrett. She may have disguised herself in sexual frippery, but she was intelligent and a calculating machine. "Garrett, you had it once. Don't waste it on the garbage at the beach."

"Heather, I will think about it. Jan invited me to Bruges."

"Oh, my God. Do you have any idea . . . ? Jan's collections are beyond belief."

All at once, Heather laced her lips with a warm, sweeping smile and extended her hand to a short, beefy man wearing a normal tuxedo coming toward them.

"Be nice, Garrett. George Rickey looks after the money. He's the genius broker who got me into all the hot-wired Internet stocks, and got me out at the top. That's his lady love, the big tall one in the Armani."

"She looks a bit uncomfortable."

Heather giggled. "Who wouldn't, wearing Armani here?"

After a fourteen hundred percent rise in her portfolio, the broker and Heather exchanged hugs and slobbering kisses. They had developed that heartfelt affection money inspires. On the border, Garrett and the large woman exchanged petty smiles. With a flourish of her whip, Heather pontifically introduced her house artist.

"This is *the* famous Garrett Lee Brant, and most of the tattoos on display are his."

The woman spoke only French and clearly did not want to shake anyone's hand.

"My lady has a touch of flu," George Rickey, smiling professionally said of Rosalind. "I think we ought to leave."

"Not before you see Garrett's body art." In an instant, Heather clicked open her chastity cage and revealed the Minotaur figure Garrett had tattooed over her shaved cleft. "And it didn't even hurt." She flaunted it in front of the woman.

"Amazing," the broker said, as Rosalind glared at him.

Garrett decided to try out his French. *"C'est très intéressant, n'est pas?"*

*"Pas pour moi, monsieur!* . . . Oh, never mind. George, I'm getting out of here before the food comes to life."

Garrett and Heather watched her broker and his infuriated amourette vanish through the Bond Voyage pergola where long-stemmed roses were being flailed against bare backsides.

"She was so rude. Garrett, I'm sorry."

"When you're rich, you never have to say sorry."

She cuddled and kissed him tenderly. "Love you, sweetie."

Like a market, there seemed to be stalls everywhere. Some women were dressed as nuns, naked underneath their black leather habits; priests in masks were taking confession; doctors and nurses, examined naked "patients."

At the buffet table, there was actual food, although none of the guests went near it. Heather served no drugs for the masses, not even a brownie.

Los Hombres de Salsa danced to the stage and began to play a melodic warm-up for a Jennifer Lopez clone in a studded irides-cent vest who was swinging her hips and breaking into *"Mi Vida Loca."*

They sauntered over to theme bars, greeting captives, pleasure purchases, mongrels, and sacrifices. "I better see if I can locate Eve."

"Find Jan, while you're at it," Heather said.

"Will do. Where'll you be?" Garrett asked through the beautiful, milling bodies.

"Try the whipping post."

**Jan had continued** to photograph the party when Eve discovered him standing behind some lighting technicians. She had taken off her smock, adjusted her makeup with a daub of Kabuki rice pow-der. Her shiny black latex pants were highlighted by the blushing pink panties. In her high-heeled boots she was half a head taller than Jan.

"You're missing the party," she said.

"Art waits for no one."

"Oh, gimme a break."

He turned from the lighting men and studied her. "Eve, you're exquisite. I was concerned about paying too much attention to you in front of Heather."

"Don't worry about it," she said, puckering her full lips. "Heather's used to it."

"No jealousy in your world?"

"It depends on whose making the decision."

"So you have certain rights."

Eve howled. "I'm a woman, I damn well better have rights."

He moved closer, taking in everything about her, photographing her in his mind. "Did Garrett mention that I invited you both for a visit to Europe? I have a house in Bruges and a villa on the Rhône, outside of Avignon."

"Really, Provence. We've been wanting to go there. Fact is, I've been studying French tapes for a year. Garrett speaks the language perfectly."

"I'll be happy to be *your* interpreter."

"Do you have a boat?"

"Yes, and it sleeps eight. We'll have picnics on the river and talk of great art while Garrett creates it."

She was intrigued by Jan. "I'll bet you have a great deal to show us."

"I have treasures for rarefied tastes." He kissed her leather cuff. "I think the trip will be good for you both."

"Some down time."

"And wonderful food. The radiant scenery, the air sweet-scented like you."

When they made their way to the tent, the noise level had peaked. They were in time for the gauntlet. Dozens of naked people were running through a group armed with whips and rods and were enveloped by the pleasurable tension of attempting to exceed human limits. Naked eerie clowns abounded, tumblers and magicians appeared out of nowhere. A sextet of men had matriculated into a full metal jacket action epic; beside them the women's choir was reaching its crescendo.

A large dungeon had been appropriated by Tantric sex specialists demonstrating their powers of breathing during lovemaking to forestall orgasm. Several grope boxes accommodated volunteers and offered anonymity to anyone who cared for a premidnight warm-up.

In her stage set—the Garden of Eden—Heather was tied to a whipping post and played the role of a naked Eve while several partners of both sexes feasted on her. Pierced tattooed peons were avid spectators, luxuriating in Heather's training: Her gymnastics years, the yoga, and her study of the Kama Sutra gave her appetites a boundless capacity.

Jan and Eve stopped to watch the exhibition of her artistry.

"God, she's beautiful," Jan said.

"Her breasts would sink the *Bismarck*. But that's what she wanted. Garrett told her a forty-two double D was massive. Well . . . lots of men like them big. Frankly, Garrett and I thought the whole plastic surgery thing was crazy."

"Do you ever get an itch for her?" Jan asked.

Eve had been waiting for this suggestive come-on. "Sure. I'd like to torture her, but I'm too much of a lady. I suppose, in a north-south way, we have an itch for each other."

"Has she asked to be with you?" he asked, emboldened by lechery and the extremes they represented.

"The thing is, when Garrett and I came together, we decided to be monogamous. What about you?"

"I have Heather now and then. But I prefer her in more intimate settings."

Eve nodded. As the clock moved closer to midnight, Eve's indifference to the frenzied carnality surrounding them was an even greater turn-on for Jan than the orgiastic maelstrom itself. She was unique; this pile of bodies weren't.

"Aren't you going to be with Garrett at the enchanting moment?"

Eve smiled cryptically. "At times like this, we play hide and seek."

"And you always find each other?"

Eve removed her corset, waved it in front of his face, and in that moment, she vanished. Jan Korteman had never seen a magic act like hers, the illusion of presence and then to dissolve. He pressed the leather vest to his lips and kissed it.

Of course Eve knew where Garrett would be.

A single narrow beam of light illuminated a painting in the art gallery and her love for him burgeoned into a sacred experience. She was silent and they both contemplated the sumptuous vision he had done of them as a celestial pair of flowers. He had painted their faces in the form of a poet's narcissus. The flower's central corona, rimmed by a bloodred band, framed their faces. It was a remarkable, ingenious work of art: Eve's long auburn hair glistened in the sun and his dark locks were down to his shoulders; his soft sage eyes, hers bright ultramarine blue, mystically contrasted. Their blissful smiles were innocent of guile.

"Come into the charm house with me," Garrett said.

"Forevermore, darling."

# CHAPTER 7

**Michel had raided Chez** Danton's larder stocks. It was the least he could do for his famished future mother-in-law. At the maple chopping block he arranged a platter of charcuterie, with finely sliced Bayonne ham, a ramekin of goose rilletes, figs, olives, cornichons, pâté and walnut-crusted chèvre wrapped in grape leaves. The bread was only a day old, but the damp cloth on top of the basket had kept it from hardening. Rosalind drank with the same lustiness as her daughter and they were already on a second bottle of Bandol.

"Better than a tuna sandwich?" he asked, placing the tray down.

"It's heaven, thank you," Rosalind said.

Jennifer turned up her face and he kissed her lightly on the lips when his cell phone rang.

"Excuse me just a moment."

"It's two in the morning, Michel."

"Sorry, Jennifer."

He listened to Pierre report from Marseille. The dead girl's parents would be flying in from Brussels and would arrive at nine in the morning.

"Call the Petit Nice, explain the situation, and get the Davises a good room. Yes, I know what it costs, but if we book them anywhere around the Quai du Port, the media will swamp them. No public announcements. Have Sylvie pick them up."

When Michel clicked off, both women were staring at him. Jennifer's face was taut with alarm.

"Ladies, please start. I had dinner before my floor show."

"Michel, you're *not* on another case?"

"No, but I had to view a crime scene earlier."

"Who, what?" Jennifer demanded.

"A young girl was found in La Ciotat on the beach of Claude's hotel."

"Davis sounds like it could be English or American," Rosalind said.

"Yes, she's American. Ladies, do please eat something. I'm suffering from the effects of a 1935 Armagnac and sleep deprivation."

As if Jennifer on her own weren't enough of a handful, he now had the very sharp-witted, sharp-tongued Rosalind to provoke her. He had skillfully dealt with murders for years, but he didn't know if he could cope with these two women.

**Michel's apartment, a** three-bedroom affair with a maid's wing, was a rambling warren of irregular chambers on the Rue Goyrand with one bathroom. The large wrought-iron terrace on the top floor was, however, a glory, for it overlooked the Fountain of the Four Dolphins. The harmonious tones of splaying water danced through his dreams every night. The concierge was asleep, but her uncongenial cat peered at him through the shabby window curtains.

Michel waited for the lift, a girdled cell that rasped on hairy cables. The women had walked up the four flights. He felt like a single pallbearer as he maneuvered Rosalind's elephantine hulk of luggage into the lift. When he finally arrived at his flat, he had to unsnap metallic buttons, then release its zippered compartments to ease it through the doorway. He left it in the long hallway. The women were talking in the guest room.

"Big boy is in the foyer. Rosalind, forgive me, but I've got to get sleep."

"Of course, pet, happy dreams."

He didn't bother hanging up his clothes, but deposited them in a clump in the handsome, newly furnished bedroom, and collapsed.

After he had closed the bedroom door, the women began disassembling the case. They had already changed into their nightdresses when Jennifer dissuaded her mother from taking a bath. Like a conspirator, she spoke in a hushed voice.

"You're too tired. Believe me, it's safer to go to bed festering than to take a chance in the bathroom."

Rosalind was startled. "I don't understand."

Jennifer stepped sat down on the brand-new queen-sized bed she'd purchased for her mother's visit. She stepped out of her slippers revealing a black and blue big toe.

"I broke it twice on the little ledge that rises at the bathroom entry. It's practically invisible to the naked eye, so wear slippers or clogs; the step into the bathroom is deadly. The orthopedic surgeon showed me how to set my toe. I just snap it back into place. Mother, the French may be great engineers, but they can't build a bathroom or plumb to save their lives."

"But de Lesseps created the Suez Canal," Rosalind said.

"That may be so, but they can't design a bathroom. The tubs are so deep and narrow, you have to be a hurdler to get in and out. You see, it's set too high. Most of them are three feet high. Michael Jordan could get in and out with no sweat, but not us mortals. There's no margin for error. Never get dreamy in the tub or you can fracture your skull getting out.

"Your legs and toes are also going to get tangled up with the shower attachment. You can knock yourself out with the shower coils or be strangled; if you stand, the shower head turns like a rainbird and the place looks like an irrigation ditch afterwards. But I'm working on a separate shower. It's there, but not yet plumbed?"

For once Rosalind was daunted. "I see. . . ."

"I'm not through. Except for the bathroom here, and the one at the farm, there is no such thing as a hook in French bathrooms."

"What are you supposed to do, throw your clothes on the floor?"

"You tell me. The French claim to have invented civilization, but not door hooks. I also put hundred-watt bulbs inside. The first in the history of France. I had to special-order them."

"God, Jennifer, I forgot all of this. I haven't been back for twenty years. I dress France in romance."

"Everyone forgets these things. They're like bad dreams. Now what about the paper?"

"I've got six rolls of triple Charmin rolls, unscented, in big boy."

Jennifer was aghast. "Is that it?"

"No, I went to Costco, ordered a case, and sent it UPS."

Jennifer embraced her mother with the passion of a lover. "I can't tell you how I've dreamt of this. Oh, Mother, bless you. The toilet paper here is a true horror. It's okay if you want to sand furniture, but not as a wipe. I've been to the homes of wealthy people and they've got these cheesy dispensers that deliver one flimsy piece at a time. Like it's rationed. And it's never near the toilet. You can break an arm reaching it or fall on your face."

"*C'est affreux.*"

"Exactly, it's shocking."

"Now, what about electric plugs?"

"I brought an assortment."

"Well, I can put them on for you. I've had to learn."

"Do you have extension cords for the hair dryer?" Rosalind, unnerved, asked.

"You're safe there, but if you decide to travel, I've got a sixty-foot one that you can break down into fifteen-foot lengths. Now, never dry your hair in the bathroom, except here. Either you'll blow the building's fuses or electrocute yourself."

"Lovely options. What happened to you during the terrible December storms?"

"Brittany and Paris were a mess, but we were okay this time. In any case, Nicole is too smart to let the electric company ruin her business. She has back-up diesel generators at the farm and the restaurant."

Before they kissed good night, Jennifer switched on the window air conditioner. "They came from Germany . . . Siemens. It was a battle royal with Michel. He thinks they're unhealthy and the concierge said they were unsightly."

"That's a new one, the deconstructed aesthetics of air-conditioning. Well, pet, I'm glad you're whipping him into shape."

"It'll take a lifetime, Rosalind."

With a half-laughing yawn, Rosalind said, "And so we say *au revoir* to the glory that was once France."

# CHAPTER 8

**Garrett and Eve had** left Heather's party when the guests began losing control. Neither of them enjoyed the spectacle of brutality and degradation that ensued. They had seen enough of these contretemps in the past. By two-thirty they were back in Venice and asleep.

But Garrett was restless all night. Dreams of dead people in which he was either the instrument or the collaborator pervaded the nightmarish landscape of his mind, blackening the palette of his artistic visions. At about eight, he awoke startled, and quietly left the bed, careful not to disturb Eve. He crept up the spiral staircase to his studio. From the terrace, indecisive stains of sunlight speckled the canals like gas vapors. In the surrounding homes, big-screen TVs were tuned to the Rose Parade. Bleary images of slaughtered flowers in the service of bombastic corporate floats incensed the artist. America had always been sell-crazy, but art retained a purity.

With a nervous shiver, Garrett decided to remove the dust sheets from his paintings. He hadn't looked at them for months and wondered if they were as good as he thought. The cold-eyed appraisal of the artist considering his own work was a solemn moment. Garrett had slashed his canvases more times than he cared to remember. Without the adulation of his worshipers—Eve and Heather, now Jan—he found himself totally isolated.

The subject matter and size of his oils varied, roving from stark still lifes suspended in space to Bosch-like skulls and visionary dream portraits of Eve; masterly collages of clocks with time weeping; anatomical death heads of animals in which people were imprisoned. And of course there were the torture studies of former models. As he moved closer to inspect the work, the event that was to reshape and transfigure many lives, on the millennium morning in Venice Beach, occurred.

*Garrett's* paintings were all signed by someone with the initials *P.G.*

He retreated in shock. Garrett gradually recognized the malicious fraud. Paul Gauguin had magically supplanted himself in Garrett's spirit and stolen his talent, his genius. He had traveled through time and space to haunt Garrett and impose his will on him. While Garrett had split himself apart painting, an imposter had taken possession of him. Which of the two was real? Who was the true creator?

Gauguin, the bandit, had through some dispensation from Satan constantly tried to steal Garrett's talent.

Throughout his life, Garrett actually knew that someone was looking over his shoulder, appropriating his work, his sensibility. Suddenly the room was permeated with the sweaty spoor and the fumes of a drunken man. On the terrace, he saw Gauguin puffing on his pipe. Catching sight of Garrett, he smirked derisively. Gauguin's once-white suit was stained and he was drunk, wobbling from side to side. His skin was raw, filled with bleeding scabs, and his head appeared shrunken from the ravages of syphilis. Garrett picked up his long needles and was about to thrust them into the figure when it vanished.

**Garrett traced this** first manifestation, this spectral visit, to his period in San Antonio. There had been a reproduction of Gauguin's painting *Where Do We Come From?* on the wall of his dead tutor's room. As the man groaned, Garrett had fixated on the painting. From that moment, Gauguin's ghoulish figure appeared laughing and snarling at him.

Garrett had drifted into San Antonio some months after he had escaped from the death trap of the Albermarle Foundling Home in Oklahoma, where he had been kept in a barred cell with the most incorrigible and violent children. Providing combustion in this charnel house were rabid biters, an epileptic, a mad girl who pulled her hair out and never stopped howling. As a method of survival, Garrett collected safety pins, hairpins, grinding the points into sharp spikes. In self-defense, Garrett stuck these pins into anyone approaching him. The children and the brutish attendants called him *It*.

His only ally was an angelic boy of four or five whose name was Darrell Vernon Boynton. The child had been tossed in with this pack because of a bureaucratic error. But Boy—as he eventually came to be known—was soon adopted by a couple named Boynton, and Garrett had only come upon him later in Venice as a walk-in who wanted his penis tattooed with copperhead snakes. At a later date, Eve had done a labia piercing for Boy's girlfriend. Now these two were dead and Garrett mourned their early loss.

Before the Albermarle spring picnic, Garrett had been allowed to shower and put on clean clothes. He seized the opportunity and escaped from the park grounds. Hitching a ride into Oklahoma City, he made for the freight yards and spent several months traveling the hobo trail, which eventually took him to San Antonio.

He loved the river and the pleasant environment. Quick-witted, with a sad charm and excellent manners, he had been taken under the wing of an accomplished hobo thief who set his pins and wires to good use by teaching him how to pick locks. When the police showed up, as they occasionally did at the outlaws' encampment around San Pedro Creek, Garrett hid until the raid was over.

Not far from the Paseo del Rio, in the back alleyway of a local pharmacy, Garrett scrounged through the trash bins, found some hypodermic needles, and armed himself. He was physically and emotionally exhausted from his flight from the police. At three in the morning, he dropped his guard and fell asleep.

The following morning he was shaken awake by a sweet, smiling middle-aged woman who owned the shop with her husband. Garrett tearfully explained that his parents had had a violent fight: His father was destined for prison, and his mother would be in the hospital indefinitely with a skull fracture and other injuries.

"The doctor said she might be in coma forever."

Mabel Haskins broke down during this tearful recital of human calamity visited by Satan on Garrett. She would call the authorities, the Baptist Church of Our Savior, and see that he was cared for. Garrett pleaded with her.

"It'll be the institution for me," he responded. "And I've been there before. It's hell. Look, I'll go on with my schooling and maybe you could let me sweep up the shop, take out the trash, run errands, deliver medicine."

"I'll talk it over with my hubby. You'll take to Doc Haskins, everyone does."

Doc Haskins, the senior deacon of the Church of Our Savior, soon agreed and Garrett inveigled himself into their hearts and lives. He attended the church school, where his natural talent as an artist was quickly recognized. His drawings of Christ, the Martyr, the saints, the Blessed Virgin, his sweet contra-tenor choir voice, and his religious bent endeared him to everyone, especially the Haskinses' married daughters.

At Thanksgiving dinner, his first one outside of Albermarle, he read the lesson, joined hands with the family at the table, and announced, "I will now and always stand up for our Lord and Savior, Jesus Christ." The air rang out with "Amens," and Garrett had a family. With his seductively pious gift of gab, he owned them.

Nothing was ever too much trouble for Garrett. He washed the cars, delivered orders, and developed a passionate interest and understanding of prescription drugs. Every night, he read his new Bible, Doc Haskins's copy of *The Physicians' Desk Reference*.

All through his intolerable years at Albermarle, where he had been dumped when he was a week old, Garrett had been an avid reader, and his way with words held him in good stead at San Antonio Junior High. His principal goal, however, was to save enough money so that he could support himself and attend art school. He imagined himself in the glamorous California he saw in films and on TV and he set out to make his fortune quickly.

Every day after school, he would pick up the prescriptions to be delivered for Doc Haskins, place them in his bike basket, and make his rounds from College Street to Mustang. Most of the recipients were women home sick and ailing, their men still at work. Often, he was told the door would be left open, and he noted this.

Garrett was frequently tipped, sometimes as much as half a dollar. Occasionally, when the coast was clear, he might snatch some money out of purse, lift a cameo, a pair of earrings, a gold chain. But he was very cautious about these thefts and seldom took anything that might be obvious. He made a careful study of the personal habits of these people. He noticed that some of the female customers were occasionally sneaking men into their homes.

In six months, he had become an *investigator*. He liked the official sound of the word; it empowered him. He was extremely frugal and hid his money in an old trunk in the pharmacy's basement storeroom. His few purchases were connected to his investigative work and included a strong combination lock and a power flashlight. Stealing loose change would never be enough for the trip to California and to build what he now called the "scholarship fund."

One lazy afternoon, the revelation came to him when he spied a married white female customer in bed with a black man. He knew that her husband was deeply prejudiced and there'd be hell to pay if he found out. He had access to Doc Haskins's Rolodex. Each customer's name address and next of kin was neatly typed, and Garrett had copied every one of them in a ledger.

He used the old Royal Bluebird Mabel had given for his school reports and wrote a letter to the adulteress.

> Dear Mrs. Parsons
>    If you don't want your crazy old man to find about you and that darky whose been tarring your feathers tomorrow morning you better stick a hundred dollars in an envelope and put it under the fifth elm tree beside the San Fernando Cathedral. There'll be a flat rock beside it. So put it under that rock. If you don't you will get a whomping from your old man that'll make that pretty face look like a broken bottle.
> Your Savior

Garrett had selected this site with care. No one could observe him from either direction. It afforded him an easy escape on his bike. He watched Mrs. Hunt Parsons drive up in her Olds convertible, park, and carry out his demand. Blackmail! He had found the Silk Route to survival. He waited an hour before riding by the cathedral. He had bought himself a bottle of RC Cola and stopped to take a swig at the tree and then tipped over the rock with the toe of his sneaker. The envelope was there. He undid the strap which held his pointed stick; he had carved this hickory limb and implanted it with a six-inch roofer's nail. He speared the envelope and rode away.

During the next few weeks, his investigations had yielded another $382 from several other women. He wondered if he ought to turn his attention to some married, gay men he had seen leaving the various bars around the Governor's Palace. He'd put that on hold.

One day, making a delivery in the historic old King William District, which had been settled by German merchants at the turn of the century, he encountered Josef Renchen, the burly owner of Renchen's Pawnbroker Exchange. Mr. Renchen was a snarling, coughing machine, sputtering phlegm into a handkerchief. He had about a forty-eight-inch gut which hung like a bear's head over his Jim Bowie silver belt. Renchen grudgingly tipped him a dime after Garrett had biked across town to make the delivery.

Garrett heard the voices for the first time, some in French and German, and he beheld a wondrous carousel filled with puppets. Although they spoke, their voices weren't recorded.

"How do they do that?"

Renchen was pleased to have an audience. "I was a ventriloquist and puppet master. When I'm not coughing, I can *throw* my voice."

Garrett was awed. "And they speak in foreign languages?"

"My family and I came over from Strasbourg when I was twelve. In Alsace Lorraine, German and French is spoken."

Always interested in antecedents, Garrett asked, "Why'd you leave?"

"My father and mother were offered jobs with a traveling circus and we settled here."

"Do you have kids?"

"No," he said ruefully, "and my great knowledge of puppetry and art will die with me."

"Well, Mr. Renchen, when you're feeling better, maybe you could teach me some things. You see, I want to be an artist."

Garrett took out his sketchbook and Renchen looked through it, praising the boy's skill at rendering the architectural sites of the town and his instant portraits.

"Glorious lines. We must get you some oil paints and canvas. You need color with line, a palette!"

He was spellbound by this stranger's generosity. "You're kidding me, you wouldn't."

"Josef Renchen is a man of his word and reveres natural talent. Who knows; one day you might be a great artist and think of me kindly?"

Garrett was overwhelmed, politely thanked him, and nosed around the showcases, marveling at the chased silver buckles, jewelry, watches, rare coins and stamps, but he was transfixed by the range of cameras. Renchen dropped a pair of codeine tablets and slugged away at his elixir of terpin hydrate.

"You want to buy or trade or borrow?" Renchen demanded, crunching, now chewing codeine tablets.

"Dunno, Mr. Renchen. My aunt left me some stuff. Maybe I could bring it in and have you decide what I should do."

The cough mixture and codeine tablets had been filled from a prescription by a doctor Garrett hadn't heard of before. Dr. Pablo Xavier Rivera had a storefront office in the barrio, and Renchen was a new customer. It struck him as odd that Renchen would select Doc Haskins when there were other pharmacies much closer.

"Bring in your aunt's things and I'll have a look."

"Thank you, Mr. Renchen. One other thing before I head back to my part of town. There are no *refills* on your prescription."

"Oh, dear."

"Maybe I can help you out with that, sir."

Renchen's mouth formed the crescent of a leer, revealing a mouth filled with gold teeth. "My fortune is in my smile, young man."

"It sure picks up the light."

After completing the inventory later that day, which Doc Haskins had made his chore, Garrett siphoned off a dozen codeine tablets and a bottle of the cough elixir which he presented to Josef Renchen shortly before the man was about to close up shop. Garrett had also brought along some of his loot.

"Very thoughtful, Monsieur Garrett."

"I try to be helpful."

"Have you eaten?"

"I had a taco after school."

"Is Mr. Haskins expecting you?"

Garrett shook his head and smiled. "I told him I'd be at the library studying."

"I'd like to invite you to dinner at the house of my dear friend. I'll show you some great art in my library."

Garrett was uncertain of Renchen's motives, but decided to accept. "I could do without the fried chitlins Mrs. Haskins does every Thursday."

"I can promise you better."

"Does your friend have a phone?"

"Of course. But why do you ask?"

"In case I'm late, I have to call."

He wheeled his bike alongside Renchen and walked through the charming old neighborhood. His friend's house was a rambling Victorian situated near the Little Rhein Steak House on South Alamo. The teetering porches upstairs and downstairs looked as though they might collapse at any moment. The interior was hardly any better. What light there was in the fusty foyer came from a huge Germanic porcelain chandelier with tiny candle bulbs which cast gloomy shadows everywhere. The moldy walls were stippled with sweat and the crannies filled with insects; the scent of burning lard invaded the house like toxic vapors. A communal dining table with splintered supports was more like a trough for the old people who boarded at the house. Four or five of them were slopping gravy over their biscuits and scooping pebbled remnants of instant mashed potatoes, then mopping up half-moons of sausage into their mouths. Ma Haskins's chitlins fry-up no longer seemed so distasteful. The spiders were also at dinner. They'd need a twister to shake them out, Garrett thought when a large woman with a coppery complexion came toward him and Renchen.

Dina Marcuro welcomed Renchen with a splash of kisses. She was a dark-haired, broad-beamed woman in her forties whose shoulders were covered with a violently colored silk shawl. When she walked, nooses of heavy gold chains and amulets jangled from her neck. She emitted the heavy scent of rose water.

"This is Garrett Brant, Dina."

Garrett briefly wondered if he might scat into a few rooms and see if there was anything around worth taking. "Pleased to meet you, ma'am."

"Nice to have you here." Dina Marcuro's raven dark eyes were mesmerizing and colossal. She had the moody, baneful air of a gypsy woman. "What a pretty boy he is, Josef. He's like a faun with those light green eyes and that thick curly black hair."

She led them into a private parlor, where a black maid awaited them. This enormous room was clean and inviting, with a mélange of objects: Statues, figurines, large locked wooden cabinets containing bric-a-brac. Everything had a coded tag, he noted. In a moment, Garrett gleaned that this was something of storage room for Renchen. Occupying pride of place on a giant round table with eight chairs, a globe dazzled with intersecting ribbons of a rainbow.

Although the boarders' dining room was dismal, Dina's parlor was immaculate. Sukie, the black maid, served them a robust dinner of sauerbraten and winey red cabbage with glasses of Liebfraumilche for the adults and a big bottle of Coke for him. Garrett learned that Dina was a medium.

"I consult the spirits," she explained. "Sometimes they consult me."

"They talk to her and she tells her group about them," Renchen added.

"Can you find out about my parents?"

"We'll see. You'll have to be very good young man."

"I'll do my best, Mrs. Marcuro."

"You'll have to be cooperative, Garrett," she continued after the plates were cleared away by the maid.

"Just tell me how."

"Well, Garrett, Josef mentioned that you work at the Haskins Pharmacy. Maybe I can get my boarders to have their prescriptions filled there."

"Doc and Mrs. Haskins would really like that."

"I'd give you a commission and tips, of course."

"That'd be wonderful."

Renchen poured her and himself another glass of wine. "You see, Garrett, Mrs. Marcuro has a number of very sick old people who live here."

"You look after them?" Garrett asked.

She gave a great sigh and her tremendous bosom inflated like water wings. "I do my best. I fill their prescriptions, take them to the doctor. And I could use someone to help occasionally with chores."

"I'm here to serve you and Mr. Renchen. What a wonderful lady you are," he said, genuinely in awe.

"Yes, she's an angel," Renchen agreed.

During the ensuing months through his thirteenth birthday, when he was given a silver buckle and a Minolta SRL by the generous couple, Garrett found a further source of income with them and expanded the scholarship fund. Through Josef Renchen, he learned photographic techniques; he was able to install a darkroom in a cubicle in Dina's capacious basement. From itinerant runaway, Garrett now had two families.

He practiced shooting with fast film in ill-lit and shadowy areas. This latest experiment in self-improvement enabled him to refine his demands for money from wayward couples. It was one thing to type a letter to some married man or woman, quite another to enclose a snapshot of ungovernable copulation. One woman paid him five hundred dollars for a negative and a man caught on film with a teenage boy contributed a thousand to the fund.

Garrett was always busy, not enough hours in the day, but he still read up on Benzedrine, phenobarbital, insulin, Nitrostat, Dexedrine, digitalis, barbiturates, and tranquilizers—drugs prescribed for the oldsters packed away in Dina's attic bedrooms. He was particularly intrigued by the side effects.

Garrett also made bank deposits—on behalf of Dina—of the welfare and Social Security checks of the boarders. Dina had a general account for these transactions and doled out money to her pensioners.

On Fridays, Dina held seminars and communicated with the dead loved ones for her tenants and a covey of outsiders who attended these spiritual gatherings. Prayer was plentiful and cash was always on hand. Josef Renchen found time to further Garrett's education by having him read the classics. They also worked daily on voice control until Garrett achieved an astounding gift for mimicking sounds.

Throughout the year, he had access to Renchen's collection of Thames and Hudson's art series, the Skira and Abrams volumes as well. Josef would patiently explain how Andrea del Sarto had mastered chiaroscuro, Leonardo vanishing-line perspective so that his paintings had depth of field; for portraits, they turned to Rembrandt and Goya; but for color and imagination there was no one who had ever painted with the originality of Gauguin.

Garrett read biographies of the artist, entranced by his devotion to his craft, his financial straits, and his suffering at the hands of colonial officials who made his life miserable in Tahiti. Uncle Josef took him to the McNay Art Museum, where Garrett stood in a trance before Gauguin's pensive *Portrait of the Artist with Idol*. In it the artist stares out defiantly at the viewer, his stark eagle eyes cold, arrogant. He has thin black eyebrows, a flowing mustache, long unkempt hair, his right thumb and forefinger appear deformed as they span a broad chin. It is a face devoid of charity, intense, self-contained.

The moment struck Garrett as a miracle when Gauguin spoke to him in English!

"You must sacrifice everything and everybody if you want to be like me."

For a moment, he was too shocked and intimidated to respond, but then he sensed the painter was waiting. "Oh, I will, I will."

The boy's training continued. Renchen taught him French and was pleased with Garrett's quickness and his willingness to practice the language and learn the grammar. They listened to classical music together, attended art lectures at the museum, and Garrett believed that this unexpected erudition would unlock the secrets of the universe.

One midwinter evening, while Dina was holding a séance, he and

Uncle Josef were in the master bedroom he shared with her. Josef had recently acquired a large poster of Gauguin's cryptic and occult masterpiece *D'où venons-nous? Que sommes-nous? Où allons-nous?"*

"Translate this for me, Garrett."

*"Where Do We Come From? What Are We? Where Are We Going?"*

"Excellent, you're a remarkable pupil. Now, Gauguin is asking, where is God, what is His meaning, why did He create us? He doesn't know, but great art asks the great questions. At the time, Gauguin was sick and penniless and he was contemplating suicide. But he had to achieve this vision first and they say he spent almost seven months on it. Possibly it is Birth, Life, and Death."

Garrett stared at the long murallike reproduction, enthralled when he heard Gauguin explaining in his own words what it all meant. Garrett felt a shimmering halo above him, a presence reflecting.

"To the right at the bottom end is a sleeping child and three women crouching. There are two figures dressed in purple who divulge their thoughts to one another. A colossal slouching figure, out of all proportion, and purposely so, lifts its arms and gapes in amazement at these two, who dare to think of their destiny. A figure in the center gathers fruit. We also have a pair of cats near a child. A white goat. An idol, its arms enigmatically raised in a kind of tempo, seems to indicate the Beyond. Then finally, I have an old woman close to death who seems resigned to her destiny. She finishes the allegory! At her feet, an exotic white bird holds a lizard in its claws. This denotes the meaninglessness of language."

Garrett knew, at that moment, he was possessed by Gauguin.

Fingers snapped in his face. "Garrett, wake up, you're in a trance."

"Yes, yes, I was under the master's spell."

"Come, Dina has prepared a late supper for us."

**Cold wursts, with** spicy mustard, goose liver, sausages, Limburger cheese, and pumpernickel and Dortmunder beer. Dina, herself, still wore a silk cape and her white turban.

"Garrett, you, Dina, and I, we have become a mutual comfort league. Trading partners. It's like the Hanseatic League that was formed between various cities in Germany: Lübeck, Bruges, Hamburg. They all gave each other preferred treatment, assisting each other through thick and thin."

He knew something was going to be demanded of him and kept quiet. "One of Dina's guests is having a very bad time. She can't breathe and she's suffering terribly."

"That's awful."

"Do you think you might get us a cup of arsenic from the pharmacy?" Dina asked.

Garrett turned away and his eyes roved over a practically new Nikon with a telephoto lens.

"With respect, Aunt Dina . . ."

"Oh, you're not going refuse me?" she asked, her voice still husky from communion with the spirit world.

They had misunderstood Garrett. "Well, Dina, sometimes Doc Haskins gets questions and calls from the police or the coroner about poisons. He's very careful about them and keeps track of them in a special poison book."

"I see," Renchen said without enthusiasm.

"Uncle Josef, please. I don't think you know what I'm trying to say."

"Go on, Garrett."

"Sukie, the maid, gives the medicine to all the sick people upstairs. See, Sukie is so busy cooking and cleaning that she doesn't know half the time who gets what pills." Their eyes fixed on him with joyful surprise. "Now suppose someone needed digitalis and was given a Dexedrine spansule—that's all speed. Or too much insulin. I mean, this happens all the time with folks. Then there's no poison or nothing that would look funny. You know, someone who is in pain and ready for the next world, well, they just conk out. No pain, no strain."

Dina touched his hand. "You're right about Sukie being forgetful. Maybe you could take over this duty for her."

"It would be a sacred trust," Uncle Josef said.

"Yes, I'd do it and continue my studies."

"In what way, Garrett?"

"Well, all the great artists paint death, don't they?"

"Of course. It would be a fulfilling part of your artistic training, a live model, then a dead one."

**Later that evening,** he had a private audience with the spiritualist. Dina spoke in the gypsy tongue, which she called Romany. She held a shiny coin on a chain and swayed it slowly from side to side. He tried to resist the gleam, but his lids grew heavy and in few moments he was under her spell, floating on a rainbow in the sky. This dazed feeling lasted only for a short time, but Garrett decided to feign entrapment. He heard noises at the table, silverware clatter, plates cracking, and a roar of thunder in the distance.

"I see your mother. She is very a pretty woman. She went under many names and she is walking the streets. She drinks, works in bars, and slips into alleys with men. They put their hands under her skirt and offer her money. One night a man in a bar where she drinks asks her for a date. She has never been with this man and she is frightened of him."

Dina began raving. *"Moarte! Vyusher . . . moxado . . . pale cido"* — *death, wolf, stained, unclean and dishonored.*

Dina's fearful voice was accompanied by a heavy downpour of rain and barrels of thunder. He forced himself to keep his eyes closed.

"Your mother tells this man that they have to get to know each other. But he says they are destined to be together. She finally agrees to go with him to his room and after she undresses and waits for him in bed, his face and body begin to change.

"He snarls at her and she realizes—"

Dina Marcuro broke off and shuddered. She saw the man being transformed into a wolf. Garrett's mother was trying to escape, but the wolf was ferocious. His hot spittle dripped on the woman's face and then his muzzle pressed against her lips and he entered her. . . .

Dina shrieked, startling Garrett, who, despite the dreamy state he had affected, was now terrified.

"Tell me what happened," he beseeched her.

Dina comforted the boy in her arms. "No harm will come to you, Garrett. I'll be here to protect you."

He was incredulous. "Did you contact my mother?"

"The spirits spoke, then vanished."

"You actually saw what happened?"

"The visit was too short," Dina replied, soothing him.

"But what happened to my mother and the man?"

Dina Marcuro had had a vision of hell. On a fiery pyre in a cavernous tomb, the woman and the wolf were entwined amid beasts and serpents. She knew that she must be cautious with this boy, for he was the child of this ungodly union.

*"Chces li tajnou vec aneb pravdu vyzvédéti."*

"I don't understand," he protested. "What do you mean?"

"Wouldst thou know a truth or mystery?" Dina said, before fainting.

**What began as** survival for Garrett, evolving into mischief, culminated in murder, but he didn't think of it in those terms. He filled his sketchbooks with the dying and the dead, the first on the scene to capture these images.

Great artists encompassed everything in their work, Gauguin informed him during the regular conversations they now had. Seminars and workshops. Sometimes Gauguin would talk about art for hours, and at others he would question his disciple. Why use the chrome yellow when a sallow orange is needed?

Garrett would be looking at a reproduction of the wonderful androgynous sculpture called *Oviri*, a ceramic work which Gauguin had done simply to buy food, and he would feel that he and his idol had established a perfect unity. In this work, a dead wolf's penis is entombed in a female.

Garrett also needed money and was prepared to make sacrifices to achieve greatness. The needle, his closest ally, always worked. Sometimes Garrett simply didn't fill the syringe and shot air into the vein, "to capture the moment," as he liked to tell Gauguin when *Le Maître* was being ornery.

Until he turned sixteen, Garrett assisted Dina and Josef in their godlike enterprise. New tenants, old and infirm, alone, abandoned by their families, came to the boardinghouse and after a time received their last rites. Cremation was the most effective method. An undertaker friend of Dina's arranged this. No questions asked.

Garrett's artistic skills had grown and he had no difficulty forging the signatures on death certificates, and other legal documents which left bank accounts and wills to the benevolent caretaker, Dina Marcuro.

Unfortunately, all of this comity, this shared purpose, changed after Josef began living with a young barmaid down on her luck who had come to pawn a watch. Both Garrett and Dina considered this a betrayal. Josef had clearly become a threat to the partnership.

Josef was very late for the Friday dinner. Dina met with Garrett and he took the necessary steps to draw up a will for Josef. Dina had countless exemplars of the pawnbroker's gothic signature.

Sukie had been given the weekend off to visit her family and the NO VACANCY sign was put up on the porch to discourage roaming salesmen. Only the bedridden and comatose guests remained in their chambers. Dina prepared a feast of Josef's favorites: rollmops, liver dumpling soup, and stuffed breast of veal, which Josef attacked with the furor of Siegfried. Wagner's *Der Ring* boomed over the speakers, and Josef, in high spirits, joined in an aria to Brünnhilde. But as he was about to assault the brandied plum pudding, he experienced severe chest pains. His face turned the color of currant jam, then gradually gave way to an ashy cinder tone. He rose up, gasping and fell from his armchair, jerking spasmodically for a minute or two, and expired.

"What did you add to the stuffing, Garrett?" Dina inquired.

"Enough nitroglycerin to blow up downtown. I think you ought to put the veal down the waste disposal and afterward add plenty of ammonia."

"Why?"

"Just in case the cops check the drain pipes."

**With the liquidation** of Josef Renchen's stock in the pawnbroking shop, Garrett had amassed twenty-five thousand dollars. He had passed San Antonio's temple of fine cuisine for many years, but never dared enter. As a tribute to his adopted family, he hosted a luncheon for the Hoskins family at the Little Rhein Steak House in the restaurant's charming Special Occasion Room.

According to a historical brochure, "the structure was utilized as an early Texas home, a boardinghouse, a German saloon, and a hangout for desperadoes." Garrett felt very comfortable with desperadoes. He had come to this gracious town alone, broke, and forlorn, and he had determined that no matter how remorseless he had to be, he would make his way in the world of art and challenge the mighty Paul Gauguin.

Garrett and the Hoskins family bade one another a teary farewell. But before leaving San Antonio, Garrett did the proper thing and called on Dina. He brought a peach pie, whipped cream, and a tin of Earl Grey tea. He watched Dina in the kitchen. To put her at her ease, he had her cut a piece of pie, lather it with cream, and he ate first.

"I'm sorry to see you going, Garrett," she said.

"Me, too, Dina. I brought a little something for you."

"You're sweet, but you didn't have to do that, honey. And I got something for you, too." She handed him a slip of paper. "This lady's name is Priscilla Carmela Adams and she lives in Pasadena. She's from here and used to be one of my regulars at the Friday medium nights. Her husband left her a pile. The *thing* is, Prissy loves art. I've written a letter of introduction to her. Said you might be calling and that you would be a greater painter than Gauguin."

"Dina, you're truly wonderful."

"Well, I know you always like to have an auntie when you're in trouble."

"I have something for you, too." Garrett's farewell gift had an ominous motive behind it, and he chided himself for his insensitive distrust. "I cherish you, Dina."

"No, you don't. I know what you are. Garrett, you're two different people and we've had a good partnership."

This treacherous gypsy had seen through him from the beginning. There was no masking what he was—what he'd become—with Dina Marcuro.

He removed an envelope from the pocket of his jaunty new blazer and continued eating his pie at the table, staring at the mysterious rainbow globe. He looked up from time to time, as she riffed through the photos of her dead boarders.

"You were taking pictures all the while."

"I had to protect myself."

"Really? Who from?"

"Maybe myself," he admitted. "I was a child in the clutches of killers."

"We were con people, bunko, nothing, until Josef brought *you* home." He had finally succeeded in getting her flustered. "Garrett, we're in Texas, we'll both go to death row. Where are the copies, the negatives?"

"I have them. Now, Dina, you just answer a question and they're yours." She nodded.

"When you did that medium stuff after I started coming here, what did you really see?"

"I never want to talk about it or relive that experience. Keep the negatives," she fired back at him, "and blackmail me."

Dina ambled to one of her red-lacquered curio cabinets and removed the sheet over it. Garrett had never seen this collection before. Inside were misshapen, grotesque, tortured figures of demons: satyrs and monks, young women with horned toads, snakelike torsos without heads.

"Your mother was a whore and your father a wolf with two heads. I thought I'd seen it all. But this was a terrifying revelation — even to me. I spared you this, until this moment."

She cringed away from him and he flung the negatives of deaths they had planned and he had executed into the fireplace.

"*Where Do We Come From? What Are We? Where Are We Going?*"

"You, you're already in Gehenna."

# CHAPTER 9

**Michel had left Jennifer** and Rosalind asleep. During the night he had heard a volcanic chorus of curses, hopping sounds, a lament, followed by thuds. Rosalind had jammed her toe on the bathroom step and elsewhere. At this rate, he'd have no one to dance with at his wedding. Perhaps when Philippe and the contractor had ended their duel, he'd call him and see what could be done.

En route to Marseille he decided to stop by Gropier's bakery. The boulangerie was still quiet and not even a disreputable drunk with a tale from his Arabian Night was present. Michel caught the *mitron* loading his truck in the alley and arranged for the youthful assistant to drop off a sack of croissants and baguettes with the concierge for the ladies' breakfast.

He nibbled a honeyed almond brioche, and in just under thirty minutes reached the undulating Corniche President Kennedy crowning the Mediterranean. At the princely Petit Nice Hôtel a porter was hosing down the driveway while the gardeners were already having a morning tipple of wine and trampling the flower beds. The commingled scent of roses, lavender, herbs, and sea air teased Michel and induced a languid mood of play, preferably sexual with Jennifer in bed beside him.

Under the awning, Sylvie Caron was waiting. She had taken his other female detective's place. Corrine had resigned to become a full-time mother. Training this ambitious new breed of detective had been a parting assignment which Michel had undertaken at the request of Richard Caron, his boss and the girl's father. Sylvie was twenty-seven and had struggled through the ranks to reach this position. Michel had heard grumbles of nepotism, but had silenced them.

The young woman, at Richard's behest, had attended the University of Lyon ostensibly to study law. Midway through, she had given up, enrolled in the local gendarme academy, passed her exams, topping all the males, and been posted to Toulouse. Five years on the streets and four shootings—drug dealers and bank robbers among them—gave Sylvie the qualifications for detective work. In a sense, she was the son Richard had never had, and now that she had pursued the same career, he was resentful.

The only obstacle to her replacing Corrine in the Special Circumstances Section turned out to be her autocratic father, who ultimately yielded to Michel's blandishments. Richard Caron was retiring at Christmas and his bloodline ought to continue in the service, Michel had said. This argument ultimately prevailed, and Michel took her under his wing.

Sylvie was limber, svelte, and had her father's hooded, impassive brown eyes. To everyone's horror she had gone for a buzz cut the previous week, the esplanade of auburn hair a casualty of impulse. But in some respects she was even more beautiful and dazzling. She had something of her father's peremptory manner and was contemptuous of flirts. A small sunflower tattoo imprinted at the seam of her cleavage seemed to repudiate her official authority and gave the impression that she belonged to the wildcat, druggie rank. But this tattoo was not frequently on view and was not a bad ad for street work.

"How's the groom's mood?" she asked.

"Ghastly. I'm swearing off drink."

"Oh, giving up your citizenship already? I heard about your performance."

"Yes, *Agence France* already reported that I've been contacted by the Folies Bergère."

"You and my father, what a pair of Blue Belles."

"He didn't take a stitch off."

"Any photos?"

"At times, Sylvie, I wish you were a man so I could wallop you."

"In the States, I could sue you for millions for that remark."

"I'll pay for your plane ticket!"

"No, no, Michel. You have to teach me everything first."

Sylvie had a feline quality and striking powers of observation which he admired. Some methods and techniques were unteachable, like her natural gift for unearthing obscure clues. Actually her playfulness had improved his mood and he cast off the dreary hangover with a container of sublime hotel coffee, reason enough for the hotel's two Michelin stars, he thought. The parents of the dead girl were still in their suite.

"Did the Belgian investigators send their report?"

"Yes, and it's trash."

He bridled. "I assumed as much. They're despicable."

Along with detectives throughout the world, Michel detested the Belgian police for their indifference, political maneuvering, and the botch they made of every important case. For years, they had ignored evidence, obvious clues that Marc Dutroux, a convicted rapist, and his wife had kidnapped four young girls. Two eight-year-olds had been murdered and two others had been found starving in an underground bunker in his house in Charleroi. Hundreds of videotapes had also been seized, starring Dutroux and his friends sexually abusing them.

Yet another case in Brussels had brought international odium. This one starred Andras Pandy, a self-styled clergyman, and his eldest daughter, who had murdered two of his wives and four of his children, along with an untold number of others. In both circumstances, there was the stench of a political cover-up.

"Dr. Laurent wants to see you after the identification."

"It would be refreshing if he could give me a specific time of death for once." As they proceeded to the Davises' villa, Michel caught Sylvie's arm. "On no account mention the acid burns or the piercing."

Melanie Davis had once been the brightest star on the Wake Forest women's golf team and had briefly played on the LPGA tour, but a broken wrist skiing had ruined her game. She was an aristocratic, sun-nurtured, supple woman, with blond hair, tan lines under her blue eyes, but she maintained the posture of crisis management. Her overwrought husband, a sulky Silicon Valley tycoon, had the pallor of his profession as a computer software designer. This accounted for the couple's expensive wardrobe of La Coste shirts, fine chambray, and the Mephistos. Michel reckoned a couple of thousand dollars for these simple morning clothes.

Mrs. Davis was currently employed as a club pro and, as Michel had surmised, her murdered daughter was one of the leading junior players in the country. Michel idly chatted with Melanie on the drive to the Special Circumstances Section center. Golf was a safe topic. Sylvie sat silently beside Jeffrey Davis in the back seat making notes.

"For some reason my putting went south," the bereaved mother said.

"I suffer from the same problem," Michel said, "and that's without breaking my wrist."

"What's your handicap?" she asked.

"My temper, probably, but it was a four a few months ago," Michel reported as though pining for a lost love.

"That's terrific," she said.

Michel respected Melanie Davis's poise and dignity under these catastrophic circumstances. The unruffled professional, nursing her emotional mate gave this woman a magisterial dignity. What we can only learn from golf, he thought.

Jeffrey Davis said vehemently, "Caroline was scratch!"

"Jeff, don't make it worse."

"It can't get any worse, Mel."

Michel decided not contradict him. They were passing Nôtre-Dame-de-la-Garde. High on the hill, the Byzantine-style basilica and its towering, ornate golden statue of the Virgin was one of the glories of Marseille. If the Davises were Catholic, he might recommend a visit and a candle lighting for their daughter.

"Before we go in for the identification, there are certain legal aspects I should explain. If the girl is indeed your daughter, then it becomes a French criminal investigation."

"What about the Belgian police?"

"Although the kidnapping took place in Belgium, the body was found in France."

Melanie sighed with relief. "Thank God for that."

Her husband snarled, "The police there don't know what the fuck they're doing."

"I'm not supposed to criticize a police force in the Interpol fraternity, but I'm retiring soon. They're corrupt swine and right-wing bastards. . . . Look, for what it's worth, the section I head has the most advanced technology in Europe."

"And how advanced are the detectives?" Melanie asked.

"Commander Danton caught the American mass murder in Provence last summer," Sylvie advised them.

"You were involved in that Snakeman case?" Jeffrey Davis asked.

"Yes, sir. My retirement present to my future wife."

"We saw a TV special on it," his wife noted.

"I didn't watch it," Michel replied, parking in his spot. He'd miss the old timbers and new facility it housed inside.

As Michel led them through the sleek corridors in the basement, passing lab technicians who looked up at the couple with him, his mood turned rancid. He signaled one of Laurent's attendants, who removed the body from a steel compartment and wheeled it up to the glass. When he lifted the plastic sheet, revealing only the girl's bloated face, Melanie Davis collapsed. Her husband caught her, struggling with his tears.

Melanie beat her fists on the glass. "I want to touch her, hold her, please."

"Is this Caroline Davis?" Michel asked.

For a moment neither could speak. Jeffrey Davis finally said, "She was thirteen last month, May eighth. I can't believe we've lost her."

"God help the woman who took my baby," Melanie screamed. "I'll chop her into pieces."

"Leave that to me," Michel said.

"Commander Danton . . . ?" Jeffrey's voice quavered.

"Yes, Mr. Davis."

"*This, this* . . . doesn't happen to people like us!"

"It's not supposed to happen to anyone."

He thrust his shoulders back and Michel could see that the slumped figure he had first encountered was structured and in grand gym shape. Sylvie steered the distraught Melanie into the cafeteria.

"Listen, Michel, I'm a problem solver. I quit college my first semester at Berkeley, rented a room, and went to work with three other dropouts. Today our company is worth thirty-seven billion dollars. I couldn't fix Mel's putting, but whoever murdered our daughter is going to be fixed. I don't care how much I have to pay to find this woman."

"It won't cost you anything but time and anguish," Michel said.

"Michel, you're retiring, what about the next guy who comes in? Is he going to be motivated?"

"I'll find the people."

Jeffrey Davis bulled against Michel as though this were a bar brawl in the making. "What are you talking about? A *woman* kidnapped Caroline."

"The woman had help. This is a *conspiracy* murder."

Like a whimpering boy beaten on the school field, Jeffrey Davis's mind was filled with extravagant notions. "I can bring in experts."

"We don't need litter and chaos. That's what your superstars will bring. This is a very complex case."

They walked to the cafeteria and Michel signaled Sylvie to remain. "It's going to be a short honeymoon for my fiancée."

"When are you getting married?"

"In two days."

"I think I'm going crazy," Jeffrey Davis said.

"No, you're going to be strong and tell me everything. I want that mind that developed your billion-dollar company to be a model of clarity."

"I'll try."

"Believe me, I won't give up until I arrest these butchers," he said, giving in to anger.

The software virtuoso stared at Michel, his bloodshot eyes drooping as though before his flat-screened monitor while formulating a new Linux or Windows.

"How can you be certain? Have you had some kind of breakthrough already?"

"Listen to me. I'm a chess player, Jeff. Groups don't do well against an individual—a single opponent."

"IBM's Big Blue beat Gary Kasparov."

"It was simply money and a machine against a man. The stakes weren't murder," Michel said. He was acquiring an impression of the case: a sense of groupings, feelings, his acute sensibility filling the canvas with forms and a structural outline. "You see, Jeff, there's always a weak coupling when there's more than one person involved in murder. Something goes wrong with one of the people: a quirk of personality, a loose hinge, jealousy, conflict, a guilty conscience."

Michel reached into his pocket, removed his wallet, and flicked a card from the stiff new Gucci wallet Jennifer had bought him.

"What's this?" Jeff asked, diverted from the conversation.

"When Melanie feels better or worse, take her to my club to hit some balls at the range. She can practice her putting on bumpy greens and you can play tennis or practice with our pro on clay courts that are as fast as mulled wine."

"How do you know I play tennis?"

"Nobody pumps iron with one hand. Your right forearm is almost as a big as Agassi's."

Jeff rolled his head from side to side as though reviving himself from an overdose of Thorazine. "I've built my company with maniacs and I was told that I was crazy."

"That's probably why the Wall Street bankers funded you."

Jeffrey Davis smiled with bitter irony. "One loose cannon meets his mate."

"That's the consensus about me here."

"How's your future wife going to handle you, Michel?"

"Not—as they say in California. Now, if you haven't had breakfast, our cafeteria can fry an egg. Try to calm your wife down. I want her to be lucid and clinical. Afterwards, Sylvie will bring you to my office."


**Admiring the view** of the harbor, Dr. Laurent waited anxiously for Michel in his office. The burly medical examiner for once seemed subdued.

"Actually, Michel, I came to a very disheartening conclusion last night when you were onstage."

"Really, you're a fan of performance art?"

"No. It's just that I actually think I'm going to miss you."

"It's too early in the day to be maudlin."

"Oh, well. I heard the girl's parents were here." Michel nodded. "This murder is grotesque. Her stomach was loaded with morphine and small traces of GHB."

"The new date rape junk?"

"Exactly. We're from the old school. Remember when you bought a young woman champagne and took your chances? Nowadays, if the young lady doesn't demand Ecstasy, someone slips Rohypnol or Gamma Hydroxy Butyrate into her flute when she's not looking. My guess is that whoever murdered the child used it as an anesthetic."

Michel switched on his computer to nuisance e-mails and inter-office memos. "And the cause of death?"

"A needle attached to a drill."

"A drill?"

"Yes, it could be a household job, but I doubt it. The needle was one decimeter, six centimeters in length, and very fine." Michel put his index finger against his pinky to visualize the measurement. "There's some indication that it might be two very fine needles soldered together. Someone put it in very neatly and cleanly into the carotid artery."

"Needles . . . like surgery?"

"In sense, but it's the wrong kind of needle configuration for surgery or for a hypodermic."

"I noticed that she had her nipple pierced. What are these kids up to?"

"No one knows," Laurent said gravely. "I had Andrea look at it under the scope. It's platinum, of all things, and had the word *amour* on it."

With reluctance, Michel pressed him. "Any evidence of sexual activity?"

"Yes, both places. But according to Timone the sperm cells are too degenerated to have any DNA validity. He says the cells are very eccentric. He plans to do an HPLC mass-spec, which will take some time.

"Then there's the saltwater adulteration. But what perplexes me are the traces of acetic acid that I swabbed from the vaginal canal."

Michel contemplated this arcane information. "Seawater?"

"I don't think so, Michel."

"The girl douched with vinegar? Very European and old-fashioned—wouldn't you think—with all the new products on the market?"

"It's a possibility and bizarre, to say the least."


**Michel refrained from** discussing the unsavory details of the post-mortem with the Davises. Their daughter's death was traumatic enough. He wanted them sharp and undistracted. With their consent, the interview was being videotaped. They both seemed resigned now and focused.

"My husband told me that you think more than one person was involved."

"Yes. But we'll get to my assumptions later. Bruges is very beautiful. Tell me about it."

"Do you know it?" Melanie asked.

"Yes, I had a friend at the Sorbonne from Bruges and we use to go biking there over school vacations. But it's not the sort of place most Americans would pick. Why did you decide to visit?"

"My Aunt Mari lives there and usually she comes to see us every summer in California. We have a house on Seventeen Mile Drive in Carmel. She's my mother's sister and my only living relative. She had a heart attack in April and I flew over to nurse her," Melanie explained. "When she recuperated, I flew back to California. I phoned her every day. But it wasn't enough to set my mind at ease. Caroline and she were crazy about each other. So, in a sense, she's more than an aunt; she's become Caroline's grandmother. I can't use the past tense yet."

"Don't worry about it."

Jeff interjected, "Caroline plays junior golf and we both thought, let's go to Bruges. We'd see Aunt Mari, then fly to Scotland so we could play St. Andrews, Carnoustie, and the whole loop of the British Opens."

"You've been to Bruges often, Melanie?"

"Oh, since I was a girl. I can't even guess how many times."

"And I've been there three, four times."

"What about Caroline?" Michel asked.

They both thought for a moment. "Once. Right, Jeff?"

"Yeah, I think Caroline was seven or eight. But it was usually in the off season, when there weren't any tournaments. Mel, we took her over Christmas—'95, '96 . . . ?"

Melanie began to sob and Jeff knelt before her and kissed her hands. "Come on, babe. We have to do this."

Michel made an effort to comfort her and in a few moments she settled into a stillness.

"Why did Caroline have her teeth capped?"

"Last year, she flipped off her surfboard and it hit her and broke her front teeth. Eventually, the dentist is going—Oh, God, there I go again. He planned to put in implants."

"I see. Now take me back to the last day in Bruges."

The family had lunched at the romantic Kasteel Minnewater Restaurant overlooking the Lake of Love, as it was known, and taken a ramble afterward, bellies filled with wine and a copious Carbonnade Flamandre, a pleasant, sweetish beer version of Chez Danton's *boeuf en daube*. Michel recalled how he and a Flemish Rubens's enchantress had thrown coins in the lake to bless their drunken weekend affair.

Melanie persevered. "My aunt has a florist shop in the Steenstraat. The Rodenstuck family has been there since 1894. Aunt Mari is one of the organizers of the *Floralies* in Ghent."

"The most prestigious flower show in Europe," Michel stipulated.

"Yes. After our walk, Aunt Mari had to return to her shop," Jeff said.

Michel allowed them to stroll through the magnificent civic sights, from the Memling Museum to the photo op on the Bonifacius Bridge, as the parents exposed their teenage golf prodigy to the treasures of the great Northern Renaissance.

"Caroline loved every moment," Jeff said, curiously defensive, as though protecting his wife and her aunt from this ordeal for a young American girl, who might have been happier hitting her wedge at the driving range in Pebble Beach.

"Did either of you or your aunt notice anyone—a couple, a group watching you at the restaurant?" They both shook their heads. "Anyone strike up a conversation?" Again they neutralized the question, and not, Michel thought, in guilty denial. "Do you remember someone coming up to you—anywhere that afternoon— asking for street directions, from a car or walking? Homeless, street people at the fish market, begging for change?" Both rejected all of his suggestions. "Did you have a guide?"

"Michel, I know Bruges blindfolded," Melanie Davis snapped.

"Fine. Now let's get to the woman you suspect kidnapped Caroline. How did it happen?"

There had been a young woman nearby among others in the Groeninge Museum. Caroline had been thirsty, had her own money and cell phone.

Melanie began, "Caroline just said, 'I'm going for a Coke. . . .' This woman looked over at her and smiled: 'Good idea, I'm dying for a drink, too.'"

Jeff added, "As Caroline and the woman were walking off, I told Caroline we'd meet up at Our Lady's Church by the Michelangelo statue."

"The *Madonna with Child,*" Michel said.

"Yes, and that was it," Melanie said. "There was a café across the street from the museum and we assumed that's where they were heading."

They described the woman. She was in her late twenties, American, with long brown hair, dark glasses, about five-eight, wearing running shoes, dark trousers, and a dark straw hat. She was attractive, carried a camera and a guidebook.

"Out of the corner of my eye, I watched this woman and Caroline talking as they walked out. Caroline was laughing and they seemed friendly."

"I have a question, if I may," Sylvie said. "Did the woman have any distinguishing characteristics, like a birthmark on her face or her hands?"

"No, none," Melanie declared.

Michel was pleased by Sylvie's initiative. They had agreed at this stage not to disclose the acid imprint on Caroline's back or that any sexual activity had occurred.

Michel took over. "Had you seen this woman before?" The Davises shook their heads. "And not afterwards?"

"No," Jeff replied. "You know, when you're sightseeing, people just spring out of nowhere. There was nothing about her behavior to make us suspicious."

Michel continued, "Was there anything peculiar, idiosyncratic about this woman? Was there some mannerism that caught your attention?"

"No," the Davises replied together.

"Are you sure she was American?" They nodded again. "How long were you away from Caroline?"

Both Davises stared, then glared at each other.

"Hold everything!" Michel said, storming to the window, turning furiously, then glaring at them. "Neither of you is responsible! So don't for a second consider pointing fingers or blaming yourselves!"

Jeffrey Davis embraced his wife.

"The museum choir was practicing Handel, and we—I—like to buy paintings—both of us love great art," he said. "Right, Mel?"

"So many rooms to fill in our enormous house."

"On Seventeen Mile Drive," Michel said.

"Yes," Melanie said, "it's not far from Maggie Eastwood's house—at Cypress Point. She was married to Clint Eastwood and we see him in town."

Michel patiently listened to the trivial irrelevancies of how the Davises were cobbling their lives together by pursuing social upgrades.

"There's going to be a sale soon at Christie's and Sotheby's of Old Masters. I'm a major client," Jeff said proudly. "And frankly, I'm fed up with the Warhols and Rothkos and the dumb Lichtenstein I bought when I got rich."

"You're considering buying van Eyck and Memling. Breughels, perhaps, and trade your other paintings?"

Jeffrey Davis nodded, then slumped down in despair. "Frankly, there's a painting in the Groeninge that I got hung up. It's by Josef Suvée, late eighteenth century. One woman is embracing another, younger one and their shadows are magically cast on the wall behind them. It reminded me of Balthus's *Music Lesson*."

Michel was well acquainted with the French master's erotic work. He had seen the painting of the teacher seducing her student. It was powerful, stunning and wanton; in its erotic realism, it had a kinship to Nabokov's Lolita, and suggested a male lesbian fantasy.

Sylvie had been observing Michel's friendly technique of interrogation. She was fascinated by his agility. He shucked oysters and came up with pearls. Would she ever know enough to become his clone?

"There is no hard evidence to suggest that this young woman who left the Groeninge with Caroline was actually involved. So why are you suspicious of her?"

They were stumped, then Jeff said, "It was too convenient and the woman disappeared. The kidnapping was on Belgian TV and in the newspapers. I took full-page ads with Caroline's picture. Aunt Mari wrote Flemish and French captions. I offered a million-dollar reward! The Belgian police did check all the hotels in Bruges looking for the woman."

"They never found her," his wife said.

"Did you take any holiday photos?"

"Yes," Jeff said. "I've got about six exposed rolls. I'll get them developed."

"I'll have one of my people go to the hotel. We'll develop them here. Now if anything else occurs to you, call me at any time."

Sylvie escorted them out and when she returned, Michel reflected and boldly put forward his premise to Sylvie. "Caroline was ordered at the restaurant like a dish off the menu. They were waiting for someone like her. I feel sure of that." He examined the photograph of Caroline: the smiling, blond, young junior golf champion. Yes, she was ordered from the à la carte menu.

"Sylvie, I want you to catch a flight to Bruges, and spend some time dining at the Kasteel Minnewater. Take your camera and play tourist. Be sure that you take snaps of the staff and any regulars."

After she left, to relax, Michel took his new Callaway driver out of the closet and cut through the bubble wrapping. He was just feeling the new grip when Melanie Davis burst back in.

"The woman was wearing a ring on her thumb. Whitish, possibly ivory."

"Excellent," Michel said with a smile.

He was embarrassed, toying with the driver at such an inopportune moment, but Melanie came beside him.

"Show me your setup."

He bent his knees, gripped the club with his left hand, then overlapped it with his right hand. She moved his right hand and he now saw that the club face was square.

"You probably hook the ball with that grip."

"Perpetually. Thank you," he added. "It's been one of the great mysteries of my life."

Melanie forced a smile to her face, pausing at the door. "Given the circumstances, I'm glad I met someone like you, Michel. Does your fiancée appreciate what you do?" She had raised the single most distressing issue in his relationship with Jennifer. When he did not reply, she shook her head. "I guess I can't blame her for hating your work."

"It's a sore point, Mrs. Davis. By the way, did you or your husband notice if the woman had a cell phone?"

Melanie became flustered. "Damn it, I forgot. Yes, as she was walking with Caroline, she made a call. I didn't see her dial, or maybe I wasn't paying attention."

"There may be other memories. But don't force yourself to think of them. It's like putting: When you put too much pressure on yourself, you miss."

# CHAPTER 10

**Eve thought of the** postmillennium cycle as the black ice period. The heavy rains in late February and early March spat off the dark Venice canals, veiling the houses in a shroud. The weather, however, had no effect on the neighborhood's ubiquitous building crews who were inside remodeling, drywalling, and installing kitchen cabinets, or the imperious decorators wearing fishermen's yellow slickers and screaming orders.

Garrett had become moody and coldly domineering. A skeleton staff ran the shops and the even rhythm of their lives took on a dissonance which devoured her. They were quarreling, and when they were occasionally landlocked in a mellow evening, she detected hostile undertones. This role reversal gained its flood tide from Heather, who was determined to split them up and banish Eve.

**To accommodate Heather's** insatiable appetites, one afternoon Garrett persuaded Eve to finally yield to her demands. She and Heather had not made love before, and Heather was relentless, curious. It was apparent though that she wanted Garrett.

During this encounter, Heather's loose mental wires fused and she berated Eve.

"You're a mannequin, a total zombie in bed, Eve." She pounded Eve's fine features with her voluminous breasts. Suddenly Heather flung her off the bed. "Before you showed up, Garrett and I had an awesome thing. I want him back! Not some lipstick dyke smearing Pond's on me. You sad sack, get the fuck out of our lives!"

"Blame yourself, Heather. It was your idea in Bangkok."

"Me? Garrett cracked up and was suicidal. I *bought* you to please him. To try to make him happy. Without me, you wouldn't exist. And never forget that."

"Garrett went to Bangkok to escape from you. He was unfulfilled."

"Oh, really. Well, this isn't the answer for me."

"At least he's painting again."

"But you're with him and I'm the spare tire."

The naked Heather, surgically cloned as Pamela Anderson, ripped off the satin bedspread. Her sweaty sex toys fell to the floor; the big red vibrator went off; it was like a cooked lobster on its back, suffering a seizure before croaking into a buttery silence. Heather flung it against the wall. With repugnance, she gaped at her Amazonian sex queen image in the full-length mirror and spat at it.

Heather screamed, "Damn you, damn you."

Eve dressed quickly. It was as if she smelled smoke. There was no way she might resolve the situation, but at the same time, she couldn't back off.

"From my point of view, it's hard to imagine you falling in love with someone like Garrett. You'll have to face it, Heather, I'm his inspiration."

"You're a monster—an aberration!"

"That may be true, but Garrett worships me."

When Eve rushed out, the virago's screeching penetrated the entire house. Rudy, the butler, sprawled on an easy chair, his feet up on an ottoman, peered over his *Wall Street Journal*. He lowered his reading glasses and his face had a torpid expression.

"Last night she had four different mates. Bart and I had to solicit on Hollywood Boulevard to nab these chickens."

Bart appeared with a pair of blushing Cosmopolitans on a silver tray. "Disgusting. She's made bloody ponces out of us. I mean, Eve, I've cracked heads, welded kneecaps for the Kray boys in London, but never have I had to *hundel* with teenage tarts."

He handed the drink to Rudy, who sipped it approvingly and said, "Delicious. . . . Eve, my dear, it was so much easier when there was only one of you."

Bart wiggled onto the ottoman and slipped in between the barefoot butler. "Oh, for the fucking glory days of Garrett on his own. Heather was happy as a lark."

"But Garrett wasn't!" Eve said, stalking out in a fury.


**Silent as a cat,** Eve crept into the house. She heard the stark, ponderous Bartók string quartet coming from upstairs. The *pizzicato* grated on her nerves and then the accelerated pace buzzed like a horde of insects. The same piece had been playing when she left for Heather's. She stood by the window gazing at the black spikes of rain pounding the waxen canals. She decided to chill out and wait until she could detect the master's frame of mind. He had been in a fury all morning. Smoking his infernal pipe, wearing a French matelot shirt and Breton fisherman's vest over his jeans. Garrett's attempt to assume the persona of Gauguin, get into his skin, gradually improved his mood. When she pasted on the droopy mustache, he settled down.

An hour of colossal Grey Goose martinis fortified her to go upstairs to face him.

"I've mixed some martinis," she said.

"I only drink Pastis or wine," he said gruffly. "Heather already phoned. And Denny is coming over with the figures."

"We'll get through the slow season, Garrett. There are other things we've got to deal with."

"Like what?"

"Like us"—her voice quavered—"and the future."

The doorbell rang, postponing the crisis. Denny Flenge, the company's general manager and enforcer, was slapping his sodden cap against his briefcase. He had been hired by Garrett years ago as a favor to Rudy, which had been as a favor to Heather.

Denny had a sheepish, fawning smile which displayed a mouth of glaring white caps designed by a Korean discount dentist. Anything was better than the floppy partial that had wiggled on his gums for years like a life raft. His tiny head, pale freckled skin, blond beard, and color-contrasted green ponytail squatted on a stump of a neck and came to rest on a pear-shaped body whose balance was regulated by a beer gut that drunkenly keeled over his belt buckle. Gold pierced hooks hung from his eyebrows, and dangling from the nib of his nose a ring swayed, reputedly human bone from Madagascar, where he claimed he and some of the locals had cooked a tourist.

"Want a drink?" Eve asked.

"Adore a whiskey neat, please. Bloody weather's only good for an all-day shag—sodomy included. I might still be in London, for all the good it does me. Wormwood Scrubs revisited."

"Beats jail."

"That it does," he said with an unrepentant sigh, then changed the subject. "You look a bit peaked. How're you, love?"

"Living for the moment," she said, pouring five fingers of scotch in a Baccarat bucket glass.

He took a short sip and she filled her martini junior vase with the watery remains.

The renovation of the Venice Boardwalk had burst forth with earthmovers killing everyone's business. The local political powers determined that tarting it up would attract free-spending tourists during the Democratic convention in August. The owners of stalls and shops were beside themselves, protesting to the city to no avail. Without foot traffic, not even stolen goods were salable.

As for Garrett's atelier, it, too, would suffer during this period of readornment.

"Accounts are seasonally shipshape except for the Boardwalk, luv."

He handed her the accounts ledger. They never used the computer and kept a spare set of cooked books for the IRS. As much as possible, Eve and Garrett ran a cash-and-carry operation. Credit cards were a necessity, but they discouraged them whenever possible and offered a bogus rebate for cash. Eve read the figures: Suntanning and massage twofers were cyclically smart; the coffee bars were kept stable by the regulars slurping their lattes when they were in for hairdressing, makeup, and manicure.

"The net profit is way off," she said.

"Yes," he agreed, "down to six grand."

"This is not good news in a shit-hot economy."

"Give us a break, Eve. Nobody's running in for a must-have

Satan piece of flash or demanding pierced clitoral hood captive beads." He drained his glass. "When the fucking workmen are out and we get some sunshine, the plebes'll be hitting the beach and we'll level out."

They spent the better part of an hour discussing a website Garrett still hadn't designed, and how to lure high school kids into the skin net. Both agreed that the local throwaway newspapers were the best source for advertisements.

"Denny . . . Denny . . ." she pondered. "I think when you see the ad people, let's throw in a prespring freebie. First ten customers get a piece of jewelry for a piercing and toss in a ten percent reduction. Do some cunning copy about being the first to flash your new pierce or tattoo on the beach for Easter madness. Kind of a Fat Tuesday come-on."

"Lovely, will do, Eve. I might round up a few of the team and make a run to Palm Springs during Spring Break and set up a stall in a suite at the Holiday Inn."

"Don't bother. I want you to trim ten people off the tattooing staff."

"That's the firing squad for some of them, Eve."

"No one ever told them that an artist's life was easy. They picked this profession."

As she escorted Denny out, he gave her a hug, and she checked his eyebrows for a loose connection. She had done all of his piercing.

"Denny, Garrett and I may be going away on a trip."

"Not to worry, my love. Big trip . . . ?"

"It could be a while. And I'd hate to think there'd be loose fingers with our finances."

"I'll whip out my seal pup club."

She knew he was serious; they both were. The stories about loose fingers at Garrett's salons were not apocryphal. Before Denny joined the staff, Garrett had been his own enforcer and used a Little League metal bat to smash the fingers of looters.

**The respite with** Denny cleared Eve's head. When she tiptoed into the studio carrying a tray of ice, Pastis 51, and a bottle of water, the doleful Bartók had been replaced by Mel Tormé's "It's a Blue World." She fixed Garrett his drink in a tall glass.

"I'm having a mood swing."

"Anything would be improvement," she said.

He smiled at her and their reflections in the mirror, licked her lips, and kissed her.

"You taste of—"

"Heather. It was a terrible idea. We truly hate each other." Eve was solemn with resignation. "I'm your slave, I'm Heather's slave. What's left for me? Garrett, I'm losing my identity."

"It's all my fault." His contrition was genuine. "I brought you into this triangle."

"I knew from the get-go that Heather was part of the equation."

"Thing is, Eve, before you came into my life, she made unbearable demands on me. I was like a send-out pizza for her pleasure and amusement. I was always down on my knees for her."

Eve's emotions were deeply engaged. "What's happening to us is too horrible. . . ."

"Humiliating and painful. You know, when Heather had her makeover, she said it was for me. To keep me interested."

"And chained."

He toyed with his itchy wig. "As if I wanted a set of hooters the size of sand dunes."

Carrying his drink, Garrett roved through his studio, studying his recent work.

"Eve . . . I've been thinking . . . the only way to *disable* a triangle is to cut off one of its legs."

Eve was triumphant. She had roused him to action, but she worried about his impetuous side.

"It's too dangerous . . . here and now!" she said. "The police would come looking for you before you got to the airport. And they'd grind *us*, Garrett."

She was finally back in control and suggested a plan.

"Before I left on my *date* with the swamp woman, Jan Kortemark called from Bruges and we had a very cordial chat," she began. "Maybe this is the way we can prune Heather and have our trip to Europe now. I've been on-line with Sabena Airlines and hotels. I also mentioned to Denny to prepare for us going, but I wanted to clear it with you."

"Good girl."

As Eve went on with a globe-trotting itinerary, he was enthralled. His lover, the lover beyond all others, had taken charge.

"We can make it for Fat Tuesday. Jan went on and on about what a hoot it was in Belgium. All those wonderful medieval towns have their own character. Garrett, we'd see new sights. It'll be good for your work. You can get closer to Gauguin, commune with him. We'll go to the museums and see his work. He'll talk to you, and explain the secrets of how his style evolved."

Garrett had a serene, dreamy expression. "I'll have the revelation."

She knelt in adoration. "My genius will find the rapture."

# CHAPTER 11

**If Philippe Danton ever** again heard the plangent names of
Stendhal, Balzac, Flaubert, or Milady Colette, he would not wait
to get to his kitchen for his Sabateur carving knife, he would simply
beat Rosalind to death with his country-squire malacca walking
stick. Yes, of course he'd heard of these people—streets and boul-
evards were named after them! What was she trying to do, test his
knowledge of Michelin's *routiers* guide? The accursed wormy
Proust she'd rambled on about might have been related to some
old restaurant client who always came in with a new girl on his
arm. An obsession with women probably ran in the sex-crazed family of this Marcel. When Philippe had been unresponsive, Rosalind
changed the subject to philosophy—Descartes and Pascal—and he
stared vacantly at her. She finally sauntered through Existentialism,
praising some madman called Sartre who had hacked out a demented document called *Being and Nothingness*.

To further compound Rosalind's disgracefully insulting behavior, she had ignored Manolete, his prize Charolais bull; *enfin* the
scatty woman refused to eat a truffled *ris de veau* he had prepared
à la Escoffier! She preferred a mussel and tapenade green salad that
Nicole had thrown together. Women don't eat sweetbreads, indeed! Trust Michel to search the world for an uncivilized mother-
in-law like this one. Well, they deserved each other!

Leaving his handsome, sumptuous herd to their grasslands in
the Camargue, the flamingos in daredevil air show flight, Philippe
was forced to stop at the ghastly old sightseer city of Aigues-Mortes
while Nicole guided Jennifer and her mother through the city's
miserable fortifications and ancient ramparts. He couldn't wait to
get back to Chez Danton and have a Pastis with René, who had

quit his temporary job working at Claude's doddering hotel. Some new murder had upset René's delicate digestion. Michel was probably knee-deep in blood and gore again.

Much as he disapproved of Nicole's driving, fearing for his pristine Mercedes SUV, he had Nicole let him off at the Place Forbin. The timpani of tourist horns was riotous. Were American cities and homes so revolting that these people had to flock to Aix in buses for the summer?

The women were to visit the new art gallery that Michel's former Sorbonne professor had opened on the Cours Mirabeau next to Façonnable, where he now bought his jeans and work shirts. He had heard rumblings from Michel that the new Chatelaine intended to put on an exposition of the masterworks Michel, *not* Jennifer, had inherited. More than a billion francs of artworks were to be displayed for these boors from New York and California and God knew where else these organisms called home. To defray the expenses and probably add to her bank account, the *dowryless* Jennifer was having Jules Chardin charge visitors an entry fee. The new queen had earmarked these funds for the building endowment of a women's residence in what had been the grand Hôtel Estaque, the finest brothel in Provence. It was all a desecration which Philippe could no longer endure.

"*Je m'excuse, mesdames,* but I have a wedding banquet to organize."

He had a brief interlude with Nicole on the cours. Nicole's luminous features were pinched and flushed as if hives were about to hatch.

"What's going on in the kitchen?"

Phillipe scowled. "The suckling pigs are arriving from Sisteron."

"That's the lamb."

"Well, you've got me so confused."

"What are you up to, Philippe?"

"I'll be checking credentials and interviewing one of those poseurs you contacted from Lyon and a few people who once worked for the *incomparable* Robuchon," he said in disgust.

To use this tone about the retired messiah of contemporary

French cuisine stunned Nicole. "Thank God, Joël came through for me."

Philippe kissed Nicole on the cheek and whispered, "After the ordeal of this afternoon, I think I'm entitled to intimate relations tonight."

"If you don't assault the contractors, the answer is yes."

"You have my word. And don't be in such a hurry this time."

"Yes, my lord, a contract is a contract," she said, twisting his earlobe.

Nonetheless, Nicole was troubled. Philippe's interviews usually resulted in abrasive quarrels. During the Paris food show, she had become painfully aware that a number of her fellow chefs had been too busy to get together; several had cut her dead. There were scattered dinner invitations and only two wine tastings. In the great cuisine circles where she had once moved like a Degas ballerina, Nicole Danton was now a pariah. She decided to pay her respects to Jules Chardin at the gallery, then dash to the restaurant in the hope of preserving what few friends remained.

# CHAPTER 12

**Michel and his team** assembled in Richard Caron's "political" room, actually a salon with a well-stocked liquor cabinet, elegantly furnished in the Provençal style with Soleiado fabrics and cushions. This was used to entertain visiting dignitaries from Paris who, under the guise of official business, used the sojourn south to hop on their mistresses for a champagne weekend. Michel had often been called upon to get tables at Chez Danton for this wolf pack of contemptible tippers. Afterward he was under siege by the staff to pony up.

The Special Circumstances Section was all present: Annie Vallon decked out in a blinding red La Croix outfit that resembled Ted Bundy's Rorschach test. Sylvie was beside her, intent on becoming an elite detective. Also in the grouping were Émile Briand, stooped and pale, avuncular but tenacious with suspects. Pierre Graslin, looking more and more like an opium addict, thin as a sun-pocked blade of grass; he had recently chucked out his long-term mistress and moved in a twenty-year-old heiress. For reasons which evaded Michel, women found Pierre seductive.

Richard Caron, the militaristic master of the legion, had a forlorn expression as he avoided eye contact with his daughter Sylvie. There was in his paternal disposition something that suggested, *My God, to think you've come to this*. Richard, the aristocrat, treated his daughter as if she might have been a streetwalker. In spite of conflict in the air, Michel knew that he had the most astute group of detectives in France or anywhere else. Sylvie, a bit anxious, would be catching a flight to Brussels that night.

The time and distance of a drive from Bruges to Marseille was discussed by Richard.

"General de Gaulle and I had some business in Brussels and afterwards we drove to Bruges. Ghent for a day. And flew back from Brussels. The roads in those days were paved by forerunners of *Homo erectus*. The cars, even ours, are probably in museums." Richard nodded to Pierre. "We're in agreement, aren't we, Pierre?"

"Yes, they had to drive."

Michel surreptitiously looked at his watch. He had to meet Jennifer by five.

"It's eight hundred kilometers to, say, Avignon," Pierre began. "With stops for gas, maybe ten hours. They'd keep at a reasonable speed."

Annie clinically said, "Caroline Davis was healthy and strong. Muscular for a thirteen-year-old—based on Laurent's report. So they had to drug her. Caroline was probably on her way to a professional career like her mother. The mother didn't make it on the pro tour, so the daughter would, if Melanie had anything to say about it. A familiar pattern—like our Sylvie and yourself, Richard."

Richard, the stern taskmaster, was taken aback by the outrageous sarcasm of this remark, but oddly this eased the tension in the meeting.

Émile finished the hard-boiled egg he had brought along. "There's nothing new I've found on the Internet porn sites . . . except the usual ooze. Frankly, Michel and I think that the porn direction is futile, Richard."

Richard asked for suggestions and unfortunately had to hear from Sylvie.

"Sir, it's clear that Caroline was a particular type the abductors were looking for."

"Why?"

"A man would have been too obvious for what they had in mind. They sent a woman to hunt."

It took a moment before everyone in the room concurred with Sylvie.

"And what, Detective Caron, did they have in mind for this child?" Richard demanded.

"Some type of experiment or ritual which had to be covered up, which is why I believe her back was seared with nitric acid."

Michel agreed with this speculation. Like a professor conducting a tutorial, he now stood up and deconstructed the text.

"We have a woman who apparently follows Caroline and lures her into a car. I would imagine she has at least one partner. Chloroform or an injection is immediately used to knock out this athletic girl. Wait, maybe a Taser gun. Caroline had no cranial damage. Even though we know the Belgians are worthless police, they have a wealthy, influential American who's on their backs — not to mention years of bad publicity and angry countrymen because of their previous negligence.

"Now, according to the Bruges investigators' report — which I believe — they actually did check the hotels from Bruges to Brussels, searching for the mystery woman. But they couldn't find her or any record anywhere — not even in a pension. I think that this band had a place in Bruges. If it's a flat, there's an elevator and inquisitive neighbors. Probably a house.

"They know the police are looking for them and Caroline. So their best chance is to leave Flanders. One of the group certainly knows France, especially Provence. Maybe he or she lives here as well. One of them is familiar with the route.

"I don't think they're American. It's a long, tricky drive from Bruges through Lille and then all across France. No, this crew won't stop to ask for directions. They know their destination. So let's assume there are two kidnappers or more, with a house in Bruges. Someone with money, very comfortable, and with a big car or an SUV.

"This brings us to Provence and the coast. Did one of them *rent* a boat — borrow or steal one — to dispose of the body? No, that weakens their position in this middle game."

"We have no reports of stolen boats," Pierre said. "I've had the uniforms checking every slip in Marseille."

"Pierre, there must be a villa with a dock and a yacht or a fishing boat in some port slip. They have the Grand Rhône to sail down and La Ciotat to use to dump Caroline."

As though in the grasp of a master storyteller, the group sat entranced by Michel, waiting for him to proceed.

"Yes, yes, that sounds good," Richard said, encouraging his luminary.

"In two days, *mes amis,* I'll be on my honeymoon, so have the gendarmes and the locals out—everywhere. I want to know if any strangers have been out to the fertilizer plants or the munitions works in Toulouse buying or stealing nitric acid."

Everyone stopped taking notes. Disputes and angry questions were squelched when Richard Caron rose from his ceremonial desk.

"For the life of me, I can't imagine why they didn't kill the girl in Bruges and toss her into a canal there. There are certainly enough of them."

"Maybe they had a *client* in Provence . . . waiting to take delivery," Annie suggested.

"No," Pierre countermanded this theory, "*they* are the clients."

Émile interposed. "I see it all! It was a ritual killing."

"They didn't drink her blood or eat her heart," Laurent boomed as he entered. "Sorry, I'm late. I had a luncheon speech to deliver. Have I missed anything?"

"Would you like to assist in *this* investigation, Laurent?" Richard asked.

"I thought I already had. And will you please call me Doctor? This familiarity is getting on my nerves. When I was in Paris—"

Michel wrapped the pompous medical examiner in a bear hug and winked at him.

"*Doctor* Laurent, have you determined how long Caroline Davis was in the water?"

"Salinity tests are being conducted in the lab. But I believe less than twenty-four hours. The deceased had very little damage from the denizens of the deep."

Now Michel changed course and goaded him. "You have three lifelines available."

Dr. Laurent looked as if he needed more. "Oh, Michel, I hope your honeymoon lasts until I retire."

"Is that your final answer?" Annie needled.

"I don't know what any of you are talking about. I'm a man of science."

"And a great one," Michel informed him. "But, Doctor, not even fish like the smell or taste of nitric acid. Have you ever smelled a bad oyster? So maybe she was in the water longer. Please continue testing."

**Michel's reserved spot** behind Chez Danton had been compromised by the monumental green marquee being installed by the contractor's tipsy workmen. Michel pulled down his sunburned PO-LICE card over the visor and triple-parked behind their rusty vans. As he walked past the once-noble boule court, he heard the screaming and reached for his Glock. Golarde raised his hands and stopped him.

"Is there a murder or a hostage situation?" Michel asked, holding off with his automatic.

The master contractor of Aix sweated through his blue overalls. It was his steeplejacks that continued to restore St-Sauveur and *hôtels particulière,* the heirloom mansions that the locals cherished even more than the tourists. Golarde was a household name of quality and nobility, beyond websites. What was more, he could plaster.

"No, just your father. Philippe was interviewing cooks. Did you see the bleeding fry cook who came from Lyon stumbling on the parking lot?"

"No."

"Well, Philippe punched him, then went after him with one of my industrial hammers. You know, Michel, I never would have taken on this lackey job if not for Nicole and you. I've pulled my men off the clock tower of the cathedral."

Michel flattered him, characterizing him as another Le Courbusier. "I'll see you at the bar for a glass of 1990 Krug."

"*Alors,* I'm not welcomed. Delantier is on point. Do you know Philippe seized my drawings, and dared to show me how to put in a fucking peg for the tent?"

Michel reconsidered. "Maybe I won't go in."

* * *

**Hauling a case** of champagne down the crowded Cours Mirabeau, Michel resembled a deliveryman. He jaywalked at Les Deux Garçons while the waiters hooted him. Once inside the Chardin Gallery, Michel spotted workmen advising the very civilized Jules Chardin about how to arrange the lighting.

Lugging the case of champagne through this magnificent interstellar space, Michel nodded to his absorbed former professor and found Jennifer on a ladder holding up the great painting of Cézanne's *Apples*. He paused, took a deep breathe. With the workmen pondering her next move, Michel, in full view, slipped his head under her skirt.

Without turning, she said, "Oh, *merde,* Michel, I had the height and weight balanced and the tolerances right."

"At least you knew it was me."

Rosalind suddenly sprang out, holding Michel's bequeathed Degas ballerinas as though it were a poster.

"Hi, ready to put your back into it, Michel?"

"You're walking very well, better than Michael Jordan, Rosalind."

"Jennifer snapped my toe back in place."

"That's one of the reasons I'm marrying your daughter. She's been saving us a fortune in orthopedic bills."

Jennifer marked the position of the painting with a pencil and signaled for a workman. She climbed down and walked to another installation. Rosalind took the opportunity to pull Michel aside.

"I suppose level floors are an American affection," said Rosalind. She put the Degas down and held on to Michel. Despite the size of her, she had a tenderness that he now knew Jennifer had inherited. "I want to say something serious to you."

"Don't worry about Jennifer. She won't be in danger again."

"She's innocent, an art professor, and she killed two people defending you."

"That's why I carry champagne to her across the cours."

As he eased the champagne peace offering to the back of the gallery, through a mill of deliveries, Rosalind was deliciously shoving people out of his way in perfect French. What a woman to have at a party. The perfect maîtresse d'hôtel.

"Rosalind, I'm so sorry that Jennifer was involved."

She pressed her strong fingers across his lips. "I know. Michel, promise me you won't resign. I've read the papers and seen the photo of Caroline Davis. I know now that what you do is critical, indispensable. There would be madness . . . unless noble men served honorable causes. Society is in chaos. Maybe it always was, but women like me channel-surf when we hear of horrors like this." Rosalind had tears in her eyes. "I just accept wars and crimes as natural."

He was astounded by her support. "May I call you Moms?"

"Yes, and I'll be back for champers."

Girding through, Jennifer pushed the back door open for more deliveries to the gallery and found Michel in a corner opening champagne. He had juggled the case, dodging cars, and the wine spewed over him.

Slopping champagne, they sprang into the gallery's bathroom. Michel's hand tugged Jennifer's panties. She licked the champagne off his face.

"I love you so madly, *chèri*," she said.

"I suppose a blowjob is out of the question. . . ."

Jennifer was not a woman to be taunted. She heaved open her blouse and thrust her breasts out of her bra. It was like a sunburst on his face after a depressing day.

"You first. . . ."

Michel lifted her through the small chasm between the *chaude et froid* taps and located a rift in the lacy seam and entrenched his tongue between her legs. She lifted his head and kissed him.

"You must be on a case, that's why you're so horny."

"Don't underestimate your magic."

She pushed him away and he was surprised. "Let's wait till later, Michel. You smell of murder."

# 2

# WHAT ARE WE?

# CHAPTER 13

**After the long flight** from Los Angeles to Brussels and the hour drive to Bruges, the graceful old four-poster in Hotel Die Swaene's royal suite provided a sanctuary for the weary travelers. Eve, the early riser, tumbled out of bed and tried to shake off her jetlag. She opened the window, leaned out, surveying the ancient city. There were flowers and evergreens everywhere and many of the houses had window boxes with red ivy. She was enchanted by the place and pleased that she had not booked them into a chain operation. The Swaene had history, the snug character of a country house. This would be a new start for Garrett, binding them closer, and a honeymoon of sorts. He would be inspired and would cast off the shadow of the malevolent Gauguin.

Over the Steenhouwersdijk, canal ferries merrily swirled and crisscrossed, and the river threw a mantilla of gray light over the city's monuments. The wind sifted off the water and the teals swam in circles chasing the bread passersby threw into the water. It was very different from her beloved Venice despite the kinship mentioned by the brochures. Her ears perked at the foreign sounds. The tortuous Flemish language had a snapping cadence and she thought of the tongue as a hooded falcon, a gargoyle in a bad dream in which a black-gloved hand was strangling the human voice. Merchants with their growling, vibrating *zzzz*'s strolled to their shops. Civil greetings and bows to the neighbors were observed in a daily ritual. The civilized air and proprieties made Eve feel as though she had entered another century. No ghetto blasters or enraged car horns soiled the ambience.

She huddled in her thin kimono print robe which Garrett had designed along with other silk-screened stunners; the temperature was in Celsius and she guessed it hung in the high thirties. Cashmere and a long-scarf day. The church, or whatever it was, resounded in a chorale concert of bells. She could not identify its name even with the hotel tourist book.

She was about to spruce up the room, shift Garrett's bags and artist cases, lay out their toiletries when there was a light tapping on the door. A smiling alert maid carried in a bouquet of flowers and, behind her, a waiter lofted a tray with courtly chased silver caps and a flask of coffee. She'd ordered eggs and smoked bacon to be served at eight in order to get on European time.

"I speak English, madame," the maid said, placing the vase on a round wooden table.

Eve tightened her robe. "Thank you so much." Eve fluffed the flowers and touched a silky, budding peony that made her want to sing. "Where are the bells coming from?"

"The carillon. The belfry's tower is from the thirteenth century and has the best view of the city. Oh, madame, I almost forget, there is a card for you.

With a light-headed gaiety, Eve read the note on Jan's embossed stationery.

## THE ARTIST HAS ARRIVED,
## LET THE WORLD PAY TRIBUTE. WELCOME.
## JAN KORTEMAN

The waiter laid out a crisp linen tablecloth.

"Good morning, Madame. *Kaffe?*" She nodded. As he poured the strong, intoxicating brew, he looked at the flowers. "These are from Mari Rodenstuck, *de bloemiste.*"

"Florist, madame," said the maid.

"Yes, the best in the world," said the waiter.

"They look like they've plucked from the Garden of Eden," Eve said.

She signed the bill but hadn't changed any money yet. Considering their warm service, she handed them a twenty-dollar bill. From their reaction, she gathered, they would drive a tractor through a Texas twister for her.

She roused Garrett. They both had to be on the same time to share the experience and embrace their symphony of freedom, their unity—without the depraved Heather Malone.

**Jan swaggered into** the small lobby. He wore a handsome full-length black leather coat with a silver silk scarf embroidered with gold eagles—a bit Gestapo, Garrett thought. Jan's ash gray eyes had a thrill-seeking deviltry. He had pomaded his long grayish hair and clustered it in a slick ponytail.

After a fistful of greetings and kisses, worthy of a papal visit, Jan drove through the charming crooked streets in his black Mercedes 600, chattering about their visit. Eve now realized that what she had assumed was an obsequious manner at Heather's party had been Old World urbanity. They would stop at his house for drinks, then dine at the Huidevettersuis, one of his local favorites.

"You're very thoughtful, the flowers are gorgeous."

"You've Mari Rodenstuck to thank for that. She's our queen of the blossoms. And you deserve them, Eve. If I may say, you are what they refer to in California as drop-dead beautiful."

"Thank you."

Garrett was silent, absorbing the scenic beauty of the ethereal medieval city which would release his artistic wings and enable him to capture the essence of the northern Renaissance as seen through the prism of his modern perspective. Gone was the grubby commerce of Venice, the barefoot savages who wanted a piece of flash on their asses or a pierce for their girls. Eve was anxious for him to begin painting in these inspiring surroundings.

"And how is our Heather? I can just imagine the bon voyage party."

"Actually, she doesn't know we're here," Garrett snapped. "Jan, if she calls, we'd be grateful if you flat-out lied—or it's going to be a short stay for Eve and me."

Jan was surprised by the acerbic tone and wanted to hear all about the quarrel. He considered himself a peacemaker and offered to broker a treaty.

Eve recalled their disastrous encounter. "Look," she stormed, "she treats us like toys she can play with when she's bored or horny."

Jan nodded and commiserated. He had met Heather in Amsterdam the previous year.

"I was doing a book on the underground's sexual mores — an oxymoron, of course. The lower depths. This was a photo essay with some text commissioned by Erotik Verlag, my publisher. I worked my way through Antwerp, Munich, Hamburg, Stockholm, and Copenhagen. Amsterdam, like hell, is the last stop.

"I discovered this very attractive woman in a sexual inferno. I have a good eye for figures and I was astounded. For a moment I naturally thought it was Pamela Anderson. On closer inspection, I realized it was a revision and it turned out to be Heather."

"Impersonation is the curse of adulation," Garrett said, putting a twist on Oscar Wilde's epigram.

"Not for everyone. You see, my dear young friends, these are special exhibitions for very decadent tastes: dwarfs, crippled people, and others. Nothing is forbidden. Spectators can join in — as they like. There is an auction. . . . And if you're prepared to pay . . . well . . . .

"I, myself, was a guest, but the admission price to these events is very high. Five thousand dollars per person is the usual rate. Heather was drinking champagne with her two English body-guards. They seem, shall we say, fey, but believe me they're dangerous men. By comparison, Heather's millennium fête was very tame indeed. Hieronymous Bosch would have left immediately," Jan added with a laugh.

**Jan pressed an** automatic garage opener and pulled into a subter-ranean vault below a canal. They could hear the river water rushing and the churning propellers of boats above. They followed Jan through a curving wine cellar that was flawless, every bin labeled in red gothic script.

"You must do very well as a photographer," Garrett observed as they entered an elevator.

Jan gave them a devious smile. "Well enough, but it helps to be *wellborn*. My father was a poor sod who went into the food business after World War Two. He'd been in a prison camp with two Jewish Americans who had some small markets when they were in civilian life. According to my late father, he convinced the Nazis that the men were Protestant.

"We had horrible food shortages in the postwar years, but through my father's connection with these two gentlemen, he opened a food market and they were able to get import-export licenses and he always had the best supply of American foodstuffs and liquor which people couldn't buy anywhere but from him. So with great reluctance he gave up his original business, which was photography and printing, and became one of the richest men in Belgium."

They took the elevator and it stopped on the first of three floors. In awe, they walked through a stupendous series of rooms with vaulted ceilings and paneled walls in burled walnut; medieval tapestries and paintings hung over Directoire tables; surrounding them were swanlike white silk sofas and velvet armchairs.

"This was originally a seventeenth-century tannery which I had gutted when I came into my fortune."

"It's breathtaking," Garrett said. "Van Eyck and Memling could have painted masterpieces here."

"Perhaps you will," Jan observed, and tinkled an old silver bell. A butler wheeled in a cart with decanters of liquors and hors d'oeuvres. "If you haven't tried our local genever, may I spoil you with one. Provided, of course, that you don't detest gin."

After four genevers and some caviar canapés, they ascended a marble staircase over which a massive crystal chandelier stood watch. Each bedroom, six or seven—Eve lost count—had its own motifs and color scheme. Everything was done in the grand Baroque style and Eve felt as if she were floating through infinite space.

The third floor held the master's prodigious studio, with a dazzling collection of antique cameras and the latest digital equipment, monitors, and an editing room. The studio was dominated by a

majestic floor-to-ceiling window which overlooked the St. Bonifacius Bridge and the Groeninge Museum, which held the masterpieces of Flemish fifteenth century painting.

Garrett was overwhelmed by the visual harmony and opulence
of the surroundings. He stopped before an easel holding a twenty-
four-by-thirty-six-inch canvas. It was blank and there was an heirloom palette and sable brushes. He picked one up and rubbed it
tenderly with his fingertips.

"You're also a painter?" Garrett asked.

"No," Jan said, "this is for you, Garrett. You can use the studio
for as long as you like."

"It's northern light as well."

Jan shook his head. "Of course. I'm a photographer and also a
patron of the arts."

Garrett was dumbfounded by Jan's aristocratic generosity. "I
don't know. . . ."

"Think about it. Talk it over with Eve."

"I don't interfere with Garrett's artistic decisions," she said
quickly.

"But *you* are his muse, Eve, and the muse has privileges that no
one else enjoys."

**At the Stammtisch,** the best table reserved for a regular like Jan
Korteman with a glowing view of the flickering boat lights on the
canals, they dined on smoked goose, velvety salmon and herring
fillets, and then a hearty civet of hare in port wine. Garrett's palate
was singing and he was ecstatic by Jan's offer. It never would have
occurred to Garrett to visit Bruges. He and Eve had turned their
disastrous emotional situation around by making this trip. Heather,
their ogre, had become the catalyst and inadvertently liberated
them. After the years of stupefying sexual degradation they had
endured at Heather's whim, they were now whole, undivided.

"I feel drunk," Eve said when they were leaving.

"It's the jet lag. Thoughtless of me to have filled you with you
all this drink."

"No, Jan, it's the gratitude we feel toward you. Your understanding and nobleness," Garrett responded, overcome by the depth of his emotion.

The patrician photographer, so European, smiled at this passionate outburst.

"Die Swaene is a charming little place, but tomorrow, while we're touring the carnival towns, my staff can move you into my house."

"Are you sure?" Eve cheeped in a small voice.

Jan kissed her on both cheeks. "Of course, my dear." He held her hand for a moment. "You're so lovely and delicate. You're a rare model of the species—unique, my dear Eve. It's no wonder Garrett fell in love with you."

She began to giggle. "Jan, we're in love with you."

"The feeling is mutual. When you're settled in, I'll show you my collection."

**Fat Tuesday . . . It** was overcast and the wind had a furor, coming in churlish gusts, like the uninvited dinner guest who smiles at the host and later seizes his wife in the bathroom. The swirling eddies dislodged the hats and masks over the disguised figures who marched in the parade along the cobbled streets of Binche. Brass bands with tuba solos cracked the eardrums of the laughing cavaliers and their women. In the taverns with their longarms of ale, and outside on the terraces, the drunken townspeople in their orange-and-yellow-striped *Gilles* costumes and white makeup might have come back to life from the sixteenth century and awaited Franz Hals or Breughel to paint them. These clowns, *blancs moussis,* were celebrated for their gross sexual pranks that were part of their tradition along with an endless train of satirical floats. Lutherans set alight an effigy of the Pope, and Catholics responded by burning Luther.

Everywhere people were dancing and kissing, screwing against alley walls. Women dressed as nuns in bras and panties outside their habits, priests wearing lipstick and falsies, an array of beautiful children behaving lewdly, the girls lifting their skirts. Their actions were flagrantly sexual and had something of the madness of the Middle Ages.

"In the States, half these people would be arrested and their kids taken from them," Garrett observed with interest.

"We're a bit more broad-minded here. In my *poaching* days, I had quite a few of these little nymphs." Jan hoped to wet-nurse the couple's lust. "They can be very submissive, anxious to please. You see, in Belgium we act out our fantasies to exorcise the demons of the year. We ridicule ourselves and our repressions. It's our Mardi Gras," Jan explained, as he continued shooting the parade with his camcorder.

"What about the parents?" Eve asked.

"Money buys honey," he replied with a titter. "You let me know if you're interested in a tasting menu. It would be very easy. . . ." He waited for Garrett to respond, but the artist pensively lingered over his beer. "I doubt if Gauguin would have refused. He had three native wives, as I recall—none of them older than fourteen." Jan caught the eye of two young girls who knew what he had in mind. In the spirit of this outrageous festival, they daintily raised their short skirts, giggled, and dashed away. "Think it over, you might find you need a model, and, when they're miniatures, they're always delicious."

Eve wrapped her coat tighter as blasts of cold air channeled down the narrow streets, swirling hats. In the tap-house garden, everyone drank a dizzying variety of the local brews in stubby glasses. "Microbreweries everywhere," Garrett said, tasting yet another—this one with a hint of cherry.

"Belgium is famous for three things: our pommes frites, and the reason for the flavor is that they're fried in lard; our incomparable beer; and lastly, our painters. Rubens painted our double-breasted women to perfection."

"Lard and tits," Eve said. "I'll have to remember that when I cook."

"Sugar, you're fine. They don't grow any finer than yours," Garrett said.

A sulky expression passed over her full lips. "Well, I guess, you'll never see me in *Playboy*."

Apparently this was something of a sensitive point with Eve.

"A woman's breasts are a fashion statement," she said with an edge to her voice.

"If you miss them, give Heather a call, sunshine," Garrett said.

Jan took her hand. "In my educated opinion, Heather is a mass-market product, and you're an original, Eve."

When they returned to Bruges, Jan told them something about his career. He had been encouraged by his father to pursue the vocation that he had denied himself. Trapped inside the frustrated millionaire was the artist's soul. He was contemptuous of the grocery business and bought Jan a Leica for his fifth birthday.

"My father knew a great deal about lighting and textures. I, on the other hand, could attract subjects. For some reason, people were charmed by the small boy with the expensive camera. I could get people to do the most outrageous things."

It was evening and Jan's studio had a peculiar mysterious atmosphere. They were drinking a fine champagne and he had told his staff to lay out a buffet in the dining room below and take the night off. He put on Scriabin's mystically chorded *Prometheus: The Poem of Fire*. The Bang and Olufson speaker system enveloped them and the acoustics had the gusto of a concert hall.

"Did you know that Scriabin intended to demonstrate the affinity between musical tones and colors? He designed something called a *clavier à lumières*." The couple were enthralled and he continued. "Colors would be projected on a screen while his music played. Unfortunately, it never came to pass. No one would put up the money."

"You would have," Garrett said.

"Indeed I would have. Now, the reason I've passed along this little anecdote is that I had my still pictures put on slides."

"I used to take photos when I was a teenager in San Antonio."

"Really?" Jan exclaimed. "What sort?"

Garrett bellowed with laughter. "I guess I'd call it the photography of indiscretion at this point in my life. In those days, it was simple, straightforward blackmail. Catching out the cheaters womping their girlfriends; or some woman going down on a black man. I had to build what I used to call my scholarship fund to get myself through art school in California."

"Everyone has to start somewhere," Eve said.

"Nothing sells better than sexual blunder," Jan agreed, tittering.

Jan sat down in a deep leather chair at a console, pressed several buttons, and a screen was automatically lowered.

"I had the means to do anything. But I chose to become the apprentice of the photographer at"—the sign on a large Baroque building flashed on the screen: DAS LEICHENHAUS—"the morgue. My father was somewhat alarmed, but I told him that if, for instance, I wanted to be a war photographer, go into an actual combat zone, say in Africa or the Balkans, I would have to get used to the sight of death so that I'd be prepared for action. One can't gear up for that sort of assignment by photographing ladies and gentlemen at their pleasure or at school graduations. There are no courses for this."

"You're right," Garrett said, reflecting on his own previous activities.

A jumble of sharply detailed black-and-white images clicked on the screen. Bodies of children, men, women, mangled, decapitated, human trunks, stabbed, strangled, shot, chopped to death, burned with acid, revealing the agonized features of the poisoned and the tortured. Cadavers that had been buried or quicklimed, skeletons that had been reassembled, formed a crazy quilt.

Heather had spoken of Jan's collection with a heightened carnal passion and now the visitors understood why their insatiable mistress had been so excited.

"Is it too strong for you, Eve?" her host inquired.

"Believe me, I've seen my share of stuff—depravity," she said, amused by the suggestion.

Garrett clasped her hand. He had a long-term experience with corpses—something like fourteen people in the Marcuro House of Death. But Josef Renchen's final moments would always haunt him. As he watched the pageant of corpses on screen, their bodies did not shock or disturb him. His detachment was an integral component of his personality. The figures were so abundant that after a while death itself evolved into a meaningless condition, the bodies icons, suggesting symbols beyond perception. Morbidity itself lost its definition amid the butchery.

Garrett, the autodidact, recalled his reading of Nietzsche. Civilized behavior was mankind's most dangerous indulgence, always working against the individual who sought to be master of the circumstances. He recognized that Jan was merely a voyeur, a thrill-seeker, testing dangerous tides. And Eve . . . ? She was his captive, but ultimately the two of them were captives of each other.

Jan Korteman enjoyed the role of narrator and director! Languid with champagne, he went on.

"Like all young European boys, I suppose in a way I was fascinated by the horrors of the concentration camps. We drove through Eupen a few hours ago. There was a camp there and my father was imprisoned for printing works verboten by the Nazis. It's part of our heritage. Americans and the Brits never really get it. Belgium was occupied not once, but *twice* during the world wars. German invaders were on our soil, debasing our way of life, and yet the Germans are not hateful and are a part of our country and language."

Onscreen, corpses gave way to a more familiar sight. Heather naked in a variety of poses.

"What exactly did Heather do at this underground exhibition?"

Jan relished Garrett's curiosity. "Oh, I never imagined it was of interest to you."

In the white beam of light, Garrett's nodding head became a silhouette on the screen. "We just wondered, since it apparently excited you." Garrett had an innate sense of how to put people in a defensive position. "You do want to tell us, don't you?"

"I don't need much coaxing," Jan said with an eerie smile. "There was bidding on a very handsome seven-foot Masai. Heather's bodyguards persuaded the competitors to back off, and Heather had her playmate for the night."

# CHAPTER 14

**The opening of the** Vercours collection of paintings was scheduled at the Chardin Gallery after Michel and Jennifer returned from their abbreviated honeymoon. As money was no object to the millionaire Dantons, Jennifer had placed ads for the exhibition in *Semaine Spectacles, Nice-Matin, Le Clarion,* and a full-page in the *International Herald Tribune.* Jennifer wanted the world of art lovers to share these masterpieces.

Over Christmas, they had decided to take to the road for their honeymoon in Jennifer's new Mercedes and drive through France, Belgium, and Italy. They would leave in late September; the tourists would be gone and the school vacations over. Emancipated from crowds, the weather still fine, they planned to visit museums and monuments, stay at romantic chateaux, and eat their way into oblivion. Months earlier, Michel had confidently predicted that his replacement in the Special Circumstances Section would be running the office by then, and he could take off six weeks before reporting to the examining magistrate as an investigator.

The murder of Caroline Davis had not altered his life. He'd still be a married man in forty-eight hours and take Jennifer away for a few days. But the image of this child refused to be vanquished. It lived within him. Her hideous death cast a pall on this happy period. Perhaps by the time he was back there'd be a concrete lead.

He had other personal torments that he could not resolve. As Jennifer was due for a final fitting with Vellancio and had asked her mother and Grace Chardin, her maid of honor, to dinner, Michel had invited Jules Chardin and Leon Stein for a drink at his apartment. He fussed at the sideboard with ice, Pastis, his Johnny Walker Black Label, and wondered if anyone would want wine. He put out a tray of hors d'oeuvres made up in the Danton charcuterie: thin slices of Jamon Serrano, cold mussels, olives, radishes, Arles saucisson, and a bowl of green almonds steeped in olive oil sprinkled with coarse Camargue salt. This would stave off hunger pangs.

He had the door open and listened to the elevator experiencing yet another coronary when it grumbled down. Jules Chardin's voice was as mellifluous as it had been when he had been lecturing on art at the Sorbonne. He greeted Michel's sullen concierge, asked about her health and the disposition of her cat. She complained that he had interrupted her program and cut through a heroic rescue by the *Baywatch* beauties. The concierge was addicted to this senseless TV import. Spengler had, of course, been right in *The Decline of the West*. Conveyed by American television, Europe had entered its intellectual winter. Yes, even with computers and the new age of the Internet, Michel saw only dog sleds in a frozen cultural tundra.

When Michel had been Jules's student, every female he had encountered at the Sorbonne was in love with him. This professor, however, was not lecherous. Jules surprised everyone after his wife died by marrying an American woman he had met at the d'Orsay Museum while consulting on the collection. He and his wife Grace now had a two year-old daughter, which amused Jules. "She makes a perfect pairing with my thirty-year-old son from Suzanne. I feel like a Hollywood producer and *alive*! A dusty professor who had to live through Grace's messy divorce while she was pregnant with Alicia. I now have three families: my original one; Grace's daughter in Syracuse; and now ours. We have two homes and I'm the subject of gossip in academic circles," he said with a buoyant laugh.

He would be sixty on his next birthday. "It's keeping you young," Michel had said when he learned of the events over Christmas.

"Well, I've resigned from the Sorbonne and I've decided to open a gallery on the Cours Mirabeau to encourage new artists."

"You're not going into the family firm?"

"No, Michel, I have no head for business. And my brother is a commercial genius."

At the end of the nineteenth century, the family had started the

Chardin Fine Art Company in Aix; this became the premier brand for artists' paints. Jennifer had found her spiritual sister in the warm and delightful Grace Chardin, and Michel had been reunited with his mentor. What struck Michel as remarkable was Jules's attitude about Michel's choice of career. "I thought you might have gone into art investigation for an insurance firm. You always had a good eye, a curious one, and never accepted things at face value."

"My fascination with murder prevented a civilized life," Michel had responded.

With his longish gray hair, horn-rimmed glasses, and expensive but unfussy blue chambray suit, set off by a checked Charvet shirt, there was an ease of manner that Jules always had brought to bear during his lectures and with his students at the Sorbonne. His smile had a sophisticated weariness and his pale blue eyes an emotional depth that calmly informed people of his intelligence.

"*Ça va, mon vieux?*" Michel asked, embracing Jules when the elevator finally arrived.

"*Oui, et vous, mon fils?*"

"Nervous." He led Jules into his apartment and fixed them both a Pastis.

"Michel, I can't tell you how much I appreciate your generosity. This exhibition is making the gallery famous overnight. I've had calls from every magazine and newspaper. *Le Figaro, Le Monde, Paris Match* are all covering the opening. Photographers are everywhere."

"It was Jennifer's idea. Frankly, I didn't know what to do with Louise's collection—donate it to the d'Orsay, sell it, or what?"

"Well, Jennifer's an extraordinary woman. Beautiful, so quick and wise. I'll say one thing for America: Their culture may be shoddy and vulgar, but their women are goddesses."

"And our ladies have become friends."

"Inseparable," Jules said. "They needed each other. In my case with an elderly family, Grace was feeling out of place."

"And with my savages, Jennifer is always in physical danger."

"Yes, Philippe's ranting behavior is an ordeal. By the way, I'm sorry I couldn't make your bachelor party."

"Well, you missed my striptease and graceful dancing."

"I thought I gave you tango lessons in Paris."

"Unless I'm drunk and with Jennifer leading me, I'm still helpless."

A booming voice intruded through the partially opened door. "You're far from helpless. I gave you wings!" Dr. Leon Stein, the other guest, burst in and made directly for the drinks table. He immediately poured himself a monster Johnny Walker, swilled it down like beer, and poured another.

Hands were shaken and the psychiatrist plopped down on the sofa beside Jules.

*"Bon soir, mes amis."*

"Are you wearing Chanel, Leon?" Jules asked.

"No, it's from my last patient," he said, beaming. "Shall I tell her to stop wearing it?" He licked his lips with postcoital satisfaction. "Age twenty-two, brunette: thirty-six, twenty-four, thirty-six. I tell you, no one fucks with the enthusiasm of a paranoid. Interesting case as well: She's suffering from Capgras syndrome. She thinks I'm the double of myself, so in her reality, it's not really *my* dick. You've heard of the devil made me do it. We now have an example of 'the double made me do it.' "

"Well, it could be a legal defense if our Leon is ever called up on charges," Michel suggested. "I'll ask Fournier what he thinks when I join the magistrate's office."

Leon Stein was uncertain about his former patient. Michel was capable of bouts of irrationality. "Please don't bother."

"I find it very reassuring that Leon is still gallantly offering himself to female patients as part of his treatment." Jules couldn't contain himself. "Anything to effect a cure."

"They tell me it's certainly preferable to electroshock," Leon replied with a hint of martyred exasperation.

*"Alors,* and Madame Stein—who we haven't seen in years—what has she got to say about your cantering?" Jules asked.

"I really haven't inquired. If she hadn't given me four lazy slugs—boom-boom-boom-boom—who drain me of every franc I earn, I might be able to see her occasionally."

"Ahh, I wondered when she'd take the fall for your conduct," Jules said, sipping his Pastis.

Michel joined in. "I may have to visit your place just to satisfy myself that she and the children aren't down the well and that Jules and I are not clinking glasses with a mass murderer."

"Michel, you don't seem to understand Leon. He couldn't get laid until he married, and he only became a shrink to undress women. So he blames his wife for his miserable life."

"No, I blame myself. I couldn't afford a divorce when I wanted one. And now that I'm finally solvent—recognized on every street because of my TV interviews—I categorically refuse to slice up my income for five wastrels." He nipped at the food tray. "Wonderful ham. Trust Michel to lay out a spread, lay a trap, for whatever it is he wants from us, Jules. We're undoubtedly here to advise him what to do—with *his* life," he added smugly, flashing his expensive caps, which had replaced the worn, cheroot-stained teeth which had only months ago inhibited smiles and given him an aura of serious-mindedness.

"Let's get to the heart of it, Michel. I assume you've come to terms with the missionary position and are properly plowing the future Madame Danton." Stein speared a pair of mussel shells together, then proceeded to shell some almonds, which he passed around. Michel declined, for now they had the scent of Chanel.

"Is this a snare or social?" Jules asked Michel.

"It better be Clos de la Violette for dinner, Jules! I held off a testosterone shot and canceled the finest blow job in Marseille for this."

"My friends, you know me much better than I know myself. It's a bit of both," Michel admitted.

"Oh, another morose evening with our deranged, *millionaire* detective," Stein said.

Smothering his mirth, Jules said, in their mock-heroic taunting, "Pull yourself together, Leon, rise to the occasion, the food will be superb."

**Despite the perfect** dinner of delicately poached turbot stuffed with new vegetables, neither of Michel's friends was really prepared for his astounding admission. They were sitting in the jasmine-scented garden with few tables still occupied, espresso, and a fine marc swirling in balloon glasses, Havanas unleashed, cut, and about to be lit, when Michel said:

"Louise Vercours was my mother. Philippe and Nicole adopted me and I've been a nervous wreck since I found out last year."

Both Jules and Leon stared at one another, hoping that this was Michel's idea of a joke, inasmuch as weddings brought out perverse behavior in French bridegrooms. The sound of them unwrapping the paper covering the sugar cubes, teaspoons stirring the coffee, and the enraged chorus of cicadas promising a very hot day, did not alleviate the distress they both felt, nor the anxiety-ridden expression on Michel's face. Both men had been acquainted with Aix's regal madam, who had been savagely murdered the previous summer. In their younger years, Jules and Leon had visited her impeccably run brothel. They had known of the close friendship between Louise Vercours and the Dantons. Michel's declaration rattled them.

Jules was the first to break the silence and affectionately laid his hand on Michel's. "It's information, Michel. How you use it is really the question."

"Exactly," Leon Stein interjected. "Michel has the Catholic guilt tendency to use anything negative against himself. You live in opposition to yourself, divided. He's covered with the thorns of ethics, sins, moral codes, whatever. You're what now—thirty-seven?" Michel nodded. The droll, adulterous psychiatrist was now serious. "Well, is it likely to affect your marriage to Jennifer? She comes first."

"It's a sin of omission," Michel said.

"Why?" Jules asked.

Stein concurred. "She loves you for what you are."

Jules sipped his cognac. "How exactly did you find out?"

"I was called in by Vincent Sardou. He was Louise's attorney and he drew up her will and arranged my adoption. He felt he ought to tell me, since I was inheriting her fortune."

"So Philippe and Nicole aren't aware that you know the truth?" Jules asked

"I haven't been able to tell them."

"Well, one thing for damn sure—you'll break Nicole's heart," Jules said. "You *are* her son."

"The other person to consider in this is Philippe. His constant growling at you is his way of concealing the affection he feels toward you. Speaking as a psychiatrist now, it's Philippe's emotionally inhibiting crutch. Michel, you were the adored, spoiled child of three parents and now you have Jennifer. What is she going to think about this? Louise ran whores, but she was a generous woman. Still, someone like Jennifer, with a different set of values, is going to be uneasy about this revelation."

"I agree with Leon. Despite the fact that you've inherited masterpieces from Louise, Jennifer feels very ambivalent about them. She told Grace in confidence that it was immoral, and unholy to own them because of Louise."

Michel ruminated over these cautions, the wisdom of his close friends.

"I'm inclined to bury my knowledge now."

As they ordered another round of drinks, Michel's cell phone rang. He picked it up and listened for several minutes. "In Pont-Aven and this evening in Arles?" His friends observed his consternation. "Let me guess . . . blondes between ten and fourteen. Yes, I'll meet you in Arles."

"Murders?" Stein asked.

"No, one attempted kidnapping of a local girl from a café in Pont-Aven yesterday. In the ladies' room, she was accosted by a woman who wore a mask and had a towel soaked with ether. A waiter saw her being dragged to a car by a man and woman. The waiter was shouting at them and they let the girl go and drove off.

"In Arles, a German girl was walking on Les Alyscamps. She'd become separated from her tour group and vanished."

The men rose and bid their good nights to the chef and his wife, who were waiting in the reception area.

"Would you like me to come along?" Stein offered.

"No, Leon. Maybe tomorrow I might want you to talk to Caroline's parents."

Michel embraced his friends and as he was about to leave, Jules stopped him.

"Don't you find all of this odd and somewhat painterly?"

"What, Jules? I'm not following your drift."

"The juxtaposition of Pont-Aven and Arles. I can't help but think of Gauguin and van Gogh painting there."

"Yes, I suppose. Thanks for your advice. I'm very grateful."

In the car, he called Jennifer on her cell phone, but it was switched off, and he left a message that he'd be late.

On the drive to Arles, Jules's curious remark reverberated like the contrapuntal dips in a fugue and Michel found himself locked in an idée fixe. The faces of Gauguin and van Gogh flashed before him as well, the absinthe-drinking in Arles, van Gogh's ear slashed, the whores, the battles between two of the giants of modern art.

As he approached, Les Alyscamps was illuminated by police floodlights, and his mind turned to the nitric acid burns on Caroline's back. Why was the acid strictly poured on her back? Was there a clue that could identify her killers, a signature? A painter destroying a canvas? He pulled himself up short and realized that his affinity with Jules might encourage him to intellectualize what had simply been the diabolical act of a psychotic monster.

# CHAPTER 15

**Life in Bruges fell** into a somber pattern dictated by Garrett so that he could have the scope to experiment, dream, and determine the course of his career. He was left alone to roam the city, spending hours at the Groeninge in rapt contemplation of the Memling and van Eyck masterworks. He would return to Jan's monumental-sized studio, sit at the window, and begin painting until late. Before concluding, he would cover his work with a cloth to avoid any discussion.

Eve remained cautious, almost invisible, a wraith, fearing that any interruption of the creative process might result in one of Garrett's stormy moods. She kept in touch with Denny Flenge in Venice and he faxed her the weekly accounts. The business was holding steady during this slow season. He had laid off nine people and the profit margin had increased. He visited their house to water the plants and pick up the mail.

Occasionally, Jan left them alone in the house and traveled to visit friends in Antwerp and Ghent. He was a constant source of encouragement to Garrett but diplomatically shied away from asking for a progress report or requesting a patron's visit to see the artist's new work.

In the middle of May, Garrett had an episode. Jan heard him shouting upstairs and wondered if there was someone with him and if the quarrel might erupt into violence. Timidly entering his own studio, Jan watched in horror as Garrett carried on an incoherent argument with an invisible figure—a ghost. Garrett's face was purple. In his frenzy, he slashed at his paintings with a twelve-inch butcher knife, rending and shredding a painting. Jan rescued some small sections and discerned a portrait. They struck him as

astounding, worthy of the Flemish expressionists of the Renaissance. Jan peered at the mutilated canvas; it was nothing less than
a masterly portrayal of the tortured face of a sailor.

"Copycat, Copycat!" Garrett, screeched. "I can't help it. It's not
my medium!"

Garrett raised a fist at the inscrutable presence, which, because
of his wild gesturing and truculent attitude, endowed it with a
tangible presence. Eyes ranging over the vast room to detect the
intruder, Jan shuddered. His automatic was in his bedside drawer
and he didn't have time to get it. Garrett went on raving.

"Listen to me, Paul, I need meat, fresh meat. Then we'll see
who's the real artist. Which of us is the original. I'll show you
where we're going, who we are. I am the seer, the visionary—not
you! You're revolting, with your ulcerated sores, your bestial smell.
You're diseased and so is your art.

"Vincent loved you and treated you like a brother in Arles. You
ridiculed him, humiliated him. But he was *the* master, not you.
You knew he'd found something—the secret of art. You gutless
bastard." As Garrett pursued his deranged tirade, it was apparent
to Jan that the phantom figure of Paul Gauguin was the visitor
who had invaded Garrett's subconscious and had evolved into his
nemesis.

". . . Derivative?" Garrett was foaming, slashing the air. "You're
the one who stole from the Impressionists. They couldn't stand
you. You couldn't clean their brushes. You had to run away to
Tahiti to fuck twelve-year-old girls. You know what, I think you
had AIDS, not syphilis!"

If only Eve were there to calm him with her love, Jan thought,
but during this haunted period she had become incorporeal, vanishing like a spirit.

With the canvasses mere shreds and Garrett flicking his log
lighter near the drapes, Jan intervened.

"My friend, let me help you find what you're looking for . . . the
missing part . . . your authentic canvas."

"Skin! Skin!" Garrett said, in a more reasonable manner, like a
man picking cheeses. Jan took the lighter from him. "Can you get
me skin?"

"Skin it will be. But now let's refresh ourselves, go out and find a way to unwind. Shall we ask Eve to join us?"

"I don't want her around her now. It's too degrading. I made a promise"—he was close to tears—"to her when we came together. I told her I would be a great artist. My work would live and she would live through me. The golden couple." Garrett miserably turned away. "She's in Ghent. I left her at the Cathedral of Saint Bavon. We were in the crypt studying van Eyck's *Adoration of the Lamb*. I asked her to make some notes and to take photos when I was there a few days ago." His glazed eyes had a martyred peculiarity. "She'd had enough of a phony like me."

"You're wrong," Jan protested. "Eve is a part of you—your quest."

Garrett smiled. "She's emancipated in some respects and a feminist most of the time. But the truth is she knows me better than I know myself most of the time."

Jan peered over the debris in his studio. "You know what the sailors say when they get to port."

Garrett was more amenable. "I sure do."

*"Liberté! Quand je suis arrivé à Marseille, J'ai couché avec trois, non quatre filles chaque nuit,"* a voice responded in perfect French.

It was deep, cynical, and seemed to originate from another part of the studio. Jan was so startled by the utterance from this unknown source that he trembled. In dread, he looked around for the man who had spoken. It couldn't have been Garrett. He had been two or three feet away from him. Was it an illusion? Some trick? Jan felt tremors travel up his neck.

"Liberty," Garrett said, clasping Jan in his arms.

Finally Jan said, "Now *I'm* hearing voices, Garrett. Let's have a night out. There's a fine old proof room that I go to when I'm searching for a vision for my own insignificant work. They brew their beer and distill their own genever."


**A bottle of** Rubbens genever sat in an ice bucket and an aproned waiter stopped his hors d'oeuvres trolley, displaying a treasure-house of smoked eel, salmon, sturgeon, mounds of caviar, baby shrimp in butter, and sliced pumpernickel. Jan gestured to Garrett, who waved him off and waited until the cart's creaking wooden wheels had passed.

The two men sat at a corner table in the taproom of the cozy Straffe Hendrick, whose timbers dated from the middle of the sixteenth century. As they toasted, the icy splinters lacing the top of their genever glasses caressed Garrett's tongue when he drank. The taproom's dark wood glimmered hazily through the mottled coats of varnish. At the bar a crowd of voluptuous, bosomy, pink-skinned women had the aspect of the models Hals used in his paintings. Through the blue haze of smoke, boisterous laughing cavaliers smoked red-tinted long meerschaum pipes; the women's blithe voices played a coy chorus, offering the gentlemen opportunities.

The *visitations,* as Garrett called them, had begun when he lived in San Antonio and been befriended by a pawnbroker and his lover, a gypsy woman, who owned a boardinghouse.

"You were telling me about the pawnbroker and Dina Marcuro's household."

"Was I? Three of these drinks and I'm getting blotto."

"But you didn't want to eat. . . . I've got a little brown bottle and a silver spoon. You could go to a stall in the gents' and refresh yourself."

"I don't do blow, but thanks.

"Josef Renchen encouraged me to be an artist. He'd been a magician, owned and designed puppets, and he loved to paint. He was also an art historian. I worked in a pharmacy delivering prescriptions and that's how I met him. He had books everywhere and we would read together and he'd explain words and concepts I didn't understand. He taught me French and how to appreciate great art.

"I read Rewald's *Impressionism,* Read's *History of Modern Art,* Schlegel. He had a photo of Laocoön, wrapped in snakes. I read and read and Josef was my guide, and there was never anything perverse or sexual. He never asked to *see* me, or to do anything. On the walls were his reproductions of his favorite Gauguin paintings. He revealed—that when no one was around—that, he and Gauguin would analyze and discuss his work and his life.

"One day, at the museum, he introduced me to Paul Gauguin and the three of us began to have conversations about painting, the vision each artist must bring if he's going to create personal, original work. Paul said I had to get out of San Antonio. It was a death trap for my creativity. He did not like cowboy art. I needed to explore, find a teacher, a college, an atelier."

When a new bottle arrived, Jan asked, "What happened to your tutor?"

Garrett became rigid. His beautifully crafted features lost their definition and tears rolled down his cheeks. He might have appeared to the crowded room as a young man who had lost his lover and was seeking advice from his older brother.

Garrett pressed his fingers together in a steeple and invented a version of Josef Renchen's death. "He was riddled with cancer, skin ashy, lips translucent like tissue paper. When I could find a vein, I was shooting him with morphine and heroin."

"You poor boy," Jan said sadly. "How many of these . . . assisted suicides did you engage in?"

Garrett's eyes seemed like the ice splinters floating on top of the genever.

"Why are you asking?"

"I want to be your biographer, your John Rewald, your Douglas Cooper. I want this new generation to hear about you."

Garrett nodded and now the tipsiness disappeared. "You've proven how much you believe in me."

"We're at a new beginning, the first year of the millennium. Yes, there have been great painters but this is the springtime of Garrett, *Le Maître*."

Garrett sprang back. "I'm flattered. . . . Jesus, I'm overwhelmed by your faith in me, Jan. And to think I met you through Heather," he added, pursing his faunlike lips with disdain. "Talk about life in a universe of chance." He moved closer in the plush booth, tightly clasped Jan's fingers, and kissed them. "In a way, you're Josef's successor. He told me after a séance with Dina that my savior would appear."

Jan was moved by the young man's faith and trust. His fascination with the situation surpassed any event he might have imagined when he himself had been learning his trade in the house of the dead. As though he were roused from a dream, Garrett's long lashes fluttered, then his demeanor became demanding and his voice authoritarian.

"I had a very angry session with Gauguin a while ago. He was drunk on absinthe—nasty, sarcastic, typically Paul. It started out with a real no-no. He wants to fuck Eve." Jan was astounded, but found the situation enticing, the possibilities endless. "That's what started the argument this time."

"Eve's met Gauguin?"

"Plenty of times. He creeps into her closet, sniffs at her underwear. He's so depraved. It's horrible. When we got back from Bangkok and I brought her home, Paul couldn't keep his hands off her. He also used to spy on her. She'd take a pee, and he was watching. I mean, it was disgusting. This Peeping Tom stuff. We're grown-ups. He'd try to touch her when she got out of the shower. Grope her when she was taking a nap.

"Gauguin's always slinking around my studio spreading rumors about Eve. That I have to watch her with Heather. It's so vulgar, all this tabloid gossip. People are entitled to a life. If they're not harming anyone, why can't they do their private things?"

Jan had never before felt such a deep kinship with anyone. He had been searching throughout his career for some person who possessed all of the life-giving elements, a combination that would answer all questions. What is true and what can be considered false? No philosopher or artist had captured this essential union or synthesized it as Garrett had. His passion for Garrett and the absent Eve was boundless.

Arm-in-arm, they wove across the winding bridges, singing, vagabonds sharing their secrets to the melodious counterpoint of the belfry's carillon, the bells light as a kiss in the darkness.

They stopped before the old Tanners' house and Jan said, "May I kiss you?"

Garrett embraced his ally, his friend, and as they were about to press their lips together, a howl tore through darkness. Three leather-bound skinheads scraped the cobblestones with steel-toed boots, kindling sparks of wrath.

"We'll shit on their faces," came from a squeaky voice.

"Piss down their throats," another jeered.

"I've a mind to chop off a cock." This voice had the abrasiveness of stone.

They were perhaps five or six feet away and Jan, paralyzed with fright, hissed to Garrett,

"Gay bashers! Run!"

But the three were already advancing, the grating of the boot toes blunt as a sneer. Garrett saw that one was big, with a larded gut, another lanky, taller than all of them, the third iron-pumped and thick as a fireplug. Jan, cowering in trepidation, raised his arm defensively to ward off the blows from the black batons they were swinging.

It happened with such speed, almost instantaneously, that Garrett's movements registered as subliminal images to Jan. Garrett was like mercury. He butted the tall man in the face, and with a dexterous touch—before the others could respond—stabbed him in the eye with a long needle, then flipped him over the side of the bridge into the canal. They heard him shout in terror as he hit the water.

The two remaining thugs were shocked, dazzled by his initiative, and seemed befuddled as Garrett made a horizontal leap into the air and kicked the shorter man in the head. He hung over the abutment of the canal, groaning, and had dropped his steel baton, which Garrett seized with the grace of dancer. He lashed out at the big man, whacking the baton against his knee, and when he fell, like a swordsman Garrett continued to whip his face with the baton, crushing bone. Chips of his skull rained out, then Garrett wrested him to his feet, rolled him against the rail, and flung him over. But this time the sound he made was not the soft slosh of water. He landed with a deadening thud on the concrete embankment.

Jan, still light-headed with adrenaline fear, was speechless and quivered like a bird.

"Take your pants down, then put your hands on the ledge," Garrett ordered the squat, bleeding, heavyset man, who was still dazed from the kick which had smashed his nose.

"Please, please!" he cried.

"Take your medicine like a fucking man and not some piss-ass. Get your pants down and show me your balls."

He fearfully dropped his leather trousers and was powerless as they drooped around his ankles.

"Hands on the ledge!"

He shakily extended his hands, and Garrett, now in a calm rage, even more terrifying than when he was in battle, methodically shattered his fingers. As the man howled from each blow, Garrett ruthlessly thumped him in the groin. Gagging in anguish, he rolled and was halfway over the canal railing. He gave a final yelp when Garrett heaved him over.

Garrett's tone was flippant now. "Bon voyage."

**Nursing brandies at** home in the shadowy light of the grand salon, surrounded by his priceless Delft and Dutch masters, Jan was flushed and still agitated. His trousers and shirt were blood-spattered, as was Garrett's face.

"It's a lucky thing Eve wasn't there," Jan said.

"Lucky for them. She took two gangbangers apart at our shops in Venice when I was out. They came for protection money, imagine."

Jan was incredulous. "Garrett, I couldn't have survived something like this. I owe you my life. For an instant, I thought I'd offer them money. Those bastards!"

"It wouldn't have helped," Garrett said.

"How did you learn to fight this way?"

Garrett smiled easily, thoroughly relaxed. "When you have a woman like Eve in your life, you have to be able to protect her. She looks after me, too. People usually assume that because I'm not pumped up, I'm a wimp. That's mistake number one, when you underestimate your opponent. I made that error once. I thought I was tough and got into a brawl with a contractor who was ripping me off. He whipped my ass.

"When I lived in Bangkok and was studying with a master tattooist, I became friends with one of his clients. Arun Mai was about my size, we weighed in at around a hundred and forty. He'd retired as the undefeated lightweight kickboxing champion. He took me under his wing and trained me to defend myself. Another friend of his was a tai chi teacher. I also learned that civilized behavior is the most dangerous habit because it's a hothouse that breeds weakness and complacency.

"The three of us used to work out, oh, and play together. Hit the bars, smoke some Thai stick, an opium pipe now and then up in Lampang. They taught me how discipline myself. When I'm at work, or take tonight, and I'm under attack, I'm absolutely focused. Everything is integrated within. Nothing blocks me or interferes. I am one with the center. There is no fear or joy or thoughts of myself, life or death, because I'm in the moment. Either you define this moment or you vanish."

Garrett's heroic stature had become Olympian. Jan restrained his emotion and reined in his gratitude in the presence of this remarkable being. As he reached for the bottle of Napoleon brandy, he heard a rustle and detected a presence.

Eve's soft laugh came from the darkness.

"And how is my great artist and his patron?" she asked.

"Feeling deserted, angel?" Garrett asked.

"I knew we'd reconnect when you got your head together and Gauguin was off your case."

Jan welcomed her back and then, after revealing how her champion had rescued them, he moved on to the subject of Garrett's artistic plight.

"Skin is Garrett's canvas," Eve said casually, almost as if she hadn't been away in Ghent and had overheard their earlier conversation.

Garrett pressed his lips against her hand. "I'll need red meat."

She growled, baring her teeth. "Then your lioness will be on the prowl and hunt."

As they flung suggestions back and forth like novices, Jan interrupted.

"Have you ever kidnapped anyone?" he asked. They admitted that they never had. "I have—and never been caught or even suspected. I developed my technique over the years. There's a *protocol*. Tell me, Garrett, do you have a specific subject in mind?"

Garrett immediately shot back his requirements. "A blonde. I want fair skin, no freckles, tender—about twelve or thirteen."

Jan beamed with pleasure. He had become active, the counselor again. "My friends, we'll pick a flower tomorrow," he said, relaxed, the gracious uncle and éminence grise. "In films, we call it a rece. Eve should stay behind because we'll need her later as our lure."

**At eight the** following morning, after a leisurely breakfast and some banter about the lurid story in the *Bruges Journal* regarding two eighteen-year-old boys on life-support systems as a result of a vicious attack and one who died in a fall from the bridge, Jan and Garrett strolled from the house to the market square. The fresh catch was being scrupulously examined by the housewives while the beer-swilling fishmongers hoarsely grumbled. Garrett's eyes alertly surveyed several young girls wandering through the stalls.

Jan led him over to Mari Rodenstuck's shop in the Steenstraat. "It's not worth scouting there. The police are floating around."

The queen of Bruges' flower emporiums had recovered from a heart attack, and Jan heard her barking orders to her assistants in the greenhouse behind the shop. Nature's treasures were for sale and the aroma of freshly watered flowers and plants was exhilarating.

Mari was complaining to a supplier about her order of tulips. Her dazzling topiary and floral display of baskets, her sheer artistry, impressed Garrett. She was a perfectionist. While Jan paid his respects and gossiped with her, Garrett roamed through the interior of the shop. His concentration found its rhythm, its orchestration, when he surveyed a series of photographs neatly pinned to the wall behind the cash register. The color prints, several of them blown up to poster size, revealed a luscious Caroline Davis posing with golf trophies; there were news stories about the golf prodigy from Carmel, California, where a headline proclaimed: CAROLINE DAVIS, LOCAL SENSATION, SHOOTS 70 AT PEBBLE BEACH.

When Jan left for the greenhouse, Garrett picked up a flower catalogue to avoid anyone observing his interest. He discreetly moved closer to the photos. Yes, the girl was lovely, her short blond hair was modishly cut like a young Gwyneth Paltrow, one of Garrett's favorite actresses. Her well-developed figure gave an inkling of breast development and she had an athlete's lithe arms and legs. Her skin was luminous, a surface fit for Rembrandt.

Jan's hardy voice intruded. "And this is my friend from California. He's an artist of genius."

Mari's sharp mouth broke into a commercial smile, revealing teeth harried to a yellowish brown by cigarettes. She wore a green waterproof smock and a frayed seaman's cap cocked over her piled gray hair. She had high-blood-pressure plum skin and, despite her dainty figure, there was a mercantile grittiness about her that did not escape Garrett's notice. He shook her damp, weathered hand and the coarseness of her nails set an uneven margin in his palm.

"Ah, an *American*," she trilled, as though his nationality were a cause for rejoicing. "I have family from there." She recounted the Davis clan's accomplishments.

"Three days ago, they arrived." She pointed to the poster. "My niece is a fabulous golfer and is going to play in the U.S. Junior Championship in July."

"You must be very proud," Garrett said with a fawning smile. "We'll think the good thought and cheer her to victory."

At this smarmy comment, Mari was aflutter, but before she could respond, Jan embraced her.

"Why aren't you with your family instead of fussing in the shop and thundering at your employees? You're killing yourself, my dear Mari."

"The staff these days don't care. Just pay them for their time so they can run to the taverns, sleep around, and dance all night at the discos. And the business can go to hell. My father would have taken a hickory stick to them."

"You must relax after your warning. Now, if I may, let's have some of the diminutive Duc van Tols, the violet ones, please, Mari, and maybe some yellow Darwins for my friend's beautiful lady."

Mari returned to the greenhouse to fill his order and Jan spoke in an undertone. "The little niece . . . what do you think?"

"It's love at first sight."

Jan gave a brittle laugh. "Really? I thought you and Eve were inseparable."

"We always find a way to share."

Jan was smitten by the possibilities and involuntarily licked his lips. The trio—no—a lush quartet, bodies all entwined, their skin matted, the cameras programed. Jan took the bouquet of tulips from Mari, kissed her on both cheeks, and she walked to the door with him.

"Why don't you take the family to lunch at some beautiful place . . . the Kasteel Minnewater, walk around the Lake of Love, and forget about the shop?" Jan said with a courtly bow.

"Jan, you're so thoughtful. Actually, I have reservations for lunch there tomorrow."

Once outside, Jan's excitement mounted. "This will be your vernissage, Garrett. We'll make history in a new medium."

# CHAPTER 16

**At one time the** Roman necropolis in Arles known as Les Alys-camps had been the most important burial site in Europe. The imperial sarcophagi vandalized over time and immortalized by van Gogh and Gauguin still possessed a macabre character. Tourists and well-organized gangs from the Camargue were ghoulishly attracted to its history of death and mourning. Arles always seemed squalid to Michel, with its maze of confounding, charmless streets, populated by scabrous, drugged hippies. The city was ingrained with slothful cops who virtually ignored rapes and brazen daylight robberies, particulars omitted by guidebooks. When Michel thought about it, he believed he could still hear the boatmen's merciless haggling for their *mortellage* after they had transported the coffins of important citizens down the Rhône River. They extracted tolls from the grief-stricken family for this gruesome service. In his mind, the laughter of the boatmen provided a shuddering counterpoint to the wails of the family.

And now that Gerta Sholler had vanished, he could hear the music of hell.

His people were all there, Annie already interviewing the tour leader, a tearful, plump nun from Munich. Sister Trude wore a kerchief and a white summer habit with short sleeves. Over a bulbous nose, her fogged bifocals did nothing to encourage Michel about her reliability as a witness. Clutching her rosary, she said, "Gerta, like the other girls, is an orphan at the Immaculate Conception in Munich. We all were looking forward to this trip for a year, and only twelve honor students could go. The girls worked so hard. Gerta was at the top of the class and group leader."

"Would she have been easily tricked?" Annie asked.

"I doubt it. We're very scrupulous and we had a travel orientation before we left. The girls were repeatedly warned not to talk to strangers, to report anything suspicious, not to stray from the group."

Nearby, Michel saw the faces of two other nuns and their young charges leaning out of the windows of the lit tour bus. A vendor was trying to flog cold drinks, and the gendarmes chased him away.

Sister Trude peered over Annie's shoulder and regarded Michel with mistrust, supposing he was eavesdropping.

"I'm the history instructor and I was in the midst of describing to the girls the miracles that took place at Les Alyscamps and how our Lord prayed here and passed among the assembly and left the mark of His knee on a rock. I was about to discuss St. Trophime's contributions as the first bishop—"

"Excuse me, sister, I'm the present-day bishop, Commander Danton of the Special Circumstances Section. Did you or any of the others notice anyone following you?"

"No, monsieur."

"Someone trying to tempt the girls with souvenirs, calissons, or ice cream?"

"There are vendors everywhere and we always take an afternoon break at a *salon de thé*. We budgeted for those treats."

"Sometimes children get distracted."

"Not our girls," she insisted.

"An attractive young man? Flirting?" Annie asked.

"No, someone would have noticed."

Michel was being signaled by Pierre but ignored his detective. "Do the girls speak French?"

"Of course, and English as well," Sister Trude replied proudly. "Our school trains those who wish to follow the holy calling of Christ to become His missionaries."

Before withdrawing, Michel made a final appeal. "Sister, I know how upset you are. Perhaps it would be better for us to send a car for you tomorrow and we can continue in Marseille. You see, we'll have to interview everyone." As he was about to turn to Pierre, he looked at the ashen face of the middle-aged nun. "Was there . . . ? Do you remember seeing a woman, maybe with a dog, walking near you?

Sister Trude was disturbed by his question and shrank back as though he were about to strike her.

"People often stop to listen when I'm lecturing." Pride before a fall, Michel thought. "When I was discussing St. Genesisus's role in saving the early Christians, I did see a woman who was at the edge of the group."

"Were you speaking German or French?"

"In France we speak French. That was one of the purposes of the trip."

"How old would you think the woman was?"

The nun was pensive. "It's hard to say; I wasn't close enough. Thirties — no, middle-aged . . . forties."

"And did she wear a hat and sunglasses? Carry a camera, possibly? Walk a dog?"

Sister Trude removed her glasses and closed her eyes. "Yes, yes, but everyone in France seems to have a dog," she protested.

"Was this a small dog?" Michel continued, waving Pierre off. "Poodle, cocker spaniel, a charming dachshund . . . no, maybe a Bichon Friese? Do you know the breed? They're small with whitish, woolly coats. . . ."

The nun wavered and her legs seemed to give out. Michel timorously put his hand on her back and grasped her as she was about to fall. He awkwardly held her in his arms, remembering the life-long strictures against ever embracing a nun. Her eyes were now coated with the glaze of trauma.

"À l'aide, vite! Un médecin!" Michel bellowed. The emergency team rushed over, and Michel eased her on a stretcher while her vital signs were checked.

"Pressure's a bit low," one of them men said. An oxygen mask was placed over her face and in a few moments she had regained her color.

"Shall I give you a ride back to your hotel?" Michel asked.

"No, I'll be all right," she insisted. "I'll return with the others on the bus."

"Where are you staying?"

"In Avignon at the hospice near St. Ruf's Abbey."

Michel helped her to her feet and assisted her to the bus.

"Since I don't have a picture of Gerta, I have one final question." Sister Trude made the cross over him. "Thank you, I am Catholic. Would you describe Gerta as pretty?"

"No, she was beautiful."

"Blond, fair-skinned?"

The nun gave a despondent nod. Michel climbed aboard the bus behind her. He addressed the frightened, but still curious, girls who were now rigidly in their seats.

"We're going to find Gerta. But I need your help, young ladies. Anyone who took a photo of Gerta—even if she was part of a group—please raise your hand." The girls waited for permission from the other nuns, who nodded. In an instant, everyone in the bus had a hand raised. "That's good news for us. Now Detective Vallon—she likes to be called Annie, by the way—will follow you back to the hospice. Even if you haven't completed a roll of film, we'll develop them for you free, return the photos and negatives, and everyone will receive three rolls of film free for your trouble. Thank you for your assistance and good night."

When the bus pulled away, he was met by Pierre, who held up his prize. On a thin metal spike, used for handling evidence, he dangled an air Taser gun.

"Our friends must've been in a hurry, to leave this behind," he said. "I'll run it back to the lab."

Émile and Annie joined them. Michel directed Annie to follow the tour bus to Avignon and begin questioning the other nuns and the girls.

"Get any pictures you can of Gerta. Annie, as you heard, these girls are exceptionally bright. Somebody must've noticed the woman. Émile, when the forensic section is finished here, get everyone into the lab. I want them working on this all night."

**At midnight Michel** tiptoed into his bedroom. He had hoped Jennifer might still be out with her mother and Grace or, in his best-case scenario, sound asleep. Unfortunately, she sat cross-legged on the bed, a highlighter poised over the *catalogue raisonné* for the forthcoming show, which was spread out over the sunflowered counterpane. Jennifer's white linen shorts were crumpled and her Stanford T-shirt had wilted, clinging to her breasts.

She did not say a word to him. Her soft green eyes were more puzzled than angry, as though she were trying to recover from some humiliating remark. He sank down in the chair recessed beside the old country pine armoire they had moved from the farm.

"I have a problem," he began.

"Cold feet . . . ? Another girl?" she asked in a plaintive tone that was at once understanding and wounded. "Tell me, Michel. It'll be better for both of us."

He rose from the chair and sat on the bed, keeping some distance between them. It was clear to him that she did not want to be touched and that humoring her would be fruitless.

"Neither, Jennifer."

"What, then? You're like a stranger. Is it my mother? I know she can get on people's nerves."

"Not mine. Roz is dazzling, spectacular. I can see you in her and something of what you might be like when you're her age. It's as though you've both stepped out of a Renoir painting to adorn my life. I can't believe that my lousy luck, the miserable choices I've made in women before you, hasn't come home to haunt me."

Jennifer seemed more surprised than pleased by the avowal. "I have a neurotic side and it was dormant for a while, but now it's broken out like a case of hives. I feel acutely insecure about everything."

"Forgive me. But I thought now that you've got a close friend in Grace that you wouldn't be so lonely."

"I love Grace. But I'm lonely when you're not around."

"I can't help it," Michel said, trying to remain calm and reassuring, standing up suddenly like an advocate in court. "I have a case that's a nightmare and it looks like it's just beginning."

"It can't be worse than what we went through last summer with Maddie and Boy."

"She and Boynton killed adults—not *children*."

Jennifer, too, was on her feet, moving closer to him to try to read his face.

"What? Tell me. I'm a big girl. It's what I don't know that tortures me, makes me doubt myself and us. *Moi! Je suis l'etranger!*"

"I'm insanely in love with you and if you don't know it by now, then our situation is hopeless."

"But your mistress is murder."

He recoiled in fury. "I don't have a mistress and never will have one as long as you love me, so don't goad me."

He tried to explain the situation: the failure to find a replacement; the retirement of Richard Caron; the bad blood with his daughter Sylvie; the disciples he had worked with but who required something only he could provide.

"And what is that?"

"Inspiration would be overstating what I give the section." He reluctantly switched on the air-conditioning and peeled off his sweaty clothes. "Imagination. I have the mind of a criminal—a murderer—which is why I'm stuck in this job. It's not simply a profession for me but a calling. I was hatched by my mother to solve crimes."

" 'Hatched'? What an odd word to use about being born."

For a moment, Michel, now stripped naked, his body stippled with sweat, wanted to confess, resolving the torment that no one could detect, which he endured in sleepless nights and in the recurring dreams of his actual mother—a whore, turned madam— who had bequeathed him a fortune. The insolence of his mother's gesture was yet a further source of debasement.

"Let's leave my imagery out of this. This isn't some clever linguistics seminar. A twelve-year-old blond girl was kidnapped in Arles at Les Alyscamps this evening. Pierre found the Taser she was shot with. Yesterday, a woman used ether in the ladies' room of a brasserie in Pont-Aven to snatch a girl there. A man was outside with a car, and the girl managed to break away because a waiter recognized her. I only found out when I checked in during dinner."

Jennifer was stunned. She followed Michel to the bathroom.

Realizing he was naked, he rushed ahead. "Oh, God, your mother," he whispered.

"She's staying with Jules and Grace for the night."

The great detective was perplexed. "Why? Did I offend her?"

"No, they invited her."

Michel went into the bathroom. Stripping off her clothes, she trailed after him, wary of the impetuous declensions of the unsympathetic tiles and steps.

Michel had his back to her, rooting for towels in the new linen cabinet. He turned around with a sense of terror. He dropped the new bath sheets Jennifer's mother had brought from Bed, Bath and Beyond. He thought he might be having a seizure when Jennifer yanked him into the shower. The showerhead had been changed! Water shot out as though from a Victorian steam engine and he cringed away.

"Not the water pipes exploding again?"

"No, my lover came by and stayed for hours." She soaped a washcloth with a new bar of L'Occitane lemon verbena and rubbed his chest. "Golarde, the contractor, and I are getting it on."

He clasped her by the neck. "You're lying. Golarde is gay."

She massaged fragrant lavender shampoo into Michel's scalp; then, raising her long blond hair, she slowly unraveled it. It hung down her back like an endless strings of pearls. Suddenly Michel retreated into a corner when Jennifer adjusted the new showerhead. The sound was deafening to him.

"Is the Rhône flooding again? How did we get this water pressure?"

"I have friends," she admitted.

"Duclair, the head plumber, isn't gay. He's insatiable, even worse than Stein with women. Was he in here with you demonstrating?"

"Michel, yes, Duclair installed it, but he was too busy and we didn't get it on." Like a celebrity endorsing a product, she trilled, "This is the new showerhead from Water Pik, so enjoy it."

"I've never felt water pressure like this before. In Provence you can go to prison for tampering with it. It's a crime!"

"Close your eyes." Jennifer massaged his scalp and again adjusted the showerhead, so that she could wash his hair clean.

"The concierge will report us," he burbled.

"Oh, bullshit. She'll think she's still watching reruns of *Baywatch* and it's Pamela Anderson rescuing someone at the beach."

"These rough seas you drag me in," he said, down on his knees and kneading every part of her body with wild, sometimes misguided thrusts of his tongue. "Richard contacted Paris and I'm flying to Quimper at seven. It's okay for you to come along. Brittany is a marvel. I'll take you to lunch at Rosmadec for their *Homard* in Pont-Aven. It's a lobster dish that's beyond human comprehension."

"Beyond your father's?"

"Almost everything connected with cooking is beyond him."

Jennifer had rinsed the shampoo from their hair and adjusted the temperature gauge so that it sprayed cool water on them.

"Can I buy clogs? And a pair for Roz?"

He briefly ceased his circuit over her thighs and said, "You can buy Gucci, Bally, Ferragamo, Manola Blaunik—Bruno Magli, if O.J. is visiting. Anything you want. Just come with me."

She smiled with a tender reminiscence. "This isn't a Proustian recherché Madeleine moment, but when I was a kid, Roz brought me back a pair of sabots with Gauguin's face painted on them."

"I'm sure that they're still available. Pont-Aven's favorite son is always in fashion."

"I wonder what he would have made of this industry."

"Probably licensed it to Disney."

Michel cautiously turned off the shower, becoming accustomed to how things, life, worked in his venerable surroundings which Jennifer had thrust into the twenty-first century. He opened the fogged shower door, and smugly reached for the towels.

He dried her, she him, and then, as they guardedly baffled the lethal steps, the loose tiles, the adventurers which had risen, fallen, loosened, the doorway harelip, a declivity followed by an abrupt elevation, she yanked him into bed and said, "Michel, are you ready for a frenzied blow job, followed by a deliriously horny fuck with me sitting on you, or is that out of the question?"

With a grimace, he briefly considered the proposition. "Where's the bloody plumber when you need him?"

# CHAPTER 17

**Jan Korteman's interior salon** — referred to as an examining room — was secreted in a high-ceilinged chamber that had been used by the Dutch Underground during the Nazi occupation of Flanders. The maestro touched a switch embedded in the side of a grandfather clock which presided over the entry of the studio. A long Spanish mirror with a portrait of the Infanta above it slid open with a harmonic humming. Eve raised her glass in a salute, filled for the third time with milky absinthe, which they had been drinking all evening. She was in Mount Everest spirits, pretending that the drinks had no effect on her and altitude was merely a state of mind.

A leather massage table had restraints and steel stirrups, the glass cabinets were dust-free and filled with a seductive variety of do-it-yourself-how-to-get-stoned remedies stationed in large antique laboratory jars. A leather *sommelier*-style menu hung from a brass hook.

"Is this your chat room?" Eve asked mischievously. "Can I be your date?" she mimicked Elizabeth Taylor mothering Montgomery Clift in *A Place in the Sun.*

"My dates" — Jan with a smug look — "haven't done well here."

Eve peered through the thick shatterproof glass of the cabinets like a bookkeeper.

"Cocaine, GHB, Seconals, Tuinals, and look, Garrett, here's our old maid chloral hydrate . . . a flask of ether, chloroform." She continued to gibe their host. "A few clichés . . . ecstasy . . . sorry, Jan — but nobody uses phenobarbital."

"Well, Europe is a step behind."

"Don't be insolent, Eve."

"Oh, pardon me. For once, since we got here, I don't have to moon over de Hooch's lighting and Wouwerman's trite landscapes. If I have to look at another one of his starstruck cows, I'll scream."

Garrett bowed and kissed her on the lips as Jan looked on with excitement.

"May I continue, kind sir?"

"Eve, you're in charge."

She pointed at the burly glass cabinet. "Hello, Taser. This model could bring down Mike Tyson and George Foreman without anyone throwing a punch."

"Or an ox," Jan said.

They roved through poisons and Percodans, toxins and tinctures of adder glands and emetics, while Jan sat on the table holding a pair of handcuffs, apparently his trade tool.

"How'd Heather do in here?" Eve asked in a spirit of rivalry.

"She needed training," Jan admitted. Garrett was incredulous. Jan spritely jumped off the table. His guests had no drinks and the servants were in bed. "I brought in a couple of our local prison guards for her bon voyage evening."

"Better them than us," she said to Garrett.

They stood staring at Jan and he felt old, frightened by the severe intensity of Eve with her scent of Poison commingling with a rutting sweat, her hand stroking, flicking inadvertently at her crotch, then her fingers gliding up toward Garrett's fly until his erection zoomed into a solid mass thrusting at the zipper of his jeans. In an unexpected flamenco turn she deposited herself in Jan's arms. The sinuous movement electrified him. Her dainty breasts pressed against him, buds blossoming against his chest. As Jan was about to clasp her, Eve twisted away, flinging herself onto the leather table, and with a tantalizing thrust dangled her long legs in the air.

"I'm so excited by our little project."

He ignored Garrett at his peril, Jan realized, but Eve had come on to him. "Eve, are you going to work with Garrett or would you like to assist me with my photos?"

"That's up to Garrett."

Garrett now had an absorbed expression, haunted by visualizing his creation.

"Eve might do some piercing work when I'm finished. She's also an artist, Jan."

**The essence of** Jan's kidnapping protocol was to maintain his regular habits, and after a few prelunch beers at the De Garre tavern he walked alone around the Lake of Love on the cloudless day and headed for his regular table and waiter at the Kasteel Minnewater. Franz read him the specials and Jan thought he'd eat lightly.

"Mousse of smoked trout with the port wine jelly and currant roll . . . no soup, Franz, it's too warm . . . yes, and to follow: roulade of sole with the salmon filling."

"All fish today," the waiter said with a flourish. "An excellent choice."

"The last Chablis was rude and barked afterward," Jan said in his customary quibbling.

"There's a demi Meursault not spoken for with a smile on her lips."

"Good, I have a long photo shoot this afternoon."

"*Danke*, Herr Korteman."

**It had been** agreed that Garrett would stay behind; Eve would meet the architect of their adventure. Sitting in Jan's model makeup room after her bath, she opened her case of magical unguents. With a sure stroke, she frothed up her Kabuki facial wax in jasmine oil with her facial brush and with delicate strokes applied it to her face, neck, and throat. This covered up any irregularities and her skin was like porcelain. She mixed up her liquid foundation—a combination of Makiage and Chanel—then on a glass plate added a few drops of Clinique porcelain beige foundation which was sold only in Paris. This gave her skin a healthier, more feminine texture.

Garrett couldn't control his urge and lifted her breast and sucked the nipple until she shoved him away.

"Bad boy. We have business to do, so don't try to mess around now." Her nipple continued to pulsate. "Hand me the number eight sable brush and the Sahara beige shadow. . . ." He did as he was ordered and she applied it to the sides of her nose and into the folds of her lips, which thinned her nose and created a softer impression.

She made a crease in the fold of her eyelid with the same color, applied it also to her cheekbone with her fingers, and this created a more angular look. She decided to go with a dark brown eyeliner at the base of her upper and lower eyelashes, which thickened them. She put on a Bamboo Matte eye shadow with a number ten sable brush.

She drew her eyebrows with a taupe pencil and went over them with a Chanel brow fixer. She finished off with an English eyelash curler, which eased the application and enabled her to look straight ahead. She completed this with a drop of J&J Duo eyelash adhesive and glued on six individual eyelashes to each upper eyelid, which gave her long lustrous eyelashes.

Her magic and artistry always fascinated Garrett. As she powdered her face with translucent Japanese rice powder, she added a finishing touch with Shiseido earth tone rouge. She stood up to give herself some perspective and selected off the cork-block wig stands a wig of brownish black. Garrett had paid five thousand dollars for each wig. They were the best human hair and sold by convents, where they were collected from the young women who had cut their hair before becoming nuns. With a dexterous move, Eve adjusted the springs on the sides and back of the wig to secure it against the sudden wind gusts that came up from the Lake of Love. Bruges's weather was as unpredictable as Garrett's quest to define his art.

"What do you think?" She asked, trying on a pair ivory-colored porcelain veneer teeth.

"A little too perfect, my love. Go with the uneven ones."

She snapped another set of teeth onto her canines. "And the contacts?" She roughly pushed Garrett away when he dropped down and nuzzled her. "Hey, cut it out. Everyone wants to go down on me. Jan's already a problem. Garrett, listen to me. He's been messing around in my undies drawer." Fastidious to a fault, she noticed everything. "He's also been in my clothes closet. I don't know what to do about him. He's like a jackal. I'm frightened of him."

"Don't be. It's not your fault that you have the most perfect pussy in the world."

She was in no mood for compliments.

"Garrett, this is important and you're not listening!"

"I hear you, Eve. Don't worry about Jan. Just play ball. When my work is completed, Jan will be a shadow, a negative that no one can develop."

She was even more deeply troubled. "How?"

"He'll dissolve, melt away. What's left will become part of winter's thaw."

She slipped on black leotards, cupped her tiny breasts and decided against a bra, and put on a cheap black dress with long sleeves made out of some synthetic fabric she'd bought at a flea market and was untraceable. Her last choice made her wonder which deception to take on and she selected the brown contacts, a French roast coffee bean color. With wraparound sunglasses and a dark straw hat, no one would recognize her.

She and Garrett took the elevator in silence to the garage crypt and listened to the gush of canal water slamming above and beside them, the sounds of boat horns. The garage door opened and a gray sky with its flash-camera sunbursts blinded them. Garrett was still moonstruck and aroused, craving a solitary afternoon with his Eve. But with such a momentous assignment, she was immune to the favors he had to bestow, especially when the outcome might be death. Garrett was the experienced one and she the vassal in this crime. She had a case of nerves and he was chattering.

"The light's wonderful. Look at the Beguine's house with the nuns walking out trying to find the sunlight. It's like the tropism of plants. The sisters were there in the thirteenth century. . . ."

"Garrett, spare me the romance for once. I'm going out to kidnap a girl for you! And I could get caught."

**A few moments** after she left Garrett, her cell phone rang and she quickly answered. Jan informed her that the Davis family was heading for the Groeninge Museum and he would be in his car in the alley waiting. Three days before, when Mari was in the back of her flower shop, Eve had slipped in to see the photos of the family and she had a clear image of Caroline.

Eve was a short walk away from the museum. She was in time, and Jan, on point, signaled her that they were inside. She walked slowly into the gallery, stopping at the paintings, but unlike Garrett she was sated on the dark Flemish primitive paintings. She had enough of tavern genre studies and metaphysical Madonnas. Tour groups came and went, and the traffic was constant. Some of the people wore headsets, others listened as guides lectured. In the background a choir was practicing for a concert.

Eve observed the Davis family. Caroline was restless. She wandered to the window while her parents stood entranced before Suvée's painting *The Invention of the Art of Drawing*. It was evident that the girl was bored, yawning, desperate to leave, but her parents ignored her and were having an animated discussion. Caroline's left and right hand joined in a golf grip and she took some practice swings, like a pro warming up without the club, just trying to get the feel.

"Mah-ahm, I'm thirsty," Caroline called in a whine. "I want a Coke."

Melanie Davis was about to put on her headset, then looked at her husband, who had been absorbed in the painting.

"Good idea, I'm dying for a drink, too," Eve said with a quick smile.

"Honey, we won't be much longer. Let's meet up at the Michelangelo statue," her mother said.

Eve pressed the automatic dial on her cell phone and in muffled voice said, "We're on our way."

She let the girl leave first, but gradually increased her pace, until they were out of view of her parents and walking side by side.

"Hey, my name's Eve. There's a café across the street. Let's go there—unless you can't get enough of those prehistoric pictures. My treat. I'm from California. What about you?"

"You're kidding," Caroline said with delight. "We live in Carmel. An American voice at last. Where in California are you from?"

"Down south, Venice."

"Wow, I love Rollerblading on the Boardwalk. . . ."

As Caroline approached a vendor with a wagon and a display of soft drinks, Eve turned and blocked her.

Before Caroline had a chance to make a decision, Eve had hooked her arm and they rushed across the street.

"Eve, that doesn't look like a café. . . ."

Wearing a chauffeur's black uniform and a cap, sunglasses, false beard, and wig, Jan stood before a dark blue Mercedes he had rented under a false name. The rear door abutting the curb was open and with a sense of urgency he stopped the two women.

"Your Aunt Mari had another heart attack, Caroline. She asked for you. Get in. We've got to go to the hospital!"

Speed causing confusion was the essence of Jan's protocol. With an unexpected shove from Eve, the girl was suddenly thrust into the back seat. Eve was beside her, slamming the door, the automatic locks clicking, and the car was moving away.

"My folks, Eve, I've got to call them on my cell phone."

As Caroline fumbled in her bag, Eve had already put on a surgical mask. Jan watched from the rearview mirror as she seized Caroline by the neck, twisted her so that she was secure in a headlock. Eve stuffed the ether-soaked towel over her face. The girl struggled for a moment and lapsed into shock.

"Roll her onto the floor," Jan shouted, "and cover her with the blanket. We'll be in the garage in five minutes."

Eve waited a moment, holding the towel tight around Caroline's mouth and nose before easing her gently down on the floor. If she were bruised, Garrett's wrath would be intolerable.

**Jan stood spellbound** in his enormous bathroom; he resembled a sentinel at his post and his automatic video cameras hummed. Eve shaved under Caroline's arms, then lathered her legs. Caroline was groggy after being force-fed a drink. She seemed to be wandering between sleep and spasmodic involuntarily reflexes which caused her legs to twitch.

"A phenobarbital cocktail—and you scoffed." Jan sighed complacently. "I suppose I'm old-fashioned, Eve, but I like to go with the tried and trusted."

"Jan, you're a specialist," Eve said, coaxing the hairs off the numb Caroline with a Gillette Mach3, *The Best a Man Can Get,* which she had bought at Costco at a bargain price. "I have a dumb question. Where are the servants?"

"Oh, I sent them to my farm in Maastrict for the summer. They have no keys to this house and the locks are on codes." He leaned into the tub and examined Caroline's soapy calf. She's sumptu-ous. . . ."

He helped Eve lift Caroline out of the tub and they showered her down, dried her, and wheeled her on a gurney to the studio, where the special table had been moved and the moonlight gloated. They strapped her ankles and wrists as Garrett had instructed. She would sleep until morning.

"Eve, can I stay in my own home, my studio, and nurse her through the dark hours if she should wake up?"

"I'm warning you, Jan, don't touch her. No matter what you've claimed to do before, you have no idea what Garrett is like when he's angry." He recalled how adroitly Garrett had dealt with the skinheads the other night. "She's Garrett's model, not a sex object. This is a holy quest for Garrett."

Eve switched off the main light and only a hallway lamp was on, cloaking the room in a penumbra of dark shapes. When Jan searched for her, she had vanished. Jan suddenly overheard two men's voices murmuring in French. They came into the private atelier. Bold moving shadows formed a canopy and in this murk-iness, Jan could distinguish very little. The intrusion troubled him and for a moment he thought the police had tracked them down. He crept into the recess beside the medical cabinet. A penlight flashed over Caroline's face and the child's drugged expression was illuminated, her breath a whisper.

Now, from the entry, Eve's voice snapped, "Jan's somewhere in there."

"Oh, really?" Garrett replied. "Thanks, Eve. You can leave now. I'll see you in bed." Footsteps accompanied this dismissal.

Garrett lifted Caroline's eyelids and checked her pupils with his penlight. He lifted the sheet off her, studying the immaculate, shaved body, the twitch of her limbs.

"*Elle est jeune . . . parfait pour l'oeuvre,* Garrett," a husky voice maintained.

"Yes, she's flawless." Garrett turned the sleeping girl on to her back.

"*Bien fait, mon ami.*"

"*Merci.* . . . Paul, after all our years of conflict, I'm glad we made our peace. Let me assure you that you're still encircled by admirers."

"*Ce soir c'est comme mes jours quand j'ai vécu à Pont-Aven. J'ai appris mon métier là. Alors toile, pour la peintre . . . le châssis.*"

"Yes, her skin is very tight. We may have to stretch *the canvas* with a muscle relaxant. There's probably Robaxin in Jan's pharmacy. Succinylcholine is too chancy without an anesthesiologist. No, Maid Caroline won't be a problem."

"*Votre chef-d'oeuvre est attendant.*"

"I like the sound of that. I'm ready to create a masterpiece after all these apprentice years."

Satisfied that the girl was in no medical danger, Garrett switched off the light and peered around the room. "Come out, come out, wherever you are. . . . Jan, honestly, there's nothing to be frightened of."

Jan's foreboding paralyzed him, and he thumped to his knees, trembling in the nook. He clasped his hands in supplication. "I swear I won't touch the girl, please don't hurt me. I only want to serve."

"My dear Jan"—Garrett's voice had a sympathetic cajolery— "Eve said you were marvelous today. We have so much to thank you for. Please don't be alarmed."

Jan stumbled to his feet, but remained cowering, in a stooped posture, apprehensive and incapable of making eye contact.

"Garrett, who else is here . . . besides you and Eve?" he asked with a shudder.

"A fellow artist." Garrett, amicable and concerned, took Jan's arm and walked with him into the darkened main part of the studio. "I hope there's room in your home for our new guest." Like the young lord bringing a scoundrel companion from school to the family estate, Garrett sought to make a case for the invitation. "Jan, as our host, I should warn you that my friend's genius is exceeded only by his rude, ungrateful, unmannerly, and boorish behavior. He is devoid of tact or any moral sense."

Jan was befuddled, a victim of his own perverse curiosity which had resulted in this captivity. Heather had whetted his desire with descriptions of her own erotic adventures with the couple. He had been led to believe this would be another of his rich-man's easy seductions.

After a few minutes, he roved over to his desk and sat on the edge, pondering the dilemma. The room was silent, but then foot-falls came pounding toward him. A match was struck and sparked into a flame. Hovering before him was the figure of a man with a drooping mustache, dressed in a matelot shirt, blue peasant trousers, and a cap; he used the flickering match to light his pipe. Jan felt he was blacking out and struggled to keep from losing consciousness.

*"Le Maître,* Paul Gauguin, has joined us."

*"Bon soir, Monsieur Korteman."*

# CHAPTER 18

**The strong saline wind** blustered and whined off the Atlantic, invigorating Jennifer after the flight. It chopped at the police car, its long antenna dancing like a feather. They were picked up at the Quimper airport, and the driver handed Michel the police report, which he reviewed during the twenty-mile drive to Pont-Aven. The sharp electric Breton blue colors of houses, doorways, and inns, the clumps of deep red hydrangeas the size of watermelons, mesmerized Jennifer. With windmills churning, fishermen loading their trucks, farmers peering up from their fields, this unexpected trip had delivered Jennifer into a new world. She had an eye for beauty, the unusual, contrasts. Although she loved Provence, this adventure, sullied by an attempted kidnapping, nonetheless added another charge to her love affair with France's regions. They were all distinct, and she thought of them as different suitors waiting to embrace her. Yet there was nothing regal or sexual in this perception, but rather a gathering of her natural resources and interests. If she were back in Los Angeles and had traveled east by plane for the same length of time, she'd be probably be in Albuquerque, not Brittany.

Her fingers lingered on Michel's wrist when the police car stopped at the prefecture on Boulevard Dupleix. In another day, they would be married with solemn rites, dine till they were bloated at the Danton feast, but these conventions were somehow less important than her actual experience of loving Michel. He had given her the charmed life that she never could have conceived for herself. A year ago she was a dour single woman teaching malcontents in a second-rate junior college in Ojai. Her prospects depressed her and the petty wrangle over finances every month wore her out, made her furious with herself. The undercurrent of personal and professional failure swamped her. This apparently irremediable situation had been altered by meeting Michel. She would be marrying a charming, quixotic genius, a virile gladiator, cultured and sensitive. She doted on their lovemaking, but his mind had become her passion.

She looked around at the steep streets, the intricate weed patterns of the Aven River which gushed through the town. "Do you want me to come with you? Help if I can?"

"*Merci, chèrie* . . . you see it's not my jurisdictional area. I'm considered a foreigner, and not an attractive one at that. You know, one of those lazy, dull slugs from Provence."

"The late Detective Paul Courbet."

"Yes, he was their model. They've got a female detective who interviewed the girl. I can't wait to meet her," he added without enthusiasm.

"I finally remembered to bring my cell phone, so call me when you're finished and I'll meet you at Le Moulin de Rosmadec."

"I'll try to make this quick."

Seldom given to emotional displays, especially with a phalanx of nosy local police at the entrance, others watching them inside from the windows, Michel held Jennifer in his arms and kissed her. He allowed the moment to linger, until the cynical whistles and hoots drew them apart. A middle-aged man with bony hands scarred by fishhooks, and a face of stippled red skin which required a tub of Jennifer's magical moisturizing cream, sauntered over. He resembled the local spiny marine life, small eyes and rough-shelled.

"*Alors, Provence est arrivée,*" he observed.

"*Oui.* We're used to our unhurried pastimes in Aix."

"Well, there's no shortage of Pastis and oysters here. I'm Detective Superintendent Roussel."

Michel extended his hand. "Commander Danton, and this is my fiancée, Mademoiselle Bowen. We're getting married in"—Michel looked at his new Piaget, a wedding gift from Jennifer—"thirty-one hours, which is why—I hope you understand—I brought her along."

"*Bon chance.*"

Jennifer wore a pale blue suit with a scalloped-neck yellow silk blouse which exhibited her most prominent features. Roussel helplessly but with clear appreciation peered down the lovely chasm, then bowed so low he was at the level of her kneecaps.

Roussel smiled, revealing gapped front teeth and incisors that could snap the spine of a lobster. "In Brittany, the company of a beautiful woman never requires an explanation."

*"Merci, vous êtes très gentille, Monsieur Roussel . . . à bientôt, Michel."*

When Jennifer walked off, Roussel said, "My God, where did you find her?" He shook his head with incredulity. "And an American."

"It's the hormones they put in their beef and the bioengineered vegetables. That's why our government banned them. We don't want our women looking like my fiancée. The nation would go to hell," he said smugly.

"Oh, really," Roussel mused. "They told me that you were a crackpot."

"Absolutely true. It's been confirmed by psychiatrists. The fact is she saved my ass last summer in the Boynton case."

"Oh, yes, yes, I remember all the talk about it."

"She's no one to creep up on from behind in the dark."

"Ah, of course, the celebrated karate expert and gunfighter. Actually, I'd like to bring her home . . . to enlighten Madame Roussel, teach her a few tricks."

**Michel brought him** up to date on the possible connections between the case in Bruges and the kidnapping in Arles the previous night.

"You think the same people were involved with our young girl?" Roussel asked.

"That's what I'm here to investigate."

They were joined by Detective Jeanne Brique, a frowsy, hungover detective with lank, unwashed hair, no makeup, and an intimidating stare. She accompanied them to the dreary interrogation cubicle which smelled like a wrestlers' changing room. What altered these dreary circumstances was the presence of an angelic blond child whose delicate features would in another time have been immortalized by Raphael.

"This is Suzy Marquay, age thirteen. Stand up, girl, for Commander Danton." Detective Brique's growl was not conducive to intimate revelations.

"How are you, Suzy?" Michel asked.

"I'm tired."

"I am, too. Maybe we both need some fresh air. How about a coffee or a Coke?"

Still keeping an eye on the young girl, Michel took the detectives outside and listened to them protesting about his unorthodox approach. Legal procedure required a videotape or recording of his interview.

"I know the rules of interrogation. I have Charles Fournier spluttering at me, so I'm not going to try anything unconventional."

"Oh, God," Roussel said, "I heard him lecture on jurisprudence last year. Heaven help you."

"Then you know what I'm up against. I want to get to know Suzy. Let her relax before I bring her back. I won't be long and I promise not to ask her anything specific."


**"Suzy, please let's** be on a first-name basis. I'm here to help and gather information. Call me Michel. Commander sounds so pompous."

Michel thought of phoning Jennifer as he and the girl walked through the center of town. Suzy might be more comfortable and inclined to confide in a sympathetic woman rather than a brusque female detective. The Aven River flowed down, connecting with the tidal estuary, and eventually the sea. Before this union, it encountered rapids and millraces, then, pausing like a poetic caesura, it leisurely skimmed alongside the Bois d'Amour, a ripe preserve whose towering trees were reflected in dazzling shapes on the river's surface. Michel was distracted, wondering what to do.

"Who are you looking for?" Suzy asked.

"My fiancée. She came along to keep me company. We're going to be married on Saturday."

At this, Suzy brightened. Near the restored Pension Gloanec, Gauguin's residence during his stays in the town before leaving for Tahiti, Jennifer was lining up a photograph. Trust her not to buy a pack of postcards. She had a large ominous sack stationed beside her.

"Would you like a porter, mademoiselle?"

"Oh, Michel, just in time." She saw Suzy, smiled, and said, "Hello, I'm Jennifer."

"This is Suzy Marquay."

"You bought Breton clogs," Suzy said. "In our blue."

"They match my toes. I need to defend them from Michel's bathroom."

"I understand," the girl said. "Americans don't do well with our bathrooms."

"I'm thinking of giving Jennifer a course in ballet," Michel suggested, pushing open the bright red door of the Café des Artistes.

"He's a mind-reader. Are you as hungry as I am?"

They sat in a corner table by the window. The sunshine splayed through the swaying river weeds, inventing cryptic patterns.

"Did you purposely bring me here?" Suzy asked.

"No," Michel replied. "My parents and I came here when I was about fourteen. You see, Suzy, my mother is a chef. She and my father have a restaurant in Aix, and she was friendly with one of the cooks in town. While she was learning how to prepare langoustines in a millefeuille of potatoes, my father and I roamed around the menhirs and the tombs of stones. Then when he got bored, we went fishing."

"This was the café I was sitting in when the woman attacked me."

Jennifer stared at Michel with a hint of temper. "It wasn't planned, ladies, I assure you."

They ordered crêpes au confiture and café crèmes from a waiter with thick bifocals. Suzy began to relax, but her eyes darted around nervously.

Jennifer took the girl's hand. "You've been through a terrible time, *ma petite*."

Suzy shook her head glumly. "I'm glad you came, Michel. That woman detective was driving me crazy, making me say all sorts of things that didn't happen."

He nodded at Jennifer. "We won't do that."

They learned that Suzy lived with her grandmother in a small *chaumière,* a stone house with a thatched roof. Her grandmother made fine lace tablecloths, wimples for the local ladies to cover their high coiffures, and jabots, pleated frills women attached down the center folds of their blouses. Some sold to locals, but mostly tourists when they wanted to get themselves up as Gauguin's Breton women for costume parties. Her mother, Suzy went on, visited her during Christmas and sometimes in the summer, but lived in Paris, where she ran a designer boutique.

"Our house is at the edge of the Bois d'Amour."

Michel was reminded of the murder in Bruges. Caroline had lunched at a restaurant on the Lake of Love and he wondered if there might be some obscure correlation between the two places, both named for love. He'd contact Sylvie, who was now in Bruges interviewing witnesses.

"Do you think you were followed to the café?" he asked.

"It was during the day and I didn't notice."

"Why'd you come here?" Jennifer asked. "To meet some friends?"

Suzy stopped eating her crêpe and the jam oozed down her fork.

Michel smiled with understanding. "You have a boyfriend and your grandmother doesn't like him, either."

"My grandmother doesn't like men. She says we women can live without them and be much happier."

"I used to wonder about that myself," Jennifer agreed.

"No, I don't think so. I saw the way you looked at Michel."

They ate in silence for a few moments, and Michel determined that Suzy had withheld information and was deciding how to divert him.

"Suzy, let's do this in a genuine spirit of frankness. I desperately need your help. You see, two other girls have been taken and I believe the same people are involved."

The news stunned Suzy and her full lips quivered. Even in apprehension, she was enchanting, part of her still the child, the other clasping at womanhood, which placed her in the magical in-between passage so attractive to pedophiles.

"One girl is dead, another was kidnapped last night in Arles. When I heard that someone had escaped from these monsters — *you*, Suzy — Jennifer and I arranged to fly here to see you."

"It's a gang, Suzy. You must help if you can." With a solemn expression, Jennifer said, "I won't have a moment's pleasure on my honeymoon — unless Michel can find out who these people are and why they're kidnapping *women* like you."

The moment of decision had arrived and it never failed to thrill Michel. The actual person involved as either a suspect or the victim would be balancing deceit with self-exposure. Suzy leaned her head on Jennifer's shoulder and Jennifer embraced her.

Suzy and her fourteen-year-old lover always met at eleven in the morning on Friday, an off hour at the café. She would occupy a stall in the ladies' lavatory and the young man and she would touch each other.

*"Jamais le péntération! Je suis une vierge!"*

*"Entendú,"* Jennifer said. *"Dîtes moi, mon enfante."*

Despite his experience of a case in Corsica, in which children had been lovers and killed for thrills, the sophisticated, lascivious interior life of this thirteen-year-old child astounded Michel. She had revealed none of this to the Pont-Aven detectives.

Suzy had waited for Bobbie in their regular stall before the kid-napping attempt.

"When I heard a woman knock, I slipped on my top, stuffed my bra in my backpack, and peeked through. I was going to say that I'd been ill, but I'd already slipped the latch and suddenly she spun me around and put this gag over my mouth. She had her arm under my windpipe and her hip against the small of my back. She was so quick that I couldn't defend myself. She stuffed this disgusting rag on my face and pressed my head into it.

"I swayed, pretended I was unconscious, and I thought — this woman is so strong. A man was at the back exit in a black suit and chauffeur's cap. He had a car door open. It was a black or blue, maybe British racing green, four-door Mercedes. I told Detective Brique about it."

"Did you discuss anything else?"

"No, she's hateful . . . a brute. She suggested that I encouraged this, wanted to be kidnapped to create a drama because I craved attention."

Jennifer was enraged. "What a witch." She had handled wild, lawless girls before at her college and expertly tapped into their secrets. "What did this woman wear, smell like . . . her makeup, hair?"

A disjointed report followed. The woman wore a black baseball cap, dark sunglasses, reeked of Poison. She wore a cherry lipstick, and was carefully made up. "I know the perfume because I hate the scent. Her hair . . . might have been blond. She dragged me outside and acted as if I was drunk or stoned. This at eleven in the morning, like I was her spoiled daughter and she was rescuing me."

The waiter interrupted them, lowering his tray. *"Trois marcs ici."*

As he was about to put down the drinks, Suzy rose. *"Jean, ici des cafés."*

*"Ahh, merci, Suzy, J'ai oublie."*

"Jean, the waiter, rescued you?" Michel asked.

"Yes, he thought I was stealing kitchen supplies in the storage room in the back. Bobbie sometimes does."

Michel went to his Palm Pilot, which contained Suzy's total report. "Tell me about the time connection with you and your lover. Why do you meet at eleven o'clock?"

"No one's around at that time."

"Please go on, Suzy."

"This woman had small tits—like mine—and I pinched them, dug in my nails. She winced and slapped me. By that time Jean saw what was going on and rushed over. The woman let go of me, and she and the chauffeur dashed into the car and drove off."

"I should talk to Jean."

"He didn't actually see them and he wasn't wearing his glasses."

Suzy had already examined hundreds of photos of known sex offenders at the prefecture and not identified anyone.

Michel presented his card. "Thank you, Suzy. You've been wonderful. If you remember anything . . . anything else, please call me at this number. It's toll-free." Michel peeled out some cash from a thick roll and signaled for the check. "Oh, by the way, Suzy, I forgot to mention that the American girl who was murdered has very wealthy parents. They're suffering terribly, but the girl's father is thinking clearly. He's offered a reward of a million American dollars for information about his daughter's killers. Imagine, at today's exchange rate, that's about seven and a half million francs.

"A helpful clue and it could be yours. You'd also have the satisfaction of putting these savages in prison. I'm sure you'd have TV interviews, your photo in *Paris Match*. You're prettier than most of the young models in the magazines. People would think of you as modern day Jeanne d'Arc."

The information had a pernicious effect on Suzy. Michel studied her face as she reckoned this immense sum of money. Michel was about to rise from the table when Suzy zipped open a compartment of her backpack. Out came a rumpled tissue. She unwrapped it. It held a gem, which she placed in Michel's palm.

The silver earring had a small red engraving on it and the wiry loop was still intact. He turned it on its reverse side and saw in capital letters VENICE.

"The woman dropped it. I would never tell Detective Brique about this. She called me *une salope*. Am I a slut because I'm in love?"

Jennifer hugged her. "No, of course not. She's ignorant and jealous of you."

Michel was mystified, and wondered what Suzy's reason could be for withholding evidence.

"What were you going to do with it?"

"Keep it as a souvenir of my escape."


**At the Quimper** airport in the metal-roofed shanty reserved for government business, Michel inspected the earring under his magnifying loop and suggested that the kidnappers were Italian. He handed it Jennifer, who inspected it.

"This small figure engraved on it is a Minotaur. It's American," she said, "not Italian."

He stared at her intently. "Really, what makes you think that?"

"Michel, *you're* the detective. If it was made in Italy, it would be spelled V-e-n-e-z-i-a, not V-e-n-i-c-e. This is really well made, not cheap, and sterling silver from Venice, California. Lots of funky shops there and very talented artisans."

"Venice, California," he repeated. "There's a job opening at the Special Circumstances Section. You should consider applying. I'm not at all squeamish about being married to a detective."

"Hah, that'll be the day," she said in triumph. "You really don't know the Venice Boardwalk."

"I spent most of my time in Los Angeles downtown at Parker Center. When I had time off I'd go to Dodgers games and then drive out to the Valley with some of the detectives for barbecue at Uncle Hogly Wogly."

"Maybe one day, when we visit L.A., I'll take you Rollerblading on the Boardwalk. I used to go down for the day with some of the girls when I was teaching at Pembroke. We'd play paddle tennis. Oh, yes, you'll love the duck sausage at Jody Maroni's and we'll watch the weight lifters at Muscle Beach. It's a hoot."

By deviously involving Jennifer, he had gained a measure of support which he hoped would buy him more time to work on the case. It was worth playing the fool. She listened attentively while he reported to his staff, and prepared the lab scientists for more overtime. With their flight delayed to Marseille, Michel attempted to ease the strain they were both under. Tonight they were due at a ball given by the Chardins at their estate.

"*Merde,* I've lost the connection again," he bellowed in frustration.

Jennifer understood how profoundly committed he was to his work and at this moment her complaints and reservations dissipated. She tried to avoid vicarious scenarios but was incapable of ignoring the actual events: She put herself in Suzy's position; then the German girl kidnapped in Arles flashed through her mind. The emotional ordeal of Caroline Davis's parents haunted her. The prospect of taking a honeymoon and ignoring what had occurred would be impossible, repellent. There would be no honeymoon until the case was solved.

# CHAPTER 19

**Sylvie Caron worked fourteen** hours a day since arriving in Bruges to pursue the investigation Michel had initiated. She had interviewed the local detectives, who proved unhelpful and were complacently relieved that Caroline Davis's body had been found in France. They had contacted Interpol and as far as they were concerned there the matter rested. It was no longer a Belgian problem, nor an official embarrassment. Caroline had become rather like one of those secretive boarders seldom seen, existing in a region one of the judicial functionaries referred to as *oubli* — oblivion.

Sylvie had photocopied all of the reservations at the Kasteel Minnewater for the month of May. The holiday photographs taken by Jeff and Melanie had been developed in the SCS lab in Marseille, digitized and sent by computer to Brussels, printed out, then a police courier brought them to Die Swaene, where she was staying. She showed them to the waiters and maitre d' of the restaurant who remembered the family luncheon on the fatal day. She brought them to the staff at the Groeninge Museum, but none of them on duty had noticed the Davises, and there were no witnesses to the kidnapping.

At the end of her resources, she was walking around the Lake of Love with Caroline's distraught, tearful Aunt Mari. They had finished lunch at the Kasteel Minnewater, which Mari barely touched, and sat at the same table she had been at with her family. They stopped at a mossy bench. In these woods of love, the trees flush, the flower beds insane with purple tulips darkening at the edges, the rasp of boat engines in the distant canal, paradise seemed tangible. A conversation about a hideous murder was discordant amid these surroundings. Nevertheless, Sylvie brought out the photos.

Mari adjusted her glasses. "It's obscene to see myself smiling."

"You're all happy," Sylvie rejoined.

"It was an occasion to rejoice. We had a fax—Caroline had been picked for the All-American Girls Junior Team. She's a golf prodigy. Maybe a female version of Tiger Woods."

Sylvie flinched imperceptibly. She had been at the autopsy and seen Caroline only in death.

"These group photos of the four of you are superb, much better than any of the others."

"They should be. Jan took them."

"Jan?"

"He's a very old friend and a celebrated photographer."

"Do you have his address?"

"Of course I do. We've been delivering flowers to him or one of his guests forever. He's a charming man."

Mari Rodenstuck's pinched face and the tallow cast of her skin were in marked contrast to the beaming woman in the photos who, despite her heart condition, appeared vivacious and serene.

Sylvie roved through a list of names. "Do you know Mr. Van Hemmes?"

"Yes, his wife and I are bridge partners. He's completed a month of chemo with good results."

"What about . . . there's a Mr. Werve?"

"Wilhelm lives in Ghent. He's a stockbroker and works with me at the flower show. The famous *Floralies* we have there. I'm one of the organizers."

This small-town provincial society resembled those of Provence's: a composition of people who knew each other well, their families, scandals, relatives, for years. Where could she find some opening? Michel certainly would have uncovered something useful.

"Look, I have the restaurant's reservation cards for May. These three names are always on the list."

"They all have their *Stammtisch*." Sylvie was puzzled. "They're regulars and have the same table. In fact, a day or two before I took the family to lunch, it was Jan who suggested it. I was in the shop and he came in for some flowers. He had guests visiting—I think some fellow artists—from America and I sent them a special arrangement."

"Do you have the names of the guests?"

"No, Jan collected them. I believe they were staying at Die Swaene."

"My hotel."

"My dear Sylvie, what's so unusual? I send out hundreds of these a month." With a temper flare, she said, "I have the most successful florist shop in Bruges."

"I know that Madame Rodenstuck. I'm exploring for a pattern and some incongruity in it. Caroline's kidnapping wasn't a random episode. We've had two of them in France since hers. My boss is in Pont-Aven, and the rest of our team is in Arles."

"I wish you French had been this meticulous during World War Two. Perhaps we wouldn't have been occupied as you were—if you'd acted."

"My father, madame, was in the Underground and served General de Gaulle when he was president."

Sylvie regretted her acrimonious outburst, but, even after more than half a century, patriotism was a sensitive issue with the French.

"I'm sorry, Sylvie, *mais mon père* was tortured by the Nazis."

"These wounds never heal, do they?"

"Apart from helping with your flower show, what can you tell me about Mr. Werve?"

"He's just about crippled from arthritis, but gallant still and a marvel when it comes to the telephone and getting sponsors for the show."

Sylvie scanned her list of names and wrote down brief comments.

"What about this photographer, Jan Korteman? How old is he?"

Mari thought for a moment. "Sixty, possibly a bit younger. A bachelor."

"Gay?"

"*Au contraire.* He had an American woman stay with him. I've never beheld breasts like hers. I assume they have factories that produce them in America. She was a sexpot who looked exactly like that actress on that beach series."

"*Baywatch*? It's the rage in France."

"Yes, I think so. There was publicity—even here—about some disreputable film the actress made."

"Her husband and she filmed themselves making love and someone stole the film. It's all over the Internet. They were innocent victims."

"Oh, well," she responded with declining interest.

"So Mr. Korteman's girlfriend resembles Pamela Anderson."

"I'm not an expert on this, but some of the locals thought it was her. Or her double."

"Do you know what happened to this woman who visited?"

"I assume she went back home. I haven't seen her since . . . I don't recall."

Sylvie accompanied Mari back to the flower shop, admired the imaginative designs of the florists who were preparing arrangements for a wedding. Mari was thumbing through the Rolodex at the till.

"Jan has a grand house over the canal." She wrote down the address and phone number for Sylvie. "I don't think there's any point trying to contact him."

"Why?"

"Jan goes to France in June. He has a villa there."

"Could it be in Arles?"

"No, it's just outside Avignon. I toured Provence five years ago and he had me to dinner. Beautiful gardens and sculptures. He's a collector of fine art."

"He must do very well as a photographer."

"He inherited the Korteman fortune." Sylvie waited as Michel would have and refrained from prodding her. "His father owned the largest supermarket chain in Belgium."

With speed and dexterity, Mari composed an exquisite bouquet of roses, tulips, sunflowers, and greens that had the timeless quality of a Monet painting. She presented it to Sylvie in a cane basket.

"Sylvie, I hate to admit this, but *you* have made me feel better.

You've convinced me that someone gives a damn about my Caroline"—Mari lost her self-control and sobbed—"and someone's doing something."

**On Sylvie's return** to Die Swaene, the management refused to allow her to examine their guest registry without the authorization of the police. The police needed a judicial writ and she realized that she'd be in a swamp of red tape. In her room, she tossed her clothes on the floor, slipped on a crumpled denim shirt, and took a swig of the cold bottle of genever she had bought and swallowed it with guilty pleasure.

She plugged in her laptop and went on-line. Searching. She typed in the name Jan Korteman, then clicked on his elaborate website. He was the author of seven books, all with astounding dollar prices and the injunction that the person had to be eighteen.

> *Love in Amsterdam and Hamburg, $15,000*
> *Women in Love, $17,000*
> *Men in Love, $22,000*
> *Mutilations, $29,000*
> *Women and their Pets, $31,000*
> *For Love of the Dead, $52,000*
> *Fetish and Tantra Maithuna, $94,000*

There were no sample pages or downloads of Jan's romances. All of the titles were signed limited editions. Pornography for millionaires. She printed out the page for herself before forwarding it on e-mail to Michel.

**She was on** the hunt. After a shower and a change of clothes—a red leather miniskirt and black blouse opened at the neckline to reveal her tattoo—she wandered in to the Dreupelhuisje, one of the liveliest taverns in Bruges. She had been told by the concierge it was a local favorite. She spotted an empty section at the stained old bar where a young man was serving. She knew there wasn't a corner of the earth where a pretty French bohemian couldn't get her way.

She ordered a short beer and the house genever. The glass was filled to the lip, as was the rule, which forced the patron to lean forward for a first sip and in effect bow to the barman. His eyes plundered her and she smiled.

"You bought a small bottle earlier."

"You're so observant," she said with a musical lilt in her voice. "I love Bruges. Flemish men are spectacular."

His name was Pieter and he agreed.

"I have my break in a few minutes. May I join you?"

"*Bien sûr. Je m'appelle Sylvie.*"

"*Enchanté.*"

They sat at a garden table and he was quick to light her Gauloise and ask flattering questions.

"It's impossible for you to be visiting alone."

"Ah, well, I am. I thought I was going to meet someone, but it's like the Truffaut film . . . *Jour pour Nuit.*"

"Ah, yes, the couple who keep missing each other. Maybe *our* meeting was destined."

"Wouldn't that be lovely?" She sipped the genever he had brought out. "Possibly you know the gentleman who was going to interview me. Jan Korteman."

Pieter frowned. "I should have expected you'd be looking for him." His tone was an admixture of pique and disappointment. "Jan always finds the beauties."

"Well, I haven't met him yet. It was just an interview for a photo shoot."

"I'm sure," Pieter replied with a cynical nod.

Her eyes sparkled and she smiled at the crestfallen barman. "Who knows, meeting you could be even better."

His spirits rose. "Do you really think so?"

He waffled on about his future as an engineer when he completed his studies. He was only working at bars part-time to spell regulars on holiday.

"What's Jan like?"

"International, very rich, and frankly he's a marvelous photographer. People, especially women, visit him from all over the world."

"I heard about him from an American lady."

"Heather." He extended his palms a foot from his chest. "We've never seen anything as prodigious as her."

"Really?" Sylvie touched his hand. "Were you panting?"

"No, Sylvie, a woman like you makes me pant."

"I'll try to do even better when you're through for the night."

Pieter was flabbergasted by the overture, but handled it with a sleek, lothario style. "Believe me, I won't let you down."

Sylvie ignored the lamentable schoolboy bravado and continued to wheedle him. "I can't believe the stories I've heard about Jan. Just as well I missed him."

"He certainly keeps the gossip churning. Half the people in town go into mourning when he leaves for France."

She had seen Michel build scenarios by linking fragments and she tested his technique.

"Actually, Pieter, there was an American couple visiting him—oh, I can't remember their names."

"Oh, that's probably Darrell and the enchanting Maddie. Everyone adored them. He's so interesting—a painter and she's his model and inspiration."

"Darrell and Maddie," she repeated, and suppressed her agitation. These were the names of the couple who had been on a rampage of murder the previous summer in Aix. "I'm sorry I didn't get to meet them."

"They were great," Pieter said wistfully, as though bar friendships were eternal. "Actually, she does very artistic piercings and he does tattoos like yours," he added with a leer. "She also works on Hollywood films as a makeup artist."

"How exciting."

Sylvie leaned forward and took his hand, pressing it against her breast. "Pieter, I'm so happy to have found you." She allowed him to linger on her flesh. "I would have loved to have met Maddie. I want a piercing, in a private place," she said, moving her lips close to him before reaching for another cigarette. "Did Darrell and Maddie leave their business card?"

Pieter's arousal, religious in its intensity, gave way to one of wrath when he was tapped on the shoulder by a beer-smelling soak of a bartender. Pieter gave her a hapless look.

*"Je m'excuse, mademoiselle,"* the man said, yanking Pieter to his feet. "We've got a barful of dirty glasses and angry customers. Now get your ass back before I kick it out."

# CHAPTER 20

**Garrett twitched and squirmed** all night, aflame with anticipation of the first morning's work on his canvas. They were now in a small studio bedroom, reserved for Jan's previously involuntary guests. Garrett hopped in and out of bed half a dozen times, scratching at his large sketch pad, the green-hooded reading lamp low over the table. Eve kept silent, recognizing that Garrett was in the thrall of one of his creative outbursts, fertile as spring's appearance. At times like this, she would speak only if he asked her something. Interruptions were intolerable to him, dangerous to his train of thought.

Eve checked on Caroline regularly. At about four A.M. they heard her groan. Eve dashed out to find out what Caroline needed. The house was always chilled and the damp foggy effluvium from the canals, mystical during the day, but sepulchral and frigid at night, made her grit her teeth when she slipped on a robe.

"The girl's groggy and crying," she informed Garrett.

"Don't be a soft touch and let her con you. She's been a spoiled rich kid all her life, a golf geek. You're not her caddy. Let her know she can't have everything she wants."

"I know what to do. Garrett, you've got a long day ahead, try to get some rest. I might shoot her up with a tranquilizer."

"Inject it between the toes. Whatever you do, make sure she's not bruised. I put some pillows under her ass. Jesus, I haven't seen one that supple and firm for ages."

"Good genes."

He sniggered. "Better than mine, babe."

When he dozed off, Eve glanced at the sketch pad and relished the art that would emerge. She returned a half hour later and Garrett jerked awake. He suffered from a condition called jactitation caused by the flurry of dream binges and stress. Sometimes he leaped up screaming, virtually jumping out of his skin.

"How's the princess?"

"Hungry."

"I don't want her eating and getting bloated."

**At eight in** the morning after a breakfast of soft-boiled eggs, brioches and strong coffee, Jan set up his video cameras, adjusted the lighting and screwed his Hasselblad into the tripod, moving it close to the table where Caroline lay squirming. Garrett removed the red silk handkerchief tied around her mouth. Jan had suggested duct tape, but that would have broken the skin. Caroline's blue eyes were agape and she started to scream. Garrett pressed his hand over her mouth.

"I don't want you to stretch your facial muscles. I'll explain what's going to happen. If you scream again, I promise to hurt you . . . very badly. Now blink your eyes to say yes."

She did as she was ordered and he released his powerful grip, scowling at the red marks his pressure had caused on her cheeks.

"No damage done."

Disoriented, Caroline raised her head from the table and looked at Garrett first, then circled to Jan, the cameras.

"A woman kidnapped me," she stated in a calm voice.

"Yes, Caroline, she did. I'm sure you would have refused if she'd sent an invitation."

"May I please have something to drink, sir?"

"We have Perrier. Evian, if you prefer still water."

"Thank you. Still water. You're American."

"Yes." He untied the black silk drape cords and the thick leather restraints around her ankles. He extended his hand and touched her powerful callused hand.

Jan watched the scene with the absorption of a medical student. He wheeled over a metal hospital trolley and poured a glass of water, which he handed to Caroline.

"Welcome to my home, Caroline. I know your Aunt Mari very

well. We've discussed your exploits on the golf course. She's very proud of you."

Caroline recognized him as the bogus chauffeur who had abetted the woman in her kidnapping. She'd never forget that affected English accent blanketing the original Flemish. She arched her back and shrank from him. Garrett took Jan aside and informed him that he needed to be alone to interview his subject. After a moment, Jan reluctantly left the room.

"Now, Caroline, you haven't been hurt or sexually attacked."

Garrett's friendly fraternal attitude was at once disarming and menacing. Since the photographer had brought up golf, she moved to her home grounds.

"I've got to start hitting some balls at the range. I'll be playing in the U.S. Junior Open in July. I may have a shot at finishing in the top ten if my putting and short game don't desert me."

"Golf is a game for people with strong nerves," Garrett said with a winning smile.

Caroline suppressed a troubled laugh. "Tell me."

Garrett found himself emotionally engaged—the artist enamored of his model, as Gauguin had frequently been. Caroline's fortitude in this moment of stress impressed him. She had a superb sense of how to adjust to circumstances and she gained his respect.

"Can I get up and stretch?"

Garrett helped her from the table. She was wobbly and he assisted her.

"That woman I met in the museum drugged me."

"I'm sorry, it was the only way."

Caroline, in white silk shorts and T-shirt (courtesy of Eve), tested her reflexes and began a stretching routine. Limber and athletic, she was a delight to watch. I have a goddess, Garrett reflected.

"Please, can I have something to eat? You want me to be happy, don't you . . . instead of acting like an old crab? I'd kill for a plate of bacon and eggs."

"It's too heavy, Caroline," Garrett advised her with a giggle. "We've got to get you off junk food."

"Pizza?" she said with a wink. "And I don't care if it's cold. We can nuke it."

She stalked around the studio like a sightseer and, in a matter of moments, gained a certain assurance. They weren't going to harm her and she fell effortlessly into the procedure she had been taught by her father's security personnel, who had lectured her and her wealthy circle of girlfriends and fellow students at Santa Linda, the exclusive school in Monterey:

*Don't panic. Crying won't help. Don't make threats. Never mention the police. Be self-assured but not arrogant. Make friends if you can. Cut a deal.*

"How about a piece of toast and a milkshake?" Caroline asked. "If you show me the kitchen, I'll make us all one."

Garrett smiled, enchanted by her. "What a piece of work you are."

"Grace under pressure," she said. "I've been trying to make three-foot putts since I was"—she lowered the palm of her hand to indicate half her actual height—"since I was that small."

"Mom teach you to play?"

"Uh-huh, she's a pro at Otter Rock. Look, Mr. . . . ?"

"Call me GG. I'm the son of a great painter."

Caroline laughed. "That's easy to remember and kinda cute." She snooped around, looked down at the canal several stories below. The window was flush, with no ledge. Her fingers touched her smooth hairless arms, then her legs, and she realized that she had been shaved.

"You're not going to hurt me, are you?"

"I'll certainly try not to," Garrett assured her.

She found GG unthreatening and indeed amicable. Slim, boyish, and with sculpted features and light green eyes; his short dark brown hair had been beautifully cut. He had a warmth that she had not expected and was in fact attractive. Not quite Rob Lowe, she thought, but in that *West Wing* club.

"GG, since we're fellow Americans, maybe you know who my dad is."

"No, honestly, I don't. Tell me about him."

"My dad's Jeffrey Davis. He's the chairman and founder of Janus Micro-Tech."

"I've heard of him. Bill Gates is his pal, huh?"

"I don't know about that. There's mutual respect, but they're rivals," she informed him.

"Superstar leagues."

"I guess." She wondered how to broach the next topic without upsetting the fragile balance and offending him. The camera equipment was intimidating, and the Flemish man, who had left, struck her as dangerous. "That creep's not going to do some kind of porn film of me and sell it on the Internet?"

Garrett's right hand flew to his breast in outrage. "No way, Caroline. I'm no child molester. I would never touch a young woman, a virgin. I hate molesters."

As though approaching a long putt for a par, Caroline took a deep breath. "Thank you," she cheeped in a small voice.

"I'm going to immortalize you."

This leap into the dense rough of the unknown baffled her. "Are you an artist . . . a great painter, sculptor?" she asked with enthusiasm.

He closed his eyes, imagining their collaboration. "Yes, I am, and you're going to become art. We'll work together."

His fervor was hypnotic, overwhelming to her, and she rushed into his arms and he found himself touched by her purity of heart, and held her. She lingered, struggling to feel secure, and clung to him.

"So you're going to take some pictures of me . . . like do some portraits?"

He released his grip on her. "Well, not exactly. You see, Caroline, skin is my medium."

She was suddenly wary. "Skin. . . . What are you talking about? How do you paint skin?" Her face quickly brightened and she winked at him. "Oh, like cowboys and Indians?"

"No. Not . . . not exactly. Have you ever wanted a tattoo?"

The gravity of his intention froze her.

"A tattoo. . . . No, no, never. My friend Annabelle Connors had one done in Salinas—a little red dragon on her shoulder. Her parents went ballistic and they sent her to a plastic surgeon. She went through months of laser surgery which hurt like hell to get rid of it. Even now you can see the faint outline. She's got these bubbles under her skin. Her mother is talking about a skin graft—all because of a lousy little dragon."

Garrett sat down on the table and regarded Caroline with her sorrow.

"I wouldn't do anything like that to you. I'm going to make my version of the Garden of Eden, something timeless and beautiful, eternal, an inspiration to the world."

Caroline was drowning in frantic images and found herself sucked into the grotesque aura that Garrett exuded. She detected a quality of madness that was by turns repellent and fascinating. He was like a coiled snake about to strike. His volatile moods, accompanied by sleek changes of tone, kept her off balance. Her thought pattern was instantaneous. She imagined her mother playing on the pro golf tour. When Melanie found herself with a bad lie, she'd analyze her options. Play safe and make par; go for the flag and hit a perfect shot over the lake and make birdie to win.

"GG, I want to trust you. Be my friend, please?"

His compassionate side became evident to her. "Believe me, I have nothing but tender and noble feelings toward you, Caroline."

"I can tell. GG, I'm an only child. My mother can't have any more kids. I don't have mental problems. I'm not a stuck-up little princess or a whiner. I adore my parents and my Aunt Mari. We're a family . . . and thanks to my Dad—he's a genius—he made a fortune. He's set up scholarship funds for students." She hunched her shoulders. "I can't even imagine how much, like a hundred million dollars. He's going to start an on-line university, so people of all ages from any country can take courses and get a degree. He's not going to charge them, either."

Garrett got down off the table and patiently moved to a leather wing chair. He instantly navigated through the waters she was about to chart for them.

"Scholarships." The word resonated in his consciousness. The scholarship fund in San Antonio had been funded through blackmail and Dina Marcuro's murdered lodgers. "I wish I'd had parents like yours," he said, finely gauging her temperament. "Go on, Caroline. I'm really interested in what you're saying."

"GG, if I was older, I'd love to date you and we could find out all sorts of great things about each other. But my mother and father are frantic—I am, too." Her shoulders bunched and she huddled against the window jamb. "My lovely Aunt Mari might've—God forbid—had a stroke, like that phony chauffeur told me when your girlfriend grabbed me and pulled me into the car."

He waited for the fastball.

"My dad told me and some of my girlfriends"—he noted the blush of the lie—"that if we were ever in a situation like this, to be open and friendly and to tell this person, or people . . . I'm getting confused . . . that money was no object. *Ten million dollars* was what he was talking about. To offer that. These parties could go to Brazil or wherever—oh, his associate mentioned Thailand—and have plastic surgery, if they wanted that, and nobody would ever bother them for the rest of their lives.

"Look, GG, if you have a computer or a phone, I have a special number to call. You can speak to the people at the other end." She encountered an impassive expression on his face that she couldn't read. "Call the number yourself from another phone, anywhere. Come on, give me a little slack."

"Wow, this is a lot to think about," he replied finally. "Okay. You broke me down. What kind of shake do you want? We've got maybe five different flavors. Chocolate, I'll bet."

She dropped to her knees and kissed his hand.

"You're right! Chocolate. You've just become a millionaire."


**Garrett withdrew. Caroline,** unbound, remained in the soundproof room adjoining the studio for almost an hour while he conferred with Eve, who was deeply upset by his decision. She demanded that he bring Jan into the conversation. The bluff photographer had implied during his morgue photography that he was accustomed to these cases, but Eve did not quite believe him. He had another agenda and was committed to Heather. He wanted to introduce Caroline to Tantric sexual exercise.

Garrett had no doubt that Jan and Heather had an alliance, or else Jan would not have been so indiscreet about Heather's behavior—as if anything he revealed about her might be damaging or surprising in its shock value. He and Eve clearly had plans that would clash with his.

After the discussion ended, Eve, like a battered servant, carried a tray upstairs with the blender and the ingredients for a shake.

Caroline looked Eve over and was surprised at how pretty she was. A slender blue-eyed blonde, wearing a bright gold sweater with a floppy sunflowered blouse collar outside, shiny, black leather jeans, and Mephistos. Eve, her kidnapper, was not threatening in real, undrugged life. She was a bit shorter than GG; together they must've made an angelic couple. They did not fit the image of violent, insane criminals. Caroline was bewildered by this sudden insight.

"What're you serving this time—cyanide?"

"Give me a break. Mix it yourself and we'll drink it. But on an empty stomach, you'll have gas."

Caroline moved closer to Eve, then sniffed the air.

"A woman shouldn't do this to another woman. I mean . . ." Caroline wrenched away from the tray on the large table. "I'm starting to remember all sorts of horrible, disgusting things . . . I was being bathed by you . . . your perfume . . ."

"It's Poison. Don't you like it? It's GG's favorite."

Her offhand manner infuriated Caroline. "You, you're a *traitor*. You shaved my privates and stuck your finger inside me. You had a glove on like my doctor."

"You're a virgin, Caroline."

"Hello, surprise, surprise. I guess in your crowd, a girl gets her cherry popped when she's five!"

Eve was taken aback. "I wanted to protect you from the old man—our host. He's a little too interested in you and thought he could . . . Look, it was the only way. GG and I read him the riot act. We don't tolerate sexual abuse."

"Just drugging young girls and kidnapping, right?"

The accusation pierced Eve's emotional defenses and she knew that her face reflected the distress she herself felt.

"We do things for love, Caroline, and sometimes we go beyond that, in the name of art."

# CHAPTER 21

**At Jennifer's insistence, Michel** made an appointment to have his hair cut at Denise's salon, which she considered the best in town. The dreaded Denise Casson, Aix's middle-aged femme fatale, was waiting in her shop for him. She had been Louise's closest friend and her traveling companion when the two women went trolling for young men. This activity had come to light the previous year while he was investigating Louise's murder. Michel abhorred the vulgar proprietress, and she him, but they tolerated each other. A cold peace had been established after his mother's murder.

"Come on, move, I'll wash you myself and get you out of here." She nudged him to the sink in the rear through a flotilla of housewives in various stages of dishabille and, in some cases, decomposition. She thrust a heavy black waterproof smock on him. "My God, when did you last have it cut?"

"I don't remember."

She shoved him in a chair, yanked his head back, turned on the water, and ran her hands through the tangled vines. "Looks like it was done in a pet shop in Tonga. You know, Michel, you're marrying a very beautiful woman. You should make some effort to be fashionable—*comme il faut.*"

She sprinkled him with shampoo and her educated fingers riffed pleasurably along his scalp and temples. When she completed the wash, she bulled him along to the Mistress's stall, lit like a film set and featuring a glass showcase with her trophies; the Golden Scissors Award from the 1994 Paris show held pride of place. He regarded these triumphs with skepticism and she was quick to take offense and give it.

"Great stars show their Oscars, these are mine."

"Yes, I can see that yours is a lifetime of achievements."

She threateningly switched on the electric razor. "One more word out of you, and you'll have a buzz cut and sideburns dyed green."

Denise snipped his hair like a jeweler setting a rare gem, constantly standing back to admire her skill.

"I heard about your depraved spree in Marseille. It's about time they hired a detective who caught criminals instead of someone who strips for men. By the way, have you caught the people who murdered the American girl?" He ignored her. "How about the German girl kidnapped in Arles? Did you find her yet? No? Well, why am I not surprised? Maybe your replacement will do a better job."

Despite these insults, the haircut was going well, a discernible, sculpted shape was emerging, and he chose to ignore her slander.

"Has Philippe had a talk with you?"

"About what?"

"What to do on your honeymoon night."

"No, I bought a book."

"I'll give you an interactive demonstration of what women like when I'm through cutting." She turned to the young manicurist. "Simone, get your pruning shears, the big-shot detective needs a clipping. *C'est affreux,* you can't touch a woman with those nails. They're only good for climbing trees. I'm afraid to think what your toenails must be like."

"Nobody touches my toes."

"I'll bet you've got bear claws and holes in your socks. Only an American would marry you," she rabbited on. "A Frenchwoman would never have you."

His tailor's mistress, the strapping Irmegard Kold, trooped in with her daughter Kristen. Since Michel had to invite Vellancio as a matter of form, the tailor had decided to emulate the late President Mitterand, who, at state dinners, included his mistress, their illegitimate daughter, and, to keep the ménage happy, his wife, of course. All very civilized and resonant of *parité,* the new feminist call to arms. *Liberté, egalité, fraternité* was an all-male province, a bitter leftover from the Revolution, which made no mention of women's rights.

Irmegard ran a hiking, biking, sightseeing, tour company—shuttling sloths on river barges for four-hour lunches, and launching the stout-hearted to the mountains in the Lubéron. She possessed a travel agent's brazen effusiveness; as Michel was trapped by the manicurist—unable to defend himself—she kissed him on both cheeks.

"Kristen, say hello to Commander Danton," she ordered her ravishingly sylvan, platinum blond daughter, whose willowy figure held out the certainty of anguish and paranoia for a future boyfriend. In Vellancio's favor, he treated the girl like Juliet Capulet, protective of her maidenhood. Once the beefy tailor had even pointed his rusty Beretta at an aristocratic client who wished to purchase her.

"Hel-lo." Kristen squeezed out the word as though it were a stubborn blackhead.

"*Bonjour,* Kristen."

"Did you organize your cops to take trips with us?"

"Not yet, Kristen. I'm working on it."

"Good. You look adorable with short hair, Michel."

"And don't be quoting Delilah; every clip hurts and weakens me."

Mother and daughter wore shorts, heavy boots, and their blond hair in ponytails.

"I met Jennifer's mother at Vellancio's and I'm going to give her a personal tour of the area while you and your enchantress are away."

"I owe you a debt of gratitude, Irme," he said. "If Vellancio ever threatens you, call me."

Her laughter had a boom-boom effect on her untethered bosom. "Tents under the stars," she went on expansively, "bathing and washing in streams, sunning ourselves *nu comme un ver*—as God intended us to be."

"Yes, the Garden of Eden should make everyone happy." He turned and snarled at Simone. "No polish! There's enough gossip about me."

"Relax, Michel, I was just going to buff you."

*     *     *

**Starved, and in** a growling mood, Michel stopped at Les Deux Garçons and took a table outside in the corner. His neck felt exposed, hairless, and his fingers tingled. Perhaps there was neuritis in the obscure gene pool he had been bequeathed by Louise and his American father. Someday, he might to try to track down his siblings; it was unsettling to think he had a half-brother and half-sister somewhere in America. Would they welcome him or be horrified? His reflections suddenly dissolved when, in a spinning spoke of sunlight, Jennifer appeared. She seemed to shimmer in her summer dress, of red poppies bordered with field green. A number of tourists' heads turned toward her as though enduring a tropism. She was radiantly beautiful, his goddess.

He stood up, and the voracious eyes of the people in the café followed Jennifer, waiting expectantly for some action. She kissed him and he slid over on the banquette; the prying eyes returned to their companions and newspapers.

"Denise gave you a great cut."

"All I need is an acoustic guitar and I'll do a hip-hop act."

"I'd pay to see you."

"You'd have to prostrate yourself."

"That's a high price for admission." She swiveled his head like that of mannequin. "Dynamite. I can't wait. If you lost some more weight, I think you'd resemble Scottie Pippen a little. He has these wonderful Egyptian features."

"Playing basketball and changing my skin pigmentation wasn't part of our treaty."

It was now four and he had forgotten to eat and he glared at the waiter, who was on his cell phone ordering *his* dinner at home. Jennifer, on a diet, ordered her regular Earl Grey, no pastry, and he a Pastis and saucisson sandwich.

"Your last night as a single man. Do you have any plans?" she asked.

"*Malhereusement,* I have to go into Marseille. Sylvie Caron is due in from Brussels and it's urgent."

He was on the verge of adding that Sylvie might have a lead

when a familiar couple stood over them. Jennifer stared at them for a moment, glanced quizzically at Michel, then back at the man and woman.

"How're you doing, Michel?" the man asked.

"Not as well as I'd hoped."

Before Michel could explain, Melanie Davis forced herself to smile at Jennifer. "I know we're intruding, Ms. Bowen, but we can't help ourselves."

"Oh, Jesus, I thought I recognized you. You're Caroline's parents," Jennifer said, shocked by their presence. "Forgive me."

Pulling out two cane chairs, Jeff said, "May we join you?"

"Please, please do," Jennifer said.

They sat down opposite them, ordered tea, and Jeff took a crammed folder out of his briefcase.

"We've read everything we could about the two of you—and the Boynton murder case last summer. My office is very thorough," Jeff advised him.

"Frankly, Michel, my husband and I are very impressed with your credentials."

"I don't think I'll get my PGA card, Melanie."

"For murder you already have it. In this trap, I'd put my money on you rather than Tiger Woods."

Jennifer gave her a reassuring nod. "It is a trap. Michel and I were up at four this morning and flew to Pont-Aven"—she turned to Michel, who did not signal her to desist—"and I don't think I'm compromising the investigation by telling you that Michel did that so that he could interview the young girl the couple tried to kidnap there."

"And . . . ?" Jeff asked.

"She was helpful," Michel admitted.

"Look, Jennifer, if I may, we're still here because our daughter was murdered! We understand your situation and what an invasion of your privacy this is. We know you're getting married tomorrow. But what else can we do? We can't face going home."

"Let Michel do his job," she insisted.

"Fine," Jeff agreed, "but when? After your honeymoon?"

Jennifer was under attack and in an instant controlled her displaced anger.

"There isn't going to be a honeymoon," she said with a grimace. "Just one night in Avignon after we're married and my husband will be at work the next day." With distaste she shoved away the thick folder of clippings on the table. "Frankly, I've gotten myself emotionally involved with Caroline and the other girls. I can't think of anything else."

"Do you mean that, Jennifer?" Melanie asked.

"Absolutely. Do you think we're the kind of people who could be rambling around while some freak is murdering children?"

The Davises had a resurgence of hope. Melanie picked up Jennifer's hand and kissed it.

"Please . . . don't," Jennifer protested. "I don't know what it must be like to lose a child. But a few years ago I was engaged to a man who was murdered while he was at an ATM. I can project myself. I wanted revenge and an end to it." She looked at Michel in a somber mood. "I'm about to marry a man who'll always be more married to murder than he ever will be to me. And maybe that's why I fell in love with him."

# CHAPTER 22

**The bell tower tolled** twelve noon and Aix's old quarter was a bottleneck of gawking townspeople, festive sightseers, and police barricades. Michel walked abreast of Leon Stein, Jules Chardin, and Philippe. Like four musketeers they strode into the Cathedral of St-Sauveur, down the immense Gothic nave past Saint Mitre's sarcophagus and Nicolas Froment's masterful triptych of *The Burning Bush,* revealing King René and Queen Jeanne kneeling beside the Virgin, who held the infant Jesus. Michel had been baptized and confirmed here. To complete the trinity of manhood, he was about to be married in this sacred church.

Hundreds of people were craning their necks for a look at him, smiling, nodding, all of their faces blurred. When he reached the altar, he felt faint. The police chief had arranged an escort for Jennifer's party. She would enter from the cloisters and come down the Romanesque nave. At the last moment, Rosalind had thrown a snit and hired a Rolls-Royce from some Marseille rent-a-hearse company rather than sit in the back of Philippe's new Mercedes SUV. There had been a sharp exchange between them at Chez Danton.

Michel whispered to his former psychiatrist, "Do you have any amyl nitrites with you?"

"If you were a twenty-year-old blonde on your knees in my office, I might pop one. But not in church, Michel."

"I'm having a panic attack."

"Don't worry about it. I'll give you CPR."

"My skin is clammy. Do something."

Leon peered around. "I'm glad to see Claude's here. His rich new girlfriend is one of my patients. She's always got some coke on her. Shall I ask? We can cut some lines on the Bible if you like. There's the archbishop, maybe he's got some in his surplice."

"*Messieurs, attention!*" Philippe was on them like a junkyard Alsatian. "*Silence, Jennifer vienne.*"

Stupefied with fright, Michel now idly wondered if he needed glasses, an intraocular implant, oxygen.

With the choir chirping Monteverde madrigals, the ravishing Kristen and her comely school friends paraded down the aisle with flower baskets, throwing lavender and rose petals into the air.

The veiled bride appeared in a dazzling strapless point d'Alençon lace dress with a train. Trust Vellancio to bleed Louise's fortune dry on his guileless bride. Her maid of honor was her mother; the bridesmaid, Grace Chardin.

At that moment, Michel realized that someone was missing from his party. He looked around for his mother. Nicole finally appeared from behind a medieval arras, like one of Shakespeare's assassins. She hugged him, and her silk sleeve caressed him like a butterfly wing.

"Thank the Lord you're here," Michel murmured. "I thought I was going to pass out."

"Me, too. I had to adjust the velouté sauce your father made for the Lobster Cardinal. It had the consistency of that paste Golarde uses for wallpapering. It just stuck to the spoon, invulnerable to gravity."

"What did you do?" he asked.

"I had to defrost five quarts of *fumet* to thin it. . . . Sorry to be late."

He held the small of his mother's back. Her luminous eyes held his with overpowering adoration as though he were a god. He knew then that he could never reveal that he knew the truth about his nativity. Some secrets were worth keeping. She read his mind.

"If only Louise were here."

"I have you. That's enough for me."

"We must build a little chapel at the farm for her on the brow of the poppy field. She loved the spring flare of the red."

The choral singing gave way to Debussy's wistful string quartet, which Jennifer had selected, giving Mahler a reprieve. It was one of her favorite pieces. Jennifer moved slowly, almost uncertainly toward them, nodding to well-wishers.

"I couldn't have picked a better mother than you," Michel said tearfully, watching Jennifer's advance.

"Or a better wife." Nicole studied the bride. "Maybe the three of us can live together."

"What about Papa?"

"Roz has a crush on him and I think they're on the verge of an affair."

"Wouldn't that be lovely for all of us."

"After the row about the Rolls-Royce for Jennifer, they made up. He fondled her on the *boules* court while I was boiling fish heads for the *fumet*."

"What? I thought I was having an anxiety attack before you got here. Now I'm hysterical. He hates Roz."

"It was a ruse. Think of it, Michel. The freedom I'd have. Visits to San Francisco. Nonconjugal for me, filial perhaps for you. I've read about the markets there. I so want to see it before I fall apart. They'll buy my *confits,* all of my products. I'll sell them through catalogs and on-line."

As a detective, he was intrigued by what went on in people's minds. What, he wondered would the relationship be if Philippe and Roz somehow or other managed to have a child? In theory he'd have a stepsister or -brother and the marital connection would also conjoin the individual into a brother- or sister-in-law. Yes, he knew that he was having a nervous breakdown.

Jennifer stepped up to the platformed altar with her entourage. When he glimpsed the pearl-encrusted satin bodice of her dress, he was restored to actuality. His luscious bride in her lace gown moved her hip against his to rouse him. Jennifer might have come from the Provençal Courts of Love. He stared at her as though she were Eleanor of Aquataine and he Adam de la Halle, her trouvère, about to sing a *serena*. Wearing the sensuous scent of Fracàs, his enchantress took his hand.

"*Ça va, chèri?*" she whispered.

*"Oui, tu est ravissante."*

The glum Père Lescaut began intoning the service in Latin, giving them a respite.

Jules Chardin leaned over and said to Jennifer, *"Merci, ils sont vrai Gauguin."*

She nodded to Jules and touched Michel.

"I love you. Your gown . . . you . . . I was having an anxiety attack."

"Don't. . . . I won't hurt you. I deliver my heart and my shield."

"It seems to me, I should be saying that."

"Your father brought me three paintings last night while we were still working on the hangings at the gallery. Gauguins. He found them in a storeroom at the chateau. He thought they were hideous."

"They're authentic?" Michel's voice was too loud for the priest and he realized this when Lescaut's scepter appeared out of nowhere and hit him in the gut just as it had when the priest had asked him to translate a line of Virgil's *Eclogues* in class.

"You okay?" Jennifer asked.

"Yes, Père Lescaut has a way of getting me over panic attacks." Michel's hand crept over Jennifer's palm. "You are glimmering in my eyes. Vellancio has prevailed."

"Ten thousand dollars' worth. What about the photographer? I haven't seen him."

"He can't take pictures of *high* Catholics during the ceremony."

"Think of it, Michel, we have three Gauguins from his period in Pont-Aven and the Marquesas."

*"Les bagues pour l'alliance, Michel! Vous êtes encore un toqué,"* the priest snarled.

Like a magician, Jules produced the rings from his vest pocket. Michel and Jennifer repeated their vows after the priest. When he suddenly concluded, still glaring at Michel, the groom's trance dissipated. Although his limbs were numb from hysteria, he lifted the veil off Jennifer's face, kissed her, and found his entry to paradise.

**"The priest from** purgatory," Michel's smiling, lustrous wife informed Rosalind at their posts on the reception line at the entry of the towering green and white marquee, kissing and greeting their guests.

Michel was sandwiched between Sylvie and Richard Caron but overheard.

"He beat me silly when I studied for Communion. He and my father were in the navy and came to Aix together after they scuttled the fleet." With a devilish glimmer, Michel lashed out. "But Philippe left a *fingerprint*. Apparently, he started a towering inferno in one of the battleship kitchens while learning his trade, and his navy chums use to call him Monsieur Flambé."

As the guests continued to get sozzled on the 1990 La Grande Dâme that Philippe had bought years before anyone thought of millennium madness and the fabricated hustle of champagne shortages by the producers, Michel and the Carons slipped out and he ferried them in to Nicole's office for some privacy. They had been warned by Nicole to avoid Philippe's Lobster Cardinal, and Michel brought in a taste of his mother's spectacular Lobster Américaine, which she had rolfed into a puff pastry.

"I taste velvety lobster and Armagnac," Richard said with approval. "It's indecent to cook this brilliantly."

"Yes, it's a miracle I'm not the size of a sumo wrestler and being transported to county fairs on eighteen-wheelers," Michel replied.

As a concession to her father, Sylvie wore a high-necked, beige-beaded dress. Her tattoo was not to be on view.

"Michel, I know you've got your guests . . ."

"I do, Sylvie, but let's talk about murder."

Her plane had been delayed and she had driven back to Bruges to ask more questions, offering to bribe the hotel staff; when she returned to the Brussels airport, it was three in the morning.

"I apologize for the delay."

"You should have e-mailed this information," Richard snapped.

"My computer was down."

"Stop these excuses. We're waiting, Sylvie," Richard prodded her. "In case you hadn't heard, Special Circumstances doesn't pay overtime or hand out gold stars."

"Richard, please ease up, she's doing fine," Michel said, trying to abort their sniping. Sylvie glared at her father.

"There's a local man, Jan Korteman. He's a photographer who lives in Bruges. He also has a house outside Avignon and knows the girl's aunt. It may be nothing, but I tracked him down on the Internet. He sells fetish porn in very expensive limited editions, dressed up as art."

"Another Mapplethorpe," Michel said with a sigh.

"There's no porn connected with this case at this point," Richard insisted.

"I know that, Papa, but it was the best I could do. What caught my attention was that he has a house in Provence and that he left after Caroline was abducted. He also had an American couple visiting—husband and wife, as far as I could determine. The man is going under the name of Darrell and the woman, Maddie. The man is a tattooist, his wife does piercings and is a makeup artist for films."

Richard Caron, the man who never lost his composure, shuddered. He turned to Michel, who stood rigid and impassive.

"A copycat couple," Richard suggested.

"Somehow I don't think so. Boy and Maddie weren't attracted by young girls. But I wonder if these two knew them or read about the case," he mused. He took Sylvie's hand and kissed it. "Sylvie, this was a brilliant piece of detective work. We have a name and a couple. A trinity."

She smiled grimly at her father. "The couple stayed at Die Swaene, but I didn't have the authority to get their names and addresses from the hotel. The Belgians made everything difficult for me."

"I'll get it through an Interpol warrant," Richard informed her, then gracefully bowed to his daughter, but she ignored him and bolted from Nicole's office.

When Michel rejoined the receiving line, the photographer and his assistants were still searching for him and were forced to shoot video of the guests.

"Where've you been Michel?" Lucien Virage demanded. Known as Monsieur Marriage, he was sweating like a wildebeest during the migration and in fact resembled one, with his arched back, broad-beamed slouched shoulders, and shoulder-length hair. "How can we have wedding photos without the groom?" His Nikons and light meter hung from his neck like Medusa's snakes as he arranged the wedding party.

"None of your chiaroscuro noir stuff, Lucien, and do try to keep the shadows off the bride's face," he chided the temperamental Monsieur Marriage.

"Enough, Michel! Now smile and freeze!" he said, firing off shot after shot like he was discharging an Uzi.

Rico Tarrante and his orchestra—a cross between the Gipsy Kings and the Budapest String Quartet—struck up a medley of Jennifer's favorite songs. To Michel, they sounded as if they were playing Stravinsky. Once he and Jennifer could escape from the receiving line, their first dance would be a languid rendition of "Someone to Watch Over Me."

When the stills were completed, Michel found himself tucked between Claude Boisser fawning over Irmegard and suggesting that she work as a madam at his hotel instead of wasting her time with tourists on barge trips. Vellancio, snarling at the suggestion, shielded Kristen from the rapacious former detective. Benedict was already drunkenly weaving through the hors d'oeuvres tables and was sharply intercepted by Delantier, who eased him into a chair just as he was about to fall into the pincers of crustacean sculptures. Waiters, detectives from his section, lab personnel, his new boss Charles Fournier with his wife Melba discussing the menu with Philippe, and distant relatives enveloped the happy but disoriented couple in a love-a-thon of kisses and the chaos of well-wishes.

Denise assessed his haircut and whispered, "For such a prick, you look pretty good."

Her commentary was suspended by Delantier; the general struck the brass gong.

*"Messieurs et dames, l'heure du dîner. . . ."*

At the flower-laden banquet table, Michel assisted Jennifer to her seat, then Rosalind, and finally his mother. With the look of a triumphant despot, Philippe raised his glass and made a toast to the bride and groom. The detective in Michel had invariably been asleep when it came to family matters, but he now observed Philippe sitting beside Rosalind, leaning over to touch her as if the move were unpremeditated. The horny madman and titular head of the family was loose and Michel could do nothing about it.

He and Jennifer studied the elaborate menu: it began with Nicole's Lobster Américaine, moved on to her delicate Provençal tomato vichyssoise with a nest of floating chives, then was abruptly detoured into truffled turkey, sweetbreads en papillote, filets of sole, rouget and salmon in champagne sauce. All of this merely light infantry before the fusillade of heavy artillery.

Sisteron Lamb encroute in a wild mushroom sauce joined Charolais Baron of Beef with a Châteauneuf marrow reduction; honeyed Bresse Suckling Pig stuffed with apples and apricots soaked in Calvados rested on a throne of vegetables. Alongside this were artichoke soufflés, dense aubergine Tians; tables of salads, hot rosemary-olive beignets, and mountains of cheeses.

With a smug smile, Philippe loomed over the married couple. "Now what do you think of *my* kitchen?"

"Unforgettable, Papa Philippe," Jennifer replied, frankly overwhelmed by the deluge. She rose and kissed the muscular chef. Puzzled by her sincerity, Michel was affected, compelled to reconsider the basis of the strife that endured between Philippe and himself. It had nothing to do with his discovery that Philippe was not his blood father or making passes at Jennifer's mother while his mother boiled fish heads to improve his infernal sauces.

"And you?" Philippe commanded Michel in an intimidating manner.

"I never underestimated your genius, Papa. The world of cuisine can forget Carême, Escoffier, Raymond Olivier, Robuchon, Julia Child, and the rest of the pretenders." Michel felt himself choking. "You, Philippe Danton, are the great artist, *Le Maître*." Michel leaned over and kissed the chef. "You're our Leonardo."

Stunned, flicking off a sweaty tributary from his upper lip into his Lobster Cardinal, Philippe meekly asked, "Do you really mean that, Michel?"

"Of course, I don't lie when it comes to food. *Jamais!*"

"After all these years of finding fault and humiliating me?"

"It was a joke—only a joke—that got out of hand to conceal

my admiration, my awe of your great talent. I thought you knew that."

"Oh, Michel"—Philippe was overwhelmed, on the threshold of tears—"and I thought the worst of you. It alienated us. I'm so proud of you . . . as well . . . and your detective skills. Food and love binds a family."

Michel had seen rare small buntings at the estate while the two had gone out to shoot duck.

"I assume you're saving the Ortlans for us."

"Yes, we have a supply of them at the chateau. We'll have Vellancio makes us purple velvet smoking jackets with detachable hoods and start the Danton Ortlan Club."

"You can count on me, Papa."

With these sententious remarks behind them and Philippe aglow, Michel realized how foolish he had been all these years. This man was his father, loved him, and because neither warrior would yield ground, they had shared a lifetime of antagonism. It now hardly mattered that his mother had cooked about ninety-nine percent of the wedding dinner and that his father was having a harmless flutter with his new mother-in-law.

Despite the feast being set before him, the music, the rapprochement with Philippe, the main course for Michel was still murder. He and Jennifer trundled out to the parquet dance platform and moved in an easy foxtrot, their first dance as husband and wife. Grasping his bride close to him, he beheld the ashen face of Melanie Davis, surveying the blissful scene before vanishing like an apparition in the crumbs of sunlight.

# CHAPTER 23

**Caroline was asleep, naked,** stretched out on the long table, her wrists and ankles in leather bindings. Her breathing was soft, unhurried, and her lucent skin captured the overhead light. Her muscles were firm and velvety to the touch. Garrett checked the IV glucose and water drip inserted in her arm. If she woke, he would feed her morphine with another drip. Her blood pressure registered 110/65. Unlike the normal tattoos he did in his shops, this process would be painless.

Garrett felt tender toward her and the last thing he intended to do was hurt her. He opened a new box of Medi-Touch disposables, put them on, and adjusted a pair of neurosurgeon goggles, which gave him microscopic and mid-distance vision. Otherwise, he was in his usual performance gear: a T-shirt that said GAUGUIN SALONS, his Ralph Lauren hiking shorts, and his comfy Rockports. Eve, as always, had laid out his needles and instruments — the antibacterial soap, ointments, syringes of lidocaine, novocaine, lint-free towels, inks in wells, alcohol, and glycerin — on two metal trays that attached to the table.

His English ink was mixed from powder, chased with alcohol and glycerin, until the colors of the palette pleased him. To the primary colors he added cherry red, fire, plum, magenta, Morocco pink, hot pink, jade, Sherwood green, peppermint, yellow, lemon, chrome, gold, primrose, Prussian blue, sky, and dark blue.

Before draping Caroline's buttocks and legs, he determined that the legs would be done as Corinthian columns, and be given a verdant, ocher patina; the buttocks leading to lit twin caves where bats, snakes, birds, and butterflies hovered. He'd need a lepidopterology text and remembered that one had been published post-humously by the esteemed Vladimir Nabokov.

With ideas erupting in his brain like Oklahoma twisters, Garrett now could bring into being the true satanic *garden*: chaotic, with the kinesthetic images of the astrological signs; a Dante's *Inferno* of the flesh—which would render the sentimental version of other artists as the wish-fulfillment of hacks. He was launching a new art form in the millennium, repossessing the spiritual consciousness that had been lost by a modern society devoted to money and possessions. Yes, his would be a religious act, an act of consecration.

He was aware of the fact that great art possessed a mystery that the viewer couldn't solve. Memories of seeing Hieronymous Bosch's overstated, presurrealism triptych in the Prado would not affect him. Bosch's work had been fire and storm, witchcraft and fulmination, both satire and indictment of the morals of fifteenth century burghers.

No, he, Garrett, had a grander conception, one that linked him with Gauguin's androgynous *Oviri* ceramic statue. Gauguin had painted in a noble savage style which he invented in Tahiti, freed of Western techniques. But Gauguin's paradise in Tahiti had been a fraud and as he traveled further in his quest for the primordial spirit in the Marquesas he had been infected by enigma and disease and had turned his last home in Hivaoa into a charnel house. Garrett would cast off the corrupting influence of Gauguin and liberate himself.

Sexuality was the sacred key to the conception of humanity. Garrett's work would be a pilgrimage that would solve the riddle of the dead and reclaim Golgotha.

"Beware pornography," he counseled himself, his deft strokes on Caroline's back forming an exquisite pattern. "Be lyrical and profane. The sacred idea is that we all possess male and female sexuality."

He referred to the draftsman sketches of his vision of his Garden of Eden. Unlike oil painting, which lent itself to an angry wipe of varnish or overpainting the surface white by the artist, Garrett's work on the skin left no margin for error. Once the ink had entered the skin, it remained forever. For the first section, he'd need about thirty-five hours. Then . . . let her heal for a few weeks, keep the skin moisturized while contemplating the work.

Garrett was calm, Eve close by, prepared for the unexpected when the summoned her. He realized the work had become more ambitious. He would need at least four subjects—models—for the quadripartite vaulting of the human cathedral he envisaged. His canvasses the unblemished bodies of young girls. Their seduction by Eve at schools, fairs, and tourist attractions was a sacrifice his art required.

After reaping the skins, he knew of only a small group of very wealthy aficionados who would take pleasure in his artistry. But he was in good company. Who had appreciated Vermeer before Proust had made him Charles Swann's obsession? Or the outcast Gauguin? No, the public never understood art when it was new, broke boundaries, and became revolutionary.

He checked his setup of needles. He never used commercial needles but made his own by soldering pairs of insect needles which were more expensive and had longer points. These were used by entomologists for mounting insects. He had used the delicate double zeros for the thinnest liners and zeros for color and shading.

That morning Eve had prepared them, first dipping them in an HCL base flux and smoothing the edges with a fine paintbrush before rounding the needles, which she held together with a rubber band tied tightly. With a 30X black Mikro Lupe, she scrupulously examined the points for roundness and discarded any with hooks. They were then placed in an ultrasonic Ritter Speedclave.

It was a meticulous procedure, not unlike a cardiac surgeon checking his scalpels. The fine needles, threes, fives, and sevens, were for the precise work; the fifteens to thirty-fives points had bolder increases for coloring large areas.

With a balletic swirl of his black ink artist's pen, Garrett expertly continued to draw freehand. This took him more than two hours. His Garden of Eden revealed his deepest belief that life's sexual content began here. His Adam and Eve would have both sexual organs. This heroic work would celebrate the duality of human beings, ultimately the harmony of the ideal synthesis. Eve would do the piercing for his *Mona Lisa* and express her own artistic sensibility.

Garrett would outline Caroline with a modern, electric Micky Sharpz machine. Embarked on his voyage of discovery, he decided to adopt the hand technique of the Japanese masters to give birth to a wondrous convergence.

In the Japanese-Thailand style, he wrapped the needles with thread around a smooth wooden stick, inserted the fine zero needles and fitted a rubber webbing on his thumb and the fleshy part of his left hand. He tested it and it slid easily like the bridge of a pool cue.

Listening to the music of Scriabin's *Prometheus,* Garrett knew he was possessed by divine fire. He wove the needle into the shimmering, docile flesh of Caroline Davis. They would both be famous.

Sensing a looming presence, he said, "Paul, I think it's time for you to leave."

# CHAPTER 24

**Although the ethereal Hôtel** L'Europe's penthouse, with its serpentined terraces and sweeping views of the Papal Palace and the Rhône at sunset, seemed the last place for marital discord, Michel found himself in a temper. While Jennifer was outside, a thoughtful maid had unpacked the bride's overnight bag.

*"Que-ce-que Je fais avec ça, monsieur?"* she asked, handing Michel a roll of toilet paper.

He took it from her, tipped her, and implored her not to mention this breach of etiquette to Hendryk, the solicitous general manager, who had given him this magnificent suite once occupied by royalty, presidents — Jackie O herself.

A quick inspection revealed it to be a triple exemplar of Charmin Ultra, *Softer, Stronger, Thicker,* manufactured by Proctor & Gamble in Cincinnati, Ohio. Michel strode heavily out to the terrace, where Jennifer was lining up a photograph with her new Minolta digital. He thrust the offending package in front of her lens.

"Hey! Don't."

"What do you spy with your little eye?"

"Oh, that," she said. "It's . . . it's part of my trousseau."

"Is this some kind of sick California joke?"

"You were never supposed to know."

"I'm a detective." He assumed his official demeanor. "Do you realize you need a license to import this? And as an officer of the law, I'm bound to report this to the customs authority for seizure of contraband and failure to pay excise duty. I hope you can produce the bill of lading, or is this just plain smuggling?" He shook his head. "Why take such a risk?"

"Isn't it obvious? I asked my mother to bring it."

"You may have to testify against her at the assizes court. If she's convicted, you'll both be deported."

"Maybe that's not such a bad idea. We'll see how badly you want to get laid."

"That's a steep price. My sky miles are nonexistent."

"Well," she said, slipping off her skirt, revealing startling yellow silk panties with frilly lace borders, "you better grab it while you can."

As she lay down on a chaise longue and unbuttoned her blouse, he reached out for the champagne and poured them another glass.

"Now, Jennifer, is it also true that you went to Maxime's for a steak?"

"I don't remember."

"Six people saw you eating a filet. My father would have a stroke. Do you realize what this could do to his reputation? Tell me it's not true."

She neatly hung her maize blouse on the horn of the chaise.

"It was a Côte de boeuf à la Moelle, and Maxime brought over toast points so I could sop up the marrow."

"How did you wind up there?"

"It was raining, my feet hurt, and I was lost."

"Lost—two blocks above the Cours Mirabeau? And there was no rain last week. You'll have to do better than that."

She lay back now and languidly sipped her champagne. "I was out shopping with Grace Chardin. Actually, I was picking up nightgowns and"—she snapped the elastic on her panties—"lingerie made by her lady on the Place Ramus. We were starved and she said Maxime's was one of Aix's treasures. And so it is."

"I've just made up with my father after three decades of mortal combat and now you want to ruin everything."

"All these French superior airs are getting to me. Do this, don't do that. I'm fed up with the French and their rules. The drinks in bars are such shrimpy shots, they must use eyedroppers. I don't like horse butchers, or the fact that there's dog shit everywhere."

"Do you seriously believe a Frenchman is going to walk around with a pooper scooper?" Michel demanded, outraged.

"All I'm saying is they ought to clean up their own shit."

"Anything else I should notify the Elysée Palace about while you're at it?"

"Yes, as a matter of fact. Kids are smoking everywhere. Nobody enforces the law against smoking, especially restaurants like yours. The women's clothes are designed for runts with small busts and short legs. And I'm not having a love affair with the on-line services and phones."

He could no longer restrain himself and tore off his clothes so rapidly that one of his shoes scooted down on the street and took a crazy hop. Ignoring this loss, he pounced on his new wife with the lust of a virgin who had hoarded his fantasies. He and Jennifer meshed gears with such brevity that he was mortified.

"Wow, you came so fast."

"I was in my Tour de France sprint mode," he lamely admitted. "What can I say , , , ? One look at those tanned legs, the sun line on your navel—and you don't have to do anything."

"May I ask how long it'll take you to reload?"

He felt humiliated. "Please, Jennifer, it's not like I've hit a bad tee shot and I'm asking for a mulligan. I think it would be best if I try to reclaim my shoe."

"I'll be here," she said with a dissolute leer before tearing the plastic wrapping from the Charmin. She peeled off a strand for herself and handed the roll to him. "You'll see that *absorbent* isn't an idle claim."

"Is this a harbinger of our married life?"

"Yes," she said, waving her hand blithely, "isn't it lovely? Oh, Michel, be a darling. While you snoop through my makeup kit, bring me a Prevacid. I've got acid reflux from hell from our wedding dinner."

**Jennifer was in** a deep, sated sleep when Michel skulked out at three in the morning. Glutted on sex, he could barely make it to the elevator. The croon and thwack of the night wind bailing off the Rhône brought him back to a semblance of reality. While Jennifer had been in the first bathroom in France that met with her approval, he had received a call from Sylvie with Jan Korteman's address.

He picked up the N7 outside of town, the highway empty apart from the occasional top-heavy *camion* heading for market in Marseille. Having hiked through the region all of his life, he knew this land and eagerly followed branch roads that led to crooked trunk lanes and ultimately to a gravel drive on which were half a dozen houses, some with post lights, others dark. He left his car on the verge, slipped on his shoulder holster with his Glock, and pulled out his large flashlight from under the seat.

The houses here were not numbered but fancifully named, like children born late in life, or callow mistresses who spread some version of sunshine. La Lumière, the Korteman gabled villa, stood in a small olive grove. It had a high-pitched roof and immense windows with closed black-green shutters. In the driveway, Michel noted the Belgian license plates on a Mercedes 600.

He wondered if he might expect a cluster of ferocious Dobermans with their vocal cords removed and took out his automatic. He knew very well that he had no legal right to be on Korteman's property and would fall on the tired ruse of his car having broken down if a caretaker or the owner flourished a weapon, which was not at all uncommon in this neighborhood. These homes cost millions and often were repositories of valuable antiques and art masterpieces. The late Douglas Cooper, art critic and intimate of Picasso and Matisse, had lived nearby. He had been a friend of Jules Chardin's and given Michel a tour of his collection when Michel had been a student.

Michel boldly rang the doorbell and waited with his limp apology. He was surprised when there was no answer. He went around back and decided to knock on the kitchen window. There was a darkened pool and cabañas. But what caught his attention was the small dock and no boat. Perhaps the millionaire photographer was docked at one of the ports, or an island—anywhere. He rapped on the window several times, then on impulse tried the cellar door which was to the side.

He lifted the wooden door, shone his flash, and walked down a

short flight of stone steps and into an immaculate professional photography lab and studio. The equipment was the best on the market—Leicas and Nikons. He switched on a light and saw a circular
steel staircase, painted a bold red, and climbed up to the ground
floor and through another door, which brought him to a reception
room.

"Hello, hello!" he shouted.

He started to cough. The air made him gag and his eyes smarted.
Toxic fumes were coming from somewhere. He pulled out his
handkerchief and covered his mouth. The most sensible action
would be to phone the fire department's hazardous waste unit in
Avignon, but he persisted in checking the source. He held on to
the walls and wobbled down a long dark hallway where the fumes
seemed strongest. At the end of the hallway he came into a large
mirrored bedroom with a playpen bed, room for six. He stopped
in his tracks, mystified: a black wet suit was laid on the bed, scuba
headgear and nozzle attached to an oxygen tank, and alongside this
equipment, black latex gloves and boots.

The abrasive gas vapors were now so powerful that Michel bit
his handkerchief and wiped his eyes with his sweater sleeve. He
kicked open a door and found himself in a bathroom with a vast
sunken tub. He was choking, bleary-eyed, and virtually suffocating
from the intense caustic fumes. He heard the hiss and sizzle of acid
fulminating on what flesh remained of an eyeless decomposing
skeleton with only scraps of flesh adhering to the bone.

Staggering out of this abattoir, he lurched down the corridor,
unlocked the front door, and collapsed on the grass. He struggled
to remain conscious, hit the automatic dial on his cell phone, and
got Pierre at the Section office.

"I need help."

"Michel . . . what's wrong? Are you hurt?"

"Ambulance, patch in to the Toxic Unit. I've been poisoned. I'm
outside Avignon . . . ask Sylvie . . ."

# CHAPTER 25

**On the fifth day,** Jan was invited to inspect Garrett's work. Caroline seemed to be tolerating the procedure well, and during brief respites from Dilaudid and morphine cocktails, she had periods of lucidity. Eve had purchased from an antique jeweler at a flea market a small platinum bar with AMOUR engraved on it. It was originally worn as an ankle bracelet, but the resourceful Eve trimmed and soldered it, then pierced Caroline's left nipple, and inserted it as decorative art.

"Your work is magnificent, totally original," Jan said. "The depth of colors are as fine as any oil. Garrett, this is genius. I realize you don't like the fact that Gauguin has been stalking you. And there's a good psychological reason for that. His was a new departure in art. Matisse borrowed color, the palette, and tones from him; Picasso adopted his use of myth, symbolism, and Gauguin's fetishes. Remember Picasso used mediums like carving and ceramics that Gauguin pioneered.

"But *you,* you've shaken off the shackles. You're creating a new type of art—I'd define it as the *art of crisis.* What you're doing with Caroline is a form of crucifixion for artist and model. No one in history would have had your courage and deconstructed art in order to make it a living performance. So if Gauguin looks in occasionally, it's to learn from a new master."

Garrett was speechless. It was too early to make pronouncements, but he knew that he had struck the chord he had been seeking.

"Thank you, Jan. Your support means everything to me."

Their attention was diverted by Caroline, very groggy but aware, asking for a mirror. She was helped into the main part of Jan's studio, where there were a number of them on wheels and she was able to see both her front and back. She gave a stupefied grunt and fainted.

Fortunately, Garrett was beside her and eased the girl into an ancient artifact of a wheelchair which Jan, the collector, had brought in. Garrett gently wrapped a green surgical sheet around her.

"Do you use this contraption, or is it a family heirloom?" he asked, intrigued.

"It's a prop. I have a storehouse of them, all catalogued. I use them for my books. Wooden arms and legs with ingenious but quaint articulations. I never know before a shoot if I might add some fascinating fetish. Some of my subjects even grow to enjoy them—no matter what I ask them to do with them.

"There was a wondrous porn shop in Aubagne—that's a town in Provence where the Foreign Legion is garrisoned—well, they used to specialize in things like this. I bought Victorian corsets and buggy whips, schoolmaster switches and masks from the owner. Not the glossy rubbish they sell nowadays." Jan's thin lips pursed. "Poor Gerard, what a tragedy."

"What happened to this Gerard?"

"He was murdered last year. An American lunatic went on a killing binge in Provence. I don't really know the details, but Gerard was shot in the back outside Le Sex Boutique."

Garrett checked Caroline's vital signs and decided that they both needed to rest. He lifted Caroline's lids and shone a flashlight into her eyes.

He popped an amyl nitrite to revive Caroline, then held a glass of lemonade with a straw for her. Caroline gurgled it.

"You don't want to overdo the drugs, Garrett."

"You're right. I'll ease off."

"Some of my subjects have had similar problems."

Jan stroked his hair, then sat on a stool by the gigantic window.

"You know, I'm embarrassed by my behavior. We've taken over your home, made you a hostage—"

"No, no. You've opened my eyes. I worship you, Garrett."

"Please don't." Garrett removed his green smock and picked up a scone. "I've been insufferable. We have manners back home in Venice. Teas with Earl Grey and Devon cream."

"Artists have their periods of intense concentration."

"When we met at Heather's bash . . . Eve and I weren't ourselves, really. Heather wanted us to get involved in the exhibitions. But we never would. If you hadn't been there, she might have tried to force us. Jan, having you there meant everything to me. You reinforced my belief in myself. I was doing shit tattoos that were old hat. Another dragon, a heart, MOM, tribal garbage, and you made me see the light." Garrett's melodious voice had a soft mewl, importuning. "I won't have sex with Heather ever again. The secret life we had is over. She can't accept that. At the same time, I'm indebted to her for setting me up with you. Heather loves me enough to have done that. I'm doing what I believe is my finest work."

Jan took Garrett's face in the palms of his hands and kissed him passionately.

"That was not sexual."

"Jan, I adore you," Garrett said. "I've never had a patron with your insight."

Garrett now returned the kiss, his tongue wet with agitation, but he pulled away.

"Jan, I'd like to give you everything. But I'm afraid . . . of Eve. She pretends to be submissive . . . but she's very suspicious."

"I want you *and* Eve. And I'd like to film us together. Heather told me that was impossible. I do understand that Eve and Heather have connected. But apparently it's unsatisfactory for both of them."

"I'm aware of that. Even I have to deal with infidelity." Garrett spoke in a whisper. "We have a dangerous problem with Eve. She smothers me, like Heather did." With his ink-stained fingers, Garrett stroked his host's face. "Eve is deranged. Last year, I had two women over. We were drinking tequila shooters. I really had no intention of . . . But one thing led to another and Eve caught me. I couldn't prevent what happened. I was so drunk. Eve played the gracious woman of the house, then laced their drinks with drugs and . . . there were drownings—if you can call them that—in the canal in Venice right near my neighbors.

"You see, she'll do things with Heather to spare me." Garrett pressed his lips on Jan's ear and with the kiss came the admonition. "Jan, I feel threatened all the time. Eve's deadly. If she suspects that there's anything going on between us . . ."

"Thanks for the warning. But would she mind if the artist and— what shall I call myself?—his *biographer* had an innocent tête-à-tête over a quiet dinner? Would that be possible? Come, now, it'll take your mind off your work, Garrett. You need a night out."

They wheeled the exhausted Caroline to her room and helped her into bed. As Garrett was about to strap her hands in the restraints, she turned awkwardly on her side.

"Should I give her another shot of morphine, Jan?"

"Garrett, she's unconscious. It's not as though she's going to take a walk or call anyone."

"You've got a point," he said, locking the door.

# CHAPTER 26

**When Michel opened his** eyes it was morning, of which day he couldn't be certain. He had been taken off life support, his gown changed, and now merely two oxygen tubes were in his nostrils. He was still hooked up to a range of monitors. Standing at his bedside were a group of doctors and nurses, along with some familiar faces from Special Circumstances. Threading through the group was the pale face of his wife. She had black bands under her bloodshot eyes and an expression of such alarming uncertainty that Michel forced himself to smile to reassure her. Just above the intravenous needle plugged into his wrist, she kissed his hand and he touched her hair.

"It was the dinner. I should have also taken a Prevacid."

"Please, don't get cute with me. You walked into a holding pond of nitric acid."

"That seems to be the acid of choice this summer in Provence."

"The doctors, they—I—thought you might have brain damage."

"Don't I?"

"Oh, Michel . . . Michel. I thought I'd lost you." Jennifer's steamy tears rushed down his cheeks and he felt too limp to stroke her.

"Are my parents . . . ?"

"They're in the country with my mother."

"*Madame Danton, je m'excuse, mais j'ai besoin à faire un examination,*" a bearded young doctor informed her, then took her arm, pulled the curtains, and with his team began a rigorous examination. Lights flashed in Michel's pupils, a portable X-ray machine was wheeled over; saliva and urine samples were taken. The chaos of illness engulfed him.

"You've had lung damage and it will take some time for the tissue and the membranes to heal—if they do. For the rest of your life, you have to avoid any place where there's smoking, Commander Danton."

Michel coughed and his chest burned as though his lungs were on fire.

"When can I leave?"

"We'll see how you're doing by next week."

"What day is it?"

"Tuesday."

He was shocked and fearful. "I've been unconscious for two days?"

"Yes. You were comatose when you were brought in. By the way, whoever sewed up those bullet wounds in your chest did a lovely piece of work. No adhesions."

"I send him champagne every Christmas."

"Are you always so flippant?" the doctor asked without amusement.

"Only when I'm on a murder case."

"I think you're off this one."

"May I have a quick visit with my troops outside?"

"I don't recommend it."

"Please show them in."

The doctor scowled at him, slid the curtains, and pointed his finger at Michel. "Don't scoff at the gift of life. It's not a joke."

Richard and Laurent led Émile and Annie to his bedside. There were expressions of concern, goodwill, and the favor of the gods. He listened patiently, trying hard not to cough.

"Another acid bath suicide," he suggested to Laurent.

"Absolutely, the attendant should be well tipped. He certainly got the temperature right with a fifteen normal nitric acid," the medical examiner said. "I can't do an autopsy for some time. The scraps are still too toxic."

"I couldn't tell . . . man or woman?" Michel asked.

"We don't know yet. Looks like a man, could be a woman."

Richard took his hand like a father supporting his errant son who might have been busted for drugs. He asked the question everyone wondered about: Why leave his bride's bed at three in the morning on their honeymoon night to investigate an unsubstantiated tip—provided by Richard's own daughter, no less, a novice detective—when he could have called in a squad of his investigators?

"I have an uncontrollable appetite for murder," Michel explained. "It was like leaving a glutton with a box of chocolates."

"Sylvie has been disciplined for this."

When he tried to lift himself up in protest, his body rebelled. "I'll testify on her behalf if you dare, Richard. Now where is she?"

"Out investigating, I assume, impervious to reason."

**Michel discharged himself** from the hospital on Friday morning. His chest still rumbled, but the pain had diminished. He had lost nine pounds and his face was drawn—quite handsomely, Jennifer told him—but nothing improved his mood. The quiet and solace of his apartment on Rue Goyrand and Jennifer waiting on him hardly compensated for the loss of direction in this case. He detected a mist of estrangement between them that Jennifer wouldn't address during his recuperation. Her performance was superb, reining in her deep anger. He couldn't blame her or assuage her disappointment. He had left their bed on the wedding night.

Now with time on his hands, he realized his behavior had been impulsive. Sooner or later someone would have found the corpse, which now resided in Marseille's chemical detoxification storage building. It was still unsafe to proceed with an autopsy, but Laurent, to his credit, had in place a forensic anthropologist to assist him. There was no word of Jan Korteman either in Bruges or Provence.

Richard Caron continued to interview replacements for Michel's position; Charles Fournier sent over a kilo of Beluga and a bottle of Krug as a welcoming gesture. Jules Chardin, busy at the gallery for the opening of the Vercours Collection, dropped by with his wife late.

Leon Stein appeared to offer psychological commiseration and on their third Pastis remarked, "Even though I haven't been hired, I did read Caroline's file."

"Well, Leon, I don't know that I still have the authority to pay you to do that. Richard's been close to hysteria with the Section's budget. They sent down a team of accountants from the Inspectorate in Paris and the feeling is that their report is going to be damaging."

"My finances are excellent at the moment, Michel. I even bought myself a suit at Vellancio's."

"Who would have thought you'd ever become a high roller? I guess it's a suite at the Mirage in Vegas next."

"Not for me. The hookers there are too expensive. I like being top gun in Provence."

Michel laughed and opened a large red portfolio with SCS CONFIDENTIAL stamped on it.

"The photos of the unknown victim in Avignon aren't very good. So I had them blown up. One interesting point I observed: The person in question's right ear was severed, à la van Gogh."

Stein pondered this. "That's a very gruesome pastiche. I assume the killer intended to taunt us."

"I wonder if it wasn't an artistic statement, a perverse one, admittedly . . . a kind of ritual. We have three or four people involved, definitely a woman or more than one who do the seducing and assist in the kidnapping of the girls."

"If it's a quartet, they've got a staff problem. Maybe they'll close up shop for the summer."

"I doubt it, Leon. This is *high* season. Floods of tourists, kids wandering off and getting lost."

"I see what you mean." Leon was about to light his cigar, then put it back in his case. "I forgot, you have to be smoke-free."

"Oh, the hell with it, light up and flip open the terrace doors. I might even grab a puff myself."

"We'll see if it bothers you. Now, Michel, what fascinates me is the use of acid in two cases. Why go to this amount of trouble when all you need to do is simply murder someone? Dump a body, in the case of Caroline. Or leave a dead body for someone to find.

I'll tell you my theory. Our man—and I'm sure it is a man—has secrets he'll do anything to conceal. This is what I would call a screening technique. To us it's sadistic and horrible, but it is in fact a coded message. He can't reveal whatever it is and this concealment has been a lifelong fixation."

The notion resonated with Michel. "I agree with the idea of a secret, but on the other hand this man wants to cover up a blunder of some kind and he's prepared to go to extremes to do so. What does this person do? He has a métier, some type of craft. Caroline's breast was pierced expertly. Oh, *merde*. How could I have missed it? Yes, I was getting married, and I thought everything would be screwed up in the kitchen by Philippe. I was careless. My mind wasn't on my work.

"The killer tattooed Caroline! Piercing and tattoos, ham and cheese!" Michel rushed to his desk. On a tray was the earring he had from Suzy Marquay in Pont-Aven. He handed it to Stein.

"It's an earring. So what?"

"The killer ruined the tattoo on Caroline and was so infuriated he had to eradicate it because he left his signature on Caroline's back. Turn the earring over, Leon. We've got his address. He's from Venice, California."

Stein's cigar glowed in the dusky evening light. "Yes. Now what about the German girl? It's been ten days."

"I'd given up hope. But I believe she's alive. Poor Gerta—*Ars gratia ars*. MGM's slogan. It's this fanatic's creed."

# CHAPTER 27

**After dinner, with cognacs** in the library, Garrett and Jan were joined by Eve. She was in a blithe mood and said, "Boys' night out."

The change of scenery had lightened Garrett's disposition. "No bowling," Garrett replied.

"You must have had a good time with the pretty ladies drinking genevers at the tavern. That barman Pieter always has a selection of them around. He even came on to me. He wants me to pierce him. I told him I'd need a letter from his mother."

Jan's reedy laughter echoed. "You actually sound surprised. My dear girl, you know very well that you're delicious."

Emboldened by the brandy, she sat down on his lap, nuzzled him, and kissed him daintily on the lips.

This double delight, first a few kisses from Garrett earlier in the studio and now Eve teasing him, was more than he could have hoped for. The ideal of possessing them both might eventually be possible. Where Heather's vulgar pushiness had failed, his ingratiating nature might yet prevail. The pair of them needed to be handled very delicately and he was a master of seduction. He brought out a copy of *Fetish and Tantra Maithuna* and leafed through the pages.

Eve stopped at a photograph of a beautiful Nepalese girl with a snake between her thighs. "What does *maithuna* mean?"

"That's the supreme form of intercourse and part of the magical five *m*'s of the Tantra, which means web or warp and is a holy arcane text of the Hindus. What happens in the books actually is a conversation between the god Shiva and his mistress Parvati. Shiva twists the elements around and develops an inversion of the five yields of the cow: butter, milk, urine, curds, and feces which are used for cleansing. These evolve into *mansa,* flesh; *mudra,* parched grain; *mada,* wine; *matsya,* fish; and finally *maithuna,* which is the highest phase of sexual congress.

"At Heather's party there were a few people who thought they knew something about it with their ridiculous Kama Sutra positions, but they were dilettantes."

"You're getting me hot," Eve said.

Garrett drifted back, interested.

"Well, the fact is, I spent five years in India—Calcutta, Madras, and Poona—studying with a guru while I was working on a book. Eventually, when I returned to Europe, my sex partners wouldn't leave me alone."

Eve was titillated. "Was Heather included?"

Jan sighed and with a sneer of condescension said, "I'm afraid she bored me. I couldn't raise her to my level, nor would I descend to hers. Multiple orgasmic nymphomaniacs don't need much stimulation or present challenges. You see, my friends, Heather could never feel the tangled serpent within herself, coiled and ready to strike."

He turned the page and revealed a woman with a donkey. "My God." Eve hid her face. "I'm not into . . . demented."

"I don't think this woman was, either. But it was part of her progression to hell. Why these things happen to people, no one but God can account for. *He owes us an explanation.*"

"You're right, karma won't do."

"Exactly. This girl was sold to a wealthy man and when she no longer amused him, he used to arrange these exhibitions for his friends. The *Tantra* is not designed for that sort of thing. But, look, I'm first of all an observer and a recorder of experiences. Mine isn't great art like Garrett's, but it's a visual chronicle of folly, madness, and inhumanity."

From across the room, Garrett's voice suddenly rang out. "I've had a vision!" Jan and Eve froze into silence. "The serpent in my Eden will be this Tantric God." He was fervent. "I've already outlined the snake on Caroline's back, but I wasn't sure of the character of its face."

"What is it?" Jan asked with excitement.

"This is show, not tell," he replied. "Let's go upstairs and see our little goddess."

**The key to** the door of the small bedroom was on the worktable. Garrett slid it into the lock, turned it, and stood in the doorway, baffled. Caroline was not in bed. The small doorless bathroom was empty. When he stepped into the room, he was hit on the side of the head with a paperweight and reeled back. Crouching behind the door, Caroline raised the paperweight again and as she was about to strike him, Garrett twisted away and kicked her in the stomach, knocking her down.

"You little bitch!" He was breathing heavily. He was about to chop her with the side of his hand, but as she was down, he lifted Caroline to her feet. Her linen nightdress was soaked with blood.

"You're a monstrosity," she yelled.

For a moment, he thought she might have had her period, but then he beheld the streaks of blood on the back of the dress.

He shouted. "My work! What've you done?"

"What've *you* done? You're the crazy bastard," she howled. "I tried to scrape that shit off my back. You better get me to a doctor."

Jan trembled while Garrett dragged her. "What do you want me to do?"

"Switch on the surgical lights and strap her hands down on the table. I'm going to shoot her up." He tore open a syringe pack, stabbed it full of morphine, and didn't bother to use alcohol on the tracked vein in her arm. He hitched on his magnifying glasses and turned her roughly on her stomach. "You rotten bitch. You're the monstrosity, the one who hates new art. I *trusted* you, believed in you."

His ungodly screeching fury, climbing off the human vocal register, was unlike anything Jan had ever heard. Scraped and bleeding with patches of soft scabs, Caroline's back was a catastrophe, with hanks of bloody flesh

"GG, I don't want to die."

"The canvas, you desecrated it."

Jan was beside him watching. "Is there any way you can save . . . ?"

In a fury Garrett pulled on a red rubber apron, deftly inserted a long number three needle in his tattoo machine, hit the foot peddle, and viciously turned Caroline over. Her pupils were already dilating and her eyes were ice caps in a frozen wasteland. He plunged the needle frenetically into her carotid artery as though sticking a pig on the killing floor of an abattoir. Blood jetted out of the wound, but he would not relinquish the drill.

**At eight in** the morning, Garrett appeared at the breakfast table. He was calm but watchful. Jan slid over a basket of bread. Although he had dismissed the servants when Garrett and Eve moved in, he had food deliveries every day. Garrett nodded and dipped his bread into the large cup of coffee and nibbled on it distractedly.

"We have to discuss this. I haven't moved her."

"I don't know," Garrett responded cavalierly. "Dump her in the canal, there are enough of them."

"Oh, *I'm* supposed to get rid of her body?"

"Do whatever you like." Garrett's head fell to the table. "Forgive me, I'm not myself."

"Does Eve have any suggestions?"

"No. She's too angry. She'd like to chop that little bitch into pieces and feed her to the sharks."

Jan nodded with resignation. He was as seriously compromised as Garrett. It was if someone had moved a knight on a chessboard, forking the queen which he had to lose because he was obliged to move his king.

"I've been guilty of some dangerous behavior before," he informed his guest, "but never murder. I encouraged you and helped you kidnap Caroline, so now I suggest you follow my recommendations. If Caroline is found in Bruges, I'm sure to be questioned. I have a doubtful reputation. Sex and young people. There's also my work. Those who don't understand it consider it pornography. On the other hand, I'm on good terms with the townspeople, because I spend lavishly. Still, there's a certain taint that eccentricity doesn't quite cover. Heather's visit didn't help my standing in the community."

Tears rolled down Garrett's cheeks and his fine features were twisted. "I was so close. I feel betrayed."

"Garrett, please stop." Jan tried to console the grief-stricken artist. "With the police all around, shadowing us, you won't be able to concentrate. The other thing is, we've got to confuse them."

Jan clasped Garrett's large fingers and kissed them. "I'm in the hunt—part of the charmed circle. We'll find other openings," he pronounced like a chessmaster.

**At two A.M.,** with the night sounds of the canals, the bells of the belfry, black water washing on the embankment, an occasional boat engine, the big Mercedes pulled out of the garage. Caroline had been packed in thick plastic and placed in the section for the spare tire. Eve sat in the passenger seat. Garrett had dozed off.

"We'll be at the border in a couple of hours," Jan said, and Eve squeezed his hand.

"I don't know what we'd do without you."

"You won't have to find out. It'll be the three of us."

Jan found himself in a curious, ambivalent predicament, sexually aroused by her as well as him. He would eventually have them both, he knew. It was only a matter of being patient.

"I've traveled everywhere and there's nothing in the world like the light in Provence, the clarity of the air, its scents, Eve. Garrett will have a rebirth at my villa."

"I forgot. Where is it?"

"On the Rhône River outside of Avignon. You'll have fresh fruit and vegetables from my garden, luscious cheeses. Plump olives that we'll press into salads. I promise you a holiday you'll never forget. Once we settle in, we'll find a wet place for Caroline. Eventually, when she's found—if she ever is—no one will know who she is or how she got to France."

Garrett was suddenly roused. "Jan, can you get hold of nitric acid?"

He was mystified. "nitric acid? Why?"

"My work's been ravished. I want to be the one to destroy it . . . *my* way. I'll need a few drums. . . ."

Jan Korteman had been close to murder in his past, but never actually consummated the final act. It was as humiliating as coitus interruptus. His participation with Garrett had been electrifying. Still, he had been a voyeur and photographed Caroline after the fact. The next time, he decided, he'd be the one to take charge, provide the coup de grâce.

Yes, his own work had a shocking gap, images that separated him from Goya's *Disasters of War*. He had another flash from his school days in England. He had been regularly beaten by the masters of his school. When he had protested, the headmaster had given him Thomas De Quincey's ingenious essay to read: "Murder Considered as One of the Fine Arts." Jan had written a shrewd rebuttal to this and was awarded a cane so that he could beat others. He had never used it.

During his time as apprentice mortuary photographer, he had taken pictures of the bodies that had been initiated by the exercise of another person's will. He was a mere accountant of experience. Garrett was leading him into another world, providing the dimension that had been missing. They would find other subjects for Garrett's canvas and when the artist heard what the critic had to *say*, he, Jan, would determine how and when it needed to be destroyed.

Jan already saw his own masterpiece and provisionally entitled the book, *The Deadliest Art: The Progress of Murder*. This would be a creative legacy worth devoting himself to and dying for. He had been searching for subject matter for many years, but what he actually needed was original *content*. The epiphany electrified him.

Aflutter with passion, Jan pressed the CD button. The car boomed with Berlioz's *Symphonie fantastique* as they sped into the black quintessence of night and its art.

# CHAPTER 28

**Wondrously, Michel felt better** about everything. His lungs were now capable of filling with the sweet fragrances of lavender, jasmine, and the herbs of Aix's markets. His chest no longer burned and even the occasional cough no longer made his throat feel as if it were being rubbed by sandpaper. Uncharacteristically for a Frenchman, when he lived in New York, he had developed a passion for baseball while working at Yankee Stadium his first summer. The unpredictable narrative of the game, its quixotic players, the endless number of games over a season, all appealed to him. The game itself answered his need to be told a story, and every week videos arrived from his American friends at the FBI. His beloved Yankees were floundering, but he was relieved that George Steinbrenner had not gone mad and given up all of his superlative young players for Sammy Sosa. David Justice would fill the bill.

His countrymen might spend their time reveling in the French victory over Italy in the European cup final. But Michel was immersed in baseball. The player who had stolen his heart was the gentle giant, Mark McGwire, who had now passed Mike Schmidt with his 550th home run. If McGwire, now thirty-seven, could play at this level for another five years, he might break Hank Aaron's record as baseball's greatest home run hitter. Big Mac was an inch or so taller than Michel, but they were about the same weight. With a red wig, Michel might pass for the slugger at a police lineup.

Tonight, Midsummer's Eve, was the vernissage at the Chardin Gallery for invited guests only, with hors d'oeuvres and plenty to drink. Now that the wedding was over and the refurbishment of Chez Danton had been completed, Golarde and his contracting forces were freed from Philippe's tyranny. A team had been work-ing on Louise Vercours's former brothel; rooms would be available for female university students for the autumn term. Another crew was building a studio for Jennifer at the family farm in St-Rémy, which Nicole insisted on giving to them as a wedding gift. She would still maintain her sausage factory and herb gardens. But the property was theirs. While the construction was under way, they continued to live in his apartment in Aix.

When Jennifer walked into the dining room before six in the morning, Michel was watching a baseball video, already dressed and on his feet applauding McGwire's colossal clout. Michel touched her tousled, silky blond hair hanging down over her waist and placed his palm on her firm tail, paradise in his grasp, even at six in the morning.

"Did I wake you with my cheering?"

"No. . . . Umm, you made coffee already. You're such a good guy," she said, kissing him, her breath smelling of Dr. Roche's minty dentifrice. "What am I going to do with you? If it's not Tiger Woods at the Open at three in the morning and you swing-ing your new Callaway driver, it's baseball. And no pizza."

"As long as I live, *pizza* will never be on the menu at home." He paused, then added another low blow. "Maybe you can get away with smuggling in your own toilet paper and sneaking meals at Chez Danton's competitors, but I am the ruler here. Get used to living under a tyrant."

"I love pizza," she said plaintively.

He arranged a change of menu and tone instantly. "I would have brought you breakfast in bed before I left." He watched the giant rounding the bases. "I'm living a boy's dream. I have you to make love to and McGwire to slug my fantasy home runs. If only I didn't have murders to deal with." He tore off the heel of Gropier's ba-guette which he had picked up earlier. "It's still warm."

"Thank you." She kissed his fingers and, for her first taste of the day, dipped the bread in a bowl of frothy café au lait and watched the boy-man she had married applauding. "You look like yourself again. You gave me a terrible scare. Michel, please, after this case, end it. We've got such a beautiful life ahead of us."

He became sulky. "I know. But I can't quit now."

"You were with Leon Stein for ages last night and I didn't want to interrupt you guys. Was he hiding from his wife or his girl-friends?"

"Neither. We were spinning tales." She smeared some Banon cheese on the bread and layered it with a finely cut slice of jambon de Toulouse, making a delectable little horn of it.

"Can I do one for you?"

"Thanks, I've eaten." He poured the last drops of espresso from the container, sucked a sugar cube, and sipped it slowly, prolonging his departure.

"Frankly, I'm surprised you're still here."

"I'm waiting for a fax from Venice, California—not Venezia, as you pointed out. They'll call from the office when it gets here."

The remark excited Jennifer. With any luck, Michel had located the killer. "You've got a lead!"

"The lady who left the earring for little Suzy in Pont-Aven does piercings and her boyfriend is a tattooist."

The information thrilled Jennifer and she high-fived him as Jim Edmonds hit a home run.

"Are you telling me he tattooed Caroline Davis and didn't like his work?"

"Or the critics gave him poisonous reviews. I don't know. . . . I better head to the office. *Alors,* I'm in motion."

"Michel, you'll be at the opening," she said, licking the cheese off her fingers and chasing after him to the elevator.

"I wish you and Louise had really gotten to know each other," he said, yearning for his mother, the rich sound of her voice, her elegance and worldly humor. "It's my loss."

She reached up to kiss him good-bye. "I don't understand."

"It doesn't matter."

As he closed the squeaking rusted gates, Jennifer's face was pressed against them. "Our parents are coming back from the cha-teau."

His finger was on the button. "Anything new about Roz and Philippe? Nuzzling in the meadows?"

"No, Nicole is apparently hitting her marks in the sack. Roz said your father's orgasm whoops are his way of turning *her* on."

"He's not that smart. Do they know I was in the hospital?"

"They heard something. I told your father it was a bad oyster and he was very concerned."

Michel pressed the button and the sluggish elevator peevishly inched down. He reached over and clasped Jennifer's fingers through the rusty bars.

"See you tonight, Jennifer."

**An uncharacteristic gloom** and doom Wagnernian mood infiltrated the postbreakfast assembly of the Special Circumstances Section surrounding Dr. Laurent in the vast laboratory. For the moment, the staff's dating arrangements and debt collecting, raillery and sarcasm, bartering time shares with wives and mistresses, had ceased. Michel was back to smoking stubs of Gitanes left in the terrace ashtrays

They all stared at the skeletal remains of what was once a human being. For a group of professional death inspectors and scientists of murder, the method was the message. This was a reality that made the sand under their feet too hot even with the sandals of experience.

Clumps of brackish, yellowed flesh still adhered to parts of the skull and even hardened veterans like Timone the DNA specialist, and Andrea, the svelte Eurasian sovereign of hair and fiber, had no glib remarks to make. After physical chemistry experiments on the body, Nana Orleans meditated morbidly. Roger Faure, whose toxicology report everyone had read, had adjourned his chess game with Albert Devoire because serology analysis stopped at A-Positive. For once Sophie Casel, the lab supervisor, whose giddy laughter masked her bullying, was not watching the clock and saving the government overtime.

Dr. Xavier Roux, the forensic anthropologist, had been called back from Gleneagles in Scotland. He had been trying to renew his vows with his gorgeous wife and while he was at it, lower his handicap to compete with Michel in their weekly golf game. After examining the body, he had lost some of his links color.

"I've never encountered anything like it . . . even when I was reconstructing skeletons from Egyptian tombs."

Dr. Leon Stein had also been called in to ascertain the psychological modality of the killer, and was holding forth. "According to Xavier, the killer used fuming nitric acid twice, so he must have some background in chemistry. He knows how to protect himself from burns. He might have worked in a dye factory or munitions works, whatever, but he's clearly not afraid of it."

Michel was leafing through a sheaf of faxes when Richard Caron came by. He was wearing a navy blue double-breasted interview suit with his *legion d'honneur*. He was followed by a troop of disenchanted recruits the Paris Inspectorate had shipped down to barbaric Marseille in the hope that one of them would finally pass muster and replace Michel.

Michel waved a friendly welcome to them. "Hello, everyone. I hope no one suffers from acid reflux. If you'd care to stay . . ."

He listened for an instant to the silence. Every one of his detectives had attended exhumations from quicklime to Sunday, but, under the lab lights, this acid maceration horrified them. Richard had his secretary lead the prospects back to his office for coffee and croissants while he remained to spread good cheer. It was part of his interview process.

"Do we know who this was?" Richard asked, indicating the cadaver.

"Jan Korteman, formerly a photographer," Michel said. "His dentist in Bruges sent his X-rays earlier."

Richard nodded, unsurprised. "Lovely, Michel. I finally wrangled the writs from Interpol. The police in Bruges did their job. I just got off the phone with them. They went through Korteman's house. No blood anywhere and, according to the staff who accompanied the investigators, nothing appeared to be disturbed or unusual. Korteman had two Americans staying with him for several months. Apparently a husband and wife, and they all left in mid-June.

"Thank you, Richard. . . . Now, some months earlier an American woman visited him and caused quite a stir. Sylvie reported this when she interviewed a barman in Bruges. Immigration sent her surveillance photo as well. "She looks remarkably like this actress Pamela Anderson. Her name, however, is Heather Malone."

The other detectives gathered around to look at the photograph.

"The Belgians have an exit ticket and photo for Malone, so she's clear." Michel scanned the faxes. "Now here's our problem. Interpol has identified the man who stayed with Korteman as Garrett Lee Brant. He registered at Die Swaene Hotel in Bruges with his wife, Eve. But Eve Brant never cleared immigration. I wonder how or why she failed to do this."

"With all the meetings in Brussels, people sometimes slip through the net," Richard said.

"Forgive me, Richard, but I don't agree," Michel said. "The Belgians are scrupulous about entry because of the constant terrorist threats to NATO and the European Union in Brussels. The homicide division is the weak link in their setup—not immigration."

"Good thing I'll be taking retirement," Richard said. "I'm burned out." As he was about to leave, he smiled at Michel. "We both are."

For a moment, Michel sulked. He was not burned out. He felt alive again, in pursuit.

He had one of the techs put Garrett's photo on the screen and they saw a handsome bald man, with sharp, distinct features, a fine, straight nose, and prominent cheekbones. It was a sensitive, strikingly beautiful face that a movie star or model would be happy to have. His blue eyes had a strange, sadly languid quality.

"Here's our tattoo artist."

"He's gorgeous," Sylvie said.

"I wouldn't mind handling him," Annie chirped in.

"I hope you get the chance very quickly," Michel snapped. "Now, as you're all aware from Sylvie's report, this couple has been parading around as our dead friends from last summer—Darrell Boynton and Maddie Gold.

"They met them, were pals, or Brant and his wife read about them and decided to use their identities in Bruges because they murdered Caroline Davis. Jennifer suggested that since the Brants do tattoos and piercings, Eve Brant might have been the one who pierced Maddie Gold's private parts."

More faxes were thrust into Michel's hands.

"This is incredible. No police or FBI record for either of the Brants and no military service for Garrett. This doesn't make sense. If they don't have police records, why would Eve Brant enter Belgium or anywhere illegally?" Michel mused, "They murder Caroline Davis, drive from Bruges to Provence, and heave her body off a boat near La Ciotat."

"It was a ruse to avoid detection in Bruges," Annie said.

"Maybe, Annie." Michel turned away from her. "Have the maritime authorities check their records for a boat registered to Korteman and get the name of the boat, Pierre."

Sylvie joined in, averting her eyes from the body. "On a whim, they go to Pont-Aven and try another kidnapping."

"That was impulsive and failed. They were better prepared for Les Alyscamps in Arles when they used a Taser on Gerta Sholler. Has anyone discovered anything about her?" Michel asked.

"No, not really," Annie said, flicking through a dossier. "Sister Trude went back to Munich and sent us all the school photos and records they had of Gerta at Immaculate Conception. But to answer your question, there have been no developments at all. And it's not through lack of trying."

He realized that his honeymoon night and subsequent hospitalization had slowed the investigation. He had good people under him, but they needed direction.

He referred to the faxes. "The Brants have platinum American Express cards, Visas with—my God—twenty-thousand-dollar limits! A very creditworthy couple. But Die Swaene's bill shows that Korteman paid it. Since he's no longer around to play rich uncle, alert all the credit companies. And have them notify us of any charges.

"Émile, I'd like you to have Judge Fournier prepare the injunctions for this. Now, everyone, let's be clear about this: I want the press blackout maintained. We can't have the killers know that we've found Korteman.

"I'll contact the Venice police in California and have them visit the Brants and their shop." He smiled. "Oh, listen to this my friends: The name of their business is the Gauguin Salons. Isn't that lovely? Just our luck to have Francophiles. And the owner of the property is listed as Heather Malone. Émile, when you've finished with the injunctions, contact all the airlines and see if Malone came in to France or has any reservations. We've got her passport number."

When his detectives dashed to their assignments, Michel quietly scrutinized Jan Korteman's ravaged body. A rhapsodic lyrical movement played through his mind. Had Garrett Brant murdered his wife and had someone impersonate her in Bruges, then brought Korteman into the conspiracy? Or possibly this couple wasn't the Brants at all and had killed them, stolen their passports, and were in fact doubling for dead people to veil the kidnapping of young girls.

As he sought to gather his impressions, the singular geography of the kidnappings struck him again. Jules Chardin had innocently, unknowingly, suggested a link. Arles and Pont-Aven were towns associated with Paul Gauguin, who had gone to Brittany to paint when he was broke. His appearance in Arles was at the insistence of van Gogh, who hoped to establish a painters' school of the south with Gauguin. Gauguin's visit had disastrous consequences. The two artists quarreled and this was long thought to be the reason for van Gogh slashing his ear with a razor.

Arles and Pont-Aven. Was he reading something into this, creating a propinquity that didn't exist? Was it simply a coincidence? Still, what possessed them to bring Caroline to Avignon and then travel hundreds of kilometers to Brittany and attempt to kidnap Suzy when they were settled in Jan's villa outside Avignon? Provence was ripe with young girls. Why Pont-Aven, of all places? What was the driving force?

He took a final look at Jan Korteman before the attendants came.

"This case thunders with madness, identity changes, demonic masks, and profound ambiguities," he told Stein.

"Don't forget sadism," Stein said, smiling and taking his arm. "Mr. Brant enjoys watching others suffer."

"You're right, Leon."

"Now, Michel, how does Le Petit Nice sound to you? A cold glass of Meursault with Rougets sautéed in pistachio oil."

"Wonderful." He put an arm around Stein's bulky waist. "Leon, now tell me the truth. You haven't been messing around with Xavier's wife again."

"No, it's been at least two years. She insulted me the last time we were together."

"Really?"

"She said I was wearing her out, and she's twenty-eight years old. Michel, I don't know about young people nowadays. All they want to talk about is business and gyms, but they have no stamina. I mean to say, when you're making love, isn't that supposed to be exercise—better than a treadmill?"

"No question."

"How are you doing in that department with your luscious package?"

"The world record holder for the hundred-meter dash," he said with a frown. "With Yvette, I couldn't get an erection, and now I'm a speed demon."

"That's simple to cure. When you're in the act, get the process totally out of your mind. Think of something else."

"Like what?"

"I don't know. You're a baseball fan, aren't you? Think of a game. That should slow you down."

"Baseball, while I'm with Jennifer? That's a sacrilege. They say psychiatrists are crazy, and you really prove it."

# 3

# WHERE
# ARE WE
# GOING?

# CHAPTER 29

**It had taken a** few days to locate, but Jan had friends wherever he traveled. For a price they would cheerfully procure anything. Four drums of nitric acid had been stolen from a fertilizer plant and delivered to one of the villa's outbuildings late on the third night while Garrett and Eve relaxed. They had to settle for protective wet suits and purchased them at a divers' supply house in Marseille.

After a pleasant lunch at the Brasserie de Catalans, they took a leisurely drive back to Avignon. Jan's classic Provence villa had whitewashed rough-cast walls, elegant antiques. The cushy furniture with its bright prints made the living room warm and appealing. Collages of photos and abstract paintings, which Garrett dismissed, were everywhere. While Jan was fixing drinks, Garrett throbbed with excitement and brandished one of the newspapers they had bought.

"Listen to this! There's going to be an Impressionist show in Aix on June twenty-third. Midsummer's Eve. He read:

> "Never-before-seen paintings by Cézanne, recently discovered Gauguins, Renoir, Matisse, Bonnard—all from the Vercours Collection—will be open to the public. This exhibition has been curated by Professor Jules Chardin, recently retired from the Sorbonne, and Professor Jennifer Bowen from Stanford, who also wrote the *catalogue raisonné*."

Garrett's face was illuminated by an epiphany. He took this as confirmation of his divine mission. Gauguin had met with disappointments throughout his life and travels, obstacles that had to be overcome to achieve great work, and now Garrett was being put to the test. His expertise had lain in murder, poisonings for the most part; kidnapping would be added to the repertoire. He needed models, dozens of them, hundreds, who knew?

"This is a direct message from Paul. He wants me to see this art show to inspire me. He's unfathomable, inscrutable. One minute he berates me, the next he's telling me to go on! I mean, Jan, the man is filled with contradictions."

"We're living proof of contradictions," Jan, ever droll, observed.

"Polarities create tension and bring out the best in the artist," Garrett said. "I'm on track."

He finished his cognac. "Eve and I have some work to do on Caroline. See you in the morning, my dear Jan."

In one of the outbuildings where the acid drums had been delivered, Garrett's tattoos, unconscionably damaged by the girl, were obliterated.


**The following morning,** from Jan's spacious yacht cruising past La Ciotat, Caroline Davis was buried at sea. Afterward, in a fey mood, Eve came on deck and informed Jan that Garrett was now in deep discussions with Gauguin.

She was enchanting. In a floppy straw boater and a tight denim cutoffs, Eve relaxed on a deck lounge. Jan surveyed the latitude of her long alabaster legs; the modest bosom she had complained about during their visit to Binche during Fat Tuesday was an aphrodisiac for him. He peered at the sculpted face, the elegant nose, her long red hair pinned up in a French roll. Eve's lithe figure aroused him, tortured him; he switched on the automatic pilot and joined her. He prayed that the conference between Gauguin and Garrett would last until dinner.

Although he wanted to lay his head below her and kiss her beautiful toes, he restrained himself. Eve had an aversion to a blatant approach. She gave him short shrift when she sensed him groveling. Exquisite torment. Eve could come on to strangers like that bartender Pieter in Bruges, but no one was permitted to make a move on her. In the absence of the Sun King, his queen consort ruled.

"How about a glass of Cristal, or I'll make you a perfect Grey Goose martini? I had my people stock the boat before we arrived."

She put down her Berlitz phrase book and held up a can of Diet Coke. "No, thank you, Jan. Everything's perfect." Then she grumbled. "Will I ever speak French the way Garrett does? He's so demanding. Sometimes I wonder if he's worth all the trouble."

Jan removed his gold-braided captain's hat and waved to passing yachts. "That's a decision only the two of you can make."

She turned on her side. Her pink silk T-shirt rode up, exposing the top of her buttocks. Jan gaped at her flesh, deeply aroused.

"I dunno. Garrett and Gauguin have been bickering again. I thought when I came on this trip that we'd get rid of Paul. But he's relentless. He told Garrett we have to go to Pont-Aven."

Jan had never disposed of a body, and here they had him on the move again, stalling his own murder ecstasy schemes.

"My dear lady, that's hours away by car."

"Garrett loves driving and eating at the truck drivers' stops."

*"Les routiers!"* Jan said. "Not again."

"We can say good-bye now, Jan. You're clean and so are we."

"Why Brittany?"

"If you follow in someone's footsteps long enough, you might lose them in their own concentric circles."

"I'm not sure I understand."

"You live in a linear world of cause and effect. We don't. Our worlds intersect."

He picked up her Coke and sucked at the mouth, anything to taste her sweet smell. Little bubbles of sweat dripped down her forehead over the sunblock and he wanted to lick them.

"What does Garrett want in Pont-Aven that he can't find in Provence?" he pleaded.

"A fresh canvas. The association with Gauguin means a lot to him. He fights it, but Paul always wins the big battles."

The lovely moment at sea had been ruined for Jan.

"There's the protocol for doing this."

"No, it's so easy," she cooed, leaning down and running her tongue on his earlobe. "You're delicious, Jan. If only you hadn't . . ."

He waited expectantly for the triumphant encounter to begin, but her mercurial mood swing caught him completely off balance. She viciously kicked him and he splayed on his back like a crab. She kicked him again until he was rolling on the varnished deck.

"What are you doing? Stop."

She had her foot on his windpipe and he felt his life buckling.

"You're a disgusting old man. You raped Caroline. She was a virgin canvas for Garrett. I examined her before the acid wash. This isn't about cheap, depraved sex, it's about a commitment to art. And we are the servants of art!" She glowered at him. "You and that bitch Heather are obsessed with sex. Frankly, it's disgusting. Garrett thinks Caroline went crazy after you raped her and that's why she ruined his work. She was a sensitive girl, Jan. How could you?"

When everyone had been asleep in the house, the temptation had been overpowering. Jan had clutched the girl during a drugged period between sleeping and waking. He wanted to remind Eve that he felt entitled to a reward for his deadly services.

"I had certain needs that weren't considered," he protested.

"Needs? What do you think I am, some low-life madam out to snatch kids for you to screw! For your own good, don't try anything like that again with Garrett's models."

"I acted stupidly. If you want to know the truth, the experience with Caroline was very unsatisfying." He grasped the rail and stood up shakily. "Eve, I wanted you and Garrett—not some drugged girl. Isn't that obvious?"

Eve's taut face relaxed and her mysterious smile captivated him. "We'll see, when the time is right."

**They had botched** the abduction of the young girl during the foray in Pont-Aven. A waiter had intervened and he and Eve were fortunate to escape. Jan's nerves were ragged on the drive back to Avignon and Eve was silent, angry. His protests about laying the groundwork were futile. Eve, Garrett's agent, was out of control and he struggled to find some solution. How could he extricate himself?

After a night in which his fears gave way to exhaustion, he arose to find Eve dressed and made up as he had never before seen her. She wore a gray wig, old-fashioned winged sunglasses, a washed-out print dress, and sneakers; a camera was lassoed around her high collar. A bulky purse hung from her shoulder and she personified the middle-aged female tourist.

"I took the car, got it gassed, and had everything checked." She did a little pirouette. "And I went shopping in Avignon. Do I look old enough to have a teenage daughter?"

He rubbed the sleep from his eyes and took the proffered black coffee.

During the night he had been bitten by a squadron of mosquitoes and reached under his sodden nightshirt to scratch. "Where are you going?" he asked listlessly, and sipped the coffee she'd made.

"Garrett said you and I are going to Arles. Jan, I pleaded with him and we argued. He's impossible." She closed her eyes with a flutter. "I wanna go home to California. Our Venice Canals, our house, which I love. I'm such a housewife when I'm at *chez-nous*. No takeouts and never pizza. It's such a snug nest."

"That's the best idea. Look, it didn't work out with Caroline. I blame myself and accept responsibility. Eve, we were almost caught in Pont-Aven. You and Garrett can fly direct now to Los Angeles from Marseille—"

She shook her head and there was a stern expression in her nut-brown colored contacts. "Garrett believes we have a meeting with destiny at Les Alyscamps. Van Gogh and Gauguin both painted it. Vincent's picture is the more famous of them, but Paul, our beloved Paul Gauguin, did by far the better piece of work."

Jan rubbed his bleary eyes and recoiled when she took an object out of her ugly purplish bag. She pointed something at him.

"What's that? Are you mad? He flinched, spilled hot coffee on his bare legs. "What're you doing . . . ?"

"BUPPP. It's a Taser. Fast and furious, like the Old West. One pop, and we'll have our canvas."

She opened the front door and Jan was enveloped in brilliant, blinding sunlight and his gnarled olive trees looked as though they were drunk on champagne. He cupped his hand over his brow.

"Meet our new friend, Jan."

He heard yapping, shook his head in disbelief as a friendly little Bichon Friese licked Eve's hand.

"Where did you get the dog?"

"Oh, some old man tied him up outside a butcher's shop in Avignon while he was waiting in line."

"You stole a dog? . . . In France, that's worse than murder."

"There was a long line at the butchers and this old geezer was reading his paper." She smirked at him. "Little girls love dogs like this." She picked up the dog and kissed his nose. "You little lovely." The dog licked her chin with gratitude. "His new name is Chi-Chi. Jan, a woman walking a little beauty like him along Les Alyscamps won't really be noticed, will she?"

"I think this is reckless, madness."

"Well, Jan, maybe you won't have to come along next time."


**That evening the** kidnappers were in a congratulatory mood at the villa. Festive glasses of champagne were raised in the pink guest bedroom where Gerta Sholler, name unknown at this point by the celebrants, lay slumbering on a magnificent bed with an antique faience headboard depicting the Three Graces.

Eve had patiently and cautiously tracked the group of schoolgirls and the nuns who herded and lectured them on the sultry afternoon in Arles. Sweltering tourists were shoulder to shoulder and Les Alyscamps resembled a sports stadium, its souvenir hawkers, food wagons, and troublemakers everywhere.

Eve and Chi-Chi charmed the tourists and particularly Gerta, who couldn't take her eyes off Eve and her prize pet. Eve crooked her finger and the girl charily checked on the nuns in the group, less vigilant than they had been earlier in the day.

Eve, smiling with encouragement, lured the girl to a grove of trees and chatted with her. As the platinum blond demoiselle stooped to pet Chi-Chi, Eve shot the Taser into her arm. She caught hold of her, then Jan wearing his black chauffeur's uniform came out of a thicket of bushes. They helped the girl to the Mercedes. If anyone asked what was wrong, they would explain that she had fainted.

Stroking his new model in the guestroom, Garrett regarded Jan with affection and gratitude.

"She'll be out for a few more hours," Garrett said. "Her pressure is a little low and the pulse is slow but stable." He put an arm around Jan and hugged him. "What an adventure we've led you on. You know, Eve and I are starting to feel more than friendship for you."

With his fantasy coupling suggested to him and the approach-avoidance technique on hold, Jan succumbed to this blandishment. He was aware that he must retain a degree of diplomacy and not rush or frighten his prey.

"If the three of us were actually to experiment to . . . it would relieve the tension. Don't you think? Frankly, Eve was disgusted by my behavior. Garrett, I am as well. I'm so sorry for what happened with Caroline. I never in my wildest dreams thought she'd damage your work."

"That's behind us. This new girl is even better suited for what I have in mind."

"Shall we all get cleaned up?" Eve coyly asked. "I want to put on my frilly lingerie and get silly, Jan. Do you have any preferences?"

"Why don't you surprise me?"

She ran her finger along Jan's lips. "You caught me at a good time. I want the full Tantric discipline."

"The *Tantra Maithuna.*" Jan was beside himself, envisioning the supreme moment and photographing them as he had others in his master bedroom, a chamber of mirrors.

"Will an hour give you enough time, Eve?" Jan asked.

"Garrett and I'll be there. I'm ready to bust some balls tonight."


**Jan poured a** potpourri of sweet-smelling Provençal fragrances into his large tub and while it filled, he shaved. He trimmed his fingernails and filed them flat, then coated the loofah with Verveine and scrubbed his body to a fare-thee-well. He oiled himself while drying. Sparkling in his blue-print kimono, he entered his bedroom like a baron after a victorious battle. But he was as nervous as a virgin.

Unfortunately, the lights were dimmed and the prospect of filming the action was impossible, but he told himself to do nothing to unsettle his quarry. This overture to the Roman Saturnalia he had pictured was before him. The Nubian slaves begging for pleasure instead of death?

"I hope you don't mind, but I brought up a couple of bottles of champagne," Garrett said.

"Wonderful. I hope you picked the Dom Perignon '90. It's for occasions like this."

"We got it," Eve said with a mischievous giggle, which titillated him.

She had made up her face with the translucent Japanese rice powder he liked so much; her long lashes fluttered coquettishly; a hint of rouge blushed her cheeks; the lips he couldn't wait to press against were a lustrous Chinese red. Afterward they might agree to initiate their sleeping captive next door. He had dragged the German girl through the woods until he was exhausted and bundled her into the trunk of the car, which was rank with death.

Jan hoisted his courage. Like a backer of a play, he would have his reading by the performers.

"Would you like a pipe first?"

Garrett was indifferent. "Drugs?"

"It's phenomenal opium, the highest quality. I have a Chinese friend in Marseille who supplies the Corsicans."

"We're not into drugs, but you can have a smoke," Garrett said.

"Never mind." Jan's eyes fixed on the vision before him. "Which of you would like to begin? Eve or Garrett?"

Eve gave him a wanton smile. He was mesmerized when she lifted her red silk panties. With an uncontrollable mating snort, he gazed at her pink, shaved pussy, the delicate golden miniature butterfly tattooed just above the clitoris. He was astounded by her perfection, the beauty that she had concealed from him. He drank a glass of champagne and thought he might tease them, stir things up.

"Do I detect jealousy?"

"No way, we want to share this with you," Garrett replied with a serene look. "That's what Heather's been after. The problem with Heather and her crazy makeover was about me. Heather was normal when we met. Lovely. I tattooed her and she fell in love with me. I can't explain this madness that goes on with people who have everything until they wake up one morning and want to be goddesses or somebody else."

Garrett gulped down his champagne and Jan was enthralled by this backstage dish about their sex which obsessed him.

"Heather thought I'd actually marry her. She still does! Heather will do anything to get what she can't have. I wouldn't fuck her on a bet."

Garrett refilled his glass with champagne and thrust himself back on the satin pillows. Eve was beside him and whined, "Me, too, I want some."

She took the flute and clumsily spilled some on the fresh sheets.

"Sorry. One more drink and I'll slap you till Tuesday, Eve. Now shut up."

Enthralled, Jan came closer, laying his head at Garrett's feet.

"Please, tell me what went on with Heather and Eve."

"Jan, I gave Heather my soul. But Heather humiliated Eve. Pissed on her. The works. I won't make love to another woman now that Eve and I are together. Heather can hire people. But we're not rough trade."

Eve turned her luminous face to Jan and crooked his neck in her arms. She was tearful and miserable.

"You have to understand, Jan . . . I did everything Heather asked me to do. But it wasn't enough to please her. Abuse, humiliation. *I'm nada*. Garrett's her god."

Sharing these intimate, important secrets heightened Jan's excitement. Jan felt as though he were weightless in the gravity of the unknown. He pressed his lips against Eve's. Her tender response encouraged him in this mysterious exploration. He nuzzled her neck.

"A woman's touch. Oh, God, Eve, Eve, you are everything . . . magnificent."

"You *really* want to film this, don't you?" Garrett asked.

"It would be an unforgettable memory. You know I'd give anything." Jan licked every plausible part of her and she gasped with the moment.

"So would Heather," Eve said. "If she could have Garrett again—even on film—she'd be in heaven."

"It wouldn't take much time to adjust the lighting," Jan said, swallowing in one draught another glass of Dom Perignon. Eager to capture this seduction for his collection, he whispered to Eve. She giggled, nodded, and kissed his forehead.

"Garrett, get it together, let's really make Jan happy. I'm going to do him like no else ever has."

Jan was so intoxicated by the prospect, he could hardly control the nervous palpitations throbbing in his neck and chest. Butterflies. He must calm down and establish a better breathing rhythm, wipe the images from his mind, enter the spirit of the Tantra. But an indefinite . . . alarming sensation overcame him. He felt clumsy and coarse.

"Eve, ohhhh," he crooned. "Garrett. Garrett . . . Eve." He was in the rhapsody of the ideal ménage à trois.

As Jan fondled Eve, then stroked Garrett, time and spatial relationships began to disintegrate and he experienced a form of saccade. Something had altered his optic nerve. The jerky motion of his eye created an image before it actually wanted to involve itself in the scene. The blood vessels in his brain were imploding and the brain stem connecting the cerebral hemispheres buzzed with indefinable static, breaking up the signal of the relay station. He labored to retain consciousness.

They were upon him and he identified the deadly code of assassins. For an instant, he thought he might be dreaming and floating through a glacial mass surrounded by countless galaxies of fire and ice. But the powers of apprehending what was happening faded as a living enactment of a chrysalis . . . a metamorphosing occurred.

He detected, hovering over him, two faces, transmuting their images, Janus-like in their horror, inducing these convulsions within his brain.

He was lifted onto his massage table and he beheld long, shining steel needles. He seemed to be melting, turning into fluid, as though his mind and body were in a vat, undergoing a hideous chemical deliquescence.

"You old degenerate. You're the worst kind of pervert," Eve screeched.

For an instant Jan imagined he heard the enigmatic Gauguin's voice. "Where are you going?" the artist asked.

The needles drew nearer, the points inexorably moving straight into his eyes. His body was paralyzed and the only sound he recognized in the dark cavern of oblivion was the hiss of acid.

Jan Korteman vanished. . . .

# CHAPTER 30

**Although the Chardin Gallery** was closed to the public and the sign on the door read PRIVÉE, Lucy Kahn-Smith, the self-styled freelance American art news journalist who specialized in gossip and happenings in the art world, barged in. She was not to be denied. The attendant at the door didn't quite know how to cope with her combative behavior, since the vernissage was for invited guests. He immediately called over Jules, who was busy greeting members of the local society.

"You must know my byline and who *I* am, Monsieur Chardin." The mayor was leaning over Jules with some councilmen. She withdrew a plastic press card. "My articles are in the *International Herald* and the *London Times*."

Jules was befuddled, rushed, and more guests were smothering him. "Yes, yes, of course, do please come in, madame. You'll have to check your camera."

"Certainly," she said, and another attendant gave her a ticket for the Nikon.

Like any journalist, Lucy headed for the table of hors d'oeuvres and plucked a plump curried shrimp on a toast point, reached over some people, and seized a glass of champagne before they ran out of the good stuff as was usual at gallery openings.

She gobbled a few more morsels, stuffed a couple of catalogues into her purse, and elbowed her way to Jennifer, who was being interviewed by journalists from *Le Monde, Le Figaro,* and a team from *Connoisseur,* as well as celebrated art critics from all of the major European publications. At a momentary pause, Lucy crooked Jennifer's arm.

"Professor Bowen, I'm a fellow American, please give me a break. I'm with the *International Herald Tribune* and a syndicate of other papers, please give me a minute. It'll mean such a lot . . . to me personally and every art lover back in the States."

Jennifer glanced at the frowsy woman with her ghastly green dress with dew drops, cheap beads, the wide space between her horsey front teeth, and the worn, tacky shoulder bag dangling from her limp shoulder.

"You're Ms. . . . ?"

"Lucy Kahn-Smith." A small tape recorder was immediately switched on. "I'm a great admirer of yours. I read about you last year during that murder rampage in Aix. Your pluck. I'm so proud of you being the one to show these French experts that Americans aren't philistines."

"You're right," Jennifer said.

"How did you acquire these unknown Gauguins?"

Kristin, wearing an angelic pink tulle dress and her long hair upswept, came by with a tray of hors d'oeuvres. The girl had been enlisted to help with the service when one of the waiters called in with car trouble. Through the throngs Michel appeared. He stooped down to kiss Kristin on the forehead and then leaned over to take Jennifer's hand.

"This is my husband, Michel Danton. They're his paintings. He inherited them from his godmother."

Michel was in no mood for an art show, but Jennifer and Jules had worked hard mounting the exhibition. To this end, he had rushed from his meeting with the Section, shaved and showered for the second time that day, and changed into a light mustard green suit that Vellancio had made for him, ripping his eyes out and remarking that Armani wasn't good enough to thread his needles.

He tried to avoid the woman's curry breath. "Hello," Michel said, "you are . . . ?"

"A journalist. Lucy Kahn-Smith. It's a great pleasure meeting you, sir." She put the tape recorder up to Michel. "I'm talking to Michel Danton. If you have a moment, please tell me a little about the Vercours Collection."

"My wife has written about the work in the catalogue. She'll be giving a short talk in a few minutes."

A pudgy hand reached across and snared a hunk of pâté from Kristen's tray. Although he didn't see whose face it was, Vellancio's signet ring was Michel's clue. Irmegard, wearing a chrome yellow silk creation and mauve silk blouse, towered above the rotund tailor-couturier. He straightened Kirstin's pink tulle collar.

Nicole dashed from the campsite kitchen she had installed in the back of the gallery. "Kristen, how's the food situation?"

"There was a run on the chard pie and the pissaladière," she said.

"They're coming, and some more of the pork crepinettes are on the way," Philippe said.

"The rissoles are delicious," Lucy said, spearing the last one on Kristen's tray.

Philippe smugly nodded. He was slowly changing his opinions of Americans and their taste buds. "It's my own recipe. It may eventually appear in the new *Larousse Gastronomique*. I'm debating about making it public."

"Cooking masterpieces and paintings," Lucy trilled. "It was worth flying from Paris for this," she said, unable to expand on these tributes, for the crowd had swelled to at least two hundred when Jules signaled to close the doors.

*"Messieurs et dames, bievenue,"* Jules said in his rich voice, standing at the podium. "Last year when I retired from the Sorbonne, I thought that I'd take some time off to decide what I wanted to do. I was encouraged by my wife Grace not to vegetate and at her insistence, I came to the conclusion that I could best serve the art community by opening a gallery in my hometown. This gallery would be devoted to showing the paintings of new artists who might not have a chance to have their work seen by the public.

"It never occurred to me that, through the generosity of the Danton family and Professor Jennifer Bowen-Danton, we would open with the collection of paintings assembled by the late Louise Vercours, for whom this collection of masterpieces is named. These paintings were bequeathed to Michel Danton and it was he and his wife who made this possible. We all now have the opportunity to view the unknown works of the giants of art. Now I'd like to introduce the lady who made this possible, Madame Jennifer Bowen-Danton."

Jennifer had not lectured for more than a year and she relished the opportunity. In an elegant pastel blue suit she came to the podium amid resounding applause. She was radiant with excitement. Impossible to predict the future; last year she'd been teaching rich reprobate girls and now she was a grande dame in Aix. She thought of this while making her way through the crowd.

"It's a pleasure to be here at opening of the Chardin Gallery and to play a small part in this momentous evening. Through his bequest, my husband Michel Danton has decided to share his inheritance. We have paintings that have seldom been seen, except by their previous owners, and they have never been brought together in a single hanging. I won't go into the history of each painting, which I've covered in the catalog with Jules's help.

"There were fourteen in all, ranging from Watteau's elegant lyric *Lady at Her Toilette* to three works by Aix's native son Cézanne—all collected by the late Madame Vercours. Unbeknownst to my husband and myself, his father, Philippe Danton, when going through the Vercours chateau, discovered three more paintings, which he has generously contributed to this permanent collection. These are now four magnificent works by Paul Gauguin: one from his days at the Pension Gloanac in Pont-Aven, an early version of Breton women dancing; the second is from his period in Arles when he visited Van Gogh; and finally two from his final period in the Marquesas. Along with two Bonnards, three Renoirs, a Degas, a Monet, the great Matisse *Odalisque,* and a Picasso. I am deeply honored to present them to you."

She signaled an usher, switched on the lights, and opened the doors to the main gallery.

"Please enrich your lives by having the first public view of the Vercours Collection."

Philippe's monumental chest thrust out with self-importance and he hooked arms with Rosalind and Nicole, leading the way into the airy space where the paintings hung.

"Americans, maybe they're not so bad after all," he condescendingly informed Rosalind.

"You're now a patron of the arts," Rosalind informed him. "Your name will be in museums."

"That's where my *côte de boeuf au trois poivres* belongs."

Vincent Sardou, the elderly barrister who had drawn up Louise Vercours's will and had become Michel's confidant, was flushed with excitement. He tapped his ivory-headed cane and Michel cleared a path so that he might get a better view of the art.

"Louise would have been delirious with joy," he told Michel.

"This was Jennifer's idea . . . sharing *her* art with the public. It offended Jennifer to simply keep it for ourselves—out of sight."

"She was right."

"I had an idea about how best to create some memorial for Louise and I've discussed it with Jules. We've been playing with the idea of having a bronze or a statue—"

"Louise would have hated that. She was never one for ostentation."

"That's what I felt, which is why I haven't gone forward. Now at the farm in St-Rémy, just outside Nicole's greenhouse, there's a brow of a hill filled with poppies and I was thinking of commissioning a sundial with Louise's face engraved at the center and a small plaque."

Never one to make a hasty decision, Sardou considered it. "That sounds more like Louise. Do you want her ashes . . . ? I have them in the urn in my office and I pray for her every day."

"No, you must keep them."

"Thank you, Michel. When my time comes, you can, of course, have them. Yes, I like the notion of a sundial in stone. Something like that would have pleased her. When it's ready, perhaps we can have a short ceremony. No priests," he added quickly. "Lescaut certainly made a hash of your wedding."

"He was scolding me for talking, just as he did when I was his student."

They paused in front of the Gauguin painting of the Breton women dancing. Lucy Kahn-Smith stood before it, her eyes glazed over with adoration.

"It's overwhelming," she said. "There'd be no modern art without him."

"You're probably right, but my wife would certainly make a case for Cézanne."

"Both of them giants. Thank you for allowing me in. I'm inspired," she said, walking off.

She made her way through the mass of visitors and Sardou said, "Odd woman."

"She's a journalist who crashed."

As Lucy threaded her way to the hors d'oeuvres table, she spied Kristen standing off to the side and she took the girl's hand.

"Could I take a little of the pâté for my dog?"

"Yes, what kind of dog do you have?"

"A little Bichon, and he hasn't been well."

"Really?" she said with concern.

"He's in the car out back. Come and have a look with me."

In the parking lot behind the gallery, Lucy opened the rear door carefully and slid in with Kristen.

"Chi-Chi, come and say hello to our new friend." The dog climbed over the seat and kissed Kristen then curled on Lucy's lap.

"It's Kristen, isn't it?"

"Yes."

"Is there a vet around here?"

"On Boulevard Roi René."

"I'm afraid I don't know Aix and I'll get lost. Would you please show me? I'll drop you right back," Lucy said, switching on the air-conditioning and locking the doors of the Citroën SUV she had rented.

"We won't be long?" Kristen asked.

"No, a few minutes," she said, pulling out into the evening traffic. "I've got a bottle of Coke in the ice cooler and some cups."

**Sylvie Caron hurtled** through the crowd in the gallery and apologized when she knocked someone's drink over. An ebullient Michel was surrounded by his family, and Philippe was saying, "What happened to you in Avignon?"

"Wedding dinner heartburn."

"Not from my food!" He glared at Nicole. "Probably the Lobster Américaine. It was so rich."

"Michel, sorry, but I have to see you."

With a smile, he extricated himself."

"We've got Garrett Brant. He just checked into Les Quatre Dauphins. The manager phoned the hotline number and I picked up."

"Who's coming?"

"Pierre and Émile are on the way."

"Come on, Sylvie, it'll be quicker if we walk." As Jennifer approached, he said, "Back in a minute. They're towing our cars."

"These traffic police are like Gestapo agents," she said, outraged.

"I'll give them hell."

As they scurried out, he said lightly to Sylvie, "Remind me to thank Brant. He's made it convenient. Right up the street from my apartment."

Michel felt his Glock, holstered neatly below the small of his back, a compromise with Vellancio on his new wardrobe so that there were no bulges in the jacket.

"What are you carrying, Sylvie?"

"A Beretta .22 and a .357 magnum."

"Big gun for a woman."

"I like the noise."

"Do you have cuffs?"

She jangled her bag. "I don't leave home without them."

The hotel was a small affair with perhaps a dozen rooms, favored by students and tourists on a budget. At this hour the town was choked with traffic, and his men had not yet arrived. Michel calmly opened the door, walked to the desk, and showed his police card to the clerk, who pointed to a large knapsack with a metal shoulder bar.

"Where is he?"

"He just went out to a café to get a beer. He said he'll be back in a few minutes."

"Let me have his passport."

The blue American passport was handed to Michel, who flipped open the page to the photograph and saw the same picture that Belgian immigration had sent to them.

"Did he register?" Sylvie asked.

"Yes, and he left his Visa and the passport. He'd been hiking and was very thirsty."

In five minutes, Pierre and Émile were double-parked outside the entry. Émile got out and signaled to Michel.

"Shall I have the street closed off?"

"No, not yet. Let's hope we can avoid a commotion. Have you got a cigarette?"

Émile reluctantly handed him a crumpled pack of Gauloises.

"I'm still suffering from wedding nerves."

"After all that acid you inhaled, you shouldn't be smoking."

At that moment, a lanky young man with shoulder-length black hair and wearing jeans and a T-shirt which said SITETRACKS.COM stopped at the hotel entrance. He had a sack with beers and water. Michel spun around.

"Garrett Brant."

The young man was puzzled and shrugged him off. "No, who are you?"

"I'm Commander Michel Danton of the Police Judiciare." Michel was now troubled. "Is your name Garrett Brant?"

"No." The young man's eyes were wary. "My name's Mark Breeding."

Michel brandished the passport and opened it again to the photograph. The picture inside and the man in front of him were two different people.

"Can I please see that?" he asked with concern. Michel showed it to him. "Oh, shit, someone must've flipped me."

"Where've you been?" Sylvie asked.

"Just bumming around. I hitchhiked down from Cassis and I spent the night on the beach in La Ciotat. I went to a café to wash up and eat, and left my gear outside."

"Get his backpack from the lobby, Émile, and take him into Marseille."

"Are you arresting me?" he asked, shaken.

"No, but you must have a valid passport or an identity card to remain in France."

With disgust and frustration, he took Sylvie aside. "Brant's beat us again. Do the interrogation, will you? And have Annie check around with Le Milieu's forgers. I want to know about any Americans trying to buy passports. If you turn up anything, I'll be at the gallery celebrating," he said glumly.

# CHAPTER 31

**It was generally conceded** by the staff at the Hôtel Roi René
that no one had ever laid eyes on a creature quite like this American
woman, nor had they ever heard such a voice. The concierge observed that it could cut diamonds; he had waited on aristocrats
from the Continent and England for years but never before encountered such a domineering manner, nor the bellmen as much
luggage. Heather Malone was occupying two of the grand apart-
ments because Garrett had overruled her travel agent, who had
suggested the intimate Villa Gallici or the courtly Pigonnet. Although both hotels claimed they were full, Heather's agent was
instructed to pay double the top rate.

Nevertheless, she was relatively comfortable atop this hotel, even
if it was larger and somewhat commercial, for Garrett had spoken.
She had been out of touch with him—not even a postcard—for
the last few months. Apart from a weekly phone call from Jan,
vague and unsettling, she had no idea what was going on in
Bruges. Yes, Garrett was painting again and the malevolent Eve
was charming.

She had made up her mind to have it out with Garrett and put
an end to Eve. The point was that she had been summoned. The
romantic, witty Garrett from their old days would shortly be back
in her arms. Garrett wanted, needed, desired her again, and she
would have flown to the Congo, Bosnia, into the eye of a hurri-
cane, to be with him.

She had followed her lover's instructions and was shortly to meet
him. She had never been to this peasant part of Provence—only
Cannes and a season at the Hôtel du Cap in Antibes. She was not
enamored of the French. They had an *attitude* and she couldn't

understand their absurd language. Everyone knew that English was the world's language! She'd heard that this part was pretty and that Aix had some history about it, but she was indifferent. She had enough of musty old buildings and guides who never used deodorants. If she had been calling the shots, she would have picked Italy . . . Venice for its beauty; Capri for rough wicked sex. In Capri, all she had to do was whistle and toss some lira out of her window and they'd be climbing along the window ledges or shimmying down from the roof. But it was all meaningless without Garrett.

She had brought her butler Rudy with her to break some heads or smack someone's face if it was necessary. Bart had gone to visit family in England; in any event he hated the Frogs and was a sulky traveler. Much as she adored him in Beverly Hills, she was not about to have him scarfing fish and chips, then barfing in her Learjet.

"Dress down, conservatively, please, Heather, if it's at all possible," Garrett had insisted when he called her a few minutes ago.

The travel agent had arranged for Rudy to pick up a new Mercedes at the Marseille airport. Heather Malone wasn't about to ride around in any of their sweaty, smoky, stinking cabs. Still, without her white Rolls Seraph, she'd be miserable, but would put on a brave front. To placate Garrett, she wore a modest lilac Ungaro sheath with her signature low-cut shell out of which the full G-cleft wiggled for freedom. After all the surgery she had endured, if you had tits, then flash them, she reflected. Tonight she'd have Garrett in her bed climbing all over them.

"I can't get the car through this bloody street," Rudy said after nearly mowing down a group of pedestrians. "Oi, move your arses!" he bellowed, " 'fore I run you riffraff down. Sorry, Heather, I'll have to double-park and walk you to the caff."

"Thank you, Rudy."

Her entrance into Chez Danton was met with astonished silence by the crowd of diners, followed by a beehive of buzzes. Delantier, hurrying into the vestibule, gasped. At the bar, René craned his neck so far down, he knocked over someone's red wine.

With an unctuous, sycophantic bow, Delantier said, *"Bon soir, madame, avez-vous reserveé."*

"Cut it out! Speak English, will you, if you can," she snapped.

"Of course. You have a reservation?"

Heather peered at a large booth in the rear. She whipped out a hundred-dollar bill and handed it to Delantier, whose hands shook when he clasped the crisp bill.

"My name *is* Heather Malone and I'm supposed to be meeting a gentleman."

"Madame Malone, of course."

As she was led to the booth, the customary jaded insouciance toward celebrities in France gave way to rapid-fire discussions, head-swiveling, and murmurs of, "It's her," meaning Pamela Anderson, in whose honor Heather had reconfigured her face and body. Heather loved it. When the table was pulled out, her breast grazed Delantier's chin and he almost had a stroke and orgasm simultaneously. He caught himself in time. She liked to give old geezers a little taste.

"Cocktail?"

"A super-dry, very large Grey Goose martini, two olives, and make it so cold that ice particles are floating on top."

"Of course."

She had hoped for a steakhouse like the Palm or Ruth's Chris, but had to settle for this fossilized place, which Garrett had told her served the best steaks in Aix. They'd have to prove it. The charred smell of beef momentarily reassured her. Garrett was always late, but with this freakin' traffic she'd forgive him. A few moments later, she felt better, sipping the martini, prepared perfectly. As she nibbled an olive, a figure slid beside her and she gaped at the brown eyes behind the horned-rimmed glasses, the salt-and-pepper, preppy hair, and beard, the seersucker jacket and rep tie. Garrett was not middle-aged!

*"Excuse me,"* she said, alarmed, thinking it was another "La Pam" fan.

"It's me."

"Jesus Christ, you like some down-and-out English prof at a

bust-out community college in the Valley. . . . My God, you've got a paunch."

"It's padding. Yes, I'm a professor, I teach a graduate seminar in the art of making love."

"Music to my ears."

He glanced without alacrity at her ensemble. "Is this your idea of demure dressing, Heather? I thought your Bette Midler period was behind you."

"I don't own schmatas, Garrett. Hey, I'll do a raid on Façonnable. I passed one of their outposts in this suburb, or whatever it is."

He caught Delantier's focused eyes. "I'll have one of those. Heather, this is a historic city, settled by the Romans," he notified her.

"Really, one *Gladiator* movie per summer is enough for me."

Heather held the hands she loved under the table. "What's going on . . . with all this cloak-and-dagger craziness?"

"Heather, my darling, a couple of thousand people with badges are looking for me. I'm generating some serious heat."

"Oh, shit. Well, France is no different than any other place. Money talks and bullshit walks."

"My credit cards are in meltdown because of an unfortunate incident. Not because I'm over my limit."

"I have about thirty, forty thousand in cash."

"I don't want to change money at a bank or one of their rip-off joints."

She thought for a moment. "I can give you my corporate platinum Visa. It's the HM Investments."

"That's a good start."

She yanked her billfold out of her purse and threaded through the cards under the table. "Oh, yeah, here's my ATM." She slipped the two cards to him. "The PIN is my birthday."

"An unforgettable moment in the history of Western civilization. What's the limit?"

"Depends on the local transfer bank which the computer is connected to," she said with an expert's knowledge. "There's some kind of a limit on all this and mine is fifty K, I think. After that some weasel's computer starts sending stroke messages, like the card's stolen. Listen, take a few thousand in cash. Believe me, we'll get you out of this."

"I know you will. But it's a little complicated."

She placed her hand on his zipper. "It's hard as a rock."

"It's been waiting for you," he said coyly. "It responds to its mistress's touch."

"Didn't forget me, huh? Of all the people in the world, you're the only one who gets me there. You got a grand-slam bat."

He checked the room, then furtively leaned over and slipped his tongue in her ear and listened to her coo.

"Where's your witch?"

"She's doing a little babysitting for our houseguests."

"Look, when you called me at home, I came on my magic carpet. Now please tell me you're not going to keep me running around. Is it over—with Eve?"

He chimed glasses with Heather and her face lit up.

"Pretty much so."

"Don't give me an ambiguous answer. Are *we* going to be to-gether?"

"Yes. For good, this time."

"Ohhhh, Garrett. Garrett, I could weep. I'm so happy."

"Not here. On my bare shoulder later."

"Baby, we're really overdue and I'm so ready."

She could not, however, release the image of her adversary. "What happened with that bitch . . . and where's Jan?"

"Yes, another round," Garrett informed the attentive waiter. "Where do I begin? Jan fell hard for Eve. He became a bit too intense. I'm loath to call it love—"

"He was in love with *her*!"

"*Possessed* is more like it, and its ugly sibling, obsession. One afternoon . . . while I was out at a museum, he got fresh with her and . . ."

"That snake. He assured me that he believed in your art and he wouldn't try anything."

"It's a pity he didn't memorize your instructions. Well, you know Eve." Heather's face fell. "She had one of her psychotic episodes."

Heather clasped her forehead. "She didn't . . ." Garrett nodded. "A bloodbath?"

"It was a bath of sorts," Garrett agreed.

"Are we finally rid of her? She stole you from me."

"I know, Heather, I've got a lot of fence-mending to do with you."

"Just tell me you love me and we'll be together."

"That's my plan. I don't love you, I worship you."

"Oh, God, you've answered my prayers!"

René's ghostly, nicotine-colored skin had a bit of luster for once. Heather's lavish tipping had worked wonders with his aversion to mixing martinis. With his tarnished sommelier medallion waving around his gawky neck, he presented the wine list. He had left a mob of customers at the bar in order to get a better look at this marvel. Delantier had claimed he'd had his first erection in a decade. This woman did resemble the well-known actress, but up close she was even more beautiful and buxom and she had the tigress's scent, not that he'd recognize it after a lifetime of smoking Gauloises and drinking Pastis.

"If you'd care for champagne, may I recommend La Grande Dâme. We still have some of the '90 left."

"Stick a couple on ice," Heather replied. "How's the food here?"

"*Alors,* Madame Malone, we have the finest marbled Charolais in Provence. Our steaks are considered the most superlative ones in France."

"I'll be the judge of that."

"Connoisseurs come from everywhere—"

"I'm a connoisseur of beef, booze, and lovemaking, so let it unfold."

René lowered his head like a serf before the chatelaine. He'd go to the ends of the earth for a woman like this—exquisite, outspoken, born to lead.

When Garrett was not exasperated with her, he also admired her plucky outrageousness. On her third martini, she kissed him. She wished the booth had velvet curtains like they did in the old costume movies she had seen when she was a kid: Stewart Granger or Errol Flynn or Tyrone Power would sweep the curtains closed and ravage the lady. Heather could hold her liquor like a stevedore and she imagined herself with Garrett again in one of their endless convulsive, unpredictable Arabian Nights, luxuriating in the forbidden adventures of the flesh. Once again, his ruthless but tender touch would be hers; she'd be privy to his long discussions with Gauguin. And afterward she would encourage Garrett in his hopes of immortality, she at his side, his inspiration.

She had done everything to hang on to him, even refashioning her body merely because one night when they were bombed and an old episode of *Baywatch* had been buzzing on TV, he had leaped out of bed when Pam came on screen and said, "I'd make love to her till February has thirty-one days."

At that, the reconstruction blueprint had begun: pouty lips, jawbone enhanced, new choppers, breasts which would support a camel's head, liposuction, surgeons, machines, workouts, personal trainers, transient fads with vegetable slushes, hair, roots, toxicity expunged, privates tightened—not that she'd ever had a brat, but still, a vise was preferable to hold a tool when sawing. And after all this, she had lost Garrett to his own elusive dreams and perilous fantasies.

The champagne was poured. Garrett approved and they toasted. She held back tears and said, "This is paradise regained."

"Heather, you're reading Milton?"

"You made me. Don't you remember the reading lists when we were together?"

"My darling," he said lavishly, "it'll be even better this time. I'm creating a Garden of Eden for us and the world."

"Garrett, I'm thrilled. I always believed in you. I knew you'd find the answer."

"Yes. . . ." His expression was beatific. "And I can continue my work in California. If I ever get out of France."

"That's a done deal."

Garrett knew he had made a serious mistake by not traveling with multiple passports. He had not realized what might lay ahead with Jan.

"You went to my house and got my other passports?"

"Yes, your changes, the works. Everything you'll need."

He clasped her to him. "My angel."

"Is there anything about Jan in the papers?"

"No. I'm kind of surprised. But the cops keep things quiet for as long as they can."

"Garrett, maybe we ought to go back to Bangkok for a complete makeover—fingerprints, the works."

"I don't think so. I'm doing fine."

Pad in hand, to avoid his habitual mistakes, Delantier was ready. He bowed to Heather.

"For a starter, I want giant Gulf shrimps and Thousand Island dressing with a splash of Tabasco."

"Heather, don't bust his balls." Garrett scanned the menu. "Hey, you love smoked salmon."

"That, madame, is one of our house specialties. The chef, and there he is, Philippe Danton—with his wife Nicole at the bar. She prepares a carpaccio of wild salmon and marinates it in sea salt from Aigues-Mortes and the first pressing of olive oil from her farm. It is finished with a dill perfume."

"Yummers," Heather said. "Forget the shrimp."

"Make it two." Heather looked rapturously at Garrett—this dull American, Delantier thought, when he could show this bombshell what amour was all about. "Steak, naturally. Which would you recommend?"

"La côte de boeuf à la Moelle. That is a majestic rib of beef infused with garlic, and herbs of Provence and a beef marrow reduction sauce."

Garrett took command. "*Oui, pour deux.* Medium rare, and I like the sound of the vegetable Tian with wild basil." Heather was purring, her Garrett was back in the fold. "And tell the sommelier we'll want a red. Don't bother to bring the list, we have business to discuss, just have him pick the best you have."

As the diners cleared out, glancing over their shoulders at the two dim figures in the prime booth, the bar continued its furious activity.

Jennifer, tired but elated, winnowed through, accompanied by Rosalind, beaming with maternal pride at her daughter's triumph. Philippe had never been demonstrative with this overseas alien, but he threw his arms around her.

"You've made an old navy cook a patron of the arts," he said. "I'm a big shot in Aix. Thank you, Jennifer, for persuading me to part with three paintings I utterly detested and now cherish."

*"Patron, attention,"* René hissed. "We have a couple in the mayor's booth. She is a replication of Pamela Anderson. They want the most expensive rouge we have."

"She's an incredible woman, very rich," Delantier affirmed, "with a mouse of a man."

Having parted with his three Gauguins, the profit motive reasserted itself in Philippe.

"I'll attend to it."

Garrett was unprepared for another staff member arriving at the table. He was wasting an entire work evening eating and bullshitting Heather. The image of Paul Gauguin flashed before him, surviving on wild red bananas and breadfruit day after day, because he was starving and broke. And when some money arrived, he'd rush to the Chinese market to buy cans of corned beef and feast on them, spreading the gelatinous mass on old bread he had secreted. All for art! The work was everything.

Garrett had a rush of guilt. With Heather's arm entwined, he was overcome by her generosity. Yes, Paul was a sponger, when he had to be. Why not enjoy the banquet? Gauguin would have said, *There's a time for art and a time for pleasure.*

*"Bon soir,"* Philippe said, ravishing Heather with his eyes. "I am Philippe Danton, the owner, and happy to have you here. Now, about the wine. I have 1990 Claude et Maurice Dugat Charmes-Chambertin that is as voluptuous as madame, if I may say. It will possess you with its opulent nose, its shimmering color, it will linger on the tongue, and the finish is perfect for love. I will do this in dollars, so there is no misunderstanding. The price is high, but that is to be expected for bliss. It is fourteen hundred dollars."

"Bring it, Phil," Heather said.

The women at the bar were also curious and peered at Heather. Rosalind leaned over and was flabbergasted. She quickly pulled Jennifer aside.

"It's incredible. I actually met that woman."

"Oh, stop. How?"

"George Rickey insisted that we go to her millennium madness." Rosalind shook her head with distaste. "It was a sex freak show. I've never seen so many perverts in my life."

"George?" Jennifer was incredulous. "At a sex orgy? Mother . . ." Jennifer couldn't help but laugh.

"Believe me, it wasn't my idea. Her father was a billionaire, a friend of George's. Now his daughter—this Heather Malone—is George's most important client. George said it was a command performance. He had to show his face. He bought her all the hot Internet stocks before anyone knew what was going on and she's made even more money . . . hundreds and hundreds of millions.

"Jen, she's absolutely depraved. She was wearing some leather outfit with a slit—you know where. Exposed! This woman has a Minotaur tattoo above her vagina. And I met the weirdo who did it. I've never seen such an exhibition in my life. Everybody there seemed to be pierced, tattooed—even branded! Fetishists kissing boots . . . yuck, I felt sick, made an excuse, and dragged George out of that madhouse."

René was finally back at the bar. He had spent an inordinate amount of time peeping at *that* woman. He poured Rosalind more champagne and attended to a barrage of angry customers.

Rosalind leaned close to her daughter. "Men never get over adolescence; they remain voyeurs with gray hair or no hair while their shanks turn flaccid and their bellies protrude. . . . Oh, well, here's to the fortunes of the female, and that's worth drinking to. . . ."

The tale no longer amused Jennifer. Something about it touched a loose wire which she could not quite connect.

"Roz, do you remember the tattooist's name?"

"No, but that certainly isn't him sitting with that creature." She gulped her champagne. "Where's Michel?"

"He said they were towing cars at the gallery. Which was bull. He did one of one his celebrated disappearing acts."

\*    \*    \*

**The wine and** dinner proved to be remarkable. When Garrett and Heather left arm in arm, they met Rudy huffing beside the rented Mercedes.

"Hey, Rudy."

"Huh, who're you?"

"It's Garrett, Rudy."

Rudy shook his head, bemused. "And how're you, milord?"

"Oh, hanging in. At Heather's service."

"That's glorious news, Garrett. You'll make ours a happy home again."

Rudy opened the car door and they got in. Happily, he turned to watch them kissing.

"Back to the hotel, Heather?"

"Yes. Any messages from home? George call?"

"No, there's just a big French detective wanting to see you, parked in the lobby. And I don't think it's about a traffic ticket."

"I'll be in touch," Garrett said, sliding open the door.

"When? Where?" Heather demanded, panic-stricken.

"I'll find you, my love."

"What about the stuff you need?"

"Rudy can drop it off. I'll call. Or better yet, write down your cell number and I'll tell you where to meet me. I'm staying on a . . . Actually, it's better you don't know. But it's right near the airport. Heather, be careful. You don't want to blow this for us, or lead them to me."

"Don't worry. We're in this together. I won't let anything happen to you," she said.

# CHAPTER 32

**Michel sat at the** deserted hotel bar drinking his fifth espresso. He had narrowly avoided a domestic clash with Jennifer by explaining away his absence on the perversity of his cell phone. Their conversation and the one that followed with Rosalind had disturbing implications. Rosalind had positively stated that the man dining with Heather was not Garrett, whose name—when Michel prodded her—she remembered. In fact, the fragmentary description she had given of the tattooist she had met at the millennium party was close enough to the photograph taken by the Belgians.

Escorted by her irritating English driver, whom Michel had met earlier, Heather Malone wobbled into the lobby. Michel left his stool at the bar and gazed at this sad travesty of femininity: the arch curves, the cherub lips, the disproportionate bosom. She resembled the painted dolls that small girls brought home from country fairs. The Minotaur tattoo that Rosalind had told him about was not on display, but Michel had no difficulty identifying Heather. As she and her driver headed for the elevator, Michel intercepted them.

"I gather you enjoyed your dinner. Three thousand and change," he added.

"What are you, an IRS auditor?" she snapped.

"No, I'm Michel Danton. You apparently set a record at my parents' restaurant."

Her false eyelashes fluttered like butterflies, fanning her deep blue eyes, which were masked in thick dark shadow. But she was clearly confused. "Chez Danton . . . oh, I met your father, then. What a guy. Very smooth. The food was sensational."

"I'll be sure to tell him; he lives for compliments. Madame Malone, I assume your driver told you I wanted to see you." Michel made a menacing move toward Rudy. "The next time you give me misleading information, you'll find yourself in jail. It's a felony in France."

"Look, she dashed out of the car. I cruised around and eventually she gave me a tinkle on my cell. I didn't know that was a crime. I am, after all, employed by the lady."

"Shut up and go to bed. I want to speak to Mrs. Malone alone."

Neither gave ground, until Heather finally roused herself from her stupor. "Beddy-bye, Rudy."

He glared at Michel, then got into the elevator. When the door closed, Michel said, "You can talk to me here and now in the lobby or at my office in Marseille. I'll be happy to give you a lift."

"What . . . what is it you want? I mean to say, I just got in this afternoon. Was there an article about me in the paper? Was I on TV?" He refused to be baited or bullied. "Am I on some kind of celebrity list?"

"No, your friends are. You've got quite a collection of them."

"I like amusing company. You know something, you're quite a hunk yourself. I like cops sometimes—especially when they carry nightsticks." Michel held up his wedding band. "Oh, dear, I hope the lucky lady has a degree in keeping a man happy. If she doesn't, I teach an honors seminar on the subject."

"I'll ask her to register for the fall term."

They sat down at a lounge table, and a waiter brought Heather a triple espresso and a Sambuca, which she poured into the coffee.

"I had a lot to drink tonight. You'll need a cattle prod to help me get my head straight."

"There's probably one left over from your millennium party," he said coldly.

He now had her attention and saw that the remark had frightened her. She was on the verge of asking how he could possibly know this much about her and became wary. Despite her reported consumption of alcohol at Chez Danton, she had developed a clear focus.

"Who was the man you had dinner with?"

"Just an old flame. Friend of my broker."

"George Rickey."

At that mention of his name, Heather almost fell off her chair. "I better get a lawyer and have you read me my rights."

"It's not done here. I'll have to wake the examining magistrate and bring you to Marseille. He'll be furious about it and he'll decide if you need counsel when you're in custody. I'd rather not handcuff you, so let's go now and not make a scene here."

Heather was on the verge of an emotional collapse. With tears murkily streaming down, she pleaded. "Why're you being so tough on me? I haven't done anything."

"Garrett Brant has, and we want him. Two girls have been kidnapped and an attempt was made on a third girl. One was found murdered. Where are Brant and his wife? And I want a description of her."

"Wife? I didn't know he was married," she said in a quivering voice.

"Oh, stop lying. Brant and his wife were guests of your former, dear friend Jan Korteman in Bruges. What little was left of him, I personally discovered in a *bath* of nitric acid."

At this, Heather tumbled off the chair and hit the floor in a faint. Michel knew this was not some theatrical feat learned in drama school. He had the room clerk call her man, who rushed down and popped an amyl nitrite to revive her. The two of them helped her to her suite.

"It's two A.M. Now, for God's sake, let the woman rest."

"I'll be back very early in the morning with troops."

"We'll be here. Make it noon and bring bagels and lox."

Upstairs, revived from a second ammie, and rebounding from the horrific news, Heather tumbled on her bed and immediately punched in George Rickey's number; thanks to the miracle of cell phones, he was on the line in an instant.

It was ten in the morning in San Francisco. George, sipping his latte, looked out of his enormous windows in the TransAmerica Building.

"Have you been talking to the French cops? They're hounding me."

"What? Heather, this is the second call I've had in an hour from Aix. First my lady friend and now you! What's going on?"

"What girlfriend?" Heather's fury succumbed to confusion.

"I have only one: Roz Bowen. The lady I introduced you to at your millennium circus. In between the Olympic fucking trials. She spoke French to you and wanted to leave the minute we got there. It was too much for her.

"Roz went to Aix for her daughter's wedding to Michel Danton. He's a big wheel and the dot.com for their murder investigations." George paused and gave a brittle laugh. "I've always said there are only forty people and they all know each other. Now, for chrissake, tell me what this all about?"

"Murder."

**Garrett had stopped** for a cognac at one of the charming old bars along the quai in Martigues. He listened to the locals chat about the fishing and how fortunate they were that the tourists hadn't uncovered their nest. The late Jan Korteman certainly had a painterly eye for the picturesque: Garrett was entranced by the Canal de Caronte, the sleepy lagoons, and the angled bridges. It was clear to him why Corot and Ziem had come to paint in this fishing village. The lucent mirage of water around the Pont St-Sébastien was called the Birds' Looking Glass, and the sheen reflected the buildings and bright boats anchored there. It was a place of tranquillity and meditation for Garrett when he finished work for the day.

He took his time walking along the quai to ensure that no one had followed him and that nocturnal meddlers weren't spying. He reached the boat slip, removed his shoes, and hopped aboard *L'Enchantement*. The cabin below was lit and he climbed down to the spacious lounge. All the comforts of home.

"How's it going?"

Eve was sullen. "All quiet, Captain."

"Are the guests comfortable?"

"In dreamland. Garrett, I didn't sign on as a prison guard while you romp around town with that fucking animal."

He had anticipated the emergence of her mutinous streak. "Heather and I had a steak dinner and some wine. No big deal. The gendarmes are on the prowl."

"It was just a matter of time. Did Heather bring what we need?"

"Yes. Rudy and I will work that out. The police are already on Heather's back."

"She'd never open her mouth."

"I have every confidence in her. But it would be a good idea, until we're airborne, for you to lay low and, when you see her, don't hassle her or open your big mouth."

"You bastard, you sold me out!"

"Eve, control yourself. It's a little late for a jealous tizzy. You knew when we met in Chiang Mai that I had to toe the line when it was necessary."

"She wants you to dump me."

"Tell me something I don't know."

She took his hand and kissed it. "Sorry, sorry, I'm so insecure."

"That's a condition of life, and not just ours."

Finally Eve unlocked the door of the cabin; a naked Kristin, hands and ankles strapped to the bed, lay on the pink sheet. Jan had an aversion to white and all the linen was florid.

"Her skin is fantastic. I prepared the canvas and oiled her for you."

"She's absolutely exquisite."

Eve locked the door and opened the adjoining cabin, where Gerta was asleep on her stomach and in restraints. Garrett moved his light over her back. The Garden of Eden Caroline had ruined was now perfectly tattooed on Gerta. She was magnificent and charming, not in the least fearful, and intensely curious. Now that she was out of the grasp of the draconian German nuns, she liked to have a Pastis or two when he was through working on her. She couldn't wait to see her photographs in magazines and art galleries and assured Garrett that she would tell the authorities that she had volunteered. She was proving to be the ideal model, cooperative, obedient.

"I think that's as much as I'm going do on Gerta."

Eve was astounded. "What about her buttocks and thighs?"

"There won't be enough time if I want to do Kristen. I'd hate to see your efforts wasted, Eve. I'll harvest Gerta and take it back home . . . if I can. Now that we know where my true work lies, we can find models in California. But no more trips for a while."

Eve agreed, but then she was troubled. "What about our house? It won't be cool."

"No question, my love, it's a danger zone. Heather'll find us new digs and I'll sign it over to her to sell."

"A new start," she said with excitement.

"Yes, it will be. Just a pity I didn't have the guts to do this years ago."

"It's not time lost, Garrett, it's time regained. You've come into your own, finally."


**As far as** Jennifer could tell from the luminous Baby Ben on her bedside table, it was just past four A.M. when the pounding on the door and the screams began. Michel rose, looked at her in the nether light, and took his automatic out. Rosalind was already in the hallway, her Breton sabots clip-clopping like horseshoes on cobblestone.

"You all right, Moms?" Jennifer asked.

"No, I'm not. What's going on?"

The doorbell continued to ring. Michel slipped on a linen robe. With his gun in his right hand, Rosalind was terrified, and he touched her hand, passed by, and went to see who was causing the commotion. He peered through the spy hole, but the hall lights were out as usual.

"Michel, Michel! It's me! Let us in."

He switched on the foyer light, opened the door to a hysterical scene: Vellancio, sweating like a racehorse and gasping for breath, could hardly speak coherently. Irmegard was shrieking and tearing at her hair.

Vellancio's timid wife, Bianca, gravely said, "Kristen, they've stolen her. The golden child is gone. . . ."

# CHAPTER 33

**Garrett left the boat** earlier that morning to walk Chi-Chi and bid him farewell. He, Eve, and the Bichon had become very fond of one another. Garrett secured the dog's tag, which gave his owner's name and phone number in Avignon. He hugged the dog and tied him to a post outside a popular bar. The French might beat and ignore their children, but never their dogs.

He contacted Rudy on his cell phone and arranged to pick up his gear. He knew the police would be searching for Kristen, and not hounding Heather for a day or two. They'd have Kristen on their brains, trooping around with photos of the beautiful girl and questioning her shuddering friends. Nonetheless, it was imperative to make a move. He had run out of time. Freedom was everything. He could not tolerate an institution again. No, he and Eve could never allow themselves to be imprisoned. They preferred death.

Eve's dilettante report on the Chardin Gallery's vernissage, and her superficial understanding of the new Gauguin paintings, would hardly suffice. No, his was the refined sensibility and he was emphatic about this over breakfast. He had to analyze these new discoveries himself, dissect and deconstruct them, frame them in their historical context.

Eve and he had fed the girls, keeping them separated. They reassured Kristen that they were simply doing a series of photographs and that she would be released shortly. Then they gave the girls their laced Cokes.

Eve followed Garrett on deck, holding a mug of steaming coffee. "You're very antsy. Aren't you going to work today?" She seldom asked a question like this. His art was sacred territory, inviolate. "Garrett, what's up?"

He was afraid his voice would tremble, but he had to tell her. "Darling, I'm going to have to move on."

"What? Are you serious? You can't leave the girls—your new art."

"I'm afraid *my* skin is more important than theirs. And in a sense, this was apprentice work. Once I shake off this investigation and get back to California, it won't have to be so stealthy and rushed. I'm out of my element here. There's nothing like working in your own backyard. We can take our time and do a thorough prep." He touched Eve's face with tenderness. "Venice is a paradise of homeless kids and runaways. I'll have all the models I need."

She gave him a rueful nod.

"Right now, we'd be better off on our own."

She wanted to scream but held back. "Oh, Garrett," she cried, "Heather got to you, bought you off, didn't she?"

"That can never happen. No, a detective got to Heather. She might cave in to the pressure. We can't risk that."

Eve tearfully leaned on the deck rail. The dreaded tourists the locals claimed never came had invaded their paradise. A herd of them were listening to an animated guide describing the inspiration artists found in the Birds' Looking Glass and that this was a photo op. The waves seemed to be furrowing from the voices of this rabble.

"What about me?"

"You always make out. Let me get my bearings and I'll make arrangements, send for you. That way we'll both be safe."

"Are you coming back to the boat?"

"I'm not sure. Not if I don't have to." He clasped his hands around Eve's haunted face and kissed her lips delicately. "I'll love you till the end of time."

"You're mine, Garrett."

"Be strong and serene, Eve."

When Garrett climbed down off the boat, he retained the vision of their first night together in Chiang Mai, Eve in her shimmering white beaded dress, he in his linen suit. They were sitting on the teak porch of the cottage, watching a rainbow dancing over the rice fields in Shangri-La.

* * *

**He caught Jennifer's** eye immediately. The man was stunningly handsome, with a blond ponytail, neatly trimmed mustache, and beard. He carried a snap-brim straw hat and his sunglasses were pushed up on his forehead. He wore a beautifully cut white shantung suit and a dark green shirt which provided an extraordinary contrast with his lime eyes. He smiled easily as he roved with the early group through the Chardin Gallery. He reminded Jennifer of one of the young aristocrats in *Brideshead Revisted*. What, she wondered, working her way through the visitors, must it be like to be born perfect?

Garrett had had his fill of Renoir, Cézanne, and the others on display. He stood in front of the four Gauguins, none of which was familiar. He had to absorb the master's work, inhabit his being, and time was not on his side. He referred to the catalogue. When he noticed Jennifer answering questions, he nodded to her and she came over.

"These are quite amazing," he said. "I assume I'm in the presence of Professor Bowen."

She liked his mellifluous voice and his easy manner. "It's Madame Danton now," she replied with a twinkle.

"Ah, a new bride."

"You're correct."

"This is certainly a treasure trove. None of these are in my Thames and Hudson or in any biography I've read."

"Their existence was unknown until my husband inherited the collection."

"Forgive me, but I wonder if P.G. wasn't living in Le Pouldu rather than Pont-Aven when this was painted."

"Ahh, you're a Gauguin expert."

"I'm very close to him—his work."

"Well, Mr. . . ."

"Johnny Reynolds."

"Mr. Reynolds, I've consulted with Professor Jules Chardin about these dates and they're provisional. These are questions which we hope we'll eventually solve with other experts. Still, it's very astute of you."

"It's certainly a version of the *Little Girls Dancing* and unmistakably P.G. He was always interested in little girls."

There was an eerie tenor in the suggestion, despite its accuracy. "Are you in the field?"

"No, but 'I, too, am an artist.' "

She laughed at the remark attributed to Andrea del Sarto when he was showing his work to Raphael.

"Actually, I'm an investment banker."

"That explains the ponytail."

At this he laughed. "I couldn't very well come to Aix and not see my beloved Gauguins. Maybe one day if you ever find yourself in California—Venice—you'll come and have a look at *my* work. I'd really like to know what an expert like you thinks of it."

"Do sign our book and leave a card, Mr. Reynolds, if you have one."

"Sure. Is the show going to travel—say, to California, with you lecturing?"

She was dazzled by the possibility. "You know, this is all so new. I hadn't even thought about it. But once I get my bearings, it's worth considering."

Sylvie was beside her suddenly and Jennifer detected an urgency and excused herself.

"I thought I might catch Michel."

"I don't know where he is. Any word on Kristen?"

"No, I've been assigned to do surveillance on an American woman he suspects is involved. She's been in Façonnable for the last hour buying and trying on everything. I'm afraid I've been spotted."

"Heather Malone."

"Yes, Jennifer, how did you know?"

She looked over Sylvie's shoulder at the intent face of the Gauguin aficionado. "She was at Chez Danton last night and my mother spotted her. She'd met her in California."

"Sorry to interrupt, Madame Danton, but may I see you for a moment?" Johnny Reynolds asked.

"Yes, yes."

"I think the painting of the two women you suggested in the

catalogue was done when Gauguin moved to Hivaoa in the Marquesas might have been one that he'd started in Tahiti. He had bad luck with shipping his paintings and he was afraid to leave anything behind in Tahiti."

"Yes, we'll rethink that," she replied. "The addition of the Gauguins to the show was put together on short notice."

Reynolds looked at his gold Rolex. "I've got to move on, Professor. Oh, by the way, a friend of mine was here at the opening, a journalist, and she forgot her camera in all the confusion."

"It's in the office."

He trailed after her through the mill of visitors into the cluttered office, where cases of champagne, glasses, trays, and brochures awaited collection.

"Looks like I missed quite a party."

Jennifer was distracted and grew uneasy. "Forgive me, I can't recall your friend's name."

"Julie Kahn-Smith. She checked her Nikon."

"Oh, yes." She unlocked the bottom drawer of her desk. "Here we are." She handed him the camera. "This is a beauty."

"It's the new digital model."

"Where are you headed, Mr. Reynolds?"

"Right now to Façonnable to pick up another friend."

"Oh, I thought we might have a drink or lunch if you're still around."

He considered the proposal for a moment, smiling graciously. "That's very kind of you. Unfortunately, I'm on a tight schedule."

"Well, maybe our paths will cross again and we can talk about Gauguin."

"If you ever get to Venice Beach, I'm in the book and I'll take you to lunch." He bowed his head. "I have to run before she buys out the whole store."

The moment he left her office, Jennifer tore out like a dervish and caught up with Sylvie pacing outside the gallery and watching the entry of the clothing store.

"Listen, the man I was talking to—he might be the one."

"What?"

"Sylvie, he was in a terrific hurry and he said a few things that spooked me. He'll be on the gallery's surveillance camera tape, but there's no time for that." She pointed. "Look, he's going around the corner on Rue Laroque to that Mercedes."

"Jennifer, I can't call the whole section in on this."

"He's picking up packages and a suitcase from the trunk."

"I see."

"Sylvie, he mentioned Pont-Aven and Venice Beach—and he's a Gauguin nut. It can't be a coincidence."

"We have no real description of the man."

"Do something, follow him."

"Okay," she said rushing to her Harley-Davidson. She revved the engine and turned into the street and spotted his Citroën SUV driving away. He took the A55 and she thought he was headed for the airport at Marignane, but then, to her surprise, he turned onto the D5, which led to Martigues. She zigzagged behind the shield of a truck but was exposed when he veered along the Canal de Caronte and through the Old Quarter.

He parked on the quai and she pulled off a hundred meters away. She phoned the Section's central office and gave the operator her location. Michel was in a meeting and no calls were being put through.

She locked the Harley, checked her weapons and slung her bag on her shoulder. She walked to the hatch of a small drinks stand close to the yacht she saw him climb aboard.

"*Une pression. . . .*" She was handed a mug and guzzled the cold beer. When he came ashore again, unlocked the van, she realized he was still unloading whatever it was he had picked up in Aix. The name of the large yacht was *L'Enchantement* and she made a quick note. She was too far away to make out the license number on the hull. She ordered another beer and intentionally spilled some on her jacket. The barkeep shook his head in disgust.

She had from time to time played the role of a tipsy woman and it always worked. She'd find herself with a suspect and pretend she was a *fille* out for a good time, then when the man prepared for easy sex, she would hook him. As a new member of the Section, she was expected to take the initiative. If this man wasn't Garrett, she'd apologize.

She took off her shoes and tossed them in her bag, tiptoed up the gangway, and found herself on a large varnished deck. She got down on her knees and peered through the window at the lounge-cabin below. It was empty and there were no cries from young women as she had anticipated.

When she levered herself up, his hand twisted her around so swiftly that she could not react.

"Hel-lo, looking for me?" he trilled.

Her eyes were agape. A long needle came toward her and was plunged under her breast. She fell backward and into the turbulent darkness hidden in the folds of a sunny afternoon.


**Michel had done** what he could to reassure Vellancio, Irmegard, and the Davises in his office. When they had gone, he turned to Annie and asked her to relieve Sylvie on the surveillance of Heather Malone. Two reports from Sylvie confirmed that the buxom billionaire was on a shopping spree on the Cours Mirabeau. Jennifer had called, said it was urgent, and then he looked at the message from Sylvie in a fury.

"My God, she's left Heather! What that hell's wrong with that girl?"

"Maybe she has a lead."

"What a fucking mess. Annie, get out there immediately. I want Heather found and brought in. Émile, you go to the Roi René. If she's still there, arrest her."

Pierre, who had gone missing for days at the Maritime Authority, burst into the office. "I've got Korteman's boat. The reason it took so long is that it had a corporate registration. It's owned by L'amoreuse. The name of the boat is *L'Enchantement*."

"Berthed in Martigues," Michel said.

"How did you know?"

"Sylvie apparently found out. Have all the airlines checked for reservations under Heather Malone and Garrett Brant. . . . Oh, yes, she's got some kind of English bodyguard. Rudy—the hotel will have his name. Put everyone on alert at Marignane airport."

He picked up the phone and advised the local police and medical emergency that he and the Section suspected the killer might be aboard *L'Enchantement* and to have the marine authorities close off the quais to all traffic. "On land and sea."

**Garrett observed the** Black Marias, the ambulances with their tooting Klaxons on the D5 heading for Martigues, while he was leisurely heading in the opposite direction . . . to Nice. There wouldn't be time to see the Chagall and Matisse museums. He'd have to settle for dinner at the Chantecler. Despite their Michelin stars, they'd be hard put to beat the steak he'd had at Chez Danton. He thought of the kindness of the elderly waiter and the courtly manner of Philippe Danton. He'd do something nice for them, he'd write a rave notice for the *Zagat Guide*.

Wistfully, he put Eve out of his mind.

# CHAPTER 34

**In all the years** he'd been a detective, Michel never had entered such a bizarre crime scene. Sylvie was bleeding profusely and was unconscious. The beige tarpaulin which had covered her was slick with bloodstains. The paramedics rushed Sylvie to the Timone Hospital, where a team of surgeons from the Faculty of Medicine were waiting for her.

A doctor had bagged the grotesque eight-inch steel needle from her chest and showed it to Michel before it was removed by the forensic team. It seemed to be specially forged and had a round knob on top, a small hilt; the tip had three butterfly prongs, like a piece of hardware used to hang something heavy on the wall. No one had ever seen anything like it.

Belowdecks, Kristen was drowsy, tearful, and shivering with fear. Although her physical condition was not alarming, she was also taken to the hospital. This could not be said for Gerta Sholler, who was clearly in shock—first incoherent, then lapsing into a kind of silence he had observed in autistic children. Her back had been expertly tattooed: A phantasmagoric rendition of the Garden of Eden, as imagined by a psychotic, covered her shoulders and ended at the top of her buttocks. Bats and butterflies, flying serpents, and what appeared to be astrological figures floated above Adam and Eve, both figures a hideous bloodred. What these surreal symbols meant could only be explained by the deranged tattooist.

The boat was being thoroughly searched by the techs and his team, but so far no tattooing equipment had been found, nor any personal effects.

"He's probably tossed everything overboard. Bring in the divers."

Michel was seldom given to sentimentality, but he could hardly hold back his tears when he considered the future of this orphan girl. What would become of her amid the students and nuns at Immaculate Conception in Munich? Yes, she was alive, but the psychological damage was unfathomable and would be unending. How could she pursue a normal life, marry, and have a family with this gruesome stigmata? As a professional, prospects of revenge seldom occurred to him, but this time he wanted blood.

Driving to the hospital, his mind filled with the speculations that he kept suspended during his investigations. But it was clear to him that the relentless, unspeakable barbarism of the twentieth century would have no remission in this new millennium. The horrors of war continued, the massive AIDS epidemics would wipe out entire civilizations and prove as mysterious to historians as if comets had decimated them. But on a more basic level, the theme of man's inhumanity to his fellow beings possessed an eternal life.

He checked his messages, then punched the automatic dial for Jennifer. Her warm voice was a balm and consoled him, but her information alarmed him.

"How is Sylvie?"

No one but the police knew she was wounded. "Jennifer, why would you ask?"

"I met the man who I think killed Caroline and kidnapped the others. He told me he's from Venice!"

"What?"

"Sylvie was in the gallery when I was talking to him. It was so eerie and I told her to follow him."

"How could you know?"

"He's a Gauguin fanatic and he mentioned Pont-Aven and Venice Beach almost in the same breath."

"What does he look like?"

"He's gorgeous. I've got pictures from the gallery surveillance camera."

"Fantastic."

"Oh, another thing: That American woman who said she was a journalist at the vernissage. I called my friend in Paris who does research on gallery openings . . . no one's heard of her. This Gauguin expert is smooth. He said his name was Johnny Reynolds. But what really spooked me was that Sylvie had Heather under surveillance and she was next door at Façonnable when Johnny mentioned that his friend was buying out the store. That's just what Sylvie had told me."

"It's the classic *switch* technique. One person intentionally remains under observation while the other makes the play."

"I pushed Sylvie. I know I shouldn't have. She said you'd be sore at her. Please don't blame her or hurt her record."

"No, of course not. She led us to Kristen and Gerta."

"They're alive?"

"Yes."

"There is a God." He was not about to argue the point with her. "Michel, are you still there or am I losing you?"

"I'm here."

"I need to ask a big favor."

"Whatever it is, yes."

"Great . . . Jeff and Melanie are going to join us for dinner at Chez Danton."

"I'll be there as soon as I can. Jennifer, take the videotape out of the camera and I'll have a messenger pick it up immediately."

He could not bring himself to reveal that Sylvie might be dying.


**Sylvie had been** in surgery for five hours. Her left lung and pulmonary artery had been punctured, but the massive needle had missed the left ventricle. She was moved into the IC recovery room and the doctors were guarded about her recovery. For the first time since Michel had met him, Richard Caron lost his haughty mask. He was inconsolable.

"She's everything to me," he admitted, trembling, as they peered through a glass window at Sylvie. "I simply don't understand her."

"Did your father understand why you dodged bullets for General de Gaulle when you could have taken over his firm on the bourse?"

"I hated the stock exchange. They were all corrupt."

The relationship with his mentor was ending, but the old man's inflexible tenet of "defeat with honor" had little place in this new world of compromise.

"Have we lost this butcher?"

Michel wanted to reassure him, but there had never been a serviceable ambiguity between them.

"Yes."

"You're sure?"

"Absolutely. He's a chameleon. I've never encountered anyone as elusive. I don't even have a tangible image of him. You see, it's not a question of what he looks like, it's his mind that baffles me. He's inscrutable."

They continued to observe Sylvie.

"I'm sorry to have missed Jennifer's opening. Soccer was on."

"It was a mob scene. You weren't missed."

"Is everything going well with Jennifer? I've been so panicked about retiring that I've lost the social graces, or they've deserted me."

"Look after Sylvie. I know firsthand what your friendship is worth. Make friends with her. And if she's able—and wants to stay on in the section—you ought to replace me with her."

**Delantier was not** worried about his tip. After Madame Malone's feast, the policy of scorning Americans at Chez Danton had become an occasion for exultation with him and the staff. The Americans flicked crisp hundred-dollar bills atop their Am-Ex cards. No change wanted. If he and Philippe had not despised these conquerors, they would have been rich in the seventies.

Jeffrey Davis had arrived early, been exceedingly polite with René and Delantier at the bar, and his French was acceptable.

"I know that Michel's folks own the restaurant and he and Jennifer won't allow me to pick up the check, but I'd like to tip you and pay for the wine."

"That is acceptable," René said, at his least querulous. "I have two bottles left of the 1990 Claude et Maurice Dugat Charmes-Chambertin. Last night, we had an extraordinary American couple who agreed that it's one of the finest wines they've ever tasted."

Jeff handed him his Am-Ex and said, "Add five hundred dollars—*personnel!*

It was as though he were rewarding croupiers after winning a
fortune at the tables in Monte Carlo.

When Jeff had left, Delantier merrily said: "I think Michel's marriage to Jennifer was just what Chez Danton needed."

"Jennifer! I'd kiss her hands, her feet, every part of her if it
wouldn't get me killed," René responded. "Let me buy you a drink,
Delantier."

Delantier's crimped features firmed as though in response to an
elixir of sheep glands which towed the marshland and ditches of
his face into a functioning canal, an engineering wonder.

"Buy me a *drink*? René, let's not ruin a thirty-year tradition of
contemptible mean-spiritedness by this reckless action. We still
must maintain the tipping ratio. Your share is a hundred and fifty
for your advice, and keep your drink. And by the way, be sure to
make Jennifer's martini with Ketel One and not Grey Goose. She
knows the difference, so don't be careless."


**After dinner, Delantier** wheeled the brandy cart and heated balloon glasses. He would recommend the Borderies Louzac, now a
venerable half century old. He was careful not to interrupt his
American patron's passionate conversation.

"I want to do this, Michel. I must meet Gerta, have the girl stay
with Melanie and me and we'll take it from there. Mel and I will
pay for plastic surgery for Gerta."

"This is complicated legal procedure. I don't know how you
could arrange it."

"She's finished—dead—at the school in Munich," Melanie said.
"She has no shot for a life. We can't replace Caroline and we don't
want to. But let her death help someone."

Jennifer, silent through dinner, was angered by Michel's reluctance to commit himself.

In the booth—still with a scent of Poison, Jennifer thought
throughout dinner—she put her husband on the spot. "Michel,
we've had a feast. Look, the four of us are safe and sound. Last

night Heather had dinner in the middle of Aix with Garrett's conspirator. His agent, whoever he is. At this table, damn it. Now tell us — or at least Jeff and Mel — what the hell's going on?"

"Yes, Delantier, the Louzac is an excellent choice," Michel said, waiting for him to pour and disappear.

Swirling the cognac in his glass, he said, "I don't think my brief is going to please anyone. To begin with, the suspect's photo is already with the FBI, U.S. Immigration, and the local police."

"You know his name?" Jeff demanded.

"I think I do. But I'm not going to tell you. Vigilante justice won't work. I don't want Mel visiting you in prison. Now let me continue. Jennifer, this is going to upset you, but I can't help it. Sylvie was severely wounded and is intensive care."

Jennifer fell back as though slapped. "No, no. Is she going to make it?"

"The doctors will call me if there's a change." His attention was now concentrated on the Davises. "Unless my detective, Kristen, Gerta, or the girl in Pont-Aven can identify this man, we'll have an impossible situation. In fact, my *juge d'instruction* — he's a DA-cum-judge — can't even file extradition papers."

Melanie was appalled. "Do you think he's still around?"

"My guess is he's heading home."

She clutched his hand. "You know his name and where he lives?"

"Yes, Mel. The difficulty we face is evidence. For instance can your aunt in Bruges identify him? We've sent the photo to the investigators there. This killer disguises himself. He has a wife or girlfriend who does the actual kidnapping or was used as the lure. She's not about to give him up. In any case, she's also vanished — literally into thin air. The man they stayed with in Bruges, your aunt's photographer friend, isn't around." He spared them the details of Jan Korteman's acid bath. "How can anyone point to him and how do we *prove* he was Caroline's killer?"

Jeff swigged his cognac and Delantier quickly refilled his glass. "Please, Michel, tell us, are you absolutely certain he killed Caroline?"

Michel threw up his hands defensively. "How can I be? Only he knows. But I have a strong lead. The question is, will this person cooperate?" He had implacable doubts about Heather Malone's willingness to testify. He moved into the minefield, aware of the tension and the fragility of their minds. "This person is immensely rich—maybe not quite in your league, Jeff, but this individual can hire very powerful lawyers and fight forever."

In a moment, he found himself in the thrall of a brilliant billionaire power player.

"Let's look at this hypothetically," Jeff said as Melanie's sad eyes studied him. "Because our daughter was murdered, you and Jennifer cut your honeymoon short."

"That's a fact," Jennifer said.

"Now, Jennifer's very anxious for you to leave police work." Michel nodded. "But when she found out the circumstances, she wanted you to work on this case."

"You and Mel are very persuasive and easy to like," Michel said.

"So are you. I'm sure we could be friends. You, more than anyone—certainly more than any cop in the States—know this case." Michel awaited the offer. "What would prevent you from continuing your honeymoon in, say, California?"

Melanie interceded. "You'd be our houseguests or stay anywhere you like."

"I can afford it. Purely by accident, I inherited a fortune—the paintings at the gallery and more than Jennifer and I will ever need."

Jeff Davis astutely sized up the situation. He thought he had made some inroads with Jennifer. Michel was more difficult to read.

"Okay, so you've got money. Do you have the new Gulfstream G-5, which flies close to Mach one, piloted by two former NATO colonels who flew F-14s on carriers?"

"Of course not."

"Well, the plane's standing by at the Marignane airport."

Michel flushed uneasily. His true, blood father had been an American NATO test pilot who had been killed. The prospect of flying with his brethren lay trapped in his mind. Michel was unaccustomed to the defensive role and for an instant he felt as powerless as a suspect under investigation.

"The point Jeff's trying to make, Michel, is that you're the only person in the world who can accurately brief our police—in whichever state this guy is in."

Michel turned to Jennifer and she appeared as exposed as he himself. Melanie thrust ahead in the interrogation.

"Isn't that true?"

"Yes," he admitted reluctantly.

"It's an open secret in the Special Circumstances Section that you and your boss are looking for someone to replace you," Jeff said. "You wouldn't have gotten involved if this hadn't been a complex case, would you? Say, if two drug dealers were murdered?"

Michel pointed to Delantier. "Please leave the bottle—espressos for everyone."

"Wonderful waiter, such charm," Jeff said.

"Really?" Michel asked in consternation.

"Michel, I hate to resort to gross bribery," Melanie began, restructuring her face in a smile, "but you could play Pebble Beach, Spyglass, and Cypress Point with me. I'd give you playing lessons."

He laughed with delight and embarrassment, like a giddy schoolboy. "I assume Tiger's too busy to give me a tutorial."

"God is, as well," she countered.

"It's up to my wife," Michel said with what he hoped would be agile diplomacy, but Jennifer's face was devoid of signs or symbols. He had been under the clearly mistaken impression that he could discern her moods and possessed a total knowledge of her psyche.

All their eyes were directed on her. "Let us sleep on it during a sleepless night," she said with Delphic serenity.

"Oh, if I were to go, there's one condition that's not negotiable," Michel said, reclaiming everyone's attention. "I'd have to see a Yankee game."

Michel gestured to Delantier to put the dinner on his account. He scrutinized the check and was amazed to see the waiter had for once made an error. There had been no bar bill. Let that bastard eat it himself, Michel thought as they left the table.

Once outside, the balmy air vibrated with the music the festival orchestra was rehearsing. The unclouded beauty of Aix enchanted

Michel. When the women hugged and the men shook hands, Jeff said, "You're about the oddest Frenchman I've ever met."

"It's the American blood in me," Michel retorted obscurely.

"Yeah, and I married it," Madame Jennifer Bowen Danton advised the world at large.

# CHAPTER 35

**Was it the Chantecler's** rougets in their own sauce, or the lamb saddled with the baby aubergines and baked in mozzarella, which lay heavily on the chest of the elderly woman in the wheelchair? She was steered through immigration by a distinguished English attendant. Mrs. Gladys Royce's face was bandaged but could not completely cover the ravages of disease which were unbearable to view by the authorities. Her scaly, liver-spotted hands trembled; behind her dark glasses, misty cataracts veiled her eyes.

Not even a look, she reflected as she was guided up the ramp of the Learjet.

Once she was aboard, the pilots and navigator greeted her. Rudy folded up the wheelchair and put it in an overhead compartment. Heather had boarded earlier and came out of the bathroom. She was dressed in a baggy shirt, suppressing her voluminous bosom, large men's jeans, and an L.A. Lakers cap. She had worn no makeup, just a touch of lipstick. Mrs. Royce thought she resembled a hockey mistress at an English boarding school. In an odd way, she preferred Heather as a butch tomboy rather than as a siren.

"May I get you something, Heather?" Rudy asked.

"How about bloody bullshots?"

"Mine, very spicy. And some privacy, please," Mrs. Royce added.

"Yes, ladies."

Rudy left them in the capacious lounge and went to the galley, closed the door and pondered the curious machinations of his employer. But speculation was aborted. He had a wonderful life and was too well paid to stick his nose into Heather's affairs. He was the perfect servant, always to be commanded, never to question.

He brought a pitcher of drinks with limes and celery in the glasses and retired in his rear sleeping compartment.

The captain's voice came over the PA. "We're cleared for takeoff, Mrs. Malone."

Heather switched on her control panel. "Let's get her up."

Once the Learjet lofted over the lit ships in the harbor, Mrs. Royce raised her glass to Heather's.

"You're a marvel," she said to her hostess.

"I'm a sappy, lovestruck woman who always gets what she wants."

"What's the ETA for LAX?"

"We're not going there. I've got a hankering for gumbo and dirty rice. Fried oyster po'boy with plenty of bayou heat for my angel."

"New Orleans? How come?"

"I thought this out very carefully. We don't want some little clod at immigration hassling you at LAX or JFK. I know all the guys at the airport in New Orleans. We've got a couple of refueling stops and we'll be drinking mint juleps at Commander's Palace tomorrow."

"That sounds like a plan, Heather, my dearest."

"Oh, God, I've waited years for you to come back to me. Is Eve gone for good?"

"Very definitely."

Heather nodded warily but was unconvinced even as she lay her head on Mrs. Royce's rubbery breast. "You know what we're going to have to do about Eve . . . ?"

"No, I don't."

"I have a final solution. We're going to exterminate that freak."

A quake ran through Mrs. Royce's body. She reclined her seat and reflected about the future. It was far from over. In fact, this experience in Europe was in a sense an apprentice period like Gauguin's had been in Pont-Aven before he had rejected Western art and sought greatness in Tahiti and the Marquesas.

*    *    *

**Neither Michel nor** Jennifer slept or spoke all night. At dawn, he went to the kitchen to make coffee. She was behind him.

"Do you want orange juice?" she asked.

"I don't think so."

She sat down at the cozy green breakfast table situated in an inglenook which overlooked the fountains. She leaned back on the straw chair while the Gaggia machine burbled and hissed with steam.

Michel turned to her. "What do you want to do, Jennifer?"

She had struggled, trying to examine the issues, the structures of a decision and whittle them into their basic elements. She had not come up with a revelation, only its consequences.

"Michel, you could save someone's life."

**It was a** warm, dazzling Sunday in Marseille. Vendors hawked boating souvenirs and cold drinks, and sightseers with picnic hampers and impatient children were lined up at the Quai de Belges to buy their ferry tickets for a day out to the islands. Many were reading newspapers filled with stories about the rescue of the kidnapped girls. Sylvie Caron's photograph was displayed below the headline.

At the Timone Hospital, now brimming with the familiar media dregs, their lights, cameras, and obscene treachery, Michel sidestepped them without commenting on the cases. He had never possessed the postures of a diplomat. He'd soon be gone and saw no reason to cultivate them.

Vellancio and Irmegard were in conference with Leon Stein outside Kristen's room.

"Take her on trip, preferably out of the country," Stein suggested. "Better yet, Euro Disney. Let her be a child again."

Vellancio frowned. It was, after all, high season for Irmegard's tour business. Michel wondered how they'd extricate themselves, then Irmegard threw Stein a beautiful spinning ball.

"Away from her friends?"

"We want to hire a child psychologist." The tailor calculated, always measuring, Michel thought. "Yes, we nurse Kristen and get her back on her routine."

"You must do what you think best," Stein said.

Annie Vallon, dressed for the press in a smoky gray Armani suit, came toward them. She had interviewed Gerta, but now brought up a critical aspect of Sylvie's assignment. "You should have let me do the surveillance on the Malone woman. I never would have left her."

"I know that."

"I don't care what Jennifer's suspicions were. An assignment is just that in the Section, isn't it, Michel?"

"Of course, you're right."

"Sylvie fell for the switch. Oh, what's the use? The girls are alive. Look, I've contacted Sister Trude. She and several others will be coming from Munich."

"You showed Gerta the photos of the two men?"

"Yes, she never saw the man who did the tattooing. She wore a blindfold all the time. There is a woman and her name is Eve. Gerta thought she was in her thirties. She has a very soothing voice, and she calmed Gerta down when she awoke from the Taser shot.

"There was also an indoctrination program of sorts about being part of an immortal artistic breakthrough. I didn't press her about this, because she was reluctant to go on.

"Gerta recalls country smells, the sound of horses nearby, and another man—who spoke French with a Flemish accent—Korteman, no doubt. She heard a truck and some men arrive and they were talking to him about the dangerous stuff they were delivering."

"The nitric acid."

"I'd say so. Because Gerta was carried to a shed shortly after and she said there was a strong caustic, chemical odor. After that, she was drugged again. The next thing she remembered was waking up on a boat. She lost all sense of time.

"I've recorded the entire interview. Afterwards I let the Davises see Gerta. I warned them not to mention anything in connection with the crime, and I monitored them. Gerta liked them very much and they've invited her to visit them in California. They said they'd discuss this with the mother superior of the orphanage."

For a moment, Annie lost her severe demeanor. *"Merde,* Michel. Mrs. Davis broke my heart. She's trying through Gerta to reconstruct the last days of her daughter's life."

**Richard Caron was** holding Sylvie's hand and sitting on a chair. He was virtually unrecognizable, unshaven, in old jeans and a T-shirt. A nurse was auditing the monitors. A spiderweb of wires seemed attached to every part of Sylvie. Michel leaned over the bed and she smiled grimly. Her skin was ashy, and rivers of capillaries in her eyes almost voided the color. Michel opened an envelope.

"How're you feeling?"

"Hungover," she said in a whisper.

"You'll have to give up drink. Sylvie, both girls are going to be all right, thanks to you."

"Papa told me."

Michel smiled at this first sign of familiarity between father and daughter. "I have two photos. Are you up to it?"

"Of course she is," Richard snapped.

He held the first one, moving it closer, then back. This was of Garrett, the man who had been with Korteman in Bruges.

"No."

"How about this one?" He showed her the photo of Johnny Reynolds taken by the gallery surveillance camera.

"Yes, him. It happened so fast, but he's the one."

According to Patrick, the head of the photo lab, the physiognomy of the two men had several congruences, but ultimately he also agreed that they were two different men.

"Sylvie, did he speak?"

"It was like a giggle. 'Hello, looking for me?' He's so fast, Michel."

"Shoes, clothes, smells, a cologne, hair pomade, anything?"

She shook her head. "No, the minute he stuck me, I blacked out."

Her doctor entered and without ceremony waved them all out.

*   *   *

**At the nearby** Brasserie Baudelaire, populated by doctors, the sun was so strong that most of the patrons were eating inside rather than on the terrace, which gave Michel and Richard some privacy. They were soon joined by Leon Stein.

"We ordered Croque Monsieurs and a Stella for you as well, Leon."

"Thanks, that's fine." He cut the tip of a cigar and lit it. "Richard, I've been talking to the doctors and I spent some time with Sylvie. When she recovers—and it's going to take a long time—I don't think she ought to return to the Section—or police work, for that matter."

"Leon, for God's sake, I never wanted her on the force. She won't listen to me. Michel's the only one who has any influence on her, and he recommended her—green as she is—as his replacement."

"Look, she's a natural. She's got the best instincts, better than any of the people Paris sent down for the job."

"Let's move on," Richard insisted. "My family situation and your replacement can wait. We have a case and we're losing it. Did either of the girls identify his photo?"

"Not even close," Michel replied.

"What about the woman who did the kidnapping?"

"A Chinese puzzle. Long dark hair, short blond brush cut, blue eyes, brown eyes. Kristen said it was the middle-aged American woman impersonating a journalist who kidnapped her. She had a Bichon called Chi-Chi in the car."

"Do either of you have any theories?" Richard asked, sipping his beer.

"I think I know who committed these crimes, but no one can identify them," Michel said, perplexed. "What I can't fathom is how many people are involved. It's like a theatrical troupe."

"Is there some characteristic that reminds you of Boy's killings last summer?" Richard continued.

"No, those murders had some kind of purpose: robbery, revenge, getting rid of witnesses, paving the way to his girlfriend's fortune, getting rid of a hostage. I spent time with Boynton and there was a psychological logic to his killing," Stein observed.

"Leon's right, Richard. This is an entirely different tonal arrangement. At the center of it is a frustrated artist fascinated by Gauguin. Jennifer told me the man who came into the gallery was a real authority and very charming. But somewhere along the line, he discovers that it's not so easy to be Gauguin and that he's not going to reinvent art. So he tattoos young girls, imagines it's art, and his patrons abet him in this madness."

They sat in sullen silence for several moments, drinking their beers with small pleasure.

"Now, there's something else that's been lost," Stein began. "This morning I reviewed Caroline Davis's pathology report. She was sexually molested. But neither Gerta nor Kristen was touched. Odd, don't you think? Gerta was with them longer than any of the others. Now, when we consider this conspectus—and I'm including the girl from Pont-Aven—we have four girls in all who anyone with a Lolita fixation, a true pedophile, would sell his soul for."

Leon Stein had touched a nerve as Michel knew he would.

"I believe Jan Korteman raped Caroline, the artist found out, and murdered him. Our man has a purity of vision, very different from Gauguin. He wants these virginal girls because of their skin, their coloring, but he doesn't want to have sex with them. Eve is his sex partner and she's vigilant. She must trust him. There's a deep pact between them about fidelity."

More beers were brought to the table. The men lathered their Croque Monsieurs with mustard and ate with pleasure. Richard asked the waiter for a pack of Gauloises and Michel and Leon watched him light his cigarette.

"I don't believe what I'm seeing. Richard, you're smoking after ten years?" Michel said.

"And it still gets me higher than any drug." Richard paused, savoring the smoke.

"What do you want me to do, Richard?"

"It's up to you. Charles Fournier approved your traveling to California, but his last words to me this morning were: 'Don't let

Michel get us into trouble.' Your protocols will come by diplomatic pouch, but—" Richard broke off. "Michel, forget it. You're really entitled to continue your honeymoon with Jennifer."

"What does she say?" Stein asked.

"Jeff Davis offered us a free ride on his jet."

Leon Stein laughed. "Well, why don't you go, then? And maybe while you're there, you'll see a baseball game. Get it out of your system and stop boring all your friends to death with this ridiculous infantile passion."

**The entry of** a small ebony casket lifted aboard the Gulfstream by the cargo handlers was deeply upsetting to Michel and Jennifer. She embraced Jeff and Melanie Davis, then Jeff moved away; the two women's tears intermingled. The Davises were sobbing. Both pilots and the navigator, veterans of wars, were also in tears.

Michel's bereavement was silent, but he was profoundly affected and forced himself to maintain a professional demeanor. He had been involved in hundreds of homicides, but the ghoulish murder of this innocent child marked him as nothing else had—even that of his mother, who had enjoyed the pleasures of a full life.

When Jeff composed himself, Michel took him aside. "I want you to know that I'll never give up on this case."

"Thank you." He walked down the aisle to the cockpit with the pilots, who were now awaiting clearance from the control tower.

"Mel went back to sit beside by the coffin," Jennifer said. Michel wiped her face with his handkerchief. "Jesus, I lost it."

"It was a struggle for me, too."

Suddenly Michel gasped and the thick police files he was balancing tumbled onto the lush green carpet of the plane. The last person in the world he wanted to see climb aboard the sleek, silver jet with its leather swivel seats was Delantier, mewling, "Messieurs et dames." It was like a bad dream, in actual time, real life. There the decrepit, fawning old waiter was, reeking of Bay Rum, and licking Jeff Davis's hand like a grateful sheepdog.

Michel leaned over to Jennifer. "If I have to fly with him, I'm getting off this fucking plane."

"Shush, and don't swear. Your parents sent a food hamper from Chez Danton to keep you happy. Charcuterie, terrines, cheeses, wine, your mother's cassoulet, the works."

"Maybe the garlic will kill the stench of him."

*"Bon voyage, mes amis."*

# CHAPTER 36

**After four days of** roaming back and forth like a courier between the consulate in Beverly Hills and the LAPD Pacific Division on Culver Boulevard, and trying to learn how to Rollerblade, even the charm of Shutters Hotel in Santa Monica wore off. The Foreign Office in Paris was laggardly reviewing the request for extradition writs, and Michel was bogged down in legal entanglements. He had no authority whatsoever. When he finally was able to meet the district attorney's foreign liaison officer and the detectives in Culver City, they were bemused and rankled by his interference.

Jerome Farberman, the deputy DA, had driven from downtown on freeways he described as parking lots. His air-conditioning had shorted and he was wringing wet when he came into the station's conference room. Sweat dripped like saliva from his thick eyebrows. He pressed a can of diet Coke against his forehead and heaved his briefcase on the table.

"Now, why am I here, Mr. Danton?"

"I have a suspect who eluded us in France. He's wanted in connection with two murders, one of them an American girl, kidnapping three young girls, and stabbing one of my detectives. I have two photographs and his name."

One of the detectives said, "We have the Democratic convention beginning next week, dozens of gang murders and drive-by shootings, and not enough investigators to handle our caseload."

"We have similar problems in France."

The other detective glanced at Michel's file. "Garrett Brant has no criminal record. He comes over to the station every Christmas with a turkey and toys for the kids. He has a successful business on the Boardwalk—tattooing, spa, hairdresser, coffeehouse, and other services. We've never had a complaint by him or against him."

Michel showed them the two photographs of Brant and both detectives began to laugh.

"What's so amusing?"

"Neither of them is Garrett Brant."

"You're positive?"

"Yeah, I think so," he said, rolling up his shirtsleeve, revealing the tattoo of the American flag on his forearm and below it some military insignia. "This was the Marines battalion I served in. Garrett tattooed me about five years ago at no charge."

Farberman drank his Coke and rolled his eyes to the ceiling. "Now, if you'll excuse us, Mr. Danton, we have other cases pending . . . cases with evidence."

"I've asked the consulate to send you a copy of our files."

"Thanks very much," the tattooed detective said.

As a courtesy, Michel was grudgingly given Garrett's home address, his phone number, license, and car registration, and was asked to take a hike. He had already found where Heather Malone lived. In a final futile effort, he decided to drive to her house. At his urging, the Davises and Jennifer had flown that morning to Monterey. He promised to come up the next day at the latest.

**Michel's first impression** of Venice had been of its eccentric scruffiness. While dodging bikers and skateboarders, tacky flea market stalls, cheap fast-food dives, head shops, druggies in wide-bottom jeans, street musicians, soothsayers, and healers, Michel realized that he had entered the world capital of men's ponytails, shaved heads, sleeveless shirts, and leather vests. Forests of armpit hair sprouted, pierced noses and eyebrows were a tribute to savagery, and tattoos and pastel curls seemed de rigueur. Everyone was part of some occult tribe.

The beach was filled with a mangy transient population which biking cops in shorts patrolled. He went into several jewelry marts and wondered if he might find a match to the earring Suzy had given him in Pont-Aven. It was an impossible task. Finally, like someone in quest of the Holy Grail, he encountered Jody Maroni's Sausage World. He sprawled on a bench and lunched on a Yucatán sausage and experienced a mood elevation.

He strayed through the Thomas guide he had bought at a stall and easily found the Venice Canals. He parked on Dell and walked to Garrett's house at 20017 North Linnie Close. This was a far cry from the mangy beach community he had imagined.

He had been unprepared for the charm of Garrett's neighborhood; it was swarming with ducks, birds, dogs, palms, evergreens, roses in profusion. It reminded him of one those small villages on the banks of the Seine, but without the Renoir boating-scene bars. The series of humpback bridges brought him past waterfront hedges, elegant houses, some modern, others brick, wood, shingles, all with satellite dishes. The canals had small rowboats and canoes tied to metal rings. Here and there an original bungalow peeked out like a poor relative at a banquet. He assumed the lot itself was doubtlessly worth a fortune.

Many of the houses had skylights; wind chimes tinkled; most of the patios were deserted, but everywhere he looked there were finely crafted dwellings, masterly stonework, expensive tiles, decks, roof gardens, small lush gardens, velvety emerald lawns, French windows, and barbecues.

Garrett's house was on four floors and was beautiful, painted in shades of lemon, ivory, and chrome yellow—a delight to the eye— with a well-tended front garden. Under the doorway a beautifully carved wood Minotaur, the hallmark from hell, stood guard. Michel saw that there was no litter of mail or newspapers. He rang the bell and waited. When no one answered, he peered over the trellis into the back garden. A large wrought-iron table had eight chairs, lounges were scattered, and a hammock was secured to an old oak.

He spent an hour walking around, ringing the bell from time to time, then decided to give it up.

**Heather Malone's house** in Trousdale did not immediately call to mind the glory that was Greece or the grandeur of Rome. Behind its high spiked gates, it possessed the architectural charm of an airline terminal. Michel looked up, smiling for the security camera, and pressed the buzzer of the squawk box and recognized the English voice asking his name.

"This is Michel Danton. I think we met in the lobby of the Hôtel Roi René in Aix."

"And you were bloody rude."

To Michel's surprise, the gates opened and he drove his rented Lexus up a blacktop driveway, encountering a stunning view of Los Angeles feathered in a gauzy smog. It was almost as though some amateur artist were imitating Georges Seurat's pointillist technique without understanding lighting principles. He parked around a folly of a circular garden, brimming with topiary, roses the size of melons. An ebony black door, one of a pair, at least twelve feet high, opened. Rudy's pinched face appeared.

"Best come in."

"Thank you. I apologize for my rudeness. Murder makes me lose my manners."

Heather's man was wearing a sleek, expensive black jacket, white linen shirt, and black-and-white seersucker trousers. He looked as though he were about to attend a fashion show. Michel's heels clacked on a remorseless, endless marble floor and he followed Rudy into a room that might serve as a Hilton lobby and could easily accommodate a crowd of conventioneers. There were so many seats and sofas that it became something of a puzzle to discover where they ought to sit.

"Actually, I'm glad to see you," Rudy said.

"That's another surprise."

"You want a drink or a beer?"

"A beer would be nice."

In the baronial kitchen, populated by two Viking ranges, an industrial microwave, four stainless steel Sub-Zeros, a coffee-shop counter with stools attached to the tile, the swimming pool came into view. It was freighted with pink cabañas, lounges that would be the envy of Shutters. The tennis court was red clay and hooded with lights.

"Resort living," Michel said.

Rudy opened two bottles of Watneys, took chilled glasses out of the freezer, and poured. "I've lived here so long, I don't notice."

"Is Mrs. Malone around?"

For an instant, Michel's simple question seemed to stump Rudy. He pawed at his clean-shaven head and rubbed his wrinkled skin. "There's a serious problem and I'm damned if I know what to do about it. She's missing." Michel sipped his cold beer and remained the attentive listener. This was not the moment to prod. "Three days now. I'm frantic and so is George Rickey. We've been calling each other back and forth."

"When did you leave France?"

"Almost a week ago. We flew from Nice to New Orleans. Laid over a day there, and then into Santa Monica Airport. That's where she keeps her Lear. She hates LAX."

"Why don't you contact the police?"

"Fat lot of good that would do. On the one hand, she could turn up and scream blue murder; on the other, she could be *gone*," he said ominously. "You see, Heather calls me twenty, thirty times a day, and the same with George to check on her investments. I've been with Heather getting on for fifteen years and this hasn't ever happened."

"You don't think she's traveling?"

"The plane's in the hangar and the Rolls-Royces are in the garage. Heather doesn't fly commercial or drive. She will walk to a shop entrance when I drop her off, or grumble to the theatre door, but that's the extent of it."

"Great wealth confers total choice, doesn't it? Not for the likes of us. Rudy, if I may, why don't you tell me who left Nice with you and what this is all about? You see, I, too, have a problem: Jan Korteman, who you met in Bruges, was found in a bath of nitric acid in his villa in Avignon. Before that he and Garrett and Garrett's wife—or girlfriend—kidnapped a twelve-year-old American girl. This child was also given the acid treatment to erase the tattoo Garrett scrawled on her back. Her parents are devastated. They flew me to Los Angeles so I could continue the investigation.

"Oh, yes, along the way, two other girls were kidnapped. And before I left France, a young female detective who works for me in the Special Circumstances Section was stabbed by Garrett. He barely missed her heart. She almost died and she's going to have health problems for the rest of her life."

The houseman's face was pallid and an autonomous quiver made him appear as though he had something lodged in his throat.

"Sweet Mother of God," he said finally. He supported himself on the countertop. "I better sit down. I'm feeling light-headed."

"Come, I'll help you. You ought to lie down. Are you on medication that you might need?"

He pointed to an open door. "No, get me into my sitting room."

Michel held him under the arm and assisted him to a cozy paneled room with flock armchairs and a brocaded sofa; there was a TV, various answering devices, and a surveillance monitor. On the walls were fond pictures of Rudy and another man. Michel helped him down, propped a pillow under his head. He located a bathroom behind the alcove and ran a towel under some cold water. He held it against Rudy's forehead, sat down beside him, and took his pulse.

"It's a little fast."

"Ninety a minute's about normal for me. Thank you, I appreciate this."

"Just try to relax."

"I don't think that's possible. If I talk to you about this, will I be in trouble?"

"Not unless you were an accomplice."

"I wasn't, of course. When all these horrors happened, Heather and I were here, at home in Beverly Hills."

Rudy took two aspirins while Michel made a pot of Earl Grey tea, heated scones, poured milk into a dainty pitcher, found the Little Scarlet strawberry preserves, the double Devon cream, and a silver tray. He might have been fourteen again, helping out at Chez Danton. Rudy was not technically a houseman or butler. Heather had knighted him some years ago; his title was personal assistant. His vacationing partner, Bart did the actual service.

Like many lives skittering off the rails, Heather's downfall had commenced with the death of her father, who had pursued a sixteen-year-old Brazilian girl to Rio and dropped dead before the wedding. Heather not only inherited his fortune, but also his financial wizard, George Rickey. Together, they had built the not-insubstantial five-hundred-million-dollar estate into well over a billion. Along the way, there was a sordid divorce.

"She married the wrong bloke, a drinker and druggie who had a cocktail frank for a dick. She made short work of him. . . . That's her." He pointed to a photograph of an attractive brunette woman in her thirties, standing between his partner and himself with a Christmas tree in the background. "Before the *Baywatch* makeover. Normal bosom, no fat lips. A pretty woman, I always thought."

To put the kindest construction on it, as Rudy attempted to do, Heather had a *freaky* side.

"Now, speaking for myself, being gay is quite enough for me, thank you very much. Bart and I are coming up on our twentieth anniversary. Bart's visiting his auntie and house-hunting in Derwent Water. That's the Lake District: Wordsworth, 'Tintern Abbey,' the Romantic poets, and what have you. Up north. We'll have ourselves a cozy cottage up there and open a caff: pastries, scones, and an Internet tea room. Then, after closing, it'll be darts, steak and kidney pies, and a pint at the pub. A quiet life."

Rudy daintily placed his cream first, then the jam on his scone. "Thank you for this. I'm starting to feel quite myself again."

For the English, it was put the kettle on, let's have a nice cuppa, and all the cares would vanish. Wonderful elixir, Michel thought, as Rudy continued to ramble. Michel was determined not to provide a compass.

"One day, Heather comes home from the beach and tells us that she's found the greatest man in the land. He's tattooed her. When she dropped her pants, Bart and I nearly had a stroke when we saw where it was. Clean-shaven, she was, with this fucking red Minotaur on her pubes."

The artist came to dinner shortly after. In spite of his trade and the desecration of their mistress, they both liked him.

"Garrett is simply amazing. Dazzling. When you're with him — one on one — he can do imitations, *throw* his voice, change it from male to female, speak French, and you think there's a party going on. He's also a magician, fascinating. And on top of this, he communicates with this dead French painter. I've heard them have conversations, arguments in *French*! He bewitched Heather. She was mad for him."

Heather had bought property for Garrett, set up his assortment of businesses in Venice.

Michel took out the photographs. "Does he look like either of these men?"

Rudy slipped on his reading glasses. "Honestly, I can't say. You see, Garrett is the man with a thousand faces. He never looks the same. If you give him five minutes and he's got his gear with him, you'd swear it was someone else. As I said, he's a magician."

Somehow, something went seriously wrong with this passionate love affair.

"Heather sulked around the house. No dates. Nothing. She's not much of a drinker and is anti-drugs. Then one evening Bart and I happened to be watching *Bimbo Watch* or whatever and she comes in, dragging her woes with her. She stops right there at the doorway, screams, 'I know what to do!'

"Well, Bart and I haven't a bloody clue what she's intending. Next day, I drive her to this plastic surgeon who does all the stars. Garrett's there as well. She decides she'll become a Pamela look-a-like. Nobody can reason with her. It's madness. She goes through all this surgery and comes out with a set of Koftes—"

"Translate that, please."

"Bristols. Bristol Cities, equal titties. Well, you've seen them. They're bigger than the headlights on the bleedin' Rolls. All this torture to get Garrett back."

This self-improvement course did little to repossess Garrett. "She buys his paintings. George Rickey told me on the *scha-schtill,* they set her back thousands. She puts in a gallery, lights for his paintings. Rubbish, if you want my opinion.

"Then, out of the blue, Heather announces we're flying to Bangkok. Garrett needed her. We had to go first-class Singapore Air; she carried on all the way there about what a woman does for love.

Flying commercial. The Lear doesn't have the lung power to get there in a single leap and Heather's not about to spend four days on Fiji looking for gas and parts if anything went wrong."

"Do you know why he went there?"

"Something to do with some research on ancient tattoo techniques. She catches up with Garrett and he's in the hospital. I don't know if he caught plague — or what. She sends me home and spends . . . oh, I'd guess two months there with him."

"Did she telephone you and George Rickey?"

"Every day, at any hour. Didn't miss one. Heather finally comes home, or rather I fly out because not only doesn't she not fly commercial, she doesn't fly unescorted, especially with the redesign. Men are falling over themselves to get a look at her. At first glance she does look like the girl in the TV series. Dicks are popping out of car windows. All this to make Garrett jealous.

"Once she's home, she's in a funk. She's going to kill herself. She starts sleeping around, bringing driftwood home that she's picked up at clubs. The lowest of the low. She wants Bart to ponce for her and that's most emphatically not my boy's style. We're both hysterical with her behavior. But, Michel, she pays us six figures a year, health and pension benefits — not to mention generous Christmas bonuses."

Rudy poured some hot water in the pot, stirred up the sodden leaves, and put the tea cozy back on for a moment.

"Garrett drops by now and then and he's got a girlfriend."

"Eve."

"Yes. Now, you want to talk about competition: This girl's got style and she's like a runway model; lovely features, perfect unlined skin, an English rose. Heather's the Goodyear blimp by comparison. The three of them somehow work things out and see each other. But there's undercurrents. Heather wants to get rid of Eve in the worst way."

"Look at the picture of the man again, taken by immigration in Brussels. Does this look like Garrett?"

He shook his head. "No, I don't think so."

"Is there anything else, a character feature or trait of Eve's, that's striking? Something that would explain why she'd kidnap young girls?"

"Oh, there most certainly is. She's a bloody psycho. Now, Bart and I knew this immediately and I'll tell you how. Bart was a runner for the Kray twins and his old man worked for them in London before they were put away for life."

"I don't know who they are."

"Psychos, and the people who worked for them were as well, like Bart's father. They were the mafia in London for years, until they killed one geezer too many. You're a detective, mate—even if you are French. Don't you know when you look over a suspect whether or not you've got a wacko?"

"Yes, and I've met too many of them," Michel said wearily.

"Me, too. So we are, to put it delicately, very chary when Eve is about. She doesn't throw fits or scream. She's scarier than that. She takes in everything. But she's a robot, waiting to discharge and frag everyone 'round her."

They met Jan Korteman at Heather's sexual freedom party on the evening of the millennium.

"He was a shady bastard. Sick and disgusting. We met him at some sex show in Amsterdam and he offered to be Heather's guide at no charge. Impossible for Heather to turn down."

"So had Heather given up on Garrett?"

"No, she was setting a trap—Bart and I came to that conclusion. Because the only thing Garrett really cares about—and he'd sell his mother for it—is to be a painter like Gauguin. He's told us often enough."

Rudy's cell phone dingled and he rushed to put it to his ear. "No, George, not a word. . . ." Michel signaled that he wanted to speak to him. "I've got a Frenchman here. Yes, sir."

Michel took the phone. "My name is Michel Danton. Yes, I'm the one. Correct, Jennifer is my wife and the incomparable Roz is now a family member. She's been with my parents and doing whatever she can to wreck their marriage. No, I don't think they've gone that far. I suggest you retrieve Roz before my father's record for fidelity is broken.

"What? Yes, do that. You'll enjoy Provence." There was a pause while Michel listened. "Yes, I'm as worried as you are about Heather. No, I'm certainly not suggesting you're hiding her. I know rich people vanish. Yes, I'll call you when I have news. I have your number, Roz gave it to me. What? Of course, I understand, but trading her stocks at this moment isn't an issue for her. *Au revoir, Monsieur Rickey.*"

Money, that's all anyone in America seemed to think about.

# CHAPTER 37

**Time is the cosmic** symphony of chance and reflects the pessimistic philosophical principle that nothing in the universe is ordained, apart from certain immutable mathematical principles. A triangle, anywhere in the universe, has one hundred and eighty degrees, but at infinity parallel lines can and do meet, and, in some cases, they do not exist. As often occurs in real life, and not merely in books, people miss connecting by a matter of minutes.

This was the situation with Michel. By five o'clock, when Garrett dropped Heather off at his house, Michel had been weaving his way to her Beverly Hills estate.

Heather was loaded with travel purchases, and Garrett helped his angel inside. She was unfamiliar with carrying packages. She could present small Harry Winston's boxes, certainly, but lifting actual sacks and *boxes*—that were not weights for some form of exercise dictated by her trainer—remained an activity for aliens.

She had given a new Irish definition to JAP. Garrett gaily kissed her sweaty brow as she sprawled on his settee downstairs.

"I have a certain talent for unwrapping. Give me any colored bow and I can untie it. Rudy does the schlepping."

"Well, with the tits and all . . ."

"There are certain trade-offs." He laughed and she fell into his arms, bundles and all. "I'm lugging seven pounds of silicone around, and carrying packages is contraindicated."

"You could get me a drink. Ice in the fridge, a martini."

"Bart does that. Honn-eyyy, my feet hurt, so let's send out for them."

Garrett and department stores lived in permanent enmity and, as Heather knew, he had a business to run. Garrett, testing the familiar waters and unafraid, but frazzled by his errands, had picked her up in his Aston Martin at Neiman Marcus. By the time they had reached Venice, she was exhausted by the drive.

Garrett took over. Heather loved his boss mode.

"Here's what we're going to do," he said. "I have to meet my people at the shops and tell them that we're closing down. I'll take them over to Jamie's Beach, buy them drinks and dinner, and swap war stories."

She had prevailed. "Thank God you'll never be touching the skin of beach trash again."

"I had to make a living, and it was a damned good one while it lasted."

"Yeech."

Now, Heather, leave everything downstairs. Have a soak in the tub and a nap and I'll be back for goodies."

"Oh, baby, I'm so thrilled that we're back for good, forever."

"Amen."

"It's been a nightmare without you, wondering, hoping. I love you so much."

"I didn't understand . . . *myself.*"

Horns were honking behind his double-parked car outside.

Heather rose, wobbled to the window, opened it, and screamed, "Fuck off." She stood there for a moment, making fists, then, bored with attitude, she returned to Garrett. "I don't smell sweaty pizzas. What's going on?"

"Coke deliveries. Like News at six. This is Venice! The kids feed health food to ducks, but if the parents can't cut lines by seven, they jump into the canal. I've got to move." He kissed her passionately. "Heather, keep your word—no calls to anyone—Rudy, George, promise?"

They had agreed that in Garrett's present state as the object of police curiosity—not that they'd encountered any—Heather's use of her cell phone was to be amputated.

"Have I ever gone back on my word? Betrayed you?"

"No, darling."

"By the way, my stocks are entering Jupiter. Amazing, I'm right all the time. I told George before I left for Provence, hang in, don't get the jitters . . . and guess who was right?"

"You. Now I've got drug dealers waving large guns outside, ready to shoot my car. Love you."

He leaped to the door, opened it and gave a pax sign to the dealers, and waved his key ring. "I'm coming!"

She followed him out. "Garrett, throw me a high hard one when you get back."

"You got it. Like Randy Johnson." He bowed, blew kisses at the cars stacked behind his, and shouted, "She couldn't find the keys," then zoomed out.


**Yes, it was** six P.M. and Michel had the Pastis thirst which itched through his throat, or was it the air-conditioning? Heather's gloomy, tasteless house was so cold, he could age a side of Charolais in it. Fortunately, Heather had briefly dated a Moroccan who insisted on Pastis. Rudy located the old reliable Pernod behind the bar and fixed it along with a Glenfiddich for himself.

"Except for meeting me, what else spoiled your trip to Aix?"

He let Rudy rush his own drink down and refill the glass. "Garrett."

"Did you see much of him?"

"I didn't see him at all."

"Not the man with the ponytail?"

"Listen, mate, I would've told you. I dropped off some bags on a side street off Cours Mirabeau and this bloke picked them up. That was it. He was wearing aviator goggles and a straw hat. Yes, I thought it was odd, but in France everything is off center."

"I agree, I'm not insulted. Did Garrett contact you? Did he call you?"

"A woman with a French accent—definitely not Heather—gave me instructions. Beforehand, Heather told me to expect the call from this person."

"And what were the instructions?"

"To round up a wheelchair and a portable oxygen tank and deliver it to the Hôtel Negresco in Nice. She was taking a friend of her late mother's back to California for medical treatment. The woman's name was Gladys Royce.

"I had that wretched Mercedes out at six, carried down the bags from Heather's suite at the hotel. Then I got Mrs. Royce into the wheelchair. I wheeled her through immigration to the plane and fixed them drinks when we were aboard."

"What did you do during this long flight?"

"I cooked and served. Afterwards I went back to my bunk, played my Benny Hill tapes on the VCR, and slept."

Michel fixed himself a second Pernod while Rudy sat behind the bar eroding. This was not the bar at Chez Danton and certainly not a terrace table at Les Deux Garçons where a man might while the hours simply enjoying the flutter of the plane trees and idly watching people. These happy, indolent moments weighed heavily on Michel and the separation from Jennifer tolled like the boatmen's death bells up the Rhône River when they reached Alyscamps, the cemetery at Arles.

"Rudy do you want to find Heather again—alive?"

"Bite your tongue, you Frog bastard. She got me my green card! I love her. Bart and I are like her blood brothers."

"I stopped by Garrett's place on the Venice Boardwalk. It was padlocked."

"I drove there as well. The city's improvement scheme is—surprise, surprise—behind schedule. There was a mound of sand in front that would do Luxor proud if you were visiting temples in Egypt."

"Yes, these are hostile business conditions." Michel wanted to hug this sweet man. He had found the perfect compliant witness. "Rudy, before you left for France, did you go to Garrett's house?"

"Heather did, not me. I've never been in there. Dropped her off enough times in the old days. Heather gave me some time off. She told me to be back in three hours or thereabouts . . . and I stopped for a couple of pints at the King's Head, my favorite pub in Santa Monica.

"When I come back, she was on the porch carrying down suitcases and cartons. I thought, I'm in Wonderland—Heather, carrying stuff? Maybe I've had a pint too many. And off to the Santa Monica airport we go, climb aboard the Lear. I carry my passport all the time."

Michel approached the next problem with delicacy, for there was no rushing the garrulous man. Rudy discussed English cooking as if there were such a subject. After a lull over the glories of steak and kidney pie, the topic sank to Scotch Eggs—hard-boiled eggs with a cement crust of unspeakable sausage—and he ran out of steam.

"How did Heather get into Garrett's house?"

"We have a key."

"Do you still have it?"

"Yes. I thought of going in myself, but that'd be B and E."

"You were afraid?"

He winced. "I mean to say . . . what would've happened if they was having a slap and tickle?"

Michel tapped his mate on the shoulder. "I'd certainly ring the bell first. If Garrett or Eve are there, maybe they'd tell me where Heather is. She could be in trouble, ill, had a fall, a heart attack—anything. If you were to give me the key, I could see if there was any sign of her. I've called and called, but his answering machine tape ran out."

"Yes, I know."

Indecision was Michel's ally. Once a witness was mulling over a course of action, he was lost. He followed Rudy back to the kitchen, where he was handed a single Yale lock key.

"By the way, would you have a flashlight I could borrow?"

Rudy opened a large cabinet. "We've got dozens of them. When we have an outage here, it's like finding your way on the *Titanic without* Leonardo."

"*Merci*. I've really enjoyed our visit. As soon as I hear anything about Heather, I'll be sure to contact you."

"Don't say where you got the key."

"Of course not."

"Garrett wouldn't harm Heather," Rudy said with uncertainty. Was he stating a fact or asking a question?

He saw Michel to the door. The huge trees and the moonless night enveloped the grotesque house.

"You know how to get there?"

"I take Washington Boulevard west and make a right on Dell."

"Exactly." Rudy clung to Michel. "A word of warning: If you do run into Garrett, don't confront him or give him a hard time. He's lethal. Once, after Heather got herself refurbished, a couple of muscle-bound boyos, twice his size, came on to her in a mall parking lot. I was going to call the cops, but I didn't need to. Garrett went ballistic and kicked their brains out."

# CHAPTER 38

**Heather had taken a** five-hundred-dollar hit at L'Occitane for balms, creams, lotions, and sweet essences that were always present in her own digs. As she ran the Jacuzzi, tossing in a mélange of pine, jasmine, and verbena, she considered a retrofit. Perhaps a total change. She'd have her breasts reduced to, say, a conservative 36D; maybe augment a little bone to the nose, which she thought a little too retroussé, and go for an aquiline style more in keeping with the current starved-model look. She could never achieve the gaunt, hollow-cheeked famine mien. Still, she'd check out the surgeons in Bangkok and make some adjustments while Garrett was recovering.

She switched on the sound system; to her horror, some high-pitched chorus was singing madrigals. They'd have to go, but she was stuck with the CD because Garrett's sound system was too complicated for her. Speakers and tape decks were everywhere in the house, a mechanical mysteryland.

She fixed herself a Ketel One on the rocks and almost chipped the acrylic off one of her nails, handling the sharp ice cubes. This help-yourself lifestyle garbage was not for *her*. Finally she arrived in the tub and had the quiet moment she had been dreading.

Reflection.

It was impossible to avoid. She was not a criminal lawyer, nor a detective, but ignoring questions did not dispose of their half-life. She preferred to accept Garrett's account of the events that occurred in Europe. Jan had kidnapped the girls: raped and murdered the American one. It was, of course, horrifying and abhorrent and Jan deserved to be punished. Furthermore, when he threatened to accuse Garrett as his accomplice and attacked Eve, what could she do but kill him in self-defense?

If the cops—particularly the rough French bastard from Provence—didn't believe the story and pursued Garrett, Mr. Johnny Cochrane would find himself with a million-dollar retainer and their heads would be spinning. No one was ever going to take Garrett away from her again.

At this juncture, she concluded her speculations, switched them off like a TV, for with Eve banished, these last few days had been a moonlit honeymoon. Garrett wanted to paint her in Tahiti and the Marquesas. What a trip! She had her lover back. She was drunk with happiness.

Garrett had been a problem like no other. But he was worth risking everything for. In any case, conscience was theoretical and she couldn't be bothered with it. Now they were going to share everything, and to show how earnest she was, she had given him the code to her offshore accounts. No, this time, she wouldn't hold a whip over him.

When they returned from their world trip, she'd put her house on the market and he would sell the Venice retreat and they would build their dream palace with a studio and gallery for him. Drying herself in the mirror, she was swallowed up by her fantasies and gave herself a wink. Pamela should look this good.

She put on a bathrobe and lay down on the bed. She found a volume switch, got rid of the madrigals, and fell into a wondrous postshopping sleep.

**"I'm hungry and** horny," Heather said aloud when she awoke. It was a bit after nine. The gloaming over the canals gave the water an iridescent luster. She switched on the TV.

"Yadda, yadda, yadda," she mimicked some dumb talking-heads program.

Her heart skipped a few beats when she heard his footsteps on the staircase. He was beside her and she gave him hugs and mushy kisses.

"It was Jamie's southern fried chicken special night, so I picked up a dinner for us."

"Yummers. Oh, you're just plain fucking, mind-blowingly wonderful."

"Give me a few minutes, I have to check my phone machine, the tape's on overload."

"Can I do anything to help?"

"What're you in the mood for?"

"I'd like to see the wardrobe room. You said you'd show it me."

"Sure, I'll unlock it and see you there in a few."

"You going to dress me up in something special?"

"I can't wait to."

Garrett walked her down the stairs, took out his keys, and switched on the lights in the enormous clothes room, which ran the entire length and width of the house. She had never been inside and was stunned by the enormity of the collection of clothes and accessories.

"Every whip and restraint known to man or beast," she said.

"Oh, Heather, you know me. I try to stay current, and I'm a sucker for Mr. Fetters's catalogue. Now go explore and let me get my stuff done and I'll be back."


**Garrett's usually tidy** office was cluttered with cartons of mail which he shoved aside to form an aisle, but he could barely get inside. He placed his set of new passports and tickets on the desk, hit the play button on his machine, and rifled through the faxes which had accumulated like single socks.

In white anger, he read the faxes, then played his messages, most of which were from Bangkok. He could hardly control his breathing, rushing out in spurts. The phone rang and he picked it up.

"Mr. Brant?"

"Yes."

"My name is Amphur," a woman's voice said. "I'm calling from Bangkok. I'm with Dr. Pridi Taksin's clinic and we've been trying to contact you for days."

He tried not to scream. "I'm reading the faxes."

"Sir, we're trying to schedule you."

"Who said anything about scheduling me?"

"Let me look at my notes. Please bear with me, sir. I'm new on the staff. Yes, Mrs. Heather Malone spoke with the doctor five days ago on—"

"Never mind. Tell him . . ." Rage had deprived Garrett of voice and reason. He put down the phone, reeled into his chair, and cried out. Nothing, not even Caroline's butchering of his work, had caused such cataclysmic pain within him. He was severed, torn apart, drawn and quartered. It was as though he had been placed on a medieval wheel of torture. His arms and legs went numb in dread.

Heather's giggly voice rang from the floor above. "Wow-wowie! Bolt the foundation. We're going to have a seven-pointer!"

The tigress was on all fours, crawling down the stairs. "Grrrrr-grrrr."

"Be right there. Go back upstairs and I'll dress you."

"Yes, master."

Much as he hated drugs, he remembered Eve had some coke in a drawer and he found it, cut a pair of thick lines, and snorted them with an old soda straw. He waited a moment and the rush kicked in. He finally wrenched himself out of the chair and went back upstairs.

"What happened?" she asked. "Bad news?"

"I'm not sure."

"Well, I'll call the fucking lawyers right now."

"No, it's okay. There was a call from Bangkok."

"The Oriental Hotel?"

"Yes," he agreed.

"It was a surprise. I booked us for our wedding reception and the Shangri-La in Chiang Mai for our honeymoon."

"Old places don't leave quietly, do they?"

She held off, trying to gauge his mood. "Are you ready for fun and games?"

"Oh, you bet. Let me grab a quick shower and then we'll get into something real heavy. The full Tantric adventure."

"Can I have it in writing?" she sniggered.

They walked through the wardrobe room, and Garrett, always knowledgeable about his inventory, selected a black leather hood, riveted across the face, which was connected to straps that buckled over the back laces. Heather examined the locks on the collar and the two metal rings. She closed the mouth zipper and detached the blindfold buckles over the eye frame.

"I want to watch you do your dirty deeds."

"Paul Gauguin might like to observe, too," he said, stroking her hair.

"The more, the merrier. Oh, God, you turn me on."

"I'll bring the rest of the war gear upstairs."

"A harness and sling—I hope."

"Heather, you'll be pleased."

"Christ, I'm so hot. I'm drenched already."

"I think the studio is the place. We can use the spotlights."

"Mirror, mirror on the wall . . ."

"Heather gets it all," he said, amused. He handed her his key ring. "This is the master, gets you in everywhere."

"I'm honored by your trust—finally."

"See you soon. Fried chicken after."

He went back into his office. There would be time to pack later and go out to pick up some equipment he had forgotten. Now he would settle all the old business before making his foray into the unknown.

**After a conversation** with Paul, Garrett put on his favorite Gauguin mask, meticulously copied from the artist's self-portrait with idol. It had gravitas, a melancholy pensiveness that eloquently declared: *Here I am, a deep thinker, meditating on the future of art and how I will change it and* your *lives.*

Heather was in the studio, the spots on dim but placed so that they illuminated Garrett's paintings. She was enthralled, and when he crept up, she was pleasantly startled.

"Oh, Paul's here. Garrett, you are up to some serious shit? The whole troupe's out, our very own voyeur, I'm so excited."

"I thought you'd enjoy this."

She dropped the bathrobe. "I shaved so that we could see the Minotaur throbbing."

"We'll follow him through the labyrinth."

"Yes, yes."

He secured the leather mask over Heather's head, tied the laces, attached a studded collar, ensuring that it wasn't too tight. She put out her hands for him to lock the leather hand restraints, and he cuffed them on a chain belt. Her bright blue eyes froze with anticipation at his every expert move. He tied a noose harness around her bulging breasts, dimpled with sweat, and kissed them.

"I knew, I knew! If I waited long enough, I'd have you back. Your soul."

She waited while he attached the seat sling, engaging the chains to the rafter beam and screwing in the suspension bar. He stopped its sway, eased her on, and adjusted the thick leather straps around her firm thighs.

"Oh, this is bliss, ecstasy," she said.

"Are you comfortable?"

"Yes. Orgasms have that effect on me."

He pushed her and she swayed as though on a kid's park swing.

"I got rid of the Alfred Deller Consort madrigals. What would you like to hear?"

"You're so thoughtful. I'll bet you don't have any Joni Mitchell oldies."

"Wrong again. And I didn't pirate them off Napster." He was sensitive to the royalty issue of artists. "I remember how much you loved her, and after our breakup I didn't have the heart to trash them."

"Garrett, I'll give you the world."

From behind Heather, a smoky voice thundered.

"I already gave it to him, sister," Eve snarled. "You think you can buy a soul!" Heather turned to the voice as a whip snarled across her back.

Heather screamed. "Garrett, stop her. You promised she'd never come back!"

He giggled. "I must have forgotten to cancel her visitor's pass."

Festering with rage, Eve said, "Listen, bitch, you're the only one who can hurt Garrett. The witness who can tie him to Jan. In a moment of pathetic weakness he 'fessed up and told you I murdered Jan and kidnapped the girls."

And now, with the whip whooshing and the echo of flaps as it thrashed against flesh, the havoc of the moment, the screaming of the women's voices, their hatred poisoning the air, a bestial metamorphosis traveled beyond the legacies of mind and rationality into an immeasurable weather storm system, beyond human dimensions.

"I am his woman. Only I can make him the great artist he was destined to be. I'm the missing part."

Heather felt herself choking, before silence stifled and stilled the pain of loss.

# CHAPTER 39

**Michel hadn't eaten since** his sausage that afternoon, but he was not hungry. He slipped his car into a driveway on Dell. Let it be towed. He had a headache from the Pastis, belched as he walked over the bridge, and turned left into the street called Linnie Close. Lights were on in most houses for the eleven o'clock news and he paused to watch ESPN's baseball roundup on a big-screen TV. The Dodgers were tied in an extra-inning game. No news yet of the Yankees.

Garrett's house was dark and no neighbors were on the prowl or taking out garbage. He rang the doorbell several times. When he was satisfied that nobody was home, he turned the key in the lock. If he was caught by anyone but Garrett, he had a hoary excuse: At the request of a worried friend, he was checking to see that Garrett was all right.

"Garrett, Garrett. Eve . . . Eve . . ." he called, and waited, shining the flashlight around the living room. He was surrounded by rows and rows of finely carved bookshelves, some oversized, holding an enormous collection of art books. The stereo was on, madrigals being sung beautifully. Madrigals and madness, he thought, unholstering his Glock.

The downstairs living room was orderly, with a remarkable collection of quality antiques that bespoke genuine, cultivated taste, flair—intellectualism. The walls were filled with excellent reproductions of Gauguin's paintings. On the long wall over the sofa, Gauguin's enigmatic masterwork hung in an ebony frame: WHERE DO WE COME FROM? WHAT ARE WE? WHERE ARE WE GOING?

Off to the side was a dining room and buffet; the kitchen had granite tops and was mostly stainless steel. In a corner overlooking the canal was a breakfast table.

Michel stealthily crept up the stairs and walked into an office. The shutters were closed and the room was disordered with cartons. A desk lamp was on and a fax machine gurgled with incoming pages.

He sat down on the swivel chair and picked up six passports, an assortment of IDs, licenses, and a travel folder. Five of the masterly forged passports were blank, the sixth revealed a photo of a man who strongly resembled Gauguin. It was made out to Paul G. E. Henri, a reversal of Gauguin's given names. There was a one-way ticket on a freighter, the SS *Hades,* embarking from San Pedro at four A.M. the following day. It was now eleven-thirty. Garrett must be out picking up some last-minute travel requirements. On a shelf were eight pocket-sized tape recorders.

The phone rang and Michel waited for the answering machine to pick it up. A voice came on with a cultivated British-Oriental accent.

"Garrett, hello, this is Dr. Taksin. I'll be leaving the office in a few minutes. My assistant phoned earlier and was disconnected. I need to know if you plan to go ahead with the surgery. It won't be as complicated as the first reassignment. In fact you'll be up and on your feet in about a week and only male. Now, I'm holding payment from Heather which she wired to us. I've provisionally scheduled you for Monday, August fourteenth at six A.M. Please be good enough to call or fax us. I'm looking forward to seeing you and Heather. There's a new restaurant on the Chaya Praya I want to take you to."

A cold sweat trickled down the back of Michel's neck. The mystery was pierced and he shivered at the realization.

Garrett *was* Eve.

The doctor in Bangkok had delivered her.

Two actual people existed within this tragic, tortured creature whose frustrations led him/her to act out these roles. He had also assumed the persona of Paul Gauguin, and these multiple personalities eventually combined to murder Caroline Davis.

Still thunderstruck by the doctor's revelation, Michel scanned some of the faxes, most of them from the Taksin Intergender and Sexual Reassignment Clinic in Bangkok. He skimmed through a folder of Garrett's medical records and learned that Garrett Lee Brant was a product of genetic demons and chaos. The divided self had been made whole by an unnatural surgical elision, creating Eve. The knowledge chilled Michel.

Garrett was a hermaphrodite, the rarest type, with neither sex dominant. Although living and functioning as a male, he had been operated on by Dr. Taksin in Bangkok, so that both sexes now existed and functioned. Eve had become a perverse extension of Garrett's sexual ambivalence and created a balance in what was a fragmented personality. At the bottom of this was anarchy, ruled by a misguided passion for artistic achievement which could never flower.

Either out of sympathy or some irrational libidinous drive, Heather Malone had fallen in love with *it*. She and others had colluded with Garrett in this twisted, tormented madness.

Michel stuffed the passports and the steamship ticket in his jacket pocket. He climbed stealthily to the floor above and shone his light into the eerie clothes room. He stood bewildered, shaking his head, surveying old theatrical costumes, masks of Gauguin, an assortment of leather and latex attire, aisles of men's and women's clothes, wigs on blocks, makeup, dentures, shoes and boots of every description, with lifts and Cuban heels, and a variety of props which baffled him.

On the next floor, there was a large bathroom, a Jacuzzi tub in the center, and the air inside was redolent of the familiar odors of Provence.

In the bedroom, three duffel bags were packed and a suitcase was open. A lamp that was a carved reproduction of Gauguin flickered on low beam. On the table with a bookmark was a copy of Alain De Botton's book *How Proust Can Change Your Life*.

Michel grumbled at this astounding perversity juxtaposed with scholarly pursuit. Everything about Garrett Lee Brant was outside his comprehension. Garrett's plane of irrationality had no gravitational force in Michel's universe.

He ascended the red spiral staircase and found himself in an artist's studio. Brushes, paints, palettes, rolls of canvas, worktables. The shutters were closed in the gallery. Michel looked at the feeble imitations of masterly works by Gauguin, Cézanne, and some dark Italianate studies. These were the art school daubs of a fair copyist. Other paintings revealed a strong graphic sense but a flat color palette, at best the work of a Sunday painter, devoid of vision and originality. Michel found it inconceivable that Brant or, for that matter, anyone might consider him a serious artist.

Yet, in some way, Garrett's artistic inclination began to make sense to Michel. The passion for art lived within him, but the talent for it was stillborn like his sexual makeup. The duality, a doppel-gänger, inspired the disguises and brought to light the fact that Garrett was someone assuming identities because he had none. This need for definition had become the murderer's quest.

Moving slowly down the long room with its raised skylight, Michel recoiled when he encountered the naked figure of a woman in a monstrous leather mask. She was suspended from a chain and handcuffed. The body was still warm; the scent of sweat and rut-ting fluids pervaded the room. The woman's figure could only be Heather Malone's.

It was now five past midnight, and Michel decided not to touch the evidence. He would phone the police when Garrett arrived for his travel documents and baggage. Sitting in this slaughterhouse, engulfed by madness, the music changed and Ravel's ghostly *Pa-vane* began to play.

Michel suddenly turned. Coming in from the roof garden, ac-companied by a charivari of voices, bits of conversation in English and French, was the figure of man. Michel thought that this was a homeless old drunk looking for a squat who had climbed up from a fire ladder he hadn't noticed. There was a curdled body stench, and smoke from a pipe. The figure was Paul Gauguin and it ap-peared as though by magic. The thick mustache, the red and black Breton vest, the broken nose, and the staring eyes were shocking.

The figure saw Michel immediately.

"I wasn't expecting company. In any case, you're a bit late. I'm not accepting any commissions. Now what are you doing here?"

Michel tossed a silver earring to Garrett, who made no effort to catch it.

"Eve dropped this in Pont-Aven when she attempted to kidnap Suzy."

"So much for improvisation. I'm not responsible for her behavior."

"Garrett, I hope you don't have any prejudices against lawyers. You're going to be spending a lot of time with them."

He shook his head disdainfully. "I don't think so. I'm leaving for Tahiti in a few hours."

"Not without your tickets and passport. I don't understand much of this, but murdering Heather—your golden goose—really doesn't make sense to me."

"She liked rough sex. There was a *triangle* and Heather knew what she was getting into. Eve came home and found us. Heather threatened to turn me in. She wanted to *exterminate* Eve."

Michel heard a bloodcurdling sound, then realized it was Eve, the voiceless soprano.

Eve seemed to emerge out of Garrett's flesh, his skin. Garrett's phantom persona became a tangible presence, terrifying Michel. He had never conceived of such a transformation.

"Heather tried to separate us and now you are," she screamed. "I'm part of him. What no one understood is that I completed him. And nobody's going to split us apart."

Voices filtered from other parts of the room. Michel wasn't certain if he was seeing double, but two shadowy figures appeared, and when he shone his flashlight along the wall, searching for the room's light switch, they vanished. He heard the sound of liquid sloshing and smelled turpentine.

For several moments, he was disoriented, then he charged out of the room, down the stairs, and found cartons blocking him on the staircase. He heard, smelled, then saw a crackling fire approach. In the clothes room, flames were already creeping over the racks and masks. He felt a sudden sting and realized that he had been speared with a needle just below the back of his neck. He staggered forward, hit his head against the doorway, and rolled to the ground.

Overwhelmed by panic, he yanked the needle out of his shoulder blade, grasped the stair rail, and levered himself to his feet, but lost his balance and pitched down the flight of stairs, crashing on the wide landing step.

Garrett was already there, kicking him in a frenzy. Michel rolled away, felt for his gun, and fired it at him repeatedly. But Garrett vanished again.

In the spreading flames coming from different directions, he now spied Garrett's figure holding a duffel bag, and he lunged at him. As they grappled on the floor, Garrett pulled another needle from a sheath strapped to his calf and again tried to stab him.

. Michel seized Garrett's wrist and turned the needle on him, plunging it into his throat. Michel rolled off him and then, to his astonishment, Garrett rose, hand at his throat, a whirling dervish, reeling backward, his clothes on fire.

Michel tottered to the front door, opened it, and turned, only to see Garrett in the middle of the inferno, twisting in a mad dance, devoured by a halo of flames.

# CHAPTER 40

**Apart from some bruises**—no broken bones—and a few stitches in his shoulder, Michel's most serious pain came from the tetanus shot. His arm felt as though it had been gored. He had given the LAPD detectives an edited version of the events: He had interviewed Heather Malone's assistant at her home and learned that she was missing and he feared for her safety. However, Rudy was reluctant to contact the police. Michel decided to stop by Garrett's house late that night. When he approached the front door, he had heard a woman screaming, in peril. Smoke was coming from inside and Michel had broken into the house. He rushed to the top floor in an attempt to rescue the woman, when he encountered Garrett.

Heather Malone was suspended from the rafter and had apparently been tortured to death. Garrett had poured turpentine through the house and already started the fire on the top floor. When Michel identified himself, Garrett attacked him, stabbed him with a needle, and tried to escape. The two had struggled. Michel had fought for his life and, during the battle, Garrett had fallen into the fire.

The moment Michel was outside, he called the fire department using his cell phone and they responded promptly. But because of the limited entry to the canals, they had not been able to control the fire. The house was a sheath of flames and their efforts to extinguish it failed. But because Michel had contacted them immediately, they had been able to prevent the spread of the fire and had saved the other houses on the street and potentially the lives of other residents who might have been trapped.

Michel stood outside Linnie Close with the detectives, the fire chief, and local TV camera crews. He refused interviews and, to make himself even more unpopular with the media, only spoke French. All that remained of the house with the Minotaur was the concrete foundation and smoldering timbers. It was still too hot and dangerous to send investigators in to recover the charred bodies.

"It's the wildest story I've ever heard," the detective with the marines tattoo remarked. "I guess I'll have to find another place to get a tattoo."

"The whole neighborhood could've been lost, and the people cut off, if not for him," the fire chief said, shaking Michel's hand.

**Before leaving for** the airport, Michel telephoned Rudy, who began to bleat like an old sheep.

"I knew she was dead, I knew it," he said. "Oh, dear me, I don't know what I'm going to do."

"Rudy, you might be in Heather's will."

The prospect of wealth uprooted his grief and his sobbing abruptly ceased.

"Wouldn't that be glorious?"

**Michel decided to** surprise Jennifer and the Davises. With a bag of peanuts in his lap, he took the puddle-jumper up to Monterey. He needed some time to compose himself and to decide what to tell Melanie and Jeff Davis. He rented a Lexus again and easily followed the directions the clerk had given him. Turning off the highway, he descended the hills and entered the bewitching town of Carmel. He was enchanted by the small village, with its elegant shops and art galleries, and was overwhelmed by the view of the ocean. At the beach, he turned right, and gave his name to the guard at the entry to Seventeen Mile. After a brief phone call he was admitted to the caviar that American wealth feasted upon every day.

Driving now in a daze, overwhelmed by the crashing surf, the foaming blowholes, the rocky coast, and the verdant fairways of

Pebble Beach, he tried to vanquish the hideous vision of Garrett and *Eve* Brant, the aberrations that had driven them to murder. Gone were the masks, the disguises, the role-playing. People who wanted to be anyone but themselves. Maybe now he could resume his life and keep his promise to Jennifer. But he wondered if he was ready to leave this work and considered the possibility that this case might never have been solved if he hadn't pursued it.

The gates of the vast Davis estate were already open when he pulled up. He was confronted by a regal manor house, monumental cypress trees, gardens overflowing with flowers, and the majesty of the sea. He was led to the terrace by the Davises' houseman. With the symphony of waves, the efflorescence of sunshine, he felt deluged by the Olympian harmonies of this natural beauty. Jennifer and Melanie were on the deck below at the swimming pool which overlooked the ocean.

"Michel, I would have met you in Monterey. Why the hell didn't you tell us you were arriving?" Jeff asked.

"I didn't know when this case would be over."

"Is it?"

"Yes, the killer burned to death last night. *It* is gone, Jeff. I know Caroline's fate will always be with you and Melanie. But at least you'll know that she was avenged."

The ladies, both tanned and in bikinis, came up the brick steps. They had overheard.

Melanie Davis tearfully wrapped her arms around him and he grimaced in pain.

"Are you injured?"

"Just a jab from the car door."

Jennifer came beside him, her face solemn and lovely, and he kissed her with tenderness.

Melanie held on to Jeff's hand and composed herself. "You've got seven days of golf with me at Pebble Beach and lunch with Jennifer at the club."

"And I've got us a field box for the Yankee-Angels series in Anaheim after that," Jeff informed him.

Michel's boyish, callow dreams awaited him. But the brave front of Melanie and Jeff made him shudder as their pain transferred to him. Losing Caroline, a child he'd met only in death, cast a murky cloud over the moment. Like the killer of the girl, he, too, experienced a sense of loss which transfigured him and he thought he must smile to reassure them, himself and his wife. But the victory of vengeance was expunged. Murder cases might be solved, but they also retained an infinite life of their own.

Jennifer turned to him and pulled him off to the side.

"Do you understand why this all happened? What it was all about?"

He doubted whether he could ever explain the complex perversity of this case or the essence of madness.

"Art. Someone without talent wanted to be an artist. The world is full of them."

"I want to go home . . . to Provence and be alone in our place. Walk down the Cours Mirabeau and meet for coffee at Les Deux Garçons."

"We'll see about that. But first let me check my starting times."